THE ROADHOUSE

When aspiring actress Charlie Carver learns that her cousin Annabelle has died, she immediately leaves Melbourne to fly home to the remote family roadhouse east of Alice Springs. But after her mother suffers a heart attack and is airlifted out for life-saving surgery, Charlie is left to take the reins of the struggling family business, alongside friends old and new, including captivating local stockman Mike. The authorities declare Annabelle to have taken her own life, but when a woman's body turns up at an abandoned mine site, Charlie begins to wonder what else is being covered up, and why. Beginning a search for the truth, a perilous bush chase ensues that threatens her own life, causing her to wonder whether she ever knew Annabelle at all.

KERRY McGINNIS

THE ROADHOUSE

Complete and Unabridged

AURORA
Leicester

First published in Australia in 2019 by
Penguin Random House Australia

First Aurora Edition
published 2020
by arrangement with
Penguin Random House Australia

The moral right of the author has been asserted

A catalogue record for this book is available
from the British Library.

ISBN 978–1–78782–262–7

Published by
Ulverscroft Limited
Anstey, Leicestershire

Set by Words & Graphics Ltd.
Anstey, Leicestershire
Printed and bound in Great Britain by
T. J. International Ltd., Padstow, Cornwall

This book is printed on acid-free paper

*This one is for Ivy, Alan and Sandra,
to celebrate our Sunday smokos.*

1

I came home to Garnet Soak following an absence of five years. My mother had rung me from the tiny Northern Territory roadhouse to say that my cousin Annabelle had killed herself.

My first dazed reaction to this incomprehensible news was, I am ashamed to admit, a spurt of irritation. 'Typical,' I muttered, then heard my mother's voice, thin and faint as though she'd momentarily turned her head away from the mouthpiece.

'What was that, Charlie?'

'I just asked why,' I lied. 'What sort of crisis was she indulging herself in this time?'

'Charlie!' she remonstrated, her tone suddenly strong again, like the woman herself. Then she sighed. 'I don't have the details. There was a letter, apparently, but naturally I haven't seen it yet. Young Tom, the copper from Harts Range, brought the news — he's only just left. It happened yesterday but it took a while for someone to call the local authorities. She was in New South Wales, Charlie. Some little town on the coast. The police there must have got onto the ones in Alice, then they rang the cop shop at Harts Range with the news. So Tom Cleary came this morning to tell me.'

'How? I asked baldly. 'Did she jump off a cliff? Though I can't see that happening — too much damage and she wouldn't like that. Or was it an overdose? That's popular down here . . . What exactly did they tell you happened, Mum?'

'They think she just took off her clothes and swam out to sea until she drowned.' Mum sighed. 'Of course, they can't *know*, but why else would she leave her clothes? As to when it happened, they've based their timing on the tides. She left the note with her clothes, you see, all folded and weighted down with a piece of driftwood, and they hadn't been washed away. Her watch was there, and her driver's licence, but no handbag. So they think she must have left wherever she was staying with the intention of killing herself. She must've written the note and then just walked into the sea. That's the official interpretation. The note she left is addressed to me, so the police have mailed it on. There was even a stamp on it, apparently. Not that I'll get it before the weekend.'

'No.' Today was Wednesday, but the road mail that served the roadhouse and the half-dozen desert cattle stations along the Plenty River Highway only ran on Saturdays. 'So, the upshot is there'll be no certainty. Nor will we have a body to bury. How could she do that to us? Annabelle always thought of herself first, but really! Even I wouldn't have suspected she'd go this far.'

'Oh, Charlie, leave it.' Mum suddenly sounded tired. 'I know you two always had your differences but let them rest now, please. She must have been very unhappy, after all, to take such a step. I want you to come home. We'll hold a memorial service for her here, perhaps put up a

2

stone later on, but we can decide that further down the track. There's only the two of us now, Charlie, and I could really do with your support in this. You will come, won't you?'

As much as I wished to refuse the request, I knew that I couldn't. Leaving Melbourne now would mean losing the latest spot my agent had found for me — a television commercial for face cream, the money for which would supplement my current earnings as a waitress, since the secondhand book shop where I'd previously spent three days a week behind the counter had folded under the weight of its unsold paper-backs. At twenty-six, my career as an actress had not so much stalled as failed to ever make a proper take-off.

Oh, there had been small parts, but never the starring role I needed to gather the notices that ensured a steady income, so my prospects had narrowed rather than broadened. A small part in *The Students' Party*, understudy for the lead in a play that closed after two nights, a brief triumph as a harassed mother in *The Baker's Dozen* back in 1991, but if a week was a long time in politics, three years was an eternity in the theatre. Nothing substantial had followed, just a slew of advertising slots staggered between auditions that seldom went any further than the ubiquitous 'Wonderful, darling! If your name comes up, we'll be in touch.' Perhaps it was time to pack the whole acting thing in.

This wasn't a new thought for me to entertain. It had been harder somehow throughout the past twelve months to maintain the hopeful outlook

I'd once had, to convince myself that tonight, or tomorrow, or next week, I'd get my lucky break. That the stars would align for me and some perceptive director would be blown away by my brilliant talent. I'd never seriously considered any other career but perhaps it was time to face facts. There were hundreds of young hopefuls out there, many of them prettier and more accomplished than me. Yes, I'd had a dance coach, a voice coach, I'd had plenty of roles in high-school plays and had acted (when I could) in the Amateur Dramatic Society back in Alice Springs, but growing up in the bush meant a late start in my chosen field. Maybe too late for success.

'Yes, of course I'll come, Mum. I'll need to tell a few people, give in my notice at the cafe. I could catch a flight maybe Friday. Do you think you could sort out a lift for me from the Alice? Or could old Bob come in and get me?'

'I'll fix something, Charlie. Perhaps one of the stations . . . Leave it with me, and ring with your ETA. We'll expect you Friday evening, then.'

'If I can get a morning flight.' I hesitated; my mother wasn't a gushy woman but I thought I detected something in her voice. 'Are you okay, Mum? You sound a bit . . . tired.'

'It's come as a shock, that's all, Charlie. Safe flight, then. Bye now.'

'Yes, bye,' I echoed. I tried to think of something more to say but while I stood dithering she hung up and the silence was broken by the burr of the dial tone, like a faint, reproachful reminder of the distance between us.

4

I tried to remember the last time we'd spoken — something like a month ago — and that had just been to ask her to post my old copy of *Romeo and Juliet* to save me the price of a new book. And I hadn't got the part anyway.

I sighed, wondering where to start. Leaving would mean that my flatmate would have to find someone else to help with the rent while I was gone, which meant that there would be no place for me to return to. It was one more thing to chalk up to my cousin's account. Annabelle had been my elder by two years. I had shared a childhood with her, been forbidden to ever shorten her name to the more manageable Anna, and knew her to be selfish to the bone and out for whatever she could get. It had been five years since we last met and I couldn't believe that she had changed one iota since. So what could possibly have compelled her to kill herself?

A sudden memory came to me: Annabelle at thirteen, preening before the mirror in our shared bedroom with the light falling on her lustrous, jet-black waterfall of hair that hung almost to her waist. 'My name means *beautiful Anna*,' she was saying complacently, 'because I am. Uncle Jim said so. My parents must have known that when they gave it to me. Not like yours, Charlie. That's a boy's name.'

'It's Charlotte.' As she well knew. But even as I spoke I divined that it was more than my name she meant. The sweeping look that had accompanied the words, up and down like a buyer scorning the goods offered, had held to ridicule my lanky childish body, my large feet and the frizz of tight, ordinary-brown curls, made somehow worse by my wide mouth and tombstone-sized front teeth.

Annabelle's mother was Eurasian, giving her daughter's appearance an exotic edge that filled me with helpless jealousy. My cousin was petite and finely finished, with budding breasts and a discernable waist — everything that I wasn't. She was everybody's pet, unlike my awkward, brooding self. My father doted on her and seemed incapable of seeing through her lies or catching her out in any of the mean little strategies she constantly used to discredit me. Telling on her wasn't an option with my parents. My father wouldn't have believed me, while to Mum carrying tales was as bad as lying. The injustice of it all had seared my soul, aware as I was that neither my feckless father nor my impatient, no-nonsense mother could recognise the duplicity of the cuckoo in our nest.

But people like Annabelle manipulated their way through life. She was a stranger to remorse and guilt alike, as far as I could tell. The Annabelles of the world didn't stand meekly in a queue waiting for life's handouts; they marched smartly to the head and demanded what they wanted. So why had she killed herself? It was as much a mystery as the method she had chosen. Why not pills and a beautiful corpse? My cousin had loved herself too much to purposely damage her body. Perhaps she hadn't considered what prolonged immersion and the attention of sea creatures could do. Or was the idea to vanish completely, leaving only the memory of beauty behind?

That, I thought, was the more likely answer. Cynically I worded the headline I was sure she must have visualised: *Tragic death of young beauty.* Only, twenty-eight wasn't that young, was it? A moment later I felt ashamed of my callousness. Mum was right, my cousin must have been appallingly unhappy to have done such a thing. It was years since we'd spoken; perhaps now, when it was too late, the time had come for me to draw a line under past grievances and forgive her.

⋆   ⋆   ⋆

To get from Tullamarine to Alice Springs meant flying via Adelaide where, predictably, there was a delay. For a while it seemed as if I might even have to overnight in the city but my anxious calculations of the extra cost of hotel accommodation and taxi fares were cut short by the announcement that the flight would proceed after all. It was a smaller plane than the big jet that had brought me from Melbourne, and I'd lucked a window seat that gave me a firsthand overview, when we began our final descent, of the little outback town snugged into the hollow of the MacDonnell Ranges, a familiar sight for me, heralding as it did the start of many a boarding-school holiday.

It was May, with the soft blue sky and brilliant desert air of the Centre, and my heart lifted in response as my feet carried me across the tarmac.

The red earth, the spinifex-covered slopes, the solid uncompromising line of Heavitree Gap and the wide, sandy bed of the Todd River, which I knew awaited me just a short drive away, were constants of my childhood. At moments like these, I silently acknowledged, I would happily chuck it all — the city, the stage, the career that had never really gone anywhere — for the joy of being back in my own country.

Waiting in the baggage hall for my scuffed port to appear, I searched the crowd for old Bob, my mother's longtime handyman. Grumpy old Bob, with his limp and disgraceful hat that he never seemed to renew. He had been helping out at the Garnet, as the roadhouse was known, since its inception when the station of the same name had been sold off to Abbey Downs, the large company-owned property next door. My father had retained only the old homestead, which had originally done duty as a stopover and refreshment point for travellers until the present-day premises had been built. The sale had gone through in 1966, two years before I was born, so the roadhouse was a new venture then. I had spent my childhood there, within the embrace of the ancient range, in the company of my family and old Bob.

Bob had been curmudgeonly even twenty-six years before, not a man to dote on children, however winsome. I had respected the boundaries he set and was gradually admitted to his friendship, something that Annabelle had not achieved. It had been solace to me as a child, balm to my smarting ego, knowing that Bob was seemingly the one person in all the world whom my cousin had never been able to fool. Staff and travellers alike had doted on her fairy-like prettiness and angelic smile.

But there was no sign of Bob now in the press of greeters. Perhaps his colicky old Land Rover was playing up? Hitching my shoulder bag higher, I turned back to where the luggage trailer was inching its way into the concourse and almost bumped into a tall, grey-haired man with a weather-beaten face. He wore a short-sleeved white shirt with little brass crosses set into the shoulders and a familiar logo on the pocket. A smaller, white-haired woman beside him offered a smile as he spoke.

'Miss Carver? I thought so — you're very like your mother. I'm Padre Don Thornton, Uniting Church. My wife, Rae.'

We shook hands. 'Molly asked me to meet you. We're heading out on patrol, so I told her we'd fly you home. Have you much luggage?'

'Oh, that's wonderful. How kind! Thank you both very much. I was looking for old Bob. And please, call me Charlie. Luggage . . . just the one bag. Hang on and I'll grab it' — for the trolley had finally arrived — 'and this.' I handed my shoulder bag to his wife to hold while I did so. 'It's not too much, is it?'

'No, I think we can manage.' His faded grey eyes twinkled briefly. 'Might be a different story if you were fat. How tall are you, Charlie?'

'A hundred and seventy-nine centimetres. It's why I wear flats.' He took the bag I'd retrieved from the stack on the vehicle and we began to

9

walk, his wife asking about my journey. I said hesitantly, 'Mum would've told you, then, about Annabelle?'

'Yes,' Rae replied soberly. 'Poor child. Our hearts grieve for her, Charlie, and for you and Molly, of course. Were you close?'

'I haven't seen my cousin in five years. Maybe Mum has, I'm not sure. I've lived away — in Melbourne mostly. This is my first visit home since I left. So, how long have you worked in the Alice, Padre Don?

'We were posted here from Karratha three years back. Ah, here we are.' He dumped my bag on the tarmac and fished from his pocket the keys of the single-engined Cessna we'd stopped beside. 'You're bush-bred — you'll have flown in small planes before, Charlie?'

'Yes, of course. I didn't know the church had a plane though. When I was living at home we'd see old Bill Handly every three months or so, but he drove a station wagon. He was the Anglican man. And there was the Catholic bloke who went to Upatak and Red Tank — the Himans and the Mallorys are Catholic. He drove too, but he never came to the Garnet — knew we didn't belong to his flock, I suppose.'

'Well, as I said, I'm the Uniting Church bloke' — Don's eyes twinkled — 'and I go everywhere they'll have me.' He opened a hatch and began loading my gear. 'You ladies can hop in if you like while I do the checks. We'll be on our way soon — you must be longing to get home.'

★ ★ ★

10

It was the best way to arrive, I thought, watching the country unroll below me, its contours briefly overlaid by the shadow of the tiny plane. We flew north-east over Randalls Peak, the country looking bare and rocky, the trees no more than blobs on the landscape. I traced the winding course of what I thought had to be the Hale River, its dry bed lined with thicker blobs than appeared on the hills, and a myriad of other nameless creeks and gullies until the solid block of the Harts Range was below us, its hollows indented with shadow in the late afternoon light. North of us, running east, was the thin ruled line of the highway. Ruby Creek was down there somewhere, and the old goldfield, and many an abandoned mica digging — the Harts was full of minerals and semi-precious gems. Water too, according to old Bob, more valuable than anything else dug from the earth, but you had to know how to find it . . .

Padre Don pulled off his headset to call out but the engine noise drowned his words. Speech was impossible. I shook my head and he pointed below as the engine note changed and the plane banked, beginning its descent. I looked down and saw the distant complex of the roadhouse, tin roofs flashing in the sunlight, the garden trees enlarging from blobs to objects as I watched. There was dust on the road heading out between the swell of two ridges, beyond which lay the short gravel airstrip. Somebody coming to meet us.

Then we were drifting down and the details of our surroundings sprang into view — gravel

11

surface, clumps of whitewood frothing with pale green blossom overlaid with powdery red dust, the solidity of the range, the pitted surface of a boulder, then a great cloud of dust catching up to us as the plane slowed to walking pace, turned and began to taxi back to where the vehicle and its lone occupant waited.

It was Bob in the same old station wagon — no changes there, then, or in his greeting as he nodded tersely at me. 'G'day, Charlie.'

'Bob,' I said, 'how are you?'

'No good complaining.' He took the bags Don was unloading and stowed them in the back of the vehicle.

'Nobody listens,' I agreed. 'You know the padre, do you? And his wife?'

'We've met.' He nodded at them both while poking a finger up under the brim of his hat to lift it slightly in acknowledgement of the woman's presence. 'Padre. Missus. You wanna get in?'

We drove back in silence. It took only minutes but it was time enough for the familiarity of the setting to enfold me again. The long shadow of the vehicle scurrying before us, the lavender tint of the range deepening to purple as the sun sank, the smell of dust, the untidy scribble of scrub amid a white mass of dried buffel grass, the spinifex rings a dusty olive across the ochre ridges and, then, half hidden behind the roadhouse we had pulled up before, the crooked roofline of the old homestead settled deep amid the shade trees and oleander of its eighty-year-old garden.

'Welcome home, Charlie,' Bob said as he switched off the motor. 'I reckon it's about time yer came back. Molly needs yer here.' He pushed his door open and got out to unload the luggage, leaving me sitting there, stunned into silence.

2

Mum greeted us at the roadhouse door that opened onto the verandah. I checked myself for a moment at the foot of the shallow steps before mounting them, gazing up at her, Bob's strange words echoing in my mind. In my own experience my mother had never needed anyone. She was the most self-sufficient human being I had ever met, made so, I had always assumed, by my father's nature. Dead these eight years, he had been a lazy, easygoing, feckless man who let things slide and slide until the pitch of circumstances placed them beyond recovery. It had cost him the station that his grandfather had pioneered, his health, and ultimately his life when chest pain had proved to be not the indigestion he had self-diagnosed, but a failing heart sending frantic signals of impending disaster, which, like so much else, he had ignored.

Now, my searching gaze showed a tall woman with a crop of grey curls and a strong-boned face that was somewhat thinner than I remembered. She had big, capable hands and large feet (we took the same size in shoes). I suspected that when she was young her figure would have been described as 'boyish' — a term that had also been applied to mine. Her body had slackened a little with age but still retained a glimpse of its once lean grace and purpose of movement. We shared the same nose and arch of brow, though

14

my colouring was somewhat fairer, her skin having had greater exposure to inland summers. Her eyes, hazel like mine, looked tired behind her glasses as they met my own.

'Charlie.'

'Mum.' I ran up the steps and received a brief hug and a peck on my cheek. 'It's good to see you,' I said, but she was already turning away to greet the others.

'Don, Rae, how are you? Thank you for bringing her home. Bob will take your stuff over to the homestead if you'd like to come in? We'll eat here — it's easier. Charlie, can you show them through to freshen up? I have to go.'

That was my welcome, but even after a five-year absence I had expected no more. My mother detested fuss. She turned away, leaving us to enter behind her, and I saw at once that there were customers at one of the tables set out amid the stands of merchandise, a party of three men, while a fourth waited at the bar. The two Toyotas parked behind the apron of concrete fronting the fuel pumps must have belonged to them. Mum hurried to the counter to serve a beer to the waiting man, then vanished through the plastic strips hanging across the kitchen entrance, and I lifted a hand to gesture at my companions. 'If you'll follow me?'

★ ★ ★

We ate dinner on the back verandah of the roadhouse, at the long table that was permanently spread with a clear vinyl covering. Mum

15

laid out the tablemats and placed the condiment tray and I helped her bring out the meal. Cold roast lamb served with mint sauce and a salad — staff and family meals at the Garnet leant towards menus that could be prepared in advance. As it was, Mum had to leave us almost immediately to attend to a customer whose arrival out front was announced by the ting of the doorbell. Bob had joined us at the table, hatless for once, his grey hair still wet from the comb. His tanned face with its dour expression seemed a little more lined than I remembered and I caught myself wondering about his age. He had always been *old Bob*, but then, even twenty seems ancient to a child.

'Is this everyone?' Surprised, I glanced from my mother's vacated chair to Bob. 'What's happened to the cook?'

'Left last week,' he grunted. 'Molly's filling in. Told yer she could do with a hand.'

'She must be busy, then,' Rae said. 'And with this tragedy to deal with as well. Did you know Annabelle, Bob?'

'Yeah,' he said, uninformatively.

Then Mum returned, apologising, and seated herself with a little sigh. 'I'm sorry. Fuel call. Which reminds me, Bob, the generator tank probably needs filling. I thought of it earlier, then forgot again.'

He was frowning. 'I'll see to it. Them other blokes gone yet? Then why not shut up for the night? A bit late for station custom or travellers now, I reckon.'

My mother, who had always made her own

16

decisions, seemed grateful for the suggestion. 'You're probably right. We'll do that. And it'll give us the chance for a proper sit down and talk, something that's been just about impossible lately.' She sighed again, closing her eyes briefly and I felt a flicker of alarm.

'You look dead beat, Mum.'

She straightened as if to deny that momentary weakness. 'Oh, I'm fine, Charlie. A bit tired, that's all, because we're shorthanded. I lost my cook last week and then the backpacker we had left as well . . . Don, I'd like your ideas about holding a memorial service for Annabelle. But let's finish dinner first and we can talk about it over at the house. Now, who's for sweets?'

Conversation over the creamed rice dessert was confined to news from the Alice, and my flight, and my life in Melbourne. When the plates were cleared, Mum, at my insistence, took the Thorntons across to the house while I cleaned up. Bob helped, stacking and wiping dishes as if it were a normal part of his chores. I'd just rinsed a handful of silver when he broke his silence.

'She seen the doctor, Molly did, on his clinic run. Then she got herself into the Alice to visit some other quack.'

Fear lurched through me. 'Why? What's wrong with her?'

He scowled at the silver he was wiping. 'She ain't said, but somethin' is. She's always tired. And her colour ain't good — sort of greyish when we've had a busy day.' He glared at me.

'High time you came home, Charlie. Talk to 'er, make her see she can't keep this up. Ain't nobody indispensable and she's old enough to know it. If she don't ease up some, she's gonna wind up killing herself.'

I said fretfully, 'I can't help unless I know what the problem is, and she's not likely to tell me. You know what Mum's like! Is it stress, do you think? Is she worried about the business? What about Annabelle? I mean, something was obviously wrong *there* — has she been back here lately?'

'The little minx came through with some bloke about ten days back. They left again after hardly no time. Didn't even stay the night. So I dunno what that was about. Heading east they were — the Gold Coast, Molly reckoned. But she never told me why they'd come, or where from.'

'It would have to have been from the Alice, wouldn't it? Who was the man with her?'

Bob shrugged, then set down the pot he was drying. 'Some townie. All you see out here these days, backpackers and no-hopers like that useless damn cook. Riff-raff. Can't hold down a job in town so they come out here to bludge, then clear off whenever it suits 'em.'

'Have you advertised for another one yet?' I asked, momentarily diverted from the point.

'Course I bloody have,' he said, 'but they don't grow on trees. If the employment mob can find one in the Alice, he'll be out on the mail tomorrow.'

'That's good, then.' I wiped the sink down and

rinsed the dishcloth. 'I'll try and talk to Mum, Bob, and at least find out what the doctor's visit was about.' The dread word that nobody wanted to hear gibbered in the corner of my mind. It couldn't be cancer, it simply couldn't! But a tiny voice whispered, *Why not?* Why should the Carvers be exempt? Heartbreak, heart attack, suicide — why not cancer as well? What was so special about my family that fate should preserve us from that?

Abruptly I said, 'What do you suppose she wanted — Annabelle? She must've come for a purpose if she didn't even stay overnight! Was this the first time she'd been back? Last I heard, she had some office job over in Townsville, but that was years ago.'

'I wouldn't know. Molly didn't say nothin' but she weren't happy about it. An' it's the first time Annabelle'd been home in a coupla years. Made a big fuss when she got here . . . It was all: *How are you, Bob? Great to see you* . . . Didn't bother with no goodbye, but. She and Molly rowed, I reckon.'

'What about the man with her?'

He shrugged. 'Fancied himself, that one. Standover merchant, I reckon. I didn't take to him.' That didn't mean much, of course. Bob's approach to liking anybody would have made a tortoise into a racehorse. He hesitated and a look that was almost shame crossed his face. 'Matter o' fact,' he said, not meeting my eye, 'I brung the old dog over from my camp for the day.'

'*Did* you?'

'Well, I thought he might've needed seeing off.

19

I wouldn't've got no help from that dozy cook if it'd come to it.'

'It's still Jasper, then?' He'd be the third cattle dog of Bob's that I could remember, each with the single-minded savagery of the breed when it came to defending their own.

'Yeah.' He hung up the tea towel. 'The bush ain't what it was, Charlie. Full of strangers these days. I reckon it's down to the better roads. Too easy to get around now and there's some that come we could do without. Like those two. She might be Molly's niece but she's never been nothin' but trouble. Well, we've got enough of our own to deal with without that.'

'Annabelle's dead, Bob. She won't be troubling anyone ever again.'

His eyes flickered. 'Yeah. I forgot. Well, I don't s'pose you're too sorry, Charlie.'

I said as neutrally as I could, 'It's old history. Over and done with,' and took a last look about the kitchen. 'Anything else needed, or are you off now?'

'Reckon I'll pump the diesel for the genny first. You go on over.'

'All right. See you in the morning. Goodnight, Bob.'

'Get yourself a torch.' He plucked his hat off the hook near the bar and limped out.

My hand reached automatically to the shelf by the door to find one of the several which, as long as I could remember, had always lived there. The back door closed on its lock behind me and I followed the slim fall of torchlight along the path and through the gate into the older garden

20

surrounding the house that, eighty years before, had been built as the original homestead of Garnet Downs.

I found Mum and her guests drinking tea in the poky little front room that served as a lounge. The old house had three bedrooms and a long side verandah, latticed in for shade and coolness, which was used for extra bed space as required. My cousin and I had slept out there through hot summer nights, and had shared a large table at the other end for schoolwork during our primary school years.

In the lounge, the slate floor had sunk slightly but the now-empty fireplace in the chimney breast still drew well, making the lounge a snug spot in winter. Seeing me enter, Mum made to rise and I moved quickly to forestall her, helping myself from the tray on the side table.

'Did you get something sorted, then?' I asked, carrying my cup and saucer to the padded cane chair beside Rae's. 'I've been thinking — won't there have to be an inquest?'

Mum looked to Don for his opinion. 'I hadn't considered that. Tom said nothing about it, but I suppose . . . ?'

'Probably,' he agreed. 'I believe in such cases the authorities do — but it needn't change your plans, Molly. It would probably be months, maybe even a year, before they'd convene one.'

'Who would do that?' I asked.

'Well' — Rae wrinkled her brow, her hair shining silver in the light — 'a coroner's court would hold it. An inquiry into the circumstances surrounding the death, just for the record, you know. It's mostly a formality. A legal nicety. Held in whichever town the death occurred.'

'Ballina,' Mum murmured. 'At night, they think. Her clothes were found at daybreak by somebody walking the beach.'

Her words seemed to hang in the air and for the first time I felt the full horror of my cousin's act, seeing in my mind's eye the empty beach, black and silver under the stars. How desperate must she have been to have ended it there all alone in the dark water? My skin crawled. As an inlander I had no affinity with the ocean and the nameless dangers it held, and could imagine no death worse than drowning.

At that moment I forgave her the wrong she had done me; it wasn't to say I would forget it, but the knowledge that she had been driven to such lengths made my decision possible. In the final analysis she must have damaged herself far more than she had me. 'What on earth was she doing in Ballina?' I asked. 'The whole thing is just so *weird*!'

'Perhaps the letter will tell us. Charlie,' Mum said, 'What do you say to Sunday week for the service? Is that too long a wait for you? The date suits Don and it'll give me time to let people know. We'll have it in the Garnet's garden, I thought — maybe two-ish? That way we could serve everyone afternoon tea and they'd still have time enough to get home in daylight. Could you stay that long?'

'Yes, of course. There's no hurry, Mum. It looks like you could do with a hand so I'll stick around for a bit.'

'But your career — ' She stopped, then sighed, exasperated. 'It's Bob, isn't it? What's he been saying to you?'

'Oh, you know,' I answered lightly. 'Nothing's the same. The world's going to the dogs.' I nodded at Don and Rae. 'A real Cheerful Charlie, old Bob. Rain brings floods, sunshine drought, and if there's anything left over from either it'll be bushfires next . . . '

Don chuckled. 'I've met a few like that. Salt of the earth as a rule. Very well, then, Molly. I'll bring the accordion along. If there're any particular songs you'd like played, or that were a favourite of Annabelle's . . . They needn't be hymns, you know. Have a think about it.' He put down his empty cup and rose. 'We'll leave you to it now. So goodnight to you both, and thank you for an excellent dinner.'

'Yes, thanks, Molly, and goodnight. Nice to meet you, Charlie.' Rae had risen with her husband. Mum stood too and I began collecting the cups, marvelling at the ease with which the padre's wife hugged her hostess before quitting the room. I envied her assured approach; my own attempts at such closeness with my mother felt forced and awkward, while her embraces were fleeting and rare. As far back as I could remember casual hugs had never come easily to either of us.

'Leave that, Charlie,' Mum said once we were alone. 'You've been travelling all day. It'll wait till the morning.'

'It's fine, really it is, but there's something that won't wait.' With our audience gone I was blunt;

it was the only way with Mum. 'I need to talk to you. You were right about Bob. He's worried about you. He said you'd seen a doctor — what for? Are you ill?'

'It was nothing. That man! Good God, if you can't get to my age without a few aches and pains . . . Bob's worse than an old woman.'

'If it was no more than that, why did you need to see another doctor in the Alice?'

'Oh, for heaven sake! How did he find out about *that*?'

I shrugged. 'Overheard you making the appointment? What does it matter? He did, and now I want to know what's wrong. Is it' — my voice faltered — 'life threatening, Mum? You'll have to tell me if it is. I'm your *daughter*, for God's sake! Don't you think I have a right to know?'

'Oh, very well. I can see I'll have no peace until the whole world knows my business. So much fuss! It's my heart.' I must've paled for she flapped a dismissive hand. 'It's nothing major, just a bit of an irregularity. I saw some doctor at the monthly clinic at the hospital. He wants to do further tests but seems to think that a pacemaker will fix it. I'll be good as new once that's fitted.'

'And until it is?'

'Well, I'm supposed to take things quietly,' she admitted crossly, 'which is easy for him to say! As if I can spend my days lying around while the place falls down around me. But that's my problem, not yours. You've got your own career to worry about.'

'I haven't, not any longer.' At Mum's startled look, I continued. 'No, I'm serious — and it's got nothing to do with this. I've been thinking — oh, for a while now — about chucking acting. I'm not getting anywhere,' I admitted painfully, looking down to scratch at the ragged edge of a thumbnail. 'Oh, I expect I could scrape by for another year or two with waitressing and a bit of ad work, but I'm neither talented nor pretty enough for much else. I'm good for 'country image' stuff in the ad world, but that's about all. Outdoorsy-type set-ups with picnic blankets and dogs, and soon enough I'll be too old even for that.' I glanced up at her then, saying it for the first time. 'The truth is, you need more talent than I've got to make a living on stage or screen.'

Mum regarded me carefully. 'But you always said it was what you wanted. You love acting.'

'I did. I do. But sooner or later you have to face facts. It's like, well, loving art doesn't make you capable of painting a decent picture, does it? If I'm going to do it, and I made up my mind on the flight that I would, it may as well be now. So I'm not quitting because you need help, but seeing that I have, you might as well accept that I'm here to stay for a bit. Until you're well, or I find a new direction for myself. This business with Annabelle has just . . . ' — I shrugged — 'I don't know, brought it all to a head, given me the push I needed to change tack, I guess. But it was coming anyway. And speaking of Annabelle, Bob said she was back here a week or so ago. Why? What did she want? And who was the man with her?'

'A friend, she said. She called him Paul, and that's all she told me. Not that I inquired too closely.' Mum shrugged. 'Well, you know Annabelle's way with men. But her morals, thank God, are — were — her own affair. I gave up worrying about *that* a long time ago. This Paul could've been her friend, her lover, her boss — if she had one. Or she might've been his mistress, I suppose. If so, he can't have been very generous because she was after money.'

'What? She actually asked you for it?' I was outraged.

'I'm afraid it was more a demand. She seemed' — Mum hesitated — 'fairly desperate. I wish now that I had, but the truth is I couldn't help her. The Garnet barely breaks even, and I'm already paying off a loan I took out with the bank.' She sighed. 'I never intended to tell you this, Charlie, but since she's killed herself, I suppose you have a right to the knowledge, and it might help you understand what was behind her attitude to you. Her jealousy, what she did with Bryan . . . Annabelle wasn't your cousin, she was your half-sister.'

3

To say that I was dumbfounded was the understatement not of the year, but the century.

'*Sister?* How? She couldn't have been!' A swift calculation had me blurting, 'She was only two years older, so you and Dad were well married when . . . besides, Uncle Frank — '

'Yes,' Mum agreed. 'Your father cheated on him as well as me. He slept with Anmah while Frank was in Vietnam. He swore to me that it was only that one time, but for some women once is enough.'

She spoke flatly and I couldn't tell if it was a thread of jealousy or anger I discerned in her tone. My parents' marriage, once I was old enough to see it, had been an armed truce of careful civility and tight-lipped silence on my mother's part. My father had cajoled and wheedled and lost his temper and been largely ignored in the business, going his own way with madcap schemes that seldom paid off.

'Dear God!' The enormity of this latest transgression made all his other failings pale in comparison. 'His own brother! And my aunt — betraying a man who was away fighting for his country. When did you find out?'

'You were eight at the time. Of course, we'd had her since she was three.' Uncle Frank had been killed on patrol in the jungle after the battle of Long Tan and my parents had taken in the orphaned Annabelle when her mother became the victim of a hit and run one dark night in a Brisbane suburb, only a street away from the flat she was renting. Mum said tiredly, 'I got suspicious, I suppose. Jim couldn't disguise his partiality for her. I told him he wasn't being fair to you and he just blurted it out — that she was his daughter too.'

'*That* must've put a stopper on things,' I murmured, and she nodded with a wry little twist of a smile.

'He never could keep a secret, your father. I don't think he even wanted to because he always acted like owning up to the things he'd done was enough to somehow exonerate him. And the strange thing is that, no matter what it was — whether he was drinking our profits, or dabbling in some shonky get-rich-quick scheme only a fool would even look at — after a while I'd just let it go. I suppose it was just too exhausting to stay angry all the time. He wasn't forgiven but he acted like he had been, and that was good enough for Jim Carver. I think he was born without a conscience, or the ability to feel remorse.'

I felt a sudden spurt of jealousy for the man I should have despised. 'So did Annabelle know he was her father?'

Mum nodded. 'She must have. I don't know when he told her. When she turned eighteen, perhaps? He didn't make a will, as you know, so when he had the heart attack the roadhouse came to me. Annabelle told me that was wrong, that as his child she was entitled to a share, and if I wouldn't give her cash she wanted a deed to say she owned a third of the business. So she could borrow against it.'

'Unbelievable!' I muttered. 'Why was she so desperate for money, anyway?'

Mum said slowly, 'Ever since I heard she'd killed herself I've wondered if she was in some sort of trouble. She shouted at me when I told her I couldn't help her. Well, screamed really. Said I didn't understand, she had to have money. I said if she was that broke she could move back home, help out here, but that wouldn't do . . . Now I wonder if she was ill because, really, she looked quite haggard. Maybe it was worry,' Mum fretted, and sighed. 'I don't know — perhaps it was just tiredness making her so nervy. She had been travelling.' A stricken look passed across her face and she pressed the fingers of a work-roughened hand to her mouth. 'Lord, I was so angry! I wish now I'd made her tell me what was wrong.'

Less charitably and with the memory of city streets and parks fresh in my memory, I said, 'Could she have been on drugs, do you think?'

'Annabelle? No, she's too smart — was too smart — for that.'

'It's surprising who is,' I contradicted. 'It's not just the down-and-outs and deadbeats who get hooked, you know. Models, housewives, flash executive types . . . Maybe they never intended it to take over their lives, but it happens. She might've needed money to feed a habit.'

'Well, we'll never know, now.' Mum rose slowly, holding onto the chair for a moment, like a much older woman, before taking a step. 'I'm for bed. I'm glad you're sensible, Charlie. You were always the reliable one I never had to worry about. Sleep well.'

'Goodnight, Mum.' However unintentionally, her words stung. Good old dependable Charlie — always second, in looks and charm and her place in the family, and not even capable of protesting the way things were. The one good thing about it all, I brooded, was that growing up I'd at least been spared Annabelle's hand-me-downs. None of them would have fitted, even if I'd wanted frills and sashes, which I hadn't.

I went to bed in my old room, changed only by the addition of Mum's sewing machine and a wonky-legged occasional table that belonged in the lounge but had somehow found its way into the bedroom. Sleep, however, eluded me. Snatches of words uttered since my arrival kept repeating themselves in my head. Bob's blunt words: *Molly needs help.* Mum's angry voice: *She wanted money.* And the finality of my own decision: *I'm chucking acting* . . . And more pressing than all, the astonishing news that the orphaned girl whom my parents had raised beside me was actually my sister.

I wondered if my father had felt guilt for the deed that produced her, but doubted it. I had never known Uncle Frank or his wife. One dead before I was born, the other while I was too young to know she existed. How had Mum, once she knew the truth of Annabelle's parentage, managed to go on treating her in the same brisk, impartial manner she had always used towards us both? She must have loved her in her own undemonstrative way, I supposed, figuring the dates, for Annabelle would have been with us for seven years by the time I was eight. Still it was a lot to ask of any woman, and only a man as brass-necked as my father would have dared do so. Or as conscienceless . . .

★ ★ ★

I must have slept eventually, for at some point the treadmill of my thoughts had ceased and I woke to the grey light of dawn and the prolonged screeching of galahs flying about the mill and tank on the banks of the little creek from which Garnet Soak took its name. I could hear water running in the bathroom as I pulled on jeans and a t-shirt, then let myself out onto the dew-damp lawn which, I noted, badly needed cutting, to gaze around at the old shade trees and the tired lean of the morticed post and rail fence.

Roosters were crowing amid the dry grass between the mainly empty sheds, and a pair of ground doves were courting on the uneven stone pavers of the path. A flash of scarlet showed that the poinsettias, though badly in need of pruning, still flourished. The trees of course were self-sustaining, but in the Garnet's garden marigolds and petunias struggled through the weeds that had taken over the flower bed by the old summerhouse. The hose, unusually, had been left lying where it was last unrolled. Mum had never been an ardent gardener but she had always tackled the job with the same energy as she had kitchen chores. Judged by that, the garden was quite out of control. Was it really just a case of being shorthanded or was the heart problem, the 'bit of an irregularity' she had admitted to, more serious than she had let on?

I returned, frowning, to the kitchen having first coiled the hose back onto its stand. Mum was cooking eggs at the stove, the table already set for five.

'Good morning, Charlie. Still an early riser, I see. I thought the theatre might have changed that.' She flipped the toaster on. 'Could you make the tea? The kettle's just boiled.'

'You can blame waitressing for maintaining the habit,' I said, reaching for the mugs. 'Seven o'clock brekkies for shift workers. Something I thought of in the night, Mum — where did Annabelle live? She must've had a flat. Won't somebody have to go there, wherever *there* is, to collect her stuff, sort the rent, whatever?'

'If we had an address, yes. It was the first thing young Tom asked but I couldn't tell him.'

It took a moment to remember that Tom was the constable from Harts Range. 'Oh. No help to be had there, then. I just thought if she *was* ill there might be something — a prescription, perhaps, or an appointment card from a doctor . . . I suppose the police will track it down eventually, from her licence, if it's still current. She might have moved. I wonder why she took the wallet with her and not a handbag? You'd almost think she didn't want to be identified.'

'Then why leave her licence in the wallet or put my name and address on the letter?' Mum asked, sliding eggs onto toast just as Bob entered the kitchen. 'Morning, Bob. He took a photo of her away with him.'

'Who did?' I asked. 'Hello Bob.'

'Young Tom. He said the police will circulate it, see if they can find anyone who saw or spoke to Annabelle before she died.'

'Morning, Molly, Charlie, Bob.' Don had come in, followed by his wife who greeted us all, saying she'd had a lovely sleep.

Bob acknowledged my greeting and nodded at them both, 'Get a date for the service sorted, did yer, Padre?'

'Yes, we did. Sunday after next. Is this your seat?'

'Nah, this'll do me,' Bob dropped his hat on the floor beside the chair he'd chosen and reached immediately for the teapot. 'Pump's going,' he added economically and I became aware of the distant throb of an engine. 'I'll get the hoses started when I've ate.'

'I can do that. And clean in here, and sweep out the roadhouse,' I volunteered, crunching toast. 'What's the mower like to start, Bob? Toast, Rae?' I passed it. 'I notice the lawn needs a trim.'

'Easy. Just prime it,' he grunted. 'You ain't forgotten how to do that?'

I ignored this. 'When's the mail due these days, Mum? Still early?'

'Half an hour.' She glanced at the clock as she swallowed her tea. 'He'll want breakfast; his passengers too, if he has any.'

'If there is one let's hope it's our cook,' I murmured. 'I'll take it on if he doesn't turn up.'

'Thank you, Charlie. If you don't mind, that would be very helpful. Just till we can find someone.' She filled Don's cup from the pot.

'Or you get this pacemaker fitted,' I said, passing it down to him. 'Don't think I've forgotten about that, Mum. We're going to sit down and organise it today. If it needs to be done there's no point in waiting.'

'The doctor didn't say it was urgent,' she protested.

'Dad didn't think his indigestion was either,' I reminded her. 'I'm going to badger you into hospital, Mum, so get used to it.'

She frowned, as if seeing me for the first time. 'You've changed, Charlie.'

'Five years suiting myself, that's all.' Only nobody ever really did; there was always somebody or something to hamper one's choices. I grinned at her, suddenly surer of myself than I had been for a long time. 'Doormats are *so* last year — as my agent always says. Which reminds me, I need to give her a ring. Right, if you'll all excuse me' — I rose from the table — 'Where are the keys? I'd best open up and get started if the postie needs feeding. Is it still Sid Bennett?'

'*And* the same old truck,' Bob said. 'The Pope must've blessed the bloody thing, it couldn't still be running else.'

'You might want to have a word with him about that clapped-out Rover of yours, then, before it quits,' I quipped, accepting the keys from Mum. Don laughed and I felt Bob's glare follow me from the room.

34

4

The old green International I remembered pulled in before the Garnet just as I finished sweeping the verandah. Sid Bennet, stained teeth gripping his pipe stem, bristly grey moustache still covering his top lip, lifted out the canvas mailbag and headed towards me. 'Mornin', Miss. Molly about?'

'Hello, Sid.' I set the broom aside to take the bag, my gaze going past him to eye the woman climbing out of the cab. So the cook hadn't come after all. 'I didn't think I'd changed that much.'

He squinted for a second, then a smile split his face. 'Jesus! Didn't recognise you, Charlie. When did you get back?'

'Yesterday. How have you been?'

'Oh, fair to middling, you know. So, home for a visit, eh? You'll find it a bit on the quiet side I'm thinking, after the city.'

'Peaceful, is how I look at it. Just the two of you for breakfast today? I'm working the kitchen,' I explained. 'I was hoping you'd brought our new cook out today.'

He jerked his head at the woman who, I now saw, was laden with the weight of a large backpack, and was fitting another smaller one over her chest. 'I did — there she is.'

'Oh, good.' Why had I automatically expected a man? I lowered my voice. 'What's her name?'

He shrugged. 'Beauty, near as I can figure. Wog sheila, talks funny. Got your mailbag handy? I'll grab it before I eat, that way I don't forget.'

I had left the outgoing bag on the slatted seat further down the verandah. 'There you go, come in when you're ready.' Then I turned to the woman now waiting behind Sid. 'Good morning. I understand you've come to work here? I'll take you to see the boss, okay?'

I had spoken slowly and clearly, wondering, after Sid's comment, if language would prove a problem and was disconcerted to hear the careful preciseness of her reply.

'Thank you. I would like to speak, please, with the manager, before the driver he goes again, yes.'

So she could go with him if the job wasn't up to her expectations, I assumed.

'Of course. My name's Charlie — Charlie Carver. My mother, Molly, runs the roadhouse. And you are?'

'Ute.' She pronounced it *U-tee*. 'Ute Byzinoski. Is not so difficult, no? But the driver does not understand. He calls me Beauty — this is the name for a cow. Mine is Polish.'

'I see. He's probably a bit deaf. It's a noisy old truck.' She was, I judged, somewhere in her thirties, strongly built and athletic looking with pleasant if rather heavy features that added to her appearance of strength. Her lips were full, her nose broad, her teeth very white and even. Her blonde hair had been pulled back into a knot beneath a nylon hat, and she strode rather

36

than walked, shoulders braced against the weight on her back.

'You live here, too, Charlie? This is a man's name,' she observed with a slight frown.

'It's short for Charlotte. And yes, for the present I do. My mother's not very well. How long have you been here — in Australia, I mean?'

'Three months. Is the working break for me of six months. Then I return to Europe. I work in the Hague — you have heard of this place?'

'Oh, yes. I haven't been to Europe though.'

'Is very different.' She paused on the top step, her eyes lingering on the purple bulwark of the flat-topped range visible beyond the ridges and low scrub. 'Here is very dry, very . . . strange. But strong, you know. One sees the bones.'

It was an odd way to put it but I understood what she meant. 'Yes,' I agreed, 'a hard land, but beautiful. Come this way, please. I'll have to leave you with my mother because right now I should be in the kitchen.'

I hurried back to prepare a plate of bacon, eggs, tomato and toast for Sid, served him, and went out to position and start the sprays on the lawn. The tubs of geraniums that were staggered along the verandah were also dry so I watered them too, weeding as I went. Paint was flaking from the timber verandah posts and rails, and there was a patch of rust on the homemade barbecue under the big breezeway. The whole place, I thought critically, needed a face-lift, but financially it was probably an unlikely ask. A piece of guttering had come askew. I stood on the log fronting a bed of emu bush and pushed at it but it resisted my efforts.

'I'll get round to it,' Bob growled behind me and I startled, slipping from my precarious perch.

'We need a full-time maintenance man,' I said. 'Someone to paint and mow and water. The homestead fence is going to fall down anytime, and there's a sheet of tin loose somewhere on one of the sheds. I could hear it flogging when the wind got up last night.'

'I know. I ain't deaf,' he said testily. 'But there ain't no chance of hiring anyone. I came to tell you there won't be no power for a bit. I gotta service the diesel.'

'Okay, Bob.' An engine surged into life and a moment later Sid's truck pulled away. 'So, did she take the job — Ute?'

'Yeah,' he agreed gloomily. 'Wog tucker — that'll be the next bloody thing.'

I found Mum in the laundry readying a load of washing. 'Bob's turning the genny off,' I warned. 'Said he was going to service the engine. What did you think of Ute, and where is she now?'

'Settling in. She's got the end donga.' There were four demountable units at the eastern end of the roadhouse that served as accommodation for staff or travellers. 'She seems capable enough. I had her make her own breakfast. A few minutes and she had the hang of the kitchen, *and* she cleared up very efficiently after herself.' Mum had sorted the dark clothes into a basket as she spoke and now stooped to lift them.

'Here,' I said, 'let me. I'll get that.'

'Oh, don't be silly — aah!' Her face twisted as she gasped in sudden pain. She whitened and dropped the basket, bending double and clutching at her left arm, then slowly toppled over and collapsed in a loose heap on the floor.

'Mum! Oh my god, Mum!' I darted to the door yelling 'Bob!' at the top of my lungs, then raced back to my mother's prostrate form, straightening her legs and rolling her onto her side. The recovery position, I thought frantically. What else were you supposed to do for a stroke. Was it a stroke? Or a full-blown heart attack? I yelled Bob's name again and laid my ear uselessly against her chest, but it was Ute who appeared, frowning, in the doorway.

'You call very loudly. What happens? There is the problem, yes?'

'Yes! Run — the phone in the kitchen. Ring the flying doctor. The number will be on the whiteboard beside the phone. Tell them my mother's collapsed. It's her heart. Then come back. Hurry, Ute.'

Wasting no time on questions, she sped away. I grabbed an armful of dirty clothing to place under Mum's head and fumbled at her wrist for a pulse. She was very pale but seemed to be breathing okay and a moment later she sighed and her eyes fluttered open.

'Mum!' I seized her hand. 'God, you gave me the biggest fright. What happened?'

'Charlie?' She seemed dazed, but at least she could talk and she knew me. Her features looked equal too, mouth and brows level and there had been no slurring of my name. I eased her onto her back, adjusting the makeshift pillow.

'Are you in pain? Can you breathe okay?'

'Just tired, and my arm hurts . . . but the pain's easing now — better, anyway. I should . . . get up.'

'No. Stay where you are for a bit.' Uneven footsteps pounded on the path and I swivelled about expecting Ute but it was Bob, out of breath and alarmed.

'Molly,' he gasped, seeing her conscious. 'What the hell . . . you playing at, girl?

'It's okay,' I soothed. Ute must have told him. 'She's had a bit of a turn and fainted. We're calling the doctor and when she's rested a bit longer we're going to get her onto a bed until the plane gets here.'

'Oh, but I can't — ' Mum began.

I opened my mouth and Bob beat me to the draw. 'Yer can and yer will, Molly. I've had a gutful of you pretendin' there's nothing wrong when a blind man can see there is. There won't never be a better time to get yerself fixed up. Charlie can run the place and we've got ourselves a cook. You're goin' to hospital and that's flat.'

'You are, you know,' I seconded. My mother sighed, closing her eyes in tacit surrender, and that frightened me almost as much as her collapsing had.

★   ★   ★

The doctor wasted no time. The staff at the Flying Doctor Base rang back with his ETA and

40

we were out at the airstrip waiting when the plane touched down. Mum was loaded onto a stretcher, which the doctor and his pilot manoeuvred into the aircraft, followed by the bag I'd packed for her. The doctor, a bald six-footer called Clive Spears, took a few moments to reassure me that all would be well.

'It's an angina attack, and it's probably a good thing it happened. I warned her of the need to slow down, but she was never going to listen. A pacemaker is just a small procedure. We'll get it done maybe Wednesday when the cardiologist is due in town again. So a few days' bed rest first will do her no harm at all. They'll probably do some tests at the hospital — cholesterol, and maybe an angiogram to check her arteries. A thorough investigation. Try not worry too much — she'll be a new women when you get her back.' He smiled and ducked under the wing while Bob and I withdrew to the parked station wagon to watch the plane take off and arrow away into the blue above the range.

When it had vanished from sight, Bob turned the key in the ignition, saying, 'Wednesday. Well, you were gonna stay till the do next Sunday, weren't yer? So her being gone meanwhile won't muck up yer plans. She'll be home by then.'

'Maybe — but if they're thinking of an angiogram now . . . That gives them a picture of her arteries. It might turn out that Mum needs a stent, or even a bypass. Anyway, I'm not going back, Bob. I'm home for the duration.'

His eyes, squinched in their wrinkled surrounds of flesh, studied me, giving nothing away.

41

'Good,' he grunted. 'Glad to hear it, Charlie. I reckon Molly'll be too, though she won't never admit it.'

'It's what I want, too,' I said. 'It just took me a while to work it out.' I eyed him curiously as he engaged the gear and drove off. 'Something I wondered, Bob — did Mum ever let on that Annabelle wasn't her niece? Because it turns out she's my half-sister, if you can believe it.'

'No, she never did, but it figures.' He shook his head and snorted in disgust. 'He was a proper piece of work, yer dad. Did she know?'

'Annabelle? Apparently. She wanted money — that's why she came to see Mum. Money, or a means of raising it against the roadhouse.'

'Good Christ!' he muttered disgustedly. 'She was his get all right! Take — that's all either of 'em knew. No wonder Molly's in hospital.'

I remembered then and exclaimed in dismay. 'The letter! I wonder if it came and, if it did, whether Mum had a chance to read it?'

'Reckon you'd better check,' he said, coasting into the shed bay that served as a carport and switching off the motor. 'The copper's bound to want to see it too.'

★   ★   ★

The letter was waiting in the bag, which hadn't yet been emptied, addressed to *Mrs M Carver, PMB 21, Garnet Roadhouse, via Alice Springs*. The sender's name *A Carver* adorned the back flap but without an accompanying address. Much as I longed to open it, I knew I couldn't and laid it aside with a sigh. Annabelle's explanation, if that was what it was, would have to wait until my mother's return. Perhaps it was just as well, I reflected. I wouldn't have put it past her to have made her final communication accusatory in tone, a *look what you made me do* epistle, in revenge for Mum's failure to give her what she'd wanted.

By the time I'd sorted the mail and checked on Ute, already rearranging the shelves of the kitchen fridge to suit herself, the heavy beat of the diesel had recommenced and the power was back on. I started to explain what she'd need to do and was firmly interrupted.

'I have the menu, yes? They order, I cook. Is simple enough, Charlie. Your mother has the good care now, yes?'

'Yes,' I agreed feebly, and left her to it. I started the washing machine, then returned to the roadhouse where a vehicle was pulling in under the shade trees out front. I checked the cash in the till and waited for my first customer to enter.

By smoko time the roadhouse was busy. Bob had taken over at the counter, dispensing beer and cold drinks, taking requests for coffee and snacks, and scribbling down orders for meals, which he handed in to Ute through a hatch in the wall that divided the kitchen from the front room. Travellers stopped off for fuel, to browse the stand of tourist literature, to ask questions about the road and distances between places, or to purchase a postcard or one of the other small souvenirs from the shelf by the door. Finding myself unemployed, I went off to finish the house chores, starting by hanging out the wet clothes.

That done, I pulled the mower from the shed and began hunting for the whipper-snipper. It turned out to be in pieces on the bench in the workshop, obviously a work in progress that Bob was still getting around to finishing. The edges would have to wait, but the lawn couldn't. Having checked the fuel and the spark plug, I primed the mower, gave a tentative tug to the starting cord and was gratified to hear the engine roar into life.

Mowing was a soothing, repetitive task. It gave me time to think while providing an occupation that helped lessen my anxiety over my mother. The doctor's words had been more reassuring than her tired, grey-faced appearance as she'd vanished from my sight. Was a pacemaker really going to cure the 'irregularity' that Dr Spears had spoken of, or did a more serious problem lie behind her collapse? Spears was a GP, not a cardiologist. He didn't have the equipment to carry out the tests that she would have had in Melbourne, for instance. I wondered if any beyond the most basic were available in Alice Springs, and whether I should have insisted on a transfer to a city hospital. But I couldn't force her to go and I guessed, anyhow, that there was no way she would agree to it.

Sweat gathered round my neck and shoulders as the pile of lawn cuttings grew. I felt the skin of my arms tighten from the heat and belatedly realised that an overshirt would have been sensible. My skin was city pale, after all. By the time I'd finished, I was hot and the thin t-shirt was clinging to my body. I emptied the last catcher of grass, pushed the mower back to its home and went to sit in the coolest spot I knew of, the old summerhouse behind the weed-laden flowerbed. I had sedulously shunned it until now, but if I was going to stay at the Garnet for any length of time, then avoidance simply wouldn't work. Fanning my flushed face with my hat, I stepped resolutely inside the space where my life had been shattered, and my heart broken, five years before.

5

Nothing about it had changed. The floor was still flagged with irregular slabs of stone carefully butted together between sand-filled cracks; the long bench seat, with its rounded timber back and stout red-gum legs, was the same, though dusty and spider-webbed from disuse. The thatching of the roof, fashioned from spinifex packed between layers of netting was as I remembered it, and the semi-open latticed sides still drew in the cooling breezes. Someone had added a cane chair and I chose that, having first tipped it up to check for redbacks, rather than the bench where, that now-long-ago day I had chanced upon Annabelle and Bryan *flagrante delicto*.

The words, which I had never used before, hadn't sprung to mind then, of course, as I stared in disbelief and horror at the two of them. But long afterwards, my soul still writhing in shame and self-hatred at my naivety, I had looked it up. 'In blazing offence' was its literal meaning. Well, you couldn't say fairer than that, I had thought, about catching one's fiancé and cousin semi-naked in each other's arms. The look of horror on Bryan's face when he saw me had been almost as bad as the act he was engaged in. A guilty visage would have meant a conscience, but the horrified expression I had glimpsed upon his face showed only that he'd never intended for me to learn of his betrayal.

Because, I had realised, plumbing his expression in that revelatory moment, no overweening passion had brought him to this assignation in the summerhouse. The knowledge had seared through me like a flame until the beautiful edifice of trust I had built to contain my love for him was a smoking ruin at my feet. It wasn't a mistake; he hadn't simply chosen the wrong Carver girl to marry and discovered the fact too late. His expression of horror and almost ludicrous dismay at my untimely arrival plainly showed that he'd meant for our marriage to go ahead as planned, doubtless with side benefits to be supplied by Annabelle as and when the mood and opportunity took them both. In this — as in so much else where my cousin was concerned — I was, as usual, to come out second best.

And now she was dead. I wondered if my mother had cried over the news. I felt no inclination to do so, but Mum, after all, had raised her. I had seen my mother angry, I reflected, and exasperated, and sad, but I had never actually seen her weep. Not even when my father died. Stunned, yes, by the suddenness of it, and then she had just got on with things as was her wont. She had been furious with both Annabelle and Bryan over the cause of my broken engagement, bracingly sympathetic with me, and supportive when I had slapped the smirk from Annabelle's face. I had put into that blow, I could now admit, not only the fury of betrayal but the resentment of years. Because the smirk that had accompanied her careless dismissal of the act — *Well, if you're too shy to satisfy a man, what makes him off limits to someone who will?* — told me that she had planned the whole thing, including being found out.

I had wept. Buckets of tearing heartfelt sobs, an orgy of grief and pain over the shattering revelation of smashed dreams. Being told, 'Better to find out before you marry than after,' and the old standby, 'He was never good enough for you, anyway,' did nothing to ease it. I had been too upset then to even consider why Annabelle had acted as she had, but now I wondered if the deed had been borne of jealousy. Because I was acknowledged as Jim Carver's daughter and she was not. Nothing else accounted for it — she was prettier than me, cleverer too, and more popular, a flower for everyman's attention to light upon. And now she was dead.

There had to be a point somewhere between grief, of which I felt none, and 'good riddance', I thought guiltily. Annabelle had been a close blood relative, even if I hadn't previously been aware of how close. She could do me no more harm, and I was suddenly, uneasily aware that, given Mum's collapse, it would probably fall to me to speak on Annabelle's behalf at the service on Sunday. No life could matter so little that something kind and thoughtful couldn't be said about it. If —

'Hello!' a man's voice called. 'Anybody home?'

Startled, I scrambled up from my seat and looked out to see a khaki-clad figure turning a slow circle on the lawn. He called again. 'Anybody here?'

'I am,' I said, stepping out of the summer-house. 'Charlie Carver. Who are you looking for?'

'You, Miss Carver. Bob said you were over here somewhere. I'm Tom Cleary, the constable from Harts Range.'

'Oh, of course.' The khaki shirt and puggareed hat should have made that obvious. 'I was miles away.' I became belatedly aware of my dishevelled, sweat-stained appearance, and brushed at the grass cuttings sticking to my jeans. 'Sorry. What's it about, then?'

He coughed, looking awkward. 'No, I'm sorry — for your loss and to bother you at this time. The letter the deceased wrote . . . have you received it yet? The police in Alice would like a look at it, you see.'

'Oh. Yes, well, it was in the mail but I'm afraid my mother hasn't opened it yet. She was evacuated by the flying doctor this morning, before she had a chance to . . . '

'Molly's ill? I'm sorry to hear it. And you haven't opened it yourself?' His glance was disturbingly keen, like someone waiting to pounce on the tiniest inaccuracy, and I bridled.

'Certainly not! It's addressed to my mother. And I'm afraid you can't have it until she's seen it.'

'Ah. What's happened to Molly, then? You said the doctor flew her out?'

'She collapsed. Her heart,' I replied baldly. 'So I'm afraid you'll all have to wait. Even if I could,

49

I wouldn't be upsetting her now with whatever's in that letter.'

'No, I see that. Well, I hope you have good news of her soon. Please give her my best when you speak to her next. She's an institution around the range, you know.' His keen eyes assessed me. 'You live away, Miss Carver? I've not seen you before.'

'Oh, call me Charlie. No, I work — worked in Melbourne. Look, as you're here, perhaps you can tell me, will there be an inquest held for Annabelle, and if so, when?'

'Yes,' he said definitely. 'All unexplained or unexpected deaths warrant one. As to when, I'm afraid I couldn't say. You'll be informed at the time.'

'Right, thanks. Oh,' I remembered, 'Padre Don will be holding a memorial service here tomorrow week, around two-ish, if you'd like to come? And if you wouldn't mind passing it on to any of the neighbours you see in the meantime? I'll be ringing around the stations this evening. Did you ever meet Annabelle, Tom?'

'I'm afraid not. But my wife and I will certainly attend to support Molly. And I'll spread the word.' He lifted his hat and turned away.

'Thank you,' I said to his retreating form. I'd almost forgotten about ringing the neighbours. It would be cheaper after seven but there was one call I had to make immediately. It was hours now since the doctor's plane had left the Garnet strip, so I went indoors to ring the hospital to inquire how Mum was doing.

She was resting comfortably, according to the

nurse who took the call. I asked if I could speak with her and was told she was sleeping at the moment. The news set off immediate alarm bells. The idea of Mum sleeping during daylight hours was so strange that I blurted, 'Is she all right? I mean — '

'She's worn out, Miss Carver. It seems to me what she really needs is a week's bed rest.' The nurse had a soft, measured voice. I pictured her as firm but kind. 'Look, try not to worry too much. Whatever caused her collapse, sleep can only help. When she wakes I'll tell her you rang, shall I?'

'That would be great. Thank you.' I replaced the handpiece and went to reassure Bob.

*   *   *

A day spent weeding, watering, wiping down the dusty shelves in the roadhouse and rearranging the stock showed me just how much my mother's hands had slipped on the reins of management. The work had plainly been getting beyond her for some time. Bob watched my progress through these chores with a sort of dour jealousy, relieved on the one hand to see the place being restored to some of its former order, but defensive about the need for my intervention.

'For heaven's sake, Bob,' I said at last, tiring of his sniping and black looks. 'It's not Mum's fault, or yours, so cut out the dog-in-the-manger act, will you? I want the Garnet sparkling for Mum when she gets home. Ute's scouring the

51

kitchen right now — that last cook you had can't have cleaned the stove once! And seeing I'm quite capable of serving behind the counter, I don't see why you can't make a start on a bit of outside repair work tomorrow. If we all pull together we'll have the place sorted in no time. It's what you want, isn't it?'

He glowered at me, grey-haired and hard-eyed, his heavy shoulders stooped from age and past labour, refusing to agree. Instead he growled, 'You've changed, Charlie. Bloody oath, you have.'

'And not before time,' I snapped, exasperated. 'You can thank Annabelle for that. Now, are you going to quit sulking and get behind me, or what?'

He surprised me then with a grudging smile. 'Oh, yeah — you're Molly's girl, all right. What d'yer want done, then? That gutter I suppose, and the loose sheet of iron on the shed?'

'They'll do for starters,' I agreed, enormously relieved that he'd come round. I knew I couldn't manage without him. 'There's the garden fence — one good push would have it over, and I noticed the side of the steps are pulling away from the verandah out front. I think the screws have gone. The whole place needs painting but we probably can't afford to do more than the timber work right now. And if that isn't enough, there're more weeds than gravel around the fuel apron. That's got to be a fire risk . . . '

'Righto, righto — I get the idea.' Almost apologetically he added, 'When you can't do nothin' about it, after a bit you stop noticing. I reckon the punters don't, but.'

'No.' I sighed. 'Well, if you're willing, Bob, we'll see what we can do to straighten things out. God knows Mum doesn't need the worry, or the extra work that Sunday, for instance, is going to make. We'll have to try and keep her from doing too much when she gets back. I've already decided I'll do the eulogy. Maybe I can ask Rae Thornton to help keep Mum occupied and sitting down?'

Bob snorted. 'Chance'd be a fine thing. That young copper find you, did he?' It was his way of asking why he'd come.

'Mmm. He wanted Annabelle's letter. I told him not before Mum had seen it and that won't be soon. God knows what she put in it.'

He scowled. 'Blamin' Molly most like, for what she was gonna do. Wouldn't put it past her. Maybe,' he added bluntly, 'you oughta read it first.'

'No, I can't, Bob. It's private. Besides, she knows it exists, so even if it says something like that, I couldn't destroy it.' I glanced at the wall clock. 'Well, I'd better get that washing in, and you've got a customer.' A vehicle had pulled into the bowser and a family were decanting themselves from it. 'I'll leave you with it,' I said, departing once more for the garden.

★　★　★

That evening, having made a list of the numbers to call, I sat down and began ringing the neighbours. Many of them had probably already

53

heard the news of Annabelle's suicide; all the local station people would have known her, and those who hadn't, like the stockmen and contractors whose work was seasonal, knew my mother. They would come for her sake.

I started with the closest — the Webbs' place, Mt Farlow — and worked east and north through the rest: Abbey Downs, Upatak, Penny Hills, Red Tank, the Red Tank Store, Kharko and Arcadia. The phone rang out at the latter station, and I would have to try them again later, while at Kharko, the biggest company property in the district, I got the bookkeeper rather than the manager or his wife. They were both in the Alice, he said, but would be home tomorrow and he'd pass the message on. I thanked him, took a deep breath and tapped in the number for Red Tank, the Mallorys' property. If Bryan was still at home and chanced to pick up the phone I would hang up. I could always call again tomorrow, but to my relief it was his mother, Kathleen, who answered with her husky smoker's voice.

'Hello. Kathleen? Charlie Carver from the Garnet.' I gave her almost no time to offer her condolences or ask, in the circumstances, the usual inquiries. 'I'm fine, thanks. How are you? Oh, you've heard? Yes, yes — a terrible shock. Actually, it's about Annabelle that I'm calling. We're holding a memorial service for her at the roadhouse, next Sunday. About two-ish, we thought, if you'd like to come? And if you wouldn't mind passing the word on to the store? Anyone who knew her, or knows Mum, is welcome. Padre Don will be running things. My mother? No, sorry, she's not here — in hospital at present, I'm afraid. Her heart. Mmm yes, look, sorry but I can't stop to talk, a million things to do. Bye.' I put the phone down, cutting her off mid-sentence before she could mention Bryan or ask anything further.

The Mallorys had five sons, of which my erstwhile fiancé was the youngest and the apple of his mother's eye. She had deplored the breaking of our engagement, seeming to think Bryan's behaviour a mere peccadillo, and one easily forgiven. I, on the other hand, had maintained with some heat that 'Boys will be boys' was neither an excuse for his actions nor a basis for forgiveness. This was the first time we had spoken since.

★ ★ ★

The house was very quiet without Mum's presence. I picked up the phone again, rang the hospital and asked for Mrs Carver. The receptionist put me through immediately. There was a click, a burst of television noise that sank away and then her voice. 'Bob?'

'It's Charlie, Mum. How are you feeling?'

'Oh, Charlie. I'm fine. I slept most of the day so I've had a good rest. That was probably all I needed, but they're not letting me out till I've seen this blasted doctor on Wednesday.'

'That's why you're in there, Mum. How's the food?'

'It's all right. More to the point, how are you

all managing? The new cook — is she worth paying?'

'Definitely. She's reorganised the fridge, and the kitchen hasn't had such a going over for years. Look, about Wednesday — do you want me to come in, be there with you for the op?'

'Of course not! It's only a local anaesthetic, the nurses tell me. Before I forget, make sure you order extra loaves this week. We'll need heaps of sandwiches for Sunday. Have you rung people yet, to tell them about the service?'

'All under control, Mum. You don't have to worry about anything. I'd better go, but Bob'd want me to tell you hello from him, too. Love you, goodnight.'

'Goodnight, Charlie. I know I can rely on you. I always could.'

I had scarcely hung up when someone rapped decisively on the frame of the screen door. I opened it to find Ute there. She switched off her torch and entered, saying, 'The time now is good, yes? I wish to make the menu, you understand, for this tea you will be having on Sunday.'

'Yes, of course. Sit down, Ute.' She had brought pad and pen and now squared them on the table before her. 'Well, I thought — '

'For how many?' she interrupted. 'First the numbers I must know. Then we put the heads alongside for what is possible to make, yes? There is no pate, no — no little goods.' She frowned. 'This is what you call the specialist meats? No olives, and the cheese — ' She grimaced, unimpressed it seemed by Kraft's ordinary Processed. 'So, how many come, and what should you wish I make?'

'Twenty?' I said. 'Maybe more. Let's work on thirty, say, because the three of us have to eat as well. And I thought mainly sandwiches — plates and plates of them. I'll order extra bread, and eggs. We'll have lettuce, cold meat, pickles, cheese, cucumbers, hard-boiled eggs. It's not deli stuff,' I said, 'but it's what people eat in these parts. And if you could make some slices and cakes to round it out — maybe a big custard tart too? It's a lot of work but I'm happy to help. I can chop and spread and wrap for you, and wash up. We'll use the big urns for tea and if they want cold drinks they can buy them.'

'So, you will not have the little fancy hors d'oeuvres with the fruits and cheeses, and smoked meat?' She frowned disapprovingly.

'Just something filling that'll see them through until they get home. It's a long drive for all but a few.'

'Threw?' she said uncertainly. 'This I do not know. Where will they see, please?'

'I mean, food that will satisfy — fill them up, you know. See them through to the next meal.'

'Oh, *through* — yes. And all these peoples know this girl — woman — who has herself killed?'

'Some did. The rest will come out of respect. It's what you do out here.'

'I understand.' She regarded me with her piercing blue eyes, her head on one side. 'And you, Charlie, you were close, yes? You feel the sadness for her? I am sorry for you.'

57

'Thank you, but you needn't be,' I said. 'I hadn't even seen her in five years. Annabelle and I, we weren't close at all.'

'But she is your family.' The disapproval was back.

'As to that, we have a saying: you can choose your friends but not your family. If it was up to me, I wouldn't ever have chosen her to be either.'

6

Wednesday morning dawned clear and cool with the early sunlight painting the range ochre and orange. I stood in the garden sipping a second cup of tea, staring at its plateaued top and worrying about Mum. I wished now that I had driven in to be with her. It was all very well to dismiss the procedure as mere day surgery but I had never known Mum to be ill with anything beyond a dose of flu, and the mere thought of her in theatre frightened me.

Bob, who was tackling the garden fence, limped into view carrying a crowbar and shovel. His repair work had got as far as the homestead and now that he was freed from helping in the roadhouse and the care of the poultry, which I had also taken over, the effects of his uninterrupted labour were becoming noticeable.

I said abruptly, 'I think I'll order five litres of paint for the front. Do you reckon that'll be enough — just for the uprights and railings?'

He squinted into the distance as he considered the question. 'Should do it. It'll need undercoating, mind. And a new paintbrush wouldn't hurt, neither. Anything in the shed'll have fallen to bits years ago.'

'Okay. You have a colour preference, Bob?'

'Yeah, not white. And not too bright neither, it'll show the dust.' Gruffly he added, for Bob could always read me, 'She'll be fine, girl. A pacemaker's nothin' major.'

'I'm not worried.'

'Course you ain't. Ute's lookin' for you by the way — something about the gas.'

'Okay.' I tossed out the last of my tea and went off to deal with it and to ring the hospital. Mum, when I was put through to her, was thoroughly exasperated.

'It isn't,' she snapped when I asked when the op was scheduled for. 'I'm waiting on the damn doctor, and he's not starting his rounds till eleven.'

'But why? What's going on, Mum?'

'Why would they tell *me*?' she asked. 'They did some sort of test yesterday, putting a line up through a vein to my heart, but all I was told — and that by a nurse, mind you! — was that maybe I wouldn't be getting the pacemaker just yet. *Doctor will explain*, she said. Like I was a child.'

'Right,' I said soothingly. 'Well, I'll ring again after lunch. Perhaps you'll know what's happening by then.'

Unable to decide whether this was good or bad news, I said nothing to Bob, resolving to phone the moment lunch was over, but long before then Ute put her head through the kitchen hatch to call me.

'Is the telephone rings for you, Charlie.'

'Thanks.' I picked up the handpiece. 'Good morning. Garnet Roadhouse. What can I do for you?'

'Miss Carver? It's Doctor Spears, from the RFDS Base.' I froze and, taking my silence for incomprehension, he continued. 'The Flying Doctor. I was out there the other day to pick up your mother — '

'Yes,' I swallowed. 'Of course, doctor. What's wrong?'

'The cardiologist who is treating Mrs Carver has sent me the results of some tests that they've run. I've been looking over them and I'm afraid her condition is a little more complicated than we all originally thought. As a result of that he won't be implanting the pacemaker. In fact — '

I interrupted his careful discourse. 'How bad is it, doctor? What did the tests show?' My own heart seemed to have slowed to a crawl, its loud, doomful thumping at odds with my gasping breaths.

He said crisply, 'It's not her heart so much as her arteries. The angiogram show that three of them are dangerously narrowed and she needs bypass surgery. It's a fairly common procedure these days. Of course it can't be done here — we haven't got the facilities — so she'll be transferred to Adelaide, which is where the specialist comes from. He'll make the arrangements and find a surgeon and schedule the op for sometime next week. It's that urgent, I'm afraid, Charlie.'

A part of me wondered how we had progressed to first names so quickly, while another section of my brain understood that it was a professional ploy to help cushion the shock of the news. Terror gibbered at the edges of reason and with an effort I pushed it back. 'That means open heart surgery, doesn't it? The risks — '

'Are far greater if intervention doesn't occur, I'm afraid. Dr Symes will have gone through it all carefully with your mother, but she really has no option — she must have the procedure.' His voice went on and on, listing the positive outcome likely for a non-smoking, non-drinking patient with good muscularity. Well, Mum certainly had that. She'd worked as hard as any man and her reward was a hospital bed and a dangerous, possibly fatal, operation.

When he'd finished counselling me, I thanked him for phoning and sat down limply on the low stool beside the workbench, thinking that I needed to ring the hospital. I'd have to go to her, and Bob would have to be told, and there was the service on Sunday, and dear God, what if the operation killed her . . . ?

'This news is bad, Charlie?' Ute's question dragged me back to the Garnet's kitchen.

'What? Oh, yes, I'm afraid it is. My mother is far sicker than we thought. Look, can you just watch for customers? I have to — ' I left without finishing, wondering if it was too late to cancel the service, and whether the two of them could manage without me for — how long? A week, ten days? And, meanwhile, what would I be using for money? The flight to Adelaide, food, accommodation — I couldn't afford it and neither, I suspected, could the Garnet.

Bob had the rails of the garden fence staggered across the lawn and was levering a leaning post back into an upright position. Seeing me come he thumped the point of the crow-bar into the earth and dragged a wrist across his sweaty brow.

'What's 'appened now?' he demanded wearily. 'A blind man could see somethin' has.'

I told him and watched the shock settle on him. 'Christ!' he muttered. 'It if ain't one thing it's another. Seems to me Molly never caught a decent break in her bloody life. But she'll pull through, Charlie. She's strong and a fighter. Kilkenny cats ain't got nothin' on Molly.'

Distractedly I grasped at the allusion, a bit of doggerel he used to recite to my younger self when spats with Annabelle had taken me to him in tears . . . 'They fought and they fit, they scratched and they bit, till 'stead of two cats there weren't any.'

'I'll have to go to town, Bob. If I take the station wagon — just there and back before Sunday — could you and Ute manage till then?'

'Course, Charlie. But wait a bit. Ring Molly first, find out when she's going south. She'd want you to keep yer head over this. Not go rushin' off for nothin'.'

'It's not nothing, Bob — it's her life,' I said sharply.

'The Garnet's her life, girl. That's what she'll be worryin' over. You ring her, see what she wants. Seems to me you ain't been bothered much about that these last five years.'

There was enough truth in his words to stop the furious reply on my tongue and I swallowed, saying feebly instead, 'She wanted me to leave.'

'Yeah, she did. Yer needed recovery time, she

said. But did it have to take five years — and in all that time not one visit? So now you're back, you listen to what Molly wants for once. Seems to me I'm the only one round here ever thinks about her needs.' He glared at me, his mouth as tight as a trap.

'Are you?' I spat. 'Well, let me tell you, Mum never *needed* anyone. Even you. You think I wanted to stay away? That scraping by on shitty part-time jobs, and knowing I was getting nowhere because I haven't any real talent for acting, was fun?' What had he expected me to do, I wondered wildly. Come running home and by so doing admit to failure in yet another sphere? 'I stayed because I had to.'

I was shouting, I realised. And I could tell by the flash of hurt in his eyes that the thrust about not being needed had hit home. I was suddenly horribly ashamed of myself. He had been with us forever, as faithful and uncomplainingly loyal to Mum as the guard dog he sometimes resembled. He loved her, I saw then. How blind was I not to have seen it before?

Bob treated my tirade with the contempt it deserved. He turned his shoulder and picked up the bar. 'Ring her,' he repeated stolidly, and resumed work with the post.

★   ★   ★

I waited until the evening, not so much because it was cheaper then, but to allow us both time to absorb the news. Mum had, predictably, worked out the reason for the delay.

64

'You'll have heard from the doctor, then, Charlie?'

'Yes. Doctor Spears rang. He explained about the tests. What did the specialist say?'

'Pretty much the same, I imagine,' she responded dryly. 'It's the operation or a heart attack, apparently. It's been scheduled for a week from today at the Queen Elizabeth Hospital in Adelaide. I'll go in as a public patient and there's some sort of transport assistance scheme that he said I'd be eligible for. That's quite a relief.'

'Yes.' It would certainly help but was unlikely to extend to relatives of the patient. 'Mum, don't you think we should talk about this? I mean, of course it's your decision but the risks . . . I was thinking I'd drive in tomorrow and — '

'No, Charlie,' she said firmly. 'There's no need. Besides, I want you there, running things for me. Of course there are risks! *Living* is a risk, but does that mean we should all wish ourselves unborn? I understand it's quite a lengthy operation, but Doctor Symes sees no reason why I shouldn't get through it. I'm basically healthy and he said the surgeon he has in mind is first class. He's already rung him and the man's displaced another, less urgent case in my favour.' I was silent for she'd obviously made up her mind. Apparently satisfied that I wasn't about to argue further, she continued on. 'Now, listen — about the Garnet. You might want to jot this down because there're a few things coming up that you'll have to deal with while I'm away. Ask Bob if you get stuck, but he's not so good when it comes to record keeping, and tax time's coming around again . . . '

7

In the morning I apologised stiffly to Bob for shouting at him. He grunted in reply, plainly not yet ready for olive branches. I said coldly, 'You were right. She doesn't want to see me. When's the fuel tanker coming?'

'Monday. If you need him to bring gas, yer want to order it today.'

'Right.' I added it to my list of things to do, the weightiest of which was 'Write something for service'. By Saturday night I was in despair and still had nothing more to show than a few jottings about Annabelle's parentage (untrue) and schooling. Beyond that I couldn't think of a single thing to say; I hadn't loved her, I wouldn't miss her, and she wasn't going to leave an irreparable hole in my life. I'd simply have to wing it, and if I dried up mid-sentence, I'd just have to pretend that grief was responsible. I must have learned *something* in the five years I'd wasted on acting.

By midday Sunday I was too busy to worry about it. In the usual way of things Saturday had seen few travellers at the Garnet, but Sunday saw a solid stream of people pulling in for fuel and refreshments and a break from the road. One of the fuel pumps jammed, and after a fruitless twenty minutes of tinkering, Bob used a felt pen to scrawl OUT OF ORDER across the bowser before hurrying back to serve impatient customers. Ute and I were fully occupied in the kitchen, filling and wrapping sandwiches, and assembling cups for afternoon tea. Bob already had the tables out and the urns filled with water. The roadhouse had only a modest number of chairs but he had improvised long bench seats made of planks of timber over logs scattered about on the lawn. They'd do for the service and the tea, he'd said roughly, and any bugger objecting to 'em could sit on the grass for him.

Padre Don and his wife flew in a little after one o'clock. Bob fetched them from the airstrip and, over a cup of tea, Don laid out the order of service for me.

'I visited Molly last night,' he said. 'She looks well rested, and she seems positive about this operation she's having next week. She asked if I'd play 'In The Sweet By And By' for Annabelle. I thought around three songs would do. Would you like to choose the others, Charlie?'

'Hymns, you mean?' I asked doubtfully. 'I'm not sure I know that many, padre.'

'Just ordinary songs. Annabelle must have had favourites. Of course, whether I'd know them is another thing.'

'Well,' I ransacked my memory. 'What about that Armstrong hit, 'What A Wonderful World'? Do you know that.'

He hummed a few bars. 'Yes, I do. That's easy. And another one?'

''I Should Be So Lucky'. She was always singing that. Or do you think it'd be a bit insensitive?'

He frowned. 'I'm not sure I know — '

'Yes, you do, Don,' Rae interposed. 'It goes like this.' She began to sing and in a few moments he was bobbing his head in time and humming along.

'You're right. That's the music sorted, then. I've planned just a short service, then we'll have the songs and a prayer. As Molly's not here, would you say a few words, Charlie? Just a bit about your cousin — an anecdote or favourite memory would do. I'm a bit disadvantaged celebrating the life of someone I didn't know.'

I drew a breath. 'Yes, I will. Now, are you staying overnight? You're more than welcome if you'd like to.'

'Thank you,' Don said, 'but I need to get back. Rae came up with an idea about that though.'

'Yes?'

Rae smiled. 'It's wonderful how God works things out. I'm sure you'd love to see your mother before she flies south, and I just happen to know that young Mike Webb's in the Alice today and heading back out tomorrow. He's head stockman at Abbey Downs. So, how would you like to fly in with us this afternoon, see Molly tonight and get a lift home next day? I know you're busy here but you'd be back by lunchtime. What do you think?'

'Oh, Rae, that would be great. Thank you! I'll take you up on that.' And Bob be blowed, I thought. If anything went wrong with the op it could be my last chance to see Mum — even if it meant being rebuked for disobedience.

Half an hour later the neighbours began arriving
in traybacks and station wagons. Some I knew,
like George and Bess Himan from Upatak, the
Maddisons from Arcadia, and Kathleen Mallory
and three of her married sons. Bryan, I was
relieved to see, wasn't among them. Kathleen's
husband had died falling from a windmill
platform, and Con, the eldest boy, had managed
the property ever since.

Tom Cleary introduced me to his wife,
Marilyn. She, like Ben Damson, the manager of
Kharko, and his wife, Sue, were strangers to me,
as were the young couple from the Red Tank
store. I forgot their names the moment Kathleen
finished introducing me, being more intent on
excusing myself than listening.

The full stock camp from Mt Farlow arrived,
piled into the back of the truck driven by old
Spider Webb. Despite knowing him all my life,
for he'd been a crony of Dad's, I'd never heard
his proper name, and was a little disconcerted to
find myself pulled into a rum-smelling hug when
I greeted him.

'How you doing, Charlie? I was sorry to hear
the news.' His powerful old arms squeezed my
ribs, and the bristly grey beard was like wire
against my cheek. 'Your dad woulda been
heartbroken today. I don't see Molly anywhere.
How's she taking it?'

'She's in hospital, Spider. Her heart's playing
up.'

'That's too bad,' he said and thumped his

own barrel chest. 'Gawd, she's only a nipper compared to me.' He was, I judged, well into his seventies and looked as hale as a man twenty years younger. The gate clicked again and I glanced around to see a stranger heading towards me. Somebody must have pointed me out to him.

I nudged Spider. 'Who's this?' The man wore the ubiquitous station uniform of jeans, boots and Akubra, the clothes tidily pressed.

'New manager from Abbey Downs. Been in the job since March. Kevin . . . Kevin . . . ' He frowned, shook his head and said, 'Nup, lost it. Looks like he's brung his camp too. Guess they're like mine, all customers of Molly's.'

'Yes,' I said and went forward to greet him but was interrupted because Don had just appeared beside the small table set up near the replaced fence on which a candle, a miniature brass cross and his bible lay. He caught my eye, nodded, then raised a hand, calling, 'A bit of hush please, everyone!'

The crowd gradually fell silent and began to spread themselves among the benches just as Abe and Rose Pennon and their three children hurried into the garden. The Pennons were from Penny Hills and they, along with the few contractors, and a travelling saddler who'd been working at Kharko, brought the running total in my head up to twenty-five. About the number I'd calculated on.

'Sorry, Charlie.' Rose, harried and flustered, with a grizzling toddler in one arm, aimed a kiss at my cheek. 'Flat tyre, and the jack collapsed on Abe. Held us up.'

Abe's right hand, bandaged and cradled protectively in his left, looked sore but Padre Don had begun the service, so I settled myself beside Rose, wondering how Bob was faring. Ute was minding the roadhouse, having declined to attend.

'For why?' she had asked practically, when I'd told her she was welcome. 'I did not know this woman. I will bring the tea when is finished.' I wished my own decisions could be as clear and decisive.

Padre Don spoke with the ease of long practice, and when it came time for the songs, his long fingers danced across the accordion buttons, his voice lifting with his wife's to give a lead to the rest of us. 'In the sweet by and by, we shall meet on that beautiful shore . . . ' Rose squeezed my hand, her voice soaring sweetly, and when the hymn was done we sang the other songs, introduced by Don as favourites of the person whose life we celebrated. Then it was my turn.

I made my way to the front. I felt a moment of paralysing indecision as my gaze roved over the assembly before me; a sea of hats and jeans mingled with the brighter shades of women's clothing. The sun shone and the lawn was green and fresh-looking from a recent watering. Bob was staring at me. He gave an encouraging nod and it seemed to free my tongue. I drew a steadying lungful of air and breathed slowly out, organising my thoughts; after all, I needn't say anything I didn't mean.

'My cousin Annabelle grew up with me in the homestead right behind you,' I began. My voice sounded weak; I cleared my throat, projected it further. 'She was an orphan, for her soldier father died in Vietnam, her mother in a road fatality . . . ' I sketched in her primary years, her time in boarding school.

It sounded more like a work resume than a eulogy. I moved a hand behind my back and clenched it, starting again. 'Annabelle was very beautiful, clever too — she always did well at school — but something must have been missing from her life for her to have decided to end it. I've been away from home, out of touch with her for some years, so I can't say what it was that made her so dreadfully unhappy, but she must have had a reason to do what she did. She was smart, sensible, so whatever had happened to her . . . ' I couldn't see an end and the sentence tailed off.

I cleared my throat. 'Self-murder is a deed of desperation, leaving questions one can never answer. It's a cruel act both for those who suffer it and those who remain, but today' — I looked at the faces before me, wrinkled, tanned, fresh, young and old, none knowing when their own time would come — 'we should remember not the deed itself but the unknown reason behind it. Those of you who knew and loved my cousin shouldn't blame Annabelle for leaving us the way she did. There can be no blame, only grief for the unhappiness she suffered. Thank you all for coming today. It means a lot, especially to Molly who is presently in hospital.'

Don closed the service with a prayer then, and as if she'd been listening behind a door, Ute appeared in the garden with the first tray. Glad to escape, I moved to help her, but Kathleen Mallory followed me into the roadhouse. I gritted my teeth knowing I couldn't rebuff her offer to help carry the platters out to the table.

'That was a good send-off for her, Charlie,' she said in her husky tones that always had me suppressing the desire to cough. 'You spoke well of her. Shame Molly couldn't be here. How is she?'

'Not well. She's having a heart operation next week.'

Kathleen tutted. 'Sorry to hear it. Give her my best next time you speak. They do say troubles come in threes. So how have you been?' She glanced at my left hand. 'No ring yet? Well, I know somebody who'll be mighty pleased to hear that. He's been waiting for you to come home. He — '

I stopped in the doorway, forcing her to a halt behind me. 'Kathleen,' I said coolly, 'I don't want to know. I have no interest whatsoever in getting back with Bryan. He acted despicably, and if you can't see that then I'm sorry for you. Now, if you'll excuse me, I have a meal to serve.' I left her with her mouth still opening, as much on the back foot as her pushy personality would ever let her be. I felt a flush of triumph at my action. My own firmness awed me and I prayed it would be enough to end the subject for all time.

74

After that I was kept busy pouring coffee for those who didn't want tea, refilling plates and the urns themselves, and being introduced to those I hadn't met. Bill Maddison, a quiet, wire-thin man told me earnestly that he'd have brought his fiddle if he'd known there was to be music, but the padre had done well with his squeeze box. Others spoke of Annabelle, some even lamenting the loss of her beauty.

'What a waste. Best-looking sheila this country's ever seen,' George Himan sighed, oblivious to his wife's glare, though her kick to his shin elicited a pained, 'What the hell's that for, woman?'

I left Bess quarrelling with him in a repressed undertone. Bob was standing in a group that included Spider Webb and the policeman. I looked for Ute and found her in the roadhouse serving a traveller who'd pulled in for fuel.

'I thought we'd closed?'

She shrugged. 'The man is banging on the door. He cannot go without the fuel, no?'

'I don't suppose he can. Thank you, Ute. And for the eats — they were very good. I hope you had some yourself?'

'Of course. Is finished the kitchen work, so I will stay here now, yes? In case more peoples come.'

'Thank you. Our guests will start to leave soon.' I had an overnight bag ready and had added to it a few extra things for Mum, including Annabelle's letter. I would decide whether or not to hand it over when I saw her. The tea was long finished, the children, tired of the solemnity impressed upon them for the occasion, were growing rowdy before the crowd began to disperse. When the last repetitive condolence had been uttered, Don and Rae helped me carry the dirty platters and teacups to the kitchen. Bob brought in the urns, halting in the doorway to speak.

'You ready, then, Padre? I'll get the vehicle.'

'I'm going with them,' I announced. 'I'll be back tomorrow.'

'Suit yerself,' he said stolidly. 'Give Molly my best.'

'Of course I will. And thanks for your help today, Bob.' He shrugged and left to bring the station wagon to the door.

★ ★ ★

We reached the Alice in daylight and I accompanied the Thorntons to the manse beside the church where I would stay overnight.

'Should I contact this Mike Webb? *Can* I contact him?' I asked Rae. 'To let him know I'm here, I mean. I don't want him shooting off without me tomorrow.'

'I'll ring and leave a message for him now,' she said. 'He'll be staying at the backpackers' lodge. It's where all the young fellows stay — well, those who don't come to town to drink. Cheaper than the pubs, you see.'

'Thanks, Rae. I take it he's old Spider's son?'

'No,' Don, filling a kettle at the sink, answered for her. 'His nephew, or his nephew's son, I don't recall exactly. At any rate he's a Top End man.

His father owned a property somewhere up that way, but he lost it. The Webbs are a big family — Spider's father married twice, and both wives produced sons. There were triplets in the first family and, what's more, all three survived.'

'That must have been unusual for those days?'

'I would think so. Spider himself has a twin, I believe.'

Some buried memory stirred and I laughed suddenly. 'Yes — I'd forgotten. And do you know what he's called? I thought Spider was bad enough but his brother is known as Funnel. Gruesome or not?'

'It wouldn't have been his mother's choice,' Rae said, replacing the phone. She had been speaking animatedly into it and looked across to smile at me. 'I was going to leave a message but Mike was actually there. He'll pick you up at eight in the morning.'

'Wonderful, thank you, Rae.' Now all I had to do was survive Mum's displeasure at my disobeying her.

★ ★ ★

Don drove me to the hospital after an early evening meal. 'Visiting hours run till nine,' he said. 'I've a few people to visit myself first before I see Molly.'

I thanked him, appreciating his tact, and followed the painted arrows through to the wards. Mum had a room to herself and was watching television. Unnoticed, I stood in the doorway for a moment, observing her, feeling my

77

heart lurch at seeing her like this — so vulnerable in her nightie, her hair looking greyer still against the white of pillow and counterpane.

She sensed me and her eyes widened in surprise, the light glinting off her glasses as her head turned to take me in. 'Charlie!' The television winked off. 'What are you doing here? I told you — '

'Don flew me in, Mum. Don't fuss. I'm heading back in the morning. How are you?' I pecked her cheek. 'I've brought you a few more things. More nighties and some talc and extra toothpaste — there's not much in the tube you've got. I found a bed jacket too, and extra undies . . . So how are you feeling?'

'Bored.' There was a half-finished crossword next to the box of tissues on the trolley tray beside the bed. 'How did the service go today? Many turn up for it?'

'Heaps.' I enumerated them. 'The manager from Abby Downs, Kevin somebody — '

'Gates,' she supplied.

'Yes, he brought his stock camp, but not his wife — '

'He's not married.'

'Oh, okay. Old Spider had his camp with him too. Most of them sent messages for you — they hadn't heard you were in here. Ute is a real find. She made a great spread.' I gave a rundown of the food we'd served, adding, 'Don played your song and a couple of others, and I said a few words.' I hesitated. 'Mum, I brought Annabelle's letter in. The police want to see it. In fact, Tom came to the Garnet a few days ago to collect it. I told him he could have it when you'd read it. But if you don't feel ready to look at it yet, that's fine. They can wait. It isn't as if they don't already know what's happened.'

She reached a hand. 'Give it to me, then.'

'Are you sure? It might be upsetting.'

'Charlie,' she said crossly, 'Annabelle killing herself upset me — I doubt a letter can make it worse.'

It was short and to the point:

Dear Molly
I'm sorry it has come to this. It's not your fault. Please don't grieve for me. It's better this way. I love you.
Annabelle

Mum's gaze skimmed over the sheet, then she read the words aloud. 'It tells us nothing,' she complained. 'Why bother writing it if — '

'To tell you she loved you?' And it must be, I thought uncharitably, the first time Annabelle hadn't tried to blame her actions on another, but there it was in black and white: *It's not your fault.* 'It's definitely her writing, though a bit shaky in places. Still, given the circum-stances . . . '

I looked up in time to see a tear trickling down my mother's cheek. 'Oh, Mum.' I took her hand, saying fiercely, 'It's true. It's *not* your fault and she did love you. How could she not, after all your care?'

'She was such a beautiful child' — Mum gulped, her eyes overflowing — 'and so wilful and . . . and *resentful*. All her life she was resentful. Of you and me both. God knows I didn't expect gratitude, but with Annabelle there was always an underlying rancour . . . And your father spoiled her rotten, taught her to expect things as of her *right*. Oh, goddamnit!' She ripped a half-dozen tissues from their box and blotted her face. 'It was his fault she turned out such a — a viper. When I found out she was his child I did try not to let it make a difference, but in the end she damaged us all.'

I squeezed her hand, then let go to fold the letter and slip it back into its envelope. 'Well, I'll give this to the cops, much good it will do them. Now, tell me what's been arranged — I take it they'll be flying you down, ambulance from the hospital, then the plane? They're not going to discharge you to find your own way home, are they, because — '

She shook her head. 'It'll be a Care Flight, Dr Symes said. It'll bring me back too.' We talked about what the cardiologist had told her and the expected recovery time after the op, then Don knocked lightly on the open door and our privacy was over.

Later, fastening my seatbelt as he started the vehicle, I asked, 'Could we swing past the cop shop, Don? I just want to drop something in, shouldn't take a moment. They'll still be open, won't they?'

'No problem.' He waited with the engine running while I hurried in and handed the letter over to the officer manning the front desk.

'It's Annabelle Carver's suicide note. Would

80

you please give it to whoever's handling the inquiry?'

'I'll see they get it,' he promised.

It was the last we would hear of it, I thought then, and the mystery of why Annabelle had killed herself would remain just that.

8

The new, white four-wheel drive pulled up before the manse on the dot of eight the next morning. I was waiting on the porch as the driver got out, cataloguing his appearance as he walked towards me. Tall, brown forearms and face, bushman's hat, the rest of him covered in jeans, boots and cotton shirt. He came up the path to offer a firm grip and a pleasant grin. 'Mike Webb. All set, Miss Carver? G'day, Rae. How's Don these days?' The last was aimed past my shoulder.

'You're right on time, Mike. Don's not home at present but he's fine, thanks. Safe trip, then.' She had emerged from the house to put a gentle hand with its thin wedding band on my shoulder. 'And we'll hold Molly in our prayers, Charlie.'

'Thank you.' I hugged her, then added, 'And for putting me up. Please tell Don goodbye for me.' I lifted my bag and headed for the vehicle, Mike beating me to it to open the door.

'Thanks,' I said. 'I'm Charlie, by the way. I know old Spider — your uncle, is he?'

'I think he's actually a second cousin,' he said cheerfully as he walked around the vehicle to slide behind the wheel and belt himself in. 'It's a bit involved. How's Molly? I gather she's ill?'

'Do you know my mother?' I was surprised. 'I thought you were new to the district?'

He grinned. 'Put it this way — I've been working on Abbey Downs since March and the Garnet's the only place a man can get a beer. Shove those papers onto the floor if they're bothering you. I've read them.'

Mike had a pleasant face with a straight nose, topped with brown eyes and dark hair. There was a mole on his left cheekbone, I saw, and a button coming loose on his shirt.

'They're fine.' I reached for the paper; it was the *Centralian Advocate*, opened and folded at an inner page. When I picked it up Annabelle's face stared up at me, grainy in print but unmistakable. I recognised the picture — it was the photo from the lounge room. There had been two, one of each of us, taken when I was twenty. I hadn't even noticed that hers was missing. The shock of seeing her face so unexpectedly held me silent.

Mike, realising then, spoke apologetically. 'Sorry, didn't think. I should've chucked it. She was certainly a looker, your cousin.'

'She was that, and it's all right.' I remembered that Mum had said she'd given Tom a photograph. The story was brief, mentioning the manner of her death and that the NSW police were asking any member of the public who may have seen her on her final day to contact them. The item must have been picked up from an interstate publication, and run in the *Advocate* for topical interest, I thought.

'Rae told me they held a service for her yesterday out at the Garnet. Were you close?' His tone was sympathetic.

'We grew up together. But close? Not really,' I said dismissively. 'I hadn't seen her in five years.' I flipped the paper right side out and changed the subject. 'I haven't had time for TV this last week, so what's been happening in the world?'

He laughed. 'This is the Alice, Charlie. The big news, and it's three weeks old or thereabouts, is that somebody knocked off the Centre Jewellers. Got away with a swag of stuff grabbed out of the display cases that they smashed before they were interrupted.'

'They'd be insured, wouldn't they? So why is it still news?'

'Because the shop's manager died. He was camped there that night in an inner room. Must've heard them busting the glass. He was bashed unconscious, went into a coma and died two days later. A clot on the brain or something. The cops recovered a diamond ring the thieves dropped, but that's it. An ongoing case, so the media interest remains.'

'Mmm, it would. So why was he camped in the shop? And why wasn't the stuff in the safe, anyway?'

Mike shrugged as we hit the highway and the land spread wide before us. 'Bit of a sad story, really. He'd been in the job twenty years. An old bloke, just widowed. Apparently he couldn't face going back to an empty house after work so he'd made himself comfortable in the shop instead. Ate out, and kept a clean shirt in the cupboard, that sort of thing. And I suppose he reckoned that his being there made the stock safe. Or maybe he just forgot to lock it away. That's the

84

story — so what about you, Charlie? Rae mentioned you'd just come home. From where?'

'Oh, Melbourne.' It passed the time so I talked about my life in the city, of waitressing in a busy cafe and my job in the bookshop with its eccentric owner and mountains of paperbacks. 'I thought I wanted to act,' I said lightly. 'The pity of it is I was never offered a waitress's part. I had that down pat. What about you — what brought you to Abbey Downs? You know my father owned Garnet Station, back before I was born? It became part of Abbey Downs when the Goldsborough Company bought it off him.'

'Did they?' It was obviously news to him, which he confirmed by adding, 'Garnet's the outstation now. I thought it had always been that. My old man had a property too, but it was always too small to be viable. When the TB and brucellosis testing came in, it was the last straw. The seventies and early eighties were bad years for the industry — low prices, and all the new infrastructure the graziers had to comply with. Then the government regulations controlling where you could sell . . . ' He shook his head. 'Dad wasn't the only one to go bust. It meant we boys — I've got two brothers — had to shift for ourselves. Jeff went into the Department of Primary Industries. He's a stock inspector these days. Dan's in real estate in Darwin, but I decided to stick to cattlework.'

'And you like it?'

'Yeah. Thirty years ago I reckon I'd have been a drover. Too late for that now but I'm putting my own plant together.' He patted the steering wheel. 'This is the start of it. Next season I'll be contracting on my own account. A wages job these days . . . ' He shook his head. 'Nothing in it. I'm looking to the future. I want a bit more out of life than what a swag and a camp job can bring you.'

'Will you stay in the Centre, then?'

'There's work enough at present, and it helps to be known, so probably. What about you — back to the city when Molly's better?'

I filled my eyes with the view beyond the windscreen, the wide sky and raggy olive-coloured scrub springing from the red sand, with the lavender smudge of the MacDonnells beyond, and the buffel grass running like a white sea to their base. Light poured over it, sparkling off the turning leaves where the wind stirred, and the sense of space was endless. 'No,' I said. 'This is my country. I'll be staying.'

★ ★ ★

We reached the Garnet a little after eleven. The road was vastly improved since I had last travelled it five years before, the new vehicle speeding effortlessly over the gravel surface with its numerous grids. Once, there had been a rutted track and a handful of gates that drivers pulled up beside to rest, over a billy of tea, before tackling the next stretch. Cattlemen had travelled it then, and the mica miners from deep in the ranges, and wandering doggers — and before them, when it could have been little more than a pad between waters, Afghan cameleers and Aboriginal people. Now four-wheel drives from all over the continent flashed past towing trailers and camper vans, scarcely aware of the grids they crossed, while the more battered-looking station vehicles went about their daily tasks. But phones and a better road surface were, I knew, little more than cosmetics; underneath, the country remained its rugged, dangerous self.

Mike, pulling up before the roadhouse beside an old blue Land Rover, hoisted my bag out of the back and whacked it free of dust.

'Thanks,' I said. 'Will you stop and have a cuppa before you go?'

He accepted with alacrity. 'You want to keep the papers? They're today's.'

'Okay, Bob might like them, thanks. Come in and I'll put the kettle on.'

Bob was behind the counter stacking the fridge shelves and he creaked to his feet as the doorbell pinged. A pair of travellers were eating a meal at a table, and a butcher bird's liquid call sounded from the verandah, drowning the scrape of cutlery on china.

'Charlie. So yer back. How's Molly?'

'As you'd expect — organised.' I dropped the papers on the counter. 'For you. She says she's fine. Bob, do you know Mike Webb?'

'Course. G'day, Mike.'

'Bob,' he acknowledged. 'I'm just having a cuppa with Charlie, then I'm off.'

''Fore you go, then, have a word with the old bloke over there, will yer? Reckons he knows yer boss. He's lookin' for permission to camp down Mica Valley for a week or so.'

'Yeah? Why?'

Bob shrugged. 'Gem hunting, him and his missus.'

'I don't like his chances.' Mike was shaking his head. 'Not when we're mustering. He'll be getting himself lost and we'll be having to run a search — '

'Not according to him. He was camp cook for Kevin out on Brunette Downs. Talk to him, will yer? Get him off my back — he's worse 'n a bloody blowfly.'

I went to the kitchen to say hello to Ute, who was mixing brownies, and prepared a pot of tea. When I returned with it Mike was talking to the couple, a dried-up old fellow in shorts and t-shirt and his solid, grey-haired wife, who was similarly dressed. The man's skin was leathered and wrinkled, his calves and forearms ropey with muscle.

The woman flashed a smile at me. 'G'day, love. I'm Cora. Cora Wilder. This is my husband, Len.'

We exchanged pleasantries, then Mike left them to join me at the far table.

'Is he who he claims?' I asked.

'I'd say so. He certainly knows Kevin, so he'll probably get permission. At least he asked. You get the smart alecs who don't and head off, then wind up getting themselves into trouble. It's always the station that has to save their bacon — as if we've nothing better to do.'

'What are they after, exactly?'

He shrugged, eyes crinkling as he smiled. 'Quartz, rubies, sapphires, garnets — anything that turns up, I guess. They go all over, apparently. He was telling me of this place in Queensland where you can find perfect little Maltese crosses. He said you just sieve them out of the dirt. Some sort of geological anomaly, I guess. He didn't know how or why they formed.'

'It's an odd hobby.'

'Oh, I don't know. Beats trainspotting or collecting matchboxes in my book. Maybe,' he suggested, 'we could have a look down the valley ourselves one day? You never know, might be fun to find a ruby.' He drained his cup. 'Well, I suppose I'd better get going. Thanks for that, Charlie. I've enjoyed meeting you. I just wish it could've been for a happier reason.' He stood and offered his hand.

'Thanks.' I shook it. 'And for the ride out.'

'My pleasure.' He fitted his hat. 'And think about that ruby, eh? You must get a day off sometime. We could take a picnic lunch, enjoy ourselves.'

I smiled, heartened by his obvious interest. 'Maybe.'

'See you, Charlie.'

'Maybe,' I repeated. And it was suddenly warming to think that I probably would.

Pending word from the Abbey Downs manager, Len Wilder asked permission to camp at the soak on the creek behind the homestead. Bob, to whom the question was put, raised a brow at me and I shrugged.

'Well, okay,' he said grudgingly. 'Don't be leaving a mess though, and watch your fire. Country's dry enough to burn.'

'I appreciate that,' Len replied. 'Drop by anytime for a cuppa and a yarn — you'll be welcome. If it's okay with you, we might take a look round the ridges tomorrow. I saw a nice out-crop of quartz there coming in.'

'But it's not a gem, is it — quartz?' I asked.

Cora's weather-beaten face lightened with a smile. 'Yeah, it is. Citrine and amethyst are quartz. Then there's rose quartz, like this.' She held out her hand to show me a heavy silver ring inset with a pink stone. 'Found that one in Queensland, up round Cloncurry, a few years back. Pretty, eh?'

'It's lovely,' I said sincerely. 'I had no idea. Did a jeweller cut it for you?'

'Nope. Len does the cutting and the silverwork. It's our summer business. He's got a workshop back in Ravenshoe and we travel round the markets selling what he makes. That's in summer. The rest of the year we're out bush, fossicking for the stones.' She looked critically at me. 'Now you — you should wear amber, or topaz. A nice piece of darkish topaz. You find some lovely bits of that in eastern Queensland.'

I looked again at the ring, admiring the workmanship. Len Wilder might have spent time cooking in a stock camp but he was a true artist. I said, 'Well, if you do find anything, I'd love to see it before you move on.' I picked up my bag and looked at Bob. 'I'll just dump my gear home, then I'll be back to relieve you. Perhaps I'll see you later, Cora.'

★ ★ ★

90

Kevin Gates rang that evening to give permission to the Wilders to visit and camp in Mica Valley. I couldn't remember ever having been there myself, but I knew there were scores of old tracks winding their way into anonymous gullies in the ranges, for mica mining had been a big thing out here in the nineteen-fifties. The valley in question had earned its name because of the many mines within it, though abandoned shafts and old camps also dotted the more accessible parts of the Harts Range. Bob took the message down to the Wilders while Ute and I cleared the dinner things away. We watched TV then, but Bob didn't return and after Ute had taken herself off to her donga I went to my room. The house creaked in the darkness, and the window frames rattled as the wind got up. It felt empty without Mum, almost alien, as if I had been gone too long to be ever welcomed back.

Restless and worried, I entered the bedroom that had once been the spare one kept for guests, until Annabelle had moved into it at fourteen. It was across the hall from mine, still with the same cream walls, and the floral curtains and lace drapes that I remembered. The bed had a cotton blanket pulled over the bare mattress and there was nothing on the walls, or, when I opened it, within the wardrobe. In the top drawer of the bed-side cupboard there was an empty diary for the year of 1985 and a lavender sachet that had lost its scent. A pair of flimsy gold sandals with a broken strap rested in the bottom one, and nothing else. Gazing at the shoes, I wondered why Mum hadn't thrown them out. They were pretty, frivolous things, with narrow soles and heels, footwear that neither she nor I could ever have worn. Annabelle, I thought unkindly, had been vain about her dainty feet; she'd owned literally dozens of shoes. A colour for every outfit. I closed the drawer with a sigh. Whatever I was seeking — and I wasn't even sure myself — there was nothing of it here. The dead woman's smooth, seamless shell remained as perfect, and hid her secrets as well in death, as it had done in life.

9

The Wilders left while we were still at breakfast.

'Interestin' bloke,' Bob commented, watching their Land Rover drive past. 'Not wasting any time, is he? Don't suppose you thought to pick up the paint while you were in town, Charlie?'

'Sunday,' I said briefly. 'The shops were shut.'

'Yeah. Forgot. I'll get the timber scraped down, then, so it's ready.'

'Okay,' I glanced out at the garden. 'The new fence looks great. I might get in a bit more weeding this evening. Those oleanders could benefit from a trim too. I thought, driving in yesterday, that the place already looks better.'

He bristled instantly. 'Well, don't go blaming Molly for it needin' the work.'

'Actually I was complimenting you,' I said, but got only a grunt in return as he went out.

'He likes to be the bear,' Ute observed as she rose to clear the table, then frowned. 'The bear — the one that has the bad head. That is right?'

I laughed. 'More or less. Bob's always grumpy. It's mostly an act.'

⋆ ⋆ ⋆

Tuesday morning I had two visitors. The first was Constable Cleary from Harts Range, who came to deliver the bundle of clothing Annabelle had left behind on the beach. It was in a sealed bag of toughened paper and had been forwarded via the Alice police.

'Just tidying up,' he explained. 'It means the local police are satisfied there's nothing further to investigate. So they return the deceased's effects to the family.'

'Right.' I took the bag and, stowing it below the counter for the time being, asked again about the inquest.

He shook his head. 'I've heard nothing but it's usually a matter of months, rather than weeks. Longer sometimes if there are a lot of witnesses. Don't worry, you'll get plenty of notice, but you know there'd be no reason for you to attend, unless you want to. It's not like you were there when it happened.'

'Right,' I said again. 'Thanks Tom.' And he went on his way.

My next caller was more rewarding — a big bluff man in an orange visibility shirt overlaid with red dust. He wore boots and shorts and a felt hat and was, he said, the boss of a Main Roads crew and was looking for a convenient camp around the soak. The old bloke out front, he said, had told him to speak to me.

'You Mrs Carver?'

'Her daughter, actually. I'm Charlie Carver. What exactly is it that that you want, Mr — ?'

'Rob — Rob Wyper. See, the thing is we're doing a couple of causeways back up the main road, one across the Garnet, and the big 'un on the Penny Creek crossing. So we need water. I'm looking for permission to use your supply for our tanker, and I'd like to set up the camp round here too, to save on travelling time. If you're agreeable, we'd grade us a clearing, say, half a kay down the road, for the vans and machinery, and maybe take our meals here if that'd suit you? Cooking ain't popular with the boys.'

Any custom was welcome so it would certainly suit, I thought. 'For how long would you stay?'

He shrugged, grinning with dust-coated teeth. 'How long's that bit of string? Depends on breakdowns, accidents, foul-ups with supplies and equipment, and sheer bloody stupidity in the workforce. A month, say, allowing for stoppages.'

'And how many men?

'Ten, and you'll have the engineer coming and going. He never stops. No camping for him.'

'I think our cook will manage that okay.'

'And the water?'

'That'll be fine. Just ask your driver to spray around here when he's filling up. I don't want the dust becoming a problem, and it might if you're running a truck back and forth.'

'Great, thank you.' He shook my hand vigorously and left, heavy boots booming on the verandah timbers.

Pleased, I went to tell Ute and found her frowning over a tin of yeast unearthed from the back of the fridge. 'Is too old,' she said forthrightly. 'You order more, yes? And I make the sweet buns and a bread we have in my country — not so bland as this you buy.'

'It's just for emergencies, in case we ever ran out of bread or the mail doesn't come.' I said. 'Mum didn't have time to bake. Besides, buns would go stale before they were sold.'

'You freeze them, of course, Charlie. In business,' she explained, 'one must grip the opportunity that comes to knock at the door. This I have learned.'

'Well, I just did — and quite a good one too. We'll have ten regular customers for all meals, from tomorrow. And they'll probably need cake or sandwiches for their smokos as well. For maybe a month? I'll be here, of course, if you get stuck.'

'Stuck, *stuck*?' she murmured, cocking her head the better to consider the word.

'I meant if you need help.'

She dismissed the idea. 'A problem it will not be, Charlie.'

I admired her certainty. In her own, much nicer, way, she was very like Annabelle, her confidence a force that gripped (to use her own word) the world and bent it to her will.

★ ★ ★

Mum's operation was scheduled for the next day. After the other two had left for their own quarters that evening, I rang Directory Assistance for the hospital number in Adelaide, then punched it into the phone. When she answered, Mum sounded alert and as close as the next room rather than half a continent away.

'Charlie! Something wrong?'

'Of course not, Mum. I just wanted to check how things are going. You're okay? How was your flight? There's been no delay with things?'

'The op's still happening tomorrow if that's

96

what you mean, and I'm fine. So was the flight, except they had me lying down all the way. They say I'll be out in a week. What about your end — how are you going?'

'Oh, we're jogging along okay. The fuel truck's due Friday. The boss in charge of a big Main Roads camp on the highway came in today. They're building causeways over the Garnet and Penny creeks, and he wants to base the camp here, have them take all their meals with us, and cart water from the soak. Best part of a month he thinks. Naturally I agreed.'

'That's good. And the new cook? Will she be up to that amount of constant work?'

'She will. She's great.' I grinned, remembering our earlier conversation. 'Very keen to grip new opportunities.' Sobering, I added, 'I gave Annabelle's letter to the cops in town, Mum. And Tom Cleary brought her gear back today, the clothes she left on the beach. He also said when I asked about the inquest that we wouldn't have to attend unless we wanted to.' I hesitated, then offered, 'I could go if you think it necessary, but I don't see what it would achieve.'

'Probably nothing,' she agreed. 'Look, every minute costs. Tomorrow will be fine. I'm not worried about the op and you shouldn't be.'

'Well, I am,' I said. 'I love you, Mum. I'll call tomorrow.' I hung up before she could object, glad I'd said it, and wondered why it should be so hard. She had always ignored or turned aside from emotion. It wasn't in her to show more than a brusque affection — a brief peck on the cheek, a one-second embrace — but perhaps, I

97

reflected, that was down to my father's behaviour, his habitual deceit killing off feelings that should have come easily and naturally to her.

Sighing, I reached for the TV remote, then my eye fell on the bag of clothing I'd brought back from the roadhouse. Morbidly I opened it. What did one wear — or take off — in order to drown oneself? And what should I do with the items now? It raised again the question of where Annabelle had stayed in Ballina, where (presumably) her handbag and other belongings remained. They would have to be sorted and dealt with once the police found the location. If it had been a rented room, I thought, then its landlord or lady should have reported a missing guest, particularly once her death hit the news, though I supposed it was possible he or she had said nothing about a temporary traveller and simply kept whatever was left behind to cover any money owed. But one paid up front these days, so that would apply only to the dishonest. At any rate Annabelle could hardly have taken anything with her into the sea, so life's other essentials — handbag, toiletries, cosmetics — had to be somewhere.

I upended the bag onto the occasional table beside my chair, revealing a red chiffon top that was very Annabelle with its shoestring straps and a series of soft, draped folds. It was followed by white capri pants, lacy black panties and bra, and a pair of acid green pumps with narrow heels. She'd always liked colour and, due to her small size, was, I remembered, seldom without heels.

They seemed an odd choice for a beach but maybe she'd had more on her mind than practical considerations. By feeling the pants pockets I located the watch, placed there, I presumed, for safety. It was one of those fashion watches, its face and band awash with glittering stones; again, very Annabelle. Why take that with her to a rendezvous with death and not the handbag? Did time matter, if life didn't?

Sighing again, I swept it all back into the bag, which I eventually deposited in the empty wardrobe in her room. It seemed too final somehow, to just throw it out.

⋆　⋆　⋆

The following day dragged. The roar of diesel motors and the to-ing and fro-ing, as well as the dust raised by the grader clearing the new campground half a kilometre up the road, signalled the arrival of the Main Roads camp. Later, the water truck was driven past the roadhouse and homestead on the narrow track that led down to the soak. There came the distant throb of the pump filling the tanker, then its return. I stepped outside to check but the driver was spraying the track as I'd asked. Satisfied, I returned to my tasks. All ten of the men arrived for lunch and seemed happy with the meal. Rob, the last to go, asked if we'd do cut lunches for them from tomorrow.

'We can't be driving back from the job every day to eat.'

'No, of course not. If you've got any bread in

the camp perhaps you could bring it in tonight? We've some,' I said, 'but ten lots of sandwiches every day . . . I'll double the order to the bakery but it won't get here until Saturday.'

'See what I can do,' he promised.

In the afternoon I tackled the vastly overgrown and straggly oleanders that had once been a neat hedge across the front of the homestead garden. With the door and windows open I was close enough to hear the phone and both dreaded and longed for it to ring. Would the surgeon call to tell me the operation had gone well, or only to inform me as next of kin that my mother's heart had stopped in theatre, or that some hideous complication had occurred? Hardly aware of my task, only of the need to keep busy, I sawed and cut, tossing the discarded branches to one side until I became aware of Bob's frowning presence beside me.

'What the hell are yer doin', Charlie?'

'What?' I looked from him to the shorn shrubbery. 'Getting it under control again. It's meant to be a hedge, not a forest, Bob.'

'No gloves,' he said, 'no glasses. Yer do know that stuff's bloody poisonous? The sap, the leaves, the wood. Yer can't leave it lyin' round neither. Kill a goat, that will.'

'So we'll burn it when it dries,' I said impatiently. 'Get off my case, Bob. I'd said I'd cut it back and I am.'

'Hmmph,' he said. 'Smoke's poisonous too, yer know. Look at your hands — sap all over 'em, if you had a cut it'd be in it . . . Why don't you go wash and find a pair of gloves?' Gruffly, he added, 'She'll be okay, you know. Tough as nails, Molly is. She'll come through this. Won't help her to learn you poisoned yerself, but. Do nothin' for her recovery that would.'

His kindly tone made my chin quiver and he patted my arm. 'Go on, girl, wash that stuff off, then come and have a cuppa. Ute was looking for you, too. I'll finish here later, if you like.'

I sniffed, went to wipe my damp eyes, then remembered the sap. 'It's okay, I'll do it. But you're right, it's a silly risk. Thank you, Bob.'

★ ★ ★

A little after five, the phone in the roadhouse, which was on the same line as the house phone, rang. I said, 'Hello?' in a breathless gasp and heard a woman's soft voice reply.

'Is that Charlotte Carver speaking?'

It had to be the hospital. 'Yes. What . . . Is my mother — ?'

'She's fine. She's come through the op well and she's stable, Charlotte. I'm Cathy Martin, her nurse. Before she went to theatre she made me promise to ring you once she was out.'

'And she's okay?' I broke in. 'When can I speak to her?'

'Well, perhaps tomorrow. It's a big op, you know, and the drugs will make her drowsy. She's sleeping now but everything's going well so far. She's out of Recovery and in ICU at present. Try not to worry too much, eh?'

'Thank you. If — when she wakes give her our

love, won't you, mine and Bob's? Tell her I'll ring.'

'I'll do that. Bye now,' and she was gone.

Bob watched me replace the phone. 'Okay?'

'Yes.' I exhaled a long breath of relief. 'Everything's fine, she made it.'

'Told yer,' he said. He tugged down the brim of his hat and limped out to sweep the apron of concrete before the pumps. Having the road constantly sprayed reduced the dust, but it did mean that vehicles tracked the damp earth onto the cement apron every time they drove in to fuel up.

What felt like the weight of the building slipped from my shoulders. Bob was right — he usually was. Tough as nails didn't begin to describe Mum. She'd be out of hospital and home before I knew it, all of today's worries forgotten.

10

Thursday evening I checked with the hospital again. Mum sounded groggy and tired, complaining that she did nothing but sleep. I kept the call brief. Friday she was brighter, her complaint this time centred on some apparatus they were making her blow into to check her lung function. Tomorrow, she said, she was leaving ICU for the ward where, she hoped, the nights would be a bit quieter. She sounded querulous, which I thought a better sign than her earlier weariness.

The fuel tanker turned up in the afternoon. I'd finished work on the hedge by then and the Main Roads crew were changing from anonymous workers to known faces. Ute was handling the extra work well. We had developed a system of self-service where the men fetched their own cutlery and food, and delivered the dirty plates back to the hatch.

Friday night was busier with stockmen from the closer stations turning up, and among them I was absurdly pleased to see Mike Webb. It made for quite a crowd until a few of the older Main Roads men left. I was kept busy serving with no time for more than a greeting but Mike seemed content to sit and wait. He'd commandeered a stool near the bar and when the rush eased, and the volume of noise around the card game at one of the tables gave us privacy, he hitched his elbows onto the counter.

'How've you been, Charlie? And Molly — how did the op go?'

'She came through it and is doing well, thanks. Back in the ward tomorrow, which I guess means the worst is over.'

'That's good. Must've been tough on you both, I imagine — being so far away.'

'For me, yes. For her, I really don't know.' The honesty of my answer surprised me. He cocked an eyebrow and I said recklessly, 'We have issues, my mother and I. I've never really been close to her. Actually, between her and Annabelle we're one screwed-up family.'

'That so? What about your dad? Is he still around?'

'He died, eight years ago.' I shrugged. 'He was a chronic gambler, and a drinker — not your ideal husband, or father.'

'Ah.' Mike nodded. 'That would be the reason he got out of the station?'

'I suppose. It happened before I was born. Three generations' worth of Carver sweat and toil, but he couldn't hold it. I suppose Mum could see even then that she'd wind up in a tent if it was left to him, so she got her hands on what cash she could and started this business. It provided a livelihood and paid for Annabelle's and my schooling. The rest he just frittered away.'

'But she stuck with him.'

'Yes, well, her generation did, however hopeless the marriage.' I frowned. 'Why are we talking about this, anyway? Let's change the subject to you.'

'Ah well, that's simple.' He grinned. 'I've got the weekend off. Doesn't happen often during a muster, but the chopper's due its hundred hourly so it went into the Alice this morning. We finished the yardwork this arvo and I'm not due back at the station till Sunday. I chucked my swag on so I could camp here tonight, and I wondered if you'd care to maybe come and hunt rubies with me tomorrow?'

I felt a tingling pleasure — so I hadn't been wrong thinking he liked me. I said, affecting puzzlement, 'Its *hundred hourly*? What does that mean, exactly?'

'It means that after every hundred hours of flying, helicopters get their innards pulled apart and checked over. It's a safety measure — the law according to CAA, aviation's god. Now, I've answered your question so it's my turn to get one from you — that's how it works. So, will you come, Charlie? Early start, picnic lunch, home by five-ish. What do you say?'

'It sounds enticing, Mike. I'd love to.' I had a brief moment wondering if it was fair to go off, leaving Bob and Ute to cope, but damnit all, I thought rebelliously, they were being paid to work, but I wasn't. 'I'll bring the lunch,' I said, 'if you provide the transport.'

'It's a date, then.' He looked pleased with himself. 'Is old Len still out there?'

'The fossicker and his wife?' I shrugged. 'As far as I know. There's no reason for him to drive back in here if he was leaving the area though.' The Garnet was five kilometres off the main road. 'Why?'

'Just gauging the possibilities,' he said airily. 'Kevin reckons you could hide a diamond in a sand dune and the old boy'd find it. Knows as much about rocks and gems as any geologist. All self-taught. If he's still about it raises the odds on your ruby turning up.'

I laughed. 'What an optimist. Of course, he could've broken an axle and be stuck somewhere with not a gem in sight.'

'Pessimist,' he teased. 'If the ruby proves elusive, perhaps we'll find him instead and get some tips for next time.'

So he was already envisaging a next time. The thought, along with the memory of his engaging smile, carried me through the evening and was with me still as I prepared for bed. Inevitably then my thoughts turned to Annabelle. *She's some looker*, Mike had remarked, but her death guaranteed that this time there could be no comparison between us. I was only too aware that with her in the room no normal man would give me a second glance. I had known it and so had she, and even separated by half a continent the knowledge had affected me. It was why the dating I had done in Melbourne had led nowhere. You needed confidence to be interesting, and trust to build a relationship on. I'd had neither, but perhaps this time it could be different? It was too soon to tell if the attraction between us would last, though it was undeniably there, on my side anyway. But he *had* asked me, I thought.

I fell asleep smiling, and sometime later was jolted awake from a dream about shoes, of all things. Wondering where that could have come from led me to think of the parcel of clothes Annabelle had worn to the beach. My subconscious must have been at work but the message remained unclear. There was something . . . something about shoes. Could *that* be the reason behind the dream, which was now a hopeless fading memory? What was wrong with her shoes apart from them being heels, which one normally wouldn't wear on a beach, but would this necessarily hold true of a person bent on suicide? Surely shoes would be unimportant then — one wouldn't be thinking about the difficulty of walking in sand. Well, I might, I conceded, but not Annabelle. Practicality came a slow second to appearances with her.

Then I had it. The colour was wrong. With a scarlet top and white pants, why had she worn green shoes? Annabelle, who had footwear to co-ordinate with every dye known to man? There was no way she wouldn't have packed matching shoes for each outfit in her bag. I lay thinking about it, picturing her in the clothes, the pretty floaty top and cotton pants, and the green shoes. Visualising her narrow waist, her dainty ankles, and the polished line of her collarbones that would have been revealed by the shoestring stra —

I sat bolt upright then, a hand flying to my mouth. The black lace bra was wrong, too! Of course she would have worn a strapless one with that blouse, and flesh-coloured at that. How had I not seen it before? And would any woman about to don white pants choose black underthings to wear with them?

My mind raced. It meant — it *had* to mean that the clothes were planted, left on the beach with the letter and watch, to suggest something that had never happened. The world spun as I considered the only possible conclusion supposing my theory was right. No wonder her handbag had been missing! She had kept it. Annabelle hadn't killed herself, she'd simply staged her disappearance to make us think that she had. It would also explain why no landlord had reported her missing. If she had checked out and taken her luggage with her . . .

Dawn had almost arrived before I slipped back into sleep, only to jerk awake within minutes to re-examine yet again the idea the night had thrown up. Was I reading too much into a choice of clothing? Who would believe that anyone bent on suicide would care what she wore? Only they didn't know Annabelle as I did. Tossing restlessly, I was suddenly stilled by another thought. Why had she done it? Being presumed dead was final, not a situation that once arranged one could easily reverse. So, why? Why had she felt the need to disappear into the anonymity of death? Was she, in fact, in trouble as Mum had feared and, if so, how bad was it? Or — another possibility — was fear behind it? If some man had threatened her (with Annabelle, any trouble would concern a man) why wouldn't she just go to the police?

The first bird calls sounded as the east lightened, and still I was no wiser. I rose and dressed and ate breakfast, wishing, as I buttered toast and sipped tea, that I could confide in someone. I couldn't bother Mum with it, and Bob wouldn't be convinced by the subtleties of dress; besides, he lacked the patience to consider possible motives. Strangely enough it was Ute, presently cooking breakfast for Rob's crew and Mike in the roadhouse kitchen, I would have chosen to tell. Her solid common sense and unflappability would have provided the perfect sounding board, but this was a family matter, so that was out too. I shrank from taking my suspicions to Constable Cleary, for most likely they were no more than that. If, I realised, the police couldn't prove that she *had* killed herself, then neither could I prove that she hadn't. Besides, it might be wise to discover the reason before involving them.

I cut sandwiches, raided the smoko supplies for cake and filled a couple of thermoses before seeking out Bob to inform him that I was taking the day off.

'Good idea,' he said, wrong-footing me from the start, for I had expected if not opposition then only grudging agreement to my plan. 'A day out'll do yer good. Young Mike, is it? Where yer headin'?'

'Fossicking,' I said, 'in the ranges. Back tonight. And he's not that young. Thirty, I'd guess.'

He cackled; there was no other word for it. 'Wait till yer my age, girl. Fifty'll look young to yer then.'

'How old *are* you, Bob?' The sky was blue behind him, the sprinkler head ticking as it

moved back and forth spraying the lawn, the end
of one of its arcs spattering the lopped oleander
hedge. The laughter left his face and he scowled
forbiddingly at me.

'Ain't none of yer business,' he said, and
stalked off.

11

I was still giggling when Mike strolled out through the roadhouse's back entrance, putting on his hat as he came.

'Good morning, Charlie. You look happy.'

'So I am. I've known old Bob since I was a toddler and I've only just found out how to get rid of him. I could've done with the knowledge when I was a teenager.'

'Yeah? How's it work, then?'

'Ask him his age.' I proffered the cooler bag. 'I'm ready if you are.'

He took the bag. 'Let's see, hat and gloves? Check. Tucker, water, shovels, billy? Check. A sieve — borrowed that from the station,' he added in parenthesis. 'Good to go, then. All aboard the Ruby Cruiser for an educational *and* entertaining tour of our lesser-known beauty spots.'

'Oh yes?' I smiled at his nonsense. 'What makes it educational exactly?'

'Well,' he began, steering me around the corner shrubbery to his vehicle and flourishing open the passenger door, 'I hope we are going to learn more about each other, and with you being native to these parts there may be some aspects of its history — pioneer, geological, whatever — that will enliven our exchange of views.'

'Right. And of course you're going to show me how to fossick. You do know how, don't you?'

111

'How hard can it be?' he asked airily. 'Chuck the dirt in the sieve and shake — see what you get. Isn't that how it's done?'

'I think,' I said, repressing an answering grin, 'we'd best hope we run across Len and his wife before we start.'

It was a beautiful June morning, cool enough for me to be glad of my long-sleeved shirt. A slight breeze ruffled the dustladen foliage of the thin scrub, and the bulk of the range stood clear and aloof beyond the trees, a dreaming lavender shape, its top ridged with buttresses of seamed rock. Mike's vehicle reached the main road and we headed east along it, eventually catching up with the heavy machinery of the road camp, and the graded detour they had made around the section covering Penny Creek where the new causeway would go.

'How's Molly getting on?' Mike asked, breaking the little silence that had fallen between us.

'She seems to be doing well. But you wouldn't know — she's always fine, according to her. Today's the third since the op. I've been wondering, once she gets out of hospital, if I might persuade her to spend a week in the Alice before coming home. I know the flying doctor's always available but if something went wrong . . . well, it's still a long wait. Strokes, heart attacks — you can die in minutes from them.'

'I'm sure it won't come to that. I can see why you'd worry though.' He glanced across at me. 'Did your cousin not know about Molly's health when she did away with herself?'

'I shouldn't think so. Mum's . . . ' I hesitated. 'She's a very private person. I doubt anyone but old Bob knew, and that's only because he cares deeply about her.'

'Are you saying that your cousin didn't?' Mike asked cautiously.

'Annabelle cared mostly for herself,' I said tartly, then winced. 'Sorry, that wasn't kind of me. I'm afraid it's true though. My parents adopted her when she was three and it wasn't . . . it didn't make for a very happy relationship, for any of us. Not wholly. She was difficult even then, Mum said. Very,' I sought the word, 'demanding, I suppose. Not just of material things but of affection, attention, people's time. She couldn't bear to be overlooked for a moment. It didn't help that she was so beautiful. She always expected more than her due, and people usually gave in to her expectations. My father did, anyway.' I shrugged. 'With looks like hers you don't need manners, or . . . or niceness. Things just drop into your lap,' I added, a shade bitterly.

'I see. She doesn't sound very . . . ' Tactfully he left the sentence unfinished and shrugged. 'Siblings don't always get on.' He spoke neutrally and for some reason his refusal to criticise Annabelle annoyed me.

'She wasn't my sibling,' I snapped and immediately contradicted myself. 'Actually, she was. She's my half-sister, something I only recently learned. Look, it's a lovely day. Can we please talk about something else?'

'Fine by me. Any ideas on a destination? Shall

113

we just try the first turn-off and see where it leads? Or look for where old Len went? His tracks ought to be plain enough to follow if we spot where he left the road.'

'Why don't we see which comes up first? So, what's Kevin Gates like? Mum said he was unmarried. Isn't that unusual for a manager? Who looks after the homestead?'

We spoke of Gates, and Mike's job and other stations he'd worked on, his gaze flicking constantly to the right until he suddenly jammed on the brakes. 'There.' Two single ruts overlaid with thick buffel grass wound off the verge of the road, heading south. 'That'll do,' he said and swung onto it.

I grabbed the handhold on the dash to brace myself against the bumps. 'Did Len come this way?'

'Don't see any fresh wheel tracks but I daresay we'll find him somewhere.' A family of euros bounded away out of mallee shade beside the track, and overhead a kite hawk glided on spread wings, leading the way through gullies and low ridges into the range. The wheel ruts wound like a snake through scrub and rock and over shallow gutters, switching from red sand back to stone until the ridges rose steeply around us. The lavender of the range had changed to ochre, and by then the Land Rover was rocking rather than bumping forward.

'Don't wreck your new vehicle,' I said, ducking reflexively from the foliage of a desert oak as it swatted the windscreen.

'It'd take more than this,' he scoffed, pulling

up. 'It's a dead end though, no more track.' We got out and looked around at the rugged ridges and the narrow gully running between them. I spotted the tailings from a half-collapsed shaft driven into the hillside that showed where the mica miners had been. It was very still and the sun-warmed rocks gave off an elusive scent. I breathed it in, hearing the tiny twitter of a bird — one of the drab little wrens, I thought — from within a patch of bush. Overhead the kite hawk, or its mate, still hovered, while a shaky-paw lizard signalled me from a rock.

'Why do they *do* that?' I wondered. 'It's like it wants the hawk to see it.'

'Territorial behaviour?' Mike suggested. 'Are you ready for this ruby, Charlie?'

I grinned. 'Oh sure. How do we start?'

'This way.' He gave me the strainer to carry, took up the shovel and the water cooler himself, and we trod up along the creek to where a shrubby wattle provided a sparse, sprawling shade.

'Looks as likely a spot as any.' He set his burden down and thrust the shovel into a patch of gravel. 'Who knows? One spadeful might do it.'

I laughed. 'You haven't a clue, have you?'

'I promised you educational,' he said with dignity, 'and that's what it'll be. Us, learning together. Let's have that strainer, woman.'

We pottered around, sieving dirt and gravel and the detritus of old vegetation, moving along the side of the ridge, laughing a lot and talking, and stopping every now and then to wipe the

115

sweat from our faces and sit in the shade.

Sipping water from the cooler, I said, 'Would we even know if we did find something? I mean it's not going to be faceted and shiny, is it?'

'You hold it up to the light, I think.' Mike was sprawled back on one elbow, idly tossing up and catching again a bit of gravel from the sieve. 'Like this.' He demonstrated, squinting at it against the light. 'If it's a gem it's not opaque. Which means this definitely isn't.' He placed the tiny pebble on a flat rock and, picking up another stone, smashed down onto it. Instead of shattering under the blow, the pebble shot violently sideways and hit my wrist.

I let out an exclamation and grabbed the wounded spot.

Mike jerked to a sitting position, plainly appalled. 'Charlie! Christ, I'm sorry! I'm a bloody idiot.' His hand closed over mine as he turned my wrist to inspect the damage. 'I just didn't think — you'll have a whopping bruise. Can you forgive me?'

'Well, it's hardly mortal.' I gently reclaimed my hand, joking because he looked so hangdog about it. 'It didn't break, so maybe it's a diamond?' My wrist stung like fury but I was reluctant to add to his guilt by making a fuss.

'No,' he said gratefully, 'but you are. I can't think of another girl who, given what's happened, wouldn't be yelling her head off at me for being the thoughtless brute I am.'

'It was an accident. Come on, let's back to it. Rubies have to be earned, after all.'

We ate lunch down another track we found

that took us deeper into the range. The gully there was almost a creek, and on arrival Mike had wandered along its pale sand drifts to a curve below the bank where he began to ply the shovel.

'Digging a soak,' he said when I asked what he was doing. Standing at his shoulder I watched the hole dampen as it deepened and, in a few minutes, water was seeping into the bottom of it. He let it settle, then knelt to wash his hands and splash water over his heated face. I copied him, feeling the delicious coolness as a breeze touched my wet skin.

'How did you know the water was there?'

'Saw the tracks. See the scrapes in the sand there? Something's been digging, dingo, roo maybe. Animals are better equipped than us — they can smell the least bit of moisture.' His gaze dropped to my hand. 'How's your wrist feel now?'

'It's fine. Don't fuss.' I'd unpacked the lunches and now offered him one of the sandwiches I'd made. 'Let's eat.'

Refusing to have the subject brushed aside he said gravely, 'I would never deliberately hurt you, Charlie. I want you to know that.'

'Of course not,' I agreed hastily. 'Who does?' But the question, meant only to stave off another apology, reminded me instead of Annabelle, whom I'd temporarily managed to banish from my thoughts. Then, because he was there, and uninvolved, and also because during our morning's exertions and laughter a pleasant rapport had been established between us, I confided my suspicion that her suicide had been rigged.

He listened carefully, a slight frown between his brows, the sandwich forgotten in his hand. When I'd finished and sat sipping my tea from the flask top, he said, 'Well, supposing you're right — it's damn difficult to prove a negative. Do you want to, that's the question? If the whole thing *was* staged, what next? I doubt it's illegal to pretend to kill yourself — a misdemeanour at best as in wasting police time. If they believed you, the cops would probably say you were clutching at straws refusing to accept her death. There'd be nothing they could do, anyway. If your cousin — sorry, your sister — wants to disappear, that's her business.'

'Oh, I wouldn't tell the police,' I said hurriedly.

'Well then, who? Your mother — Annabelle's friends?'

'I wouldn't know who they were. And Mum . . . ' I bit my lip, watching him scarf down the forgotten sandwich. 'It might just hurt her more. I mean it's a cruel, rotten thing to do to someone who loves you, to put them through that, letting them think you're dead. Right now she can forgive Annabelle *because* she's dead. I don't know how she'd feel finding out that she isn't, that it was all a calculated lie. If I'm right, of course.'

'Well, what then?'

I sighed. 'I just can't help wondering why she'd want to disappear.' I hesitated, then plunged ahead. 'She was home a week or so

118

before they found her clothes. Mum said she came for money. Not just a handout, but real money — to the point of mortgaging the roadhouse, I mean. Maybe she's hiding from debt?'

'Or someone? Say a relationship had gone wrong and some man was threatening her?'

I laughed shortly. 'I thought of that but he'd be a brave man! I doubt Annabelle ever met one she couldn't handle.' But Bob had been afraid, I remembered — well, wary — of the one she was with, hadn't he? Still her beauty made fools of them all, I thought cynically.

'Ah.' Mike was scratching his cheek, his gaze on my face thoughtful. Flushing, I suddenly wished my observation unsaid. Could he possibly know about my broken engagement? It was five years ago but gossip tended to linger out here. What Melbourne would forget in a week kept its currency longer in the bush.

I reached abruptly for the thermoses and remnants of our meal. 'Come on, then, lazybones. Nobody found the Cullinan diamond by sitting about.'

12

The afternoon seemed to lack some of the sparkle the morning had held. I would have regretted sharing my suspicions with Mike save that doing so had clarified things for me. I now knew I wouldn't mention them to either the police or my mother. Annabelle's death was on record, so I'd let it stand as a fact. Her permanent absence from my own life would scarcely worry me, even if the mystery of her actions continued to niggle away at the back of my mind. Life was full of puzzles, I told myself; this was just one more, and basically none of my business anyhow.

Mike continued his enthusiastic search amid the rubble of the ages that had been brought down the gullies by the events of forgotten centuries, but for me the fun had gone out of it. I enjoyed more the meandering drives as we followed where the old mining tracks, made thirty and forty years before, led us. At Mica Valley, which we eventually reached, the ground and the sides of the hills glittered with shards and outcroppings of the mineral, and it was here, emerging from the valley as we were about to enter it, that we found Len and Cora.

Mike pulled into the shade and we got out to greet the couple, who had stopped on the track. Cora waved and I went over to her while the men shook hands and spoke, both dropping easily onto their heels in the squat the stockmen used. Cora was brown and dusty, her hair showing in stringy wisps beneath her hat.

'Fancy seeing you out here, love,' she said. She sounded tired and a bit fed up, as if the warmth of the afternoon was too much. 'Day trip, is it?'

'Yes. How's yours been — find anything?'

'Oh, a few bits. Like I said to Len though, there's a hell of a lot of rock mixed in with them. I reckon the valley's about fossicked out so we're heading back. We'll camp at the racetrack tonight — there're tanks there — and move on tomorrow. What's the news on your mum? I heard she was having some big op.'

'She's doing well, thanks,' I said, unsurprised that she should know about Molly. Out here, news, however trivial or personal, was the currency of the land. People collected it to pass on; it was one reason why visitors were welcomed so warmly, because they brought news into the isolated lives of those receiving them.

'That's good to hear.'

'Look,' I said impulsively, with a glance at the sun. 'Our thermoses are empty but we're carrying a billy if you've got tea leaves. We could boil up, have a cuppa?'

Cora hesitated, then shook her head. 'Ta, but I reckon not. Len wants to get back.'

I was surprised — an offer of tea was rarely refused — but she was right; the men were already shaking hands again. Len called a greeting and farewell to me in the same breath and a moment later the battered blue vehicle was moving off. 'That was quick,' I said, regaining my seat. 'And she seemed a bit unsettled. I wonder if they've had a row? What was he in such a hurry about?'

Mike shrugged. 'Dunno, but it is getting late. We should head back too. The good news is, Miss Carver, that we've succeeded. I just checked with Len and you are now the proud possesser of a genuine, fossicked gem.'

I gaped at him, saying, 'You're kidding, right? Not a ruby?'

'Nope. A garnet.' He handed me a tiny stone half the size of my smallest fingernail. 'I thought it looked promising but I wasn't sure. Hold it up to the light.'

I obeyed, saw a glint of red and laughed in delight. 'We did it, Mike! On our first try. But you found it, you keep it.'

'No,' he said. 'It's too small to be worth anything, but I'd like you to have it. A memento of our day. Which I have greatly enjoyed.'

'Well, thank you. That's very sweet of you. And I enjoyed it too.' I gave one last wondering look at the tiny gem and buttoned it safely into my pocket for the journey home.

We followed Len's tracks back to the highway. There we turned west, while his had gone east. 'They're camping at the racetrack tonight,' I said. Harts Range was the Garnet's closest neighbour, if a collection of empty buildings fell into that category. Tom Cleary and his wife were the only inhabitants save for race-day, which the whole district turned out for, together with the ball that followed. The last time I'd attended such an event I'd been nineteen and newly engaged to Bryan.

★ ★ ★

The road machinery, when we drove by the work site, was deserted. The men had knocked off for the day and a quick glance at the sun showed it to be later than I'd thought.

'I'd best head back tonight,' Mike said, as if also aware of the time.

'But I thought you had the weekend off?' I bit my lip the moment that the words, with their clingy connotations, were out. 'I mean, stay and have a meal at least — come over to the house and eat with us,' I added, making clear that he wasn't meant to pay.

'Thanks, Charlie, but you've fed me once today already. No, my washing's calling. If I don't get it done tomorrow it'll be dirty duds all week. It's been great today. I hope we can do it again — or something else. I'll be back,' he said, coasting to a stop before the roadhouse.

'I'd like that,' I said simply. The men from the road camp were already there, their vehicles parked to one side. 'It was a lovely day. Thank you. And for my garnet.' I touched my pocket.

'My pleasure.' He leant across the gear stick to kiss my cheek, his breath warm on my skin. 'I'd like to stay but I'd really better get back. Till next time, then.' He handed me the cooler, carried the two thermoses to the verandah, returned to the vehicle and left with a wave and a smile.

'You had the nice time, yes?' Ute asked. Her blonde hair was tied back and she was turning meat in a pan on the stove, the smell of it suddenly igniting my hunger.

'I did,' I said buoyantly. 'And we found a garnet.' I fished it out and showed her. 'Mind you it was a lot of work.' Now that it was over I felt for the first time the ache in my shoulders from my sessions with the sieve. 'Busy day?'

'The big — road trucks you call them? With the cows?'

'Road trains, yes.'

'Five today,' she said, sounding impressed. 'This is a lot of cows, Charlie — to where do they go?'

I shrugged. 'The saleyards, I suppose. They'll be headed to Alice or Darwin. There's nowhere else to send them.'

'There is much emptiness here,' she agreed, putting the pan aside to begin draining and mashing potatoes. 'Bob says it is called *bugger-all*. This is correct?'

I grinned. 'More or less. But you're not afraid of it, are you?'

She looked surprised. 'For why should I be? You are not.'

'No,' I agreed. 'I love it out here.' And, pulling off my hat, I went through to relieve Bob at the counter.

★ ★ ★

Sunday was a quiet day. I checked on Mum, who said she was doing well, and had been out of bed to shower. She sounded alert, and I deduced that the hospital was cutting back on the drugs. The men from the road camp wandered up to the roadhouse mid-afternoon to play cards and drink in a desultory fashion. One of them asked me for reading material and I found him a couple of paperbacks, but mostly they just sat around and talked. Sundays were a pain, the reader told me; he'd sooner be working than loafing around in camp.

On Monday evening when they arrived for their evening meal, there was much speculation as to what was going on further down the road. The coppers, Rob Wyper told us over the neck of the cold beer he was holding, had been buzzing back and forth all day like blowflies. Something was obviously afoot.

'Might've been a rollover,' Bob offered. 'Silly bastards not used to drivin' on gravel always hit the brakes too hard. Them HiLuxes — start a skid in one of them and you'll roll. Their centre of gravity's too damn high.'

'Could be,' Rob agreed. 'There was a covered van, might've been an ambulance went by. Too much flamin' dust to get a decent look at it.'

'It'll be on TV,' I said, but although I flipped channels that evening to catch each news bulletin, I could find nothing about an accident on the Plenty Highway. There was a row in federal parliament over funding for Aboriginal communities, another school shooting in America, an earthquake in Colombia and, on the home front, the police were no closer to finding those responsible for the death of the widowed manager of the jewellery store in Alice Springs. So, whatever had happened along the highway, nobody had as yet informed the local media.

★   ★   ★

The following morning I had barely opened the roadhouse door when Tom Cleary appeared in his dusty police vehicle.

'Morning, Tom. Lovely day.' I straightened the coir mat before the screen door and cast an eye along the verandah for overlooked bottles and cans from the previous evening. The air was crisp enough for a jumper and scented with wattle. The range loomed purple behind the twisted trunks of the mallee and the pink dust of Tom's arrival hovered between red earth and blue sky.

'Good morning, Charlie. Bob about?'

'He won't be far. Where're you heading today?'

'Just here. To see Bob.'

I gave up. He obviously wasn't about to tell me why. 'Come in, then. I'll get him.'

Haled from his task of pumping fuel, Bob stumped irascibly over to the roadhouse where the constable waited, tapping an impatient boot. I made to withdraw but Tom beckoned to me. 'No, stay — you might be able to help.'

'With what?'

'This.' He placed a small plastic evidence bag, like the ones you saw on the TV crime shows, on the counter, nudging it towards us with one finger. 'Either of you notice a recent customer wearing this? A youngish, dark-haired woman, it would've been, going back three weeks, say — maybe a month.'

'I wasn't here a month ago.' I picked it up all the same, turning it about, then froze, staring at the contents. It was a slender gold chain with a pendant in the shape of a golden harp. 'That's . . . ' I began, then stopped. 'But it couldn't be!'

'You've seen it before?' He leant towards me, suddenly gimlet-eyed.

'Yes — well, one like it. Annabelle had one — you remember, Bob?' I turned to him. 'You must've seen her wearing it. But it's obviously not hers. Where did it come from?'

'So can you identify it as the property of Annabelle Carver?' Tom pressed.

Bob bristled. 'That ain't what she said. Me, I dunno. I might've seen it, I don't pay no attention to women's gewgaws.'

Suddenly I understood. 'You've got her handbag, haven't you? And they've sent this back for identification. But they said her licence was with her clothes on the beach . . . ' Something in his face stopped me. 'Not the handbag. Her body's turned up — is that it?'

He nodded soberly. 'A body has, yes. We're trying to identify it. What about this ring, then? Seen that before?' He handed me another bag.

It was a showy piece, what could have been diamonds — or zircons for that matter — set in a rose-gold band. I shook my head. 'It looks new, but I've never seen it before. Where's the body?'

Ignoring the question, he said, 'If it should turn out to be your cousin's, do you know of anyone who would have wished her harm?'

'What?' I stared at him. 'But what's that got to do . . . Annabelle killed herself. I mean, it was your lot who said so! She swam out to sea . . . Didn't she? You told Mum — '

'We were led to believe so,' he said portentously, 'but it now seems possible that wasn't the case.'

'But — the note, the clothes . . . Why would anybody — ' I stared at him, wondering if I should mention my suspicions.

'Where'd yer find this body, then?' Bob demanded. 'It's near a month since Annabelle was 'ere, anyway, so it certainly ain't hers.'

'Unless she was killed immediately after leaving the roadhouse. Which we now think is what occurred. The body we found had been dumped in Mica Valley. A fossicker and his wife stumbled across it on Saturday and reported it that night.' I sat down on the nearest chair as if someone had winded me with a punch, remembering Cora's distracted manner, Len's disinclination to linger.

Appalled I said, 'You're talking about murder? *Annabelle?* First she killed herself, and then she didn't, and now somebody has *murdered* her? I don't believe it.'

Shocked into it, I had unwittingly voiced my private suspicions. Nor did the constable miss it; he stiffened like a hunting dog scenting prey.

'What exactly do you mean by 'And then she didn't'?'

13

There was no help for it then but to tell Tom of my midnight reconstruction of the staged suicide. Old Bob, predictably, would have none of it.

'That's barmy,' he said forthrightly. 'If she's gunna kill herself she'll not be fussing over 'er clothes.'

'But that's just it, Bob. It wasn't fussing as such — it was second nature with her.'

Cleary broke into the conversation then. 'How was she dressed when she left here, Bob? You saw her, spoke with her.'

'Yeah,' he muttered. 'I did, and the geezer with her.'

'We'll get to him in a moment. First, tell me what she was wearing.'

'I dunno,' he said crossly. 'Clothes. Somethin' blue, maybe?' It was obviously a guess. Cleary sighed with exasperation. 'It's a bloody month ago,' Bob complained. 'How the hell's a man supposed to remember who was wearing what?'

'I'll ring Mum,' I offered. 'She might recall.' Diffidently, because it was the last thing I wanted to do, I added, 'Is the body in a fit enough state to recognise? I could — '

'No.' Cleary said abruptly. 'It's not. It looks like her face copped — and anyway the insects and animals have . . . ' He left the sentence unfinished and I was glad of it. 'Unless there's some clear way of identifying her, it'll have to be dental records or DNA — and unless the DNA matches yours, it will only tell us who she's not. I understand she was your father's niece?'

'She was actually his daughter, my half-sister — something I only recently learned.'

'Better,' he said approvingly, impervious to Bob's sudden glare.

'And,' I remembered, 'she broke two of the toes on her left foot when she was twelve. The little toe and the one next to it. Would that show up in an autopsy?'

'I'll pass it on — they can X-ray the remains. Thanks, Charlie. Now, if you could give me a number for Molly, maybe she can help with the clothes.'

'No,' I said definitely. 'I'll do it. I'm not having her badgered. I'll ask and if she can't recall details that's the end of it. She's recovering from major surgery. If necessary,' I warned, 'I'll tell the hospital they're not to put your calls through.'

He held up his hands. 'All right, all right. But soon as you can, okay?'

'I'll do it now.' Daytime phone rates seemed a better deal than trying his patience too far. I couldn't see him agreeing to wait, and I wasn't certain the police didn't have the power to override any instructions I might give to keep them from interviewing Mum.

The phone seemed to both ring forever and then not long enough as I tried to frame the question without giving away the reason for asking it, but for once Mum seemed less than interested.

'What?' she mumbled. 'What do you want, Charlie?'

'Are you feeling okay?' She sounded off somehow.

'Yes, well, my head aches, and this damn bed's uncomfortable. Why are you ringing?' she asked. 'I was trying to sleep.'

'Sorry. Aren't they bringing your breakfast about now?'

'I'm not hungry. What do you want?'

'Well, only to see if you can remember what Annabelle was wearing the last time you saw her. But if you can't — '

'Of course I can,' she snapped. 'She came in a pair of those skinny jeans and a black top — though why she'd wear black the way it shows the dust . . . She changed when she showered, though, into a dress and white sandals, which are just about as silly. One step outside and . . . '

'What sort of dress, Mum? What colour was it?'

'Red, with a white ruffle from neckline to waist. It matched the red rosettes on her sandals. How can it matter anyway? Look, this is a waste of money. Ring at a cheaper time, Charlie.' The phone went down and I was left with the dial tone. At least she hadn't asked why I wanted to know.

I'd made the call from the privacy of the homestead and, thinking hard, I walked slowly back to pass her words onto the constable. He left shortly afterwards and Bob, who stood staring after him, said abruptly, 'You reckon this murdered sheila could be her?'

'I honestly don't know. If it is, how did her stuff get left on a beach in Ballina?' *Because the murderer — if there was one — took it there to throw us off the scent and account for her disappearance*, I answered myself. 'We won't learn anything until it suits the coppers to tell us. I mean, Cleary's seen the body, he already knows how it was dressed, but he didn't give us anything, did he?'

Bob cleared his throat. 'I told 'im I could take a look, see if I could recognise her. He wouldn't have it, but. Said her face was bashed in, let alone what else has 'appened since.'

I nodded. 'So that's what killed her — blunt force trauma, as they say on TV. Did someone take her there and kill her? Or was she already dead and just dumped? Maybe whoever did it believed she'd never be found?' I thought about that. 'If it *is* Annabelle, it's a perfect reason for staging her suicide in a way that could neither be proved nor disproved, and to account for her disappearance. Everybody would just accept that she died in the ocean and never washed ashore.'

'Yeah, well' — Bob pulled at the loose skin of his throat — 'I daresay we'll hear if it's her or not. How was Molly?'

I smiled ruefully. 'Cranky with me for calling. Maybe she's getting tired of hospital.'

★ ★ ★

132

We heard nothing more from Tom Cleary that day. There was no reason why he should tell us the dead woman's identity if it wasn't Annabelle. And the cotton bud sample of saliva and cheek cells he'd taken from me would take days, if not weeks, I supposed hazily, to process. In the TV shows DNA results seemed to come back overnight, but that was a highly unrealistic time frame for anything out here. Meanwhile, another mystery confronted me: consulting the calendar, I noticed a large black B had been written across the coming Saturday.

I showed Bob. 'What's this?'

'Christ! I forgot all about that.' He scratched his cheek where stubby white whiskers rasped against his fingers. He must've skipped a shave that morning. 'It's benefit night for the flying doctor. Molly holds 'em once a month. The community's raising money for a clinic buildin' at the Range. Next to the cop shop and handy to the airstrip. Jeez, I wonder whose turn it is to donate the meat for June? Molly knew all that stuff — where the rota was at. I suppose you'd better ring somebody and ask.'

'We put on a barbecue, you mean, and donate whatever it raises?'

'Yeah. There's a bit of bring-and-buy too. Cakes and jam an' stuff — the women fix it. It's the CWA behind it. Ring one of them.'

Every woman in the district would be a member of the Country Women's Association so I called Penny Hills to speak to Rose Pennon.

'Oh, hi Charlie,' she said when I gave my name. 'How're things? How's Molly doing?'

'Quite well, thanks. Getting a bit tired of hospital, I think.' We talked for a few moments before I got down to the business of whose turn it was.

'Let me see . . . The week's come round so quickly. Sue Damson from Kharko brought the meat last time so that means it's Red Tank's turn now. We all agreed a roster, you see. Saves time and duck-shuffling.' She laughed.

'I guess it does. Okay, thanks. I'll ring Kathleen, make sure she's on board. What time does the barbie usually kick off?'

'Oh, soon as the meat gets there, more or less. Say six, half past? Look, I've heaps of tomatoes at present. You want me to bring you a bucketful?'

'Thanks, that'd be lovely.'

'Good. I'll see you Saturday, then.' She broke the connection and, sighing, I braced myself for a conversation with Kathleen.

★   ★   ★

Ute, informed about the Saturday evening menu, nodded. 'So, the meat with the salads. Okay. And the bread rolls, and much of the deadorse, yes?'

'Sorry? Dead what?'

She looked surprised. 'Is what Bob says — *pass the deadorse* — this is not correct?'

'Oh, dead horse! Tomato sauce, Ute. Yes, that too, but it'll have to be bread, not rolls.'

'No. You will order the yeast, Charlie, and I will make the rolls. The mail arrives in the morning, so there is time. You have heard more from the policeman about the woman who is dead?'

'Not a word.'

'Is very sad,' she observed, 'but life is moving still.'

'It goes on, yes. With the road camp *and* the barbecue, Saturday's likely to have more than its share of it.'

'And your Mike will come too?'

I felt myself flush; I'd deliberately not let myself think that he might. 'He's not mine, Ute. I've only just met him.'

'So? Is plain he likes you.' She studied me thoughtfully. 'Seventeen is time for pretence, for sighs and tears, but you are not a silly girl now. You decide for yourself — you are the boss, yes?'

'I'll try and remember that,' I muttered, adding more loudly, 'How much yeast do you want?'

★　★　★

I rang the hospital early the following day, but it was Mum's nurse Cathy who picked up. Mrs Carver wasn't available at the moment, she told me. She was down in radiography.

My pulse quickened. 'Why? What's wrong?' In the stillness as I waited I could almost feel the nurse's hesitation before she spoke.

'Doctor's a little concerned. He thinks there's some fluid on her lungs, and wanted a picture,' she said then, picking her words carefully. 'There's no need to be alarmed, Charlie. It's all

135

right for me to call you that? Your mother's spoken of you so often I almost feel I know you.'

'Yes, yes,' I said impatiently. 'Why has this happened? And what's being done about it? Should I come down?'

'No, not at this stage. If it's pneumonia she's already been started on antibiotics. But whatever the cause it'll probably clear up in a day or two. Sadly, secondary infections aren't that uncommon following surgery. She has rather a high fever at present but I'd expect that to fall when the dose kicks in. The best thing you can do is to try not to worry. Why don't you give her a ring tonight? She'll be feeling much better by then. I'll tell her you called, shall I?'

'Please,' I said numbly, 'and give her my love.' *Probably*, the word repeated itself in my head, sinister enough to be deeply worrying.

It was hard to think of anything else after that. I didn't tell Bob — no point in both of us fretting — but the moment I got back to the house that evening I rang again. Mum, however, sounded so doped up and vague that hearing her voice did little to dispel my fears. We spoke only briefly for her breathing sounded laboured, and I hung up more concerned than when I'd called. I spent an hour or so staring at some television program wondering if I shouldn't just head for the Alice first thing in the morning and get a flight south. The phone ringing jerked me from my worries, which only intensified as the caller introduced himself as Mum's doctor.

He was calling he said, to reassure me, as my mother's nurse had mentioned my concern. Yes, there was a small hitch in her recovery, a minor infection in the wound and the X-ray he'd ordered had confirmed there was some fluid on the lungs, but they'd almost ruled out pneumonia. They were moving her into the ICU for the next twenty-four hours but he was confident that she would be okay. 'The antibiotics will suppress the infection, Miss Carver' — his voice was crisp, a man in control of events — 'and we'll also drain the fluid. That will improve her breathing so she'll be feeling much more comfortable by the morning.'

'Should I come down? I mean, intensive care . . . '

'Oh, I don't think there's any need for that,' he soothed. 'ICU *sounds* scary I know, but really it just means she's being constantly monitored.'

'But why did it happen?'

'Oh, bad luck, that's all. Hospitals are the germiest places going. It's inevitable, despite all our care, that the odd bug gets through. Don't worry, we're keeping a close eye on things . . . '

I thanked him for the call, then sat on still clutching the phone, my thoughts far away with Mum, warmed by the thought that she had spoken of me so frequently to the staff, but aghast that, for all the doctor's assurances, she was back in the ICU. I sighed then, thinking of Bob. It was only fair that he should be told.

Breakfast was my first opportunity. I watched the shock settle on his face but all he said was, 'An' the quack reckons she'll be okay?'

'He seemed very positive, Bob. A *hitch*, he called it, that's all.'

'Yeah, well, easy for him to bloody say. You goin' down?'

I'd thought hard about it overnight and shook my head. 'I'll give it a day to see if there's any improvement. If her temperature's still high tomorrow morning, then I'm off.' I looked across at Ute, listening attentively as she ate. 'You'll be able to handle Saturday night's do without me, won't you, if it comes to that?'

She frowned. 'What is 'do'?'

'The barbecue.'

'Yes, this is so, Charlie. *Do*,' she murmured reflectively. I could see her tucking the word away. 'You speak the most strange English, you and Bob. What is the *quack*?'

'What?' The phone rang and I rose to get it. 'It means doctor, only — oh, never mind. Hello?'

'Morning, Charlie. Everything okay? Only you sound a bit . . . '

'Mike!' I heard the pleasure in my tone and was instantly flustered. 'How are you? I suppose I am a bit fraught. I've had some worrying news from the hospital.'

'Your mother? What's happened?'

'Seems she's caught some sort of an infection. The doctor reckons she'll be fine but it's made us a bit anxious.'

'It would,' he agreed. 'Will you go down there? I'm happy to drive you into town if you need transport.'

'Thanks,' I said gratefully, 'but I'm giving it another day before I decide. Enough about my troubles. What can I do for you?'

'Oh, the boys were wondering about the

barbecue this Saturday. Molly's been running them regularly as fundraisers. Third Saturday of every month. I didn't know if you — ?'

'Yes, we are. Red Tank's bringing the meat and there'll be homemade rolls to go with it.'

'Can't wait.' There was a smile in his tone. 'And not just for the tucker. Thanks, Charlie. See ya.'

I smiled despite myself as I replaced the handpiece in its cradle, reflecting that Ute was right. He really was keen.

⋆　⋆　⋆

At mid-morning the police vehicle came speeding up the well-watered road. Tom Cleary slammed the driver's door, settling his hat as he strode towards the roadhouse verandah. Watching him approach, I felt Bob move up to stand beside me.

'What's the bastard want now?'

'No doubt he'll tell us,' I murmured. I raised my voice. 'Morning, Tom.'

'Good morning.' He nodded to us both, unsmiling, and I felt my heart jump. 'I'm here to let you know that we've identified the body. And I'm sorry to have to tell you that the dead woman is Annabelle Carver. I'm afraid there can be no doubt about it.'

I'd thought I was prepared but hearing the words still came as a shock. 'Then the DNA results are back?'

'We didn't need them. Molly's description of the clothes and the X-rays of the healed fractures in her toes were sufficient without them. The tests will go ahead but they'll merely confirm what we already know.'

'Yes,' I said blankly. Bob drew in an audible breath and my knees felt suddenly weak. 'Let's sit down for a bit,' I said and when we had done so, on the hard verandah seat, I stared helplessly at the constable. 'I can't get my head round it. Who could have done this? The man she was travelling with?' I knew that Bob had given the police chapter and verse on him. 'Why would he kill her? And if not him, then who?'

'We think we know that, too,' Tom said. 'That diamond ring I showed you? It was found on the body. It's been identified by the insurers as a part of the haul taken in the big jewellery robbery in the Alice back in early May. We suspect that Carver was involved, and the man with her. He must've missed it when he dumped her body.'

I gasped; his suddenly hard official voice using her surname like that turned her from Annabelle into an instant criminal. Beside me, Bob's reaction was equally shocked.

'Jesus! You sayin' she robbed — ' His mouth dropped open. 'Hang about, wasn't there a bloke killed in that business? Bashed to death, the papers said.'

Face hard, Tom nodded. 'There was. It's a double murder case now. Detectives will be flying down this afternoon to interview Molly. She's the last known person to have spoken to Annabelle.'

I said numbly, 'The doctor won't let them.

140

She's in intensive care.'

'It's murder, Charlie,' he said. 'That makes it urgent.'

'And you don't think the fact that it *is* murder, with Annabelle as the victim, won't upset her?'

He said coolly, 'I daresay the dead man's family is upset too. For which your sister is partly or wholly responsible.'

And to that I could make no answer.

14

The rest of the day passed in a blur of indecisiveness that had me losing track of simple tasks I was performing: I washed the same dishes twice, and could make no sense of the store inventory I was trying to conduct. If Mum was fit enough to understand what was going on, should I forewarn her? There was no way the police would sugarcoat the pill. While her instinct would be to protect the child she had raised, they would use the shock of the news to jar from her any crumb of knowledge she might have. That she knew nothing would be beside the point, but could I really stop them interviewing her?

Bob was caught between worry about the effect the news would have on Molly, and a sort of savage satisfaction that his own long-held reading of Annabelle's character had been justified. 'Trouble-makin' little bitch shoulda been drowned at birth. Nothin' but grief to Molly — I said it all along.' And much more of the same.

I made the call at seven p.m. and was put through to one of the nurses, who offered to take a message. 'I can't speak to her, then?'

'She's asleep at the moment. But she's much improved, Miss Carver — off the oxygen and the infection's responding to the medication. She'll be going back to the ward tomorrow or the next day. Was there some particular message I can pass on?'

Impossible to compress all that I needed to tell her into a couple of sentences, I sighed, silently admitting defeat. 'No, just that I rang. And Bob and I send our love. Thank you.'

Later the phone rang again. This time it was Mike. 'Just wondered how Molly was doing? And to ask if you've decided whether to go down to see her?'

'Oh, Mike, thanks for calling. She seems to be much improved, thank God, so I think I won't. They're talking about shifting her back to the ward soon, which is a big relief.'

'Glad to hear it,' he said, 'I don't actually want to miss seeing you Saturday. How's it going there?'

I blurted my news. 'The body Len found, Mike. It's Annabelle. So I was right all along and she didn't drown.'

'You're kidding me!' He whistled. 'God! How awful for you, Charlie. I'm sorry. So when was she killed?'

'The coppers think it happened after she left the Garnet.' I went on to tell him the whole appalling business — how the stolen ring linked her to the robbery, and the killing of the jeweller, ending grimly, 'Perhaps it's just as well she *is* dead — at least she won't be charged with murder. If she didn't kill the man, it seems that she was certainly an accomplice.'

'Holy shit!' The surprised exclamation was followed by an apology. 'Sorry. That makes it aggravated assault or something — not that it

143

matters now, I suppose. So your guess about the clothes was spot on. Any word on who her partner was yet?'

'No. His name's Paul something, that's all Mum knew. Bob's given the police a description, for what it's worth. I mean, big, dark, nasty-looking — what good is that? He'd certainly know him if he saw him again, but it's not likely, is it?' I hesitated. 'I think Bob was scared by him. He's a tough old fellow, you know — nobody's pushover. He'll wade in if he's needed. He's always stood by Mum when there was trouble, like when somebody tried to hold the Garnet up once, years ago. It was really scary — the bloke came in yelling and waving a wheel wrench and Bob tackled him, no hesitation. Almost got his head smashed in too. But I think he had the wind-up about this guy with Annabelle. Told me he didn't like the look of him from the outset and that he'd brought his dog over as back-up in case it should be needed. I suppose he *is* getting old — older,' I amended.

'And maybe he can recognise a bad 'un when he sees him,' Mike said soberly. 'Some blokes you just don't take chances with. Okay, Charlie. The camp's going out tomorrow, back home Saturday arvo. I'll see you after that. Take care.'

'You too, Mike. Bye.'

★   ★   ★

The following day Annabelle's picture appeared on television in connection with the robbery. The police wanted to learn where she'd been living

144

and were asking for public assistance. Anyone who knew the murdered woman, where she'd been working and/or staying prior to the first week in May was asked to contact Crime Stoppers. They were also very interested in speaking to the man who had been travelling with her. I fielded calls from curious neighbours expressing disbelief and condolences, or simply wanting further details. Old Spider just about summed up the local attitude with his opening remark.

'I thought your cousin killed herself, Charlie. You telling me some other bugger done it for her?'

'I'm afraid so, Spider. It was a shock to us too.'

'Christ on a bike!' he marvelled. 'What the hell's the world coming to?'

Rose Pennon asked how Annabelle had come to be where her body was found, in what the media was describing as 'a lonely desert valley, thirty kilometres from her childhood home'.

'She came home for a visit,' I explained. 'It was before I got back. She was only here for an hour or two tops. The police seem to think she was killed when they moved on — that's why they're looking for the man who was with her.'

'You mean her murderer was right there? At the Garnet? Dear Lord! If I was you, Charlie, I couldn't sleep at night. Aren't you scared?'

'Well, he's not here now,' I said. 'And he's hardly likely to return — *if* he killed her, which we don't know, do we?' I was certain in my own mind that he had, and said it only because

Rose's histrionics exasperated me.

'Well, who else could've?' she answered inarguably.

Kathleen Mallory was next, husky smoker's voice urgent with concern. 'I saw it on the news, Charlie. Horrible! And to think we thought she'd done it herself! You shouldn't be there alone — it's dangerous. One of the boys can come and stay till the police catch this killer . . . '

'Whoa, Kathleen, let's just backtrack a bit.' I knew quite well which of the boys would turn up and was having none of it. 'First off, I'm not alone. I — '

'Be sensible, Charlie. What sort of protection is one old man and a foreign girl? You could be murdered in your bed! You need a man there to — '

'I have a man — ten of them, in fact, camped on my doorstep. The Main Roads lot are here and will be for weeks, so I'm knee-deep in muscle should I need help. Which I won't. It's kind of you to concern yourself, Kathleen, but I'm fine, thank you.'

The woman had more to say but I finally got rid of her and hung up muttering ' . . . and why should being *foreign* make any difference?'

It was typical of Annabelle. Even dead she was still the centre of attention. If her murder was never solved she'd become an enduring outback legend — maybe they'd even run tours so tourists could gawp at the place where she died, I thought crossly.

★   ★   ★

146

Mum continued to improve; she was back in the ward on Thursday and on Friday afternoon told me she could be discharged next day, only it transpired that she'd have to wait until Monday for transport back to the Alice. That suited me for I intended, if I could, to organise for her to stay a few days in Alice Springs, where she'd be closer to medical help if it was needed. Taking a deep breath, I broke the news of Annabelle's complicity in the crimes of robbery and murder and felt her shock in the breathed 'Dear God!' that came faintly down the line.

'Mum, are you okay? I thought the police might already have spoken to you about it. Tom said they were going to.'

'Two policemen came to see me, yes. They told me about finding her body. I mean, I knew she was dead, but it was still a shock to . . . They said they thought she was an accomplice to robbery but nothing about murder. She wouldn't . . . All right, she was greedy and unscrupulous, Charlie, but not vicious.'

'I don't think the law draws a line between the accomplice and the actual murderer these days,' I said. 'And unless she waited outside . . . Even then, she had knowledge of the crime — either before or after it was committed, which makes her an accessory. She was wearing a stolen ring.'

'Why was she so desperate for money? How much did the jeweller lose?'

'I heard eighty thousand. It was Centre Jewellers, you know, that big place in the Mall? High-end stuff. But they'd have to fence it, and that'd cost them as well as taking time, Tom said.

He told me that the person handling the stolen goods usually makes more out of the heist than the actual thieves.' Inspiration hit me. 'Maybe they were planning to leave the country — or she was, without telling him? And she was worried about what he'd do. Perhaps the jeweller's death scared her enough that she wanted to get away from him. Could that be why she needed cash? Do you remember *anything* at all about him, Mum?'

'Paul? No. The police already asked me. I served him a meal, and Annabelle and I went over to the house to talk. I returned to the roadhouse after we quarrelled, and she went for a shower before she left. I think I told him she wouldn't be long, and I was back in the kitchen cooking when she came through, dressed differently. She didn't say goodbye — not to me or Bob. Just looked at us and left. I assume they drove off then, but I didn't go to the door to watch. There were customers waiting.'

A brief silence ensued. A part of me marvelled that it wasn't uncomfortable. My mother and I were talking, actually holding a conversation. I said thoughtfully, 'I should have asked Tom what a fencer of stolen goods would actually charge. Ten per cent, do you think, or twenty? Bearing in mind nobody's going to get the full value and what's left presumably gets split between the thieves, it's not much, is it, for the risk? Not when it includes murder.'

'Perhaps the murder wasn't intended? And with Annabelle dead there's no need to split it.'

'You're right. Grief!' I shivered at a sudden thought. 'Could he have meant all along to kill her, to keep it all for himself? It doesn't bear thinking about!'

'Well, let's not, Charlie.' She sounded weary all at once. 'Tell me how things are going at the Garnet instead. Did Bob remember the benefit night?'

We talked about the plans I'd made for it, and I retailed some of Ute's misunderstandings of the vernacular for her amusement before a glance at the clock reminded me how long we'd been on the phone.

'You should be resting,' I said. 'Bye, Mum. I'll see you soon.'

'Yes, thanks for calling, Charlie. Bye.'

Turning our conversation over in my mind, I wandered out into the garden where Bob had already set out the tables for tomorrow night and stood contemplating them. The thud of boots on slate made me glance back across the fence at the house and the man strolling calmly along the verandah towards me. He saw me notice him and waved, the action fragmented by the latticework between us.

'There you are, Charlie. Long time no see. I've missed you, girl — you've no idea how much,' he called cheerily. 'Welcome home, by the way.'

'Bryan,' I said frostily. 'What the hell are you doing here? Apart from trespassing, I mean? Was this your mother's idea?'

'Oh, come on, don't be like that. Can't a man call on his sweetie without needing prompting? But Mum's dead right, you shouldn't be here

149

alone with a killer on the loose. I'd never forgive myself if anything happened to you.'

'Very touching,' I sneered. 'But I'm not alone, and even if I were, you're the last man I'd turn to. The very last. So you can take yourself off, and don't come back!'

'You don't mean that, Charlie. Look, I'm sorry. Will that help?' His blue eyes were hopeful, his hair still the same coppery red; in fact, he didn't look to have changed at all. That was the trouble, I thought. His betrayal had sat so lightly upon him that he doubtless saw it as a boyish misdemeanour, easily excused. 'Come on, Charlie,' he coaxed, smiling. 'We've always been good mates and the very fact that you're back and not wearing a ring means you must still feel something for me.'

'Did your mother tell you that too?' I said furiously. 'You Mallorys! Your ego is beyond belief! Go! If you don't I swear I'll set Bob's dog on you. You've got five minutes.' I turned and stormed back to the roadhouse, slamming the back door loudly enough to bring Ute from the kitchen.

Her eyebrows shot up at the sight of my heated state. 'Something else is wrong, yes?'

'There will be,' I muttered direly. 'If a man comes through that door in the next five seconds you lay him out with your biggest frying pan. Got that?' And leaving her gaping after me in bewilderment, I took myself off to the storeroom to calm down.

★ ★ ★

By midday Saturday the barbecue had been scrubbed down and seating arranged around the tables under the roofed extension near the staff dongas. The kitchen, meanwhile, was giving off the enticing odour of freshly baked bread.

Ute, pulling trays of rolls from the oven, brushed off my compliment on her skill. 'Is simple, Charlie. One follows a recipe, yes? You should try — all new things you should try. Not to be the fraidy-puss. That is right?'

'Cat,' I said. 'Fraidy-cat. I just wish I had your confidence. As a matter of interest, how many languages do you speak, Ute?'

She shrugged, 'Four. For Europe is normal. Polish I learn at home. French and English at school, German for my work. English is hardest, so many idi- idiots? No, the quaint sayings?'

'Idioms.' I shook my head. 'You're amazing. Most native-born Australians can't speak more than one. Have you someone special waiting for you back home?'

'Like your Mike?' she teased, then sobered. 'There is one but he does not wait — he is married. He has family too, I am like the sweet bun for him, to eat and forget. So I come away to show him is not so easy, yes?'

'I'm sorry,' I said sincerely. 'You deserve better than that.'

She frowned. 'You think so? Me, I think we make our — what you say — luck? We earn by what we do, Charlie. If I stay I am forever mistress, not wife. So maybe I find better man and be wife. Maybe I don't, but either way I am no longer sweet bun.'

151

'I'm sure you will find someone. I just hope he deserves you. Now, what you said about trying new things . . . you're absolutely right. Do you think that tomorrow you could teach me how you make those rolls?'

15

We had a full house for the barbecue: all the stations, the road camp, and several lots of travellers who saw the notice Bob had posted up and decided to stay, asking permission to camp overnight and use the facilities.

'Five bucks a head,' he said without a blink, 'and you don't leave no mess be'ind.'

They agreed readily and later, when I remonstrated at what I considered a rip-off, asking if Mum charged for use of the ablution block, he looked up from the fridge shelves he was stacking with cans to scowl upon me.

'She don't, but she oughta. An' we ain't benefitting — you'll be cleaning the block an' the CWA's getting the dough.'

'It just seems a bit mean.'

'They're paying for protection, Charlie, not just a shower 'n a dunny. Yer won't find travellers pulling off the road just anywhere to camp, like they used to. It's got too chancy. Besides, every bugger'll have heard about the murder and it'll have made 'em extra jumpy. Safety in numbers, you know.'

'I imagine you're right.' I immediately thought of Kathleen's words on the subject and, as if I'd conjured him up, the door opened and Bryan Mallory strode into the roadhouse in advance of his brother Con, Con's wife, Amy, and their three kids. I opened my mouth but before I could speak, Bryan gave a beaming smile as if yesterday's encounter had never occurred and spread his arms as if he actually expected me to run into them.

'Long time, Charlie. You're looking well. Got a hug for an old friend?'

Kathleen was smiling smugly behind him, pushing through the knot of road-camp men to keep up. Eric, the one I'd given the paperbacks to, was forced to step hastily back to avoid her. Several other men glanced over to see who had addressed me; I seethed, silently cursing him for the attention he'd drawn to us. To order him out of the Garnet would create nothing but gossip, which I realised was probably what he was counting on.

'No,' I snapped, keeping my voice down. 'I haven't. I thought I'd made it perfectly plain I want nothing to do with you.' The aroma of cooking meat wafted into the room from the garden where Ute was handling the barbecue. I picked up a tray and, bearing it before me like a shield, ducked into the kitchen to begin loading the salads onto it. I used the back door to reach the garden and got two more loads out before he found me again in the gathering throng. He had a beer in his hand by then and his voice had lost some of its breezy assurance when it sounded again quite close behind me.

'There you are, Charlie. Look, I just want to talk,' he pleaded. 'I know you were angry back then, but that was five years ago, for God's sake! Time to let bygones be bygones, I'd have thought. I really have missed you, and I've

154

already apologised. Can't we just start again, or at least talk about things?'

I sighed with exasperation. 'There's no need to, Bryan, because there's nothing to say. Whatever we had ended right here in this garden. I've moved on and if you haven't, that's your problem. As far as I'm concerned, you're just a neighbour. We're not friends and we're certainly not lovers. Is that plain enough for you?'

He frowned, obviously perplexed by my attitude. All the Mallorys were handsome men with their deep auburn hair, light eyes and fair skin. Bryan, as the baby of the family and Kathleen's darling, was unused to being refused anything. I was amazed at my own blindness in not having recognised this weakness in him before and realised that I had not only moved on but grown too, while he hadn't. He was the same spoilt boy-man I had known five years ago, relying on his charm and his mother's indulgence to get by. Mum had been right after all: had we married, it would never have lasted.

'You can't still be holding that thing with your cousin against me, Charlie, after all this time,' he said reasonably. 'What's happened to you? You were always kind and forgiving. It's what I love about you. Fellows make mistakes — it's not the end of the world! I made one and I'm truly sorry, so you have to let it go.' The limpid blue eyes I had once adored cajoled me, but with a hint of complacency in their depths. It was how he got his way with his mother and I felt a spurt of irritation at his childishness.

155

'Get out of my way, Bryan. I've got work to do.'

He grabbed my wrist as I turned away. 'No, wait — just give me another chance, Charlie. I'll make it up to you, and I swear I'll never look at another woman — '

I slapped furiously at his arm. 'Get your hands off me!'

Mike was suddenly beside me, looking not at me but at my companion. 'Trouble, Charlie?'

'No,' I said thankfully, 'because Bryan here is going off to feed his face and find somebody else to annoy. Can you give me a hand to bring the rest of the stuff out, Mike?'

'My pleasure,' he said, without taking his eyes off Bryan. They bore a far-from-friendly gleam as he jerked his head dismissively. 'You heard her. Piss off.'

'Who the hell are you to come butting into a private discussion? Mind your own goddamn business.' Bryan's voice flared. 'You gonna make me?'

'If it comes to that,' Mike said flatly, and something in his aspect must have changed Bryan's mind for, with a muttered curse, he turned angrily away.

'Thank you,' I murmured. 'You don't really have to help. I just said that so he'd go.'

'But I want to.' Mike picked up the tray and touched my elbow, turning me towards the kitchen. 'Who is he?'

I breathed out through my nose. 'One of the Mallorys from Red Tank. I broke off our engagement five years ago. Five years, for God's sake! He's just a bit slow to accept it. I can't believe,' I said, 'that I once fancied him.' Or, I silently added, that I'd let him break my heart. It seemed Mum had been right when she had told me, with what I had seen at the time as a complete lack of empathy: 'Someday, Charlie, you'll look back and marvel at the escape you've just had.' I had thought it was her own disillusionment speaking rather than the wisdom that came from life experience and, wondering what else I'd been wrong about, I sighed.

Mike, misinterpreting the sound, said grimly, 'He won't bother you again, Charlie. I'll make sure of it.'

'It's all right. Truly it is. I was just sighing for the waste of time and emotion he cost me.' I had told him so much, I thought, I might as well tell him the rest. 'I told you we were engaged. I broke it off the day I caught them — him and Annabelle — in the summerhouse back there.' I remembered again that glimpse of her rose-tipped breasts against the white of his body. 'I'd had a catalogue sent to me in the mail so I could choose a wedding dress. I just wanted to show it to him, to see if he liked it. And there they were, having sex on the bench. And I'm pretty sure that she planned for me to find them.'

Mike's eyebrows shot up. 'Jesus, she sounds a proper piece of work! I suppose it does make it less surprising, though, that someone knocked her off. I hope the pair of them got splinters in their bums.'

The image shocked a giggle from me. He grinned and then we were both whooping with

157

laughter. 'That's better,' he said, when we'd sobered. 'Nothing beats a bit of humour. You've got a pretty laugh, Charlie. Now, where's this stuff you want carried out?'

★　★　★

The barbecue ran late. I suspected that it was a pleasant change for both the road camp and the station men to meet up with others outside their own circles, while opportunities for the station women to socialise with one another were rare enough to make each gathering eagerly anticipated. The three lots of travellers mixed in, fascinated, if their overheard questions were a guide, with the differences between bush and town living. One, at least, was avid to hear the details of the murder until Bess Himan said levelly, 'You should ask Charlie, our hostess, about that. The victim was her cousin.'

'Oh, I didn't know,' the woman exclaimed, sounding flustered and chastened. She immediately quit the group of women, taking herself off to the table where the bring-and-buy items were displayed, but still wasn't beyond earshot of Bess's parting riposte, 'Yes, well, every murder is a tragedy for someone,' which effectively closed down the subject among the rest of the women.

Mike stuck close to me and, looking round at one stage as we ate, I caught Bryan glowering at him. I saw Ute in earnest conversation with Eric and wondered what they would make of each other. He seemed quieter and more thoughtful than most of his mates, almost like Rob, the

158

boss, though a good deal younger. Tom Cleary and his wife were there but they were the first to leave. He'd have had a hard time fending off questions from the men wanting details of the murder. Nor would his wife have escaped a quizzing from the women. I wondered if there was a requirement in the force that wives not discuss their husbands' work.

'You're very quiet,' Mike said. 'Can I get you a beer, or a coffee?'

'Coffee would be nice, thanks. I don't like beer.'

'The one's coming up, the other I'll remember.' He rose from the red-gum log on which we were sitting a little apart from the rest, and made his way to the urn on the table. The barbecue coals were ash, and the uneaten rolls were drying out in their baskets. I should really get up and cover them, I thought, but I sat on listening to the hum of conversation and the bursts of laughter. People were wearing coats and some even had blankets around their shoulders for the June night was cold. Overhead the stars were bright points in the blackness, only a little dimmed by the stretch of bulbs Bob had strung between the kitchen and the summer-house roof to give light to the proceedings. The diesel thumped reliably on, so much a part of bush living that one rarely registered the noise.

I watched Mike's tall form, cast half in shadow, walk back towards me, and my heart gave a funny little flip. Was he really the one? I hardly knew him, yet I had told him things I had told no one else. That surely must count. Then I remembered Bryan and was filled with doubt. Didn't they say that women made the same mistake over and over when it came to choosing men? Would he prove to be no more trustworthy than Bryan had been?

'Penny for them,' Mike said, handing me the cup. 'You look a bit lost, Charlie. What's up — apart from Molly's health, Annabelle's death, and that nitwit who was making a pest of himself?'

I had to smile at that. 'That's enough, isn't it? It's nothing really, Mike. I was just wishing that I was more certain about things, and life in general. Braver, I guess, than I am. Like Ute. Can you see me crossing half the world on a solo holiday just to teach a man a lesson? Which is more or less what she's done. And then taking all this' — I waved a hand to encompass the broad reach of the night, and the emptiness of the land beyond the garden — 'in her stride as if it was no more than a park in the Hague? If they have room enough for parks there.'

'Perhaps not,' he agreed, 'but I can see a young girl with her heart and faith shattered, who left home for a distant city, which must have seemed every bit as formidable a challenge as another country given her background, and who made a go of it there. That takes courage, Charlie. And you stuck it out, you supported yourself, followed your dream. What makes you think any of us operate on certainty, anyway?'

'Annabelle did,' I said. 'She never had the slightest doubt. What she wanted she took.'

He snorted. 'There's a difference. Where

would society be if we all acted like that?' He squeezed my hand. 'You shouldn't doubt yourself. I think you're amazing, Charlie. The most amazing girl I've ever met.'

'You do?' I goggled at him and very deliberately he grounded his coffee cup, took my chin in his hand to tilt up my face, and kissed me.

'That's to prove it,' he said. In the shadows his half-lit face gazed down at mine, wearing a look that was part quizzical, part apprehensive. 'Well, are you going to sock me now, and add me to the nitwit queue?'

'No,' I said and, reaching up to cup his face in my hands, I kissed him back.

16

I was up early the following morning, humming over the task of making sandwiches and filling the thermoses. I had packed a bag for Mum the previous night, breaking off every now and then to relive that instant as Mike's lips met mine. We had talked and touched and made plans for today, and when he finally drove off after the rest had departed, he had kissed me again lingeringly, in a way that left me elated and unsettled until sleep had claimed me.

'I'll be back tonight,' I told my two co-workers as I scrambled through breakfast, burning my tongue in my haste to be gone. 'I'd take the cash if the banks were open, but it'll just have to wait until we bring Mum home.' Since the attempted robbery years before, the safe was emptied on a regular basis, leaving only a couple of hundred dollars for daily transactions. Mum hadn't installed an EFTPOS line and wouldn't, she had said, until the business doubled. Nobody was holding their breath for that to occur, so the calico bags of notes and coins continued to be ferried into the Alice whenever someone visited.

'You watch yerself,' Bob growled. 'Plenty of idiots be'ind the wheel these days. Drive like maniacs, some of 'em.'

'I'll be careful. I've got water, tools, and tucker. And I'm sure that Mike can change a tyre. I'll be fine, Bob.'

'You have the beautiful day, Charlie.' Ute winked at me. 'A nice drive in the country, with plenty of stops, yes? Is good as concert or museum visit.'

I grinned at her. 'Shame Eric can't take you on one too.'

She shrugged. 'I am working, but he come and we talk. Who knows? Perhaps I make him blinis. We will see.'

'Well, I'm glad everyone's happy,' Bob growled.

'Ah, lighten up, you old grumble-guts.' I surprised him with a kiss on the cheek. 'I'm off. Don't worry if I'm a bit late home.' I grabbed the lunches and headed out to the station wagon, which was fuelled and waiting in the shed.

It was a beautiful morning, chilly enough for a jumper and the woollen gloves I'd pulled on. The crisp air made a pale-blue backdrop for the lavender ranges, and a light breeze shivered the dun and olive shades of scrub and bush. The first of the men were straggling up from the camp for their slightly later Sunday breakfasts, their dusty yellow machines that would sit silent all day drawn up like sleeping monsters in the cleared bay beside the camp.

I sped past to the turn-off and a short distance west down the highway, slowing when I reached the thin track that speared away south to the new Garnet outstation. Mike was waiting beneath a mulga tree, his lean form propped against the dark trunk. He wore a fleece-lined jacket over jeans and shirt and his boots had been polished. He grinned from beneath his Akubra, pulling the door open as I stopped beside him.

'Morning, Charlie. How do you manage to look so pretty this early in the day?'

I felt myself blush. 'Do I? Thank you, Mike. Where's your vehicle?'

'Back in the mulga a bit, outta sight. I could wish I had a dog to leave with it, but it should be safe enough.'

'Like Bob's Jasper,' I agreed. 'He'd tear the leg off anyone who came near it.' I giggled suddenly. 'Bit like his master really. But a different story once you get to know him.'

'The man or the dog?'

'Both. I guess in all the ways that mattered Bob was more like a father to me than my own dad.' I pondered the matter as I drove back onto the road. 'It was always him I went to for company, or comfort, or help — a broken toy, a flat bike tyre, a sick pet. Dad wouldn't be bothered, or he'd tell you he'd do it later — only he never would — and Mum was always busy. Whenever I felt put upon, Bob was there for me. I suppose, in a way, he was my best friend till I went off to boarding school. What about you? Were you ever lonely as a kid?'

'Ah, well, I had my brothers. We're all pretty good mates. I'm probably closest to Jeff. Dan's five years younger — that's quite a gap when you're a kid, plus he's got town interests. Being a stockie, Jeff's always out on the stations. We meet up for a beer, see each other at Christmas — it's that sort of arrangement. Did you not get on with Annabelle, then, even when you were little?'

'No.' I flicked him a look. 'There's only one

queen bee to a colony and she was it. I read somewhere that the first queen to hatch in a hive stings the rest to death while they're still in their cells. Annabelle would've approved of their actions, take my word for it.'

'Ah.' His brows rose in a query. 'No word back from the coppers on how the investigation's going?'

I shook my head. 'But, talking to Mum the other day, I got to wondering if Paul — Annabelle's partner in the crime — might've killed her because she was a witness to the murder? Or that she was about to run out on him and he found out. The money she wanted — it could've been so she could leave the country.'

'It's possible,' he conceded. 'Anyway, it's much too nice a day to waste on mysteries we can't solve. Tell me what you've got planned.'

'To organise something for Mum. I want a greeter, transport, accommodation, possibly a nurse to look in on her every other day . . . Difficult to do on a Sunday, but it's the only time I have.'

'The accommodation might be a problem, but I meant more personal stuff, Charlie. Like where should we have smoko, and which park you'd like to eat lunch in, and when do I get to kiss you again?'

My heart repeated its little flip but I said sternly, 'Certainly not while I'm driving. Let's wait for smoko time to come.'

'So, then?'

'I'll think about it. You seem to have a very

165

demanding nature, Mr Webb.'

'Only with important stuff,' he deadpanned, adding, 'I love that little smile of yours, Charlie.' His brown eyes crinkled at the corners and my heart flip-flopped like a teenage girl's.

* * *

In the end we just pulled off the road and uncapped the smoko thermos in the shade of a beefwood for our cuppa. It wasn't a long stop; we couldn't afford the time. The morning had warmed up and we shed coats and gloves before continuing.

'You want me to spell you?' Mike asked after our break and I was glad to let him drive. It gave me the chance to curl sideways in my seat and watch him. The sight of his clear-cut profile framed by the side window and his strong brown hands on the wheel made something within me purr like a contented cat. I liked the way the dark hair curled about his ear (it had a moderate-sized lobe and lay flat against his head) and the strong line of his jaw. There was a tiny scar on the side of his chin, the width of my smallest fingernail, and curved in a similar arc.

'What happened there?' I leant in to touch it lightly.

'That?' He fingered the skin. 'That was Jeff's fault. He threw a gun at me.'

'A *gun*?'

'A cap gun. It was the foresight that cut me.' Seeing my look, he laughed. 'It wasn't the OK Corral or anything, Charlie. I was six and we were fighting over the gun, and in the end he chucked it at me.' A glint of chrome and glass from within the dust cloud ahead had him braking to pull the passenger-side wheels half into the table drain as the approaching road train powered past. When the dust had blown away he steered us carefully back through the gravel rill edging the road. 'The track could do with another grade about now,' he observed.

'Mmm,' I agreed, then remembered something. 'What did you mean about accommodation being difficult?'

'Just that rodeo weekend's coming up. The town will be busting at the seams with all the station people and tourists come Saturday, and they'll all have booked ahead. Didn't you know it was on?'

'I'd forgotten. Damn! Well, I'll have to think of someplace she can stay. Though a friend's house would actually be better — that way she'd have someone to keep an eye on her.'

He shrugged. 'We'll have to do some visiting when we get in, then. So, did we decide on a lunch spot?'

We wound up on a shaded bench in the Civic Centre Park, where we ate our sandwiches and drained the second thermos. Packing up again, Mike slid behind the wheel with the cryptic utterance, 'Come on. I've had an idea.'

It proved to be ice creams bought from a little convenience store half a block from the backpackers' lodge where he normally stayed, and which we ascertained was booked out — not that Mum would have been comfortable there

167

with its dorm beds and a shared kitchen. When the cones' smooth sweetness had been consumed, I heaved a sigh of completion, then used a cup of water from our drinking supply to rinse sticky hands.

'That was lovely. Now, to work. First stop the Uniting Church manse. I don't even know if the Thorntons are in town — they could be out on patrol — but I'm rather pinning my hopes on them.'

'And Plan B is?'

'Kathy Gleeson. Kathy used to cook at Abbey Downs — eight, maybe ten years back. She and Mum were friends but I don't know if they've kept in touch. I noticed an ad for her husband's business on a hoarding back there — he runs a drill rig, so they could be out of town.' I hoped that it wouldn't come to that and it didn't. The first press of the doorbell brought Rae to open it, her pleasant, elderly face breaking into a smile of welcome.

'Charlie, and Mike! How lovely to see you both. Come in, I'll put the kettle on.'

'We just had lunch actually, thanks,' I said. 'It's a one-day trip today — we're due back tonight. I'm just so glad we caught you — I half expected you'd be out on patrol.'

'Not much point just now,' she said, leading us into the living room. She patted a chairback. 'Sit down, make yourself at home. You're sure you won't have some tea?'

'No, it's fine thanks, really. Why do you say that?'

'What? Oh, the patrol — the rodeo, Charlie.

168

Everyone will be in the Alice anyway. Will the Abbey lot be amongst them, Mike?'

He nodded. 'Not me though, or the cook. Kevin'll probably come in, and the boys all have time off for it, starting Friday. The managers don't like the timing — everyone's mustering — but if you don't let the men go they'll just pull out anyway. This way at least you get them back.' He grinned, 'And a sorrier bunch you'll rarely see till the grog's out of 'em.'

I sniffed theatrically. 'Men! This is your idea of fun, is it?'

'Not mine, no. But hey, Molly'll find it easy to get a lift home.'

'Not with a bunch of drunken ringers, thank you very much!'

'So, she's coming home?' Rae interposed. 'That's wonderful, Charlie. When?'

It was the opening I needed. 'The Care Flight gets in from Adelaide tomorrow. I gather she'll be taken to the hospital here to get her follow-up appointments with the visiting cardiologist before she's officially discharged, but I'd forgotten about the rodeo and now I'm worried that I won't get accommodation for her. I want her to spend at least a week in town. I just don't feel she should be taking on a long road trip immediately.' I paused, then rushed on, 'Mum doesn't actually know about this part of the plan, but really, Rae, don't you think after a big op like that she should be close to a doctor, just for a while?'

'You're perfectly right, Charlie. And don't worry, we'll look after her for you. She can stay

169

with us for as long as she needs to. As for getting her home, I'll keep an eye out among the rodeo crowd to see if I can find somebody respectable' — her eyes twinkled — 'and sober to drive her home. Ben and Sue Damson, for instance, or maybe the Himans. They'd be happy to do it, I'm sure.'

'Thank you.' I stretched my neck, feeling the tension run out of my shoulders. 'It's so strange — I've never had to worry about Mum before. She always seemed, I don't know, indestructible. She was like a machine, never ill.' I stood up. 'Well, I suppose we'd best be going. We have to fuel up and — '

'You're sure you won't take something first? It's a wearisome drive back.'

'No, we're fine, thanks. But if you wouldn't mind, maybe we could boil the kettle and fill our thermoses?'

'Of course. Bring them in and I'll put the jug on.'

★   ★   ★

It was another half hour before we got away. Mike brought in the bag I'd packed for Mum, carrying it under Rae's direction straight into the guest's bedroom.

'I'll ring the hospital and leave my number so they can let me know when she's ready for pick-up,' Rae said. 'It'll be a slow business — the Care Flights don't usually land until around ten. If she's discharged much before noon I'll be surprised.' She returned my hug. 'Don't worry,

170

Charlie, and have a safe trip home. It's been so nice to see you both again.'

'Rae's just lovely,' I said as Mike pulled out from the kerb. 'I hope I'm half as nice when I'm her age.'

'You reckon you'll need time to achieve it?' he teased.

I flicked a fingernail against his wrist. 'You know what I mean. Head for the fuel depot. God, it's half-two already! Where does the time get to?'

17

The trip back took longer than I'd expected. I reclaimed the wheel for the first half, which included the stretch of bitumen until the turn-off onto the Plenty River Highway when we began meeting a string of road trains coming from the east. They hogged the crown of the road, forcing me to slow and move over. Mike, staring intently between the slatted bars of the trailers, said, 'They're from Kharko — I just caught an earmark. Sale bullocks. Ours aren't going off till next week. We'll load them straight after the rodeo.'

'Speaking of which, why aren't you going in for it?'

'To view or ride?'

'Either or both,' I said. 'I thought all ringers loved rodeos?'

'Nah. How many ways can you get piled off a bucking horse? Besides, I rather thought I might hang out with you.'

'Well, great — but I'll have to work, Mike. Still, it would be nice to have you around. And there're always the evenings.'

'Good. Maybe Bob can find me a job to fill in the days. Don't you get *any* time off, Charlie?'

I shrugged. 'Today's off. You can't keep office hours in a business like the Garnet. Customers come when they come.'

We stopped for a quick cuppa by the side of a

dry creek where yellowed grass spilled down the red soil bank to the coarse sand of its bed. I sifted a handful through my fingers, surprised as always at the quantity of the little spiral shells among the grains.

'I used to collect these when I was a kid.' I frowned, trying to resurrect the memory. 'From the creek near the mill. It's proper sand there, like this. The stuff in Penny Creek's more powdery, like pink talc. They were my little people, no arms or legs, but still . . .' I held one up between thumb and forefinger. 'A couple of pencil spots for eyes, then you glue some hair on. I'd cut a curl off with Mum's scissors — until she found out, of course.'

Mike's brown eyes smiled at me. 'Oh yes. How old were you?'

'Five, maybe. I had a whole little family of them.'

'And how much hair left?'

'Oh, plenty.' I pulled my hat off to run a hand through my thick curls. 'A good thing about hair like mine is it can take a lot of mangling before it shows. So there was Mum and Dad and Uncle Bob, and two little babies and me.' I smiled reminiscently. 'I thought when I grew up that I'd have two babies, you see, so they could keep each other company. Looking back I don't seem to have bothered with a husband. They lived in a tobacco tin Bob gave me. He smoked, you know, till Mum made him quit.'

'Ah, well. I collected frogs. No shortage of them up north. I tied coloured strings round their necks so I could tell which were mine.

173

Trouble is' — Mike's teeth glinted in a grin — 'frogs don't really have necks and the strings never stayed on. So maybe I just collected the same six over and over. And they escaped so often I eventually gave up on the collection. What happened to your little family?'

'I lost them. They just vanished. I always blamed Annabelle for it. My things had a way of disappearing. She claimed I was just careless with stuff, but it wasn't that. You might forget where you put things down but sooner or later you find them again. I never did.'

'That's mean,' Mike said. 'What sort of things are we talking about?'

'There was a book I loved — it went. And my little family, and a gold locket I got for my birthday. She was so jealous when I got it I was sure she'd taken it, but I never saw her wear it, so the chain *might* have broken . . . Anyway, it vanished. And there could have been other stuff too that I've forgotten about.'

'So, maybe her being involved in that robbery wasn't such a departure after all? Maybe she started out nicking your things and graduated to shoplifting, as a way of working up to a real robbery. I wonder if the jewellery shop was the first one they'd done?'

'Unless they catch this Paul we'll never know. And only then if he confesses.' I stretched and yawned. 'Still a couple of hours to home. Maybe we'd better get going again.' I drained the thermos and Mike stood up, snapping erect from his stockman's squat as if his knees were springs.

'Yeah, time to kill a metre. Want me to drive?'

I assented and we were soon on our way, crossing the Mt Farlow boundary grid into Upatack country and shortly afterwards meeting the last of the road trains. This one had no intention of ceding us an inch of space, which, as we were crossing a culvert at the time of meeting, forced Mike to head precipitously down the bank into the table drain, swearing as we pitched over the side.

'Road-hogging bastard!' I grabbed the hand-hold as the vehicle tilted alarmingly on the steep slope. The huge truck roared past, then the back of the vehicle lurched and Mike swore again.

'Bugger! Thought I'd missed it. There goes the tyre.'

The scattered bones of a beast, probably one hit and killed the previous year by another road train, had caused the blow-out. Mike eyed the wheel sitting on its rim and sighed. 'It's a write-off, or will be by the time I've shifted it. Can't change it where it is. Sorry, Charlie.'

'Don't be, it wasn't your fault. I'm glad you were driving — I might've tipped us over getting down here.' I pressed my shaking hands together, for the angle the vehicle had achieved was acute. 'I'll get the tools out.'

The tyre had a long split where the bone had gone through the case. 'Might be able to get it retreaded,' Mike said doubtfully. He rolled the spare around and fitted it. 'I could ask Kevin to take it into town on the weekend.'

'I'll see what Bob thinks.' I handed him the last nut and glanced at the sun. 'You're going to be driving in the dark.' It was thirty kilometres from the turn-off where he'd left his vehicle into the outstation where the stock camp was based.

'Doesn't matter.' He leant sideways and kissed me, the brim of his hat knocking mine off. 'That never happens in the movies.' He dusted it off and handed it back. 'Maybe that's why the gal always has hers hanging from a string round her neck?'

'I thought that was to save film and time — so the director didn't have to keep yelling 'Cut!' every time the wind blew it off. I'm glad you came today, Mike. Apart from not crashing us, I'd still be getting the nuts off if I'd had to change the tyre myself.'

'You know how, then?'

'Of course! First thing Bob taught me when I started driving.'

'Always at a lady's service,' he said, mouth downturned, 'but here I was hoping it was my company you valued.'

'Hah! Fishing for compliments now. How about I consider it while we drive?'

We parted with a long kiss at his turn-off and I drove back to the Garnet through the early darkness, dust motes dancing in the headlights, which meant that somewhere ahead there were, or had been, cattle on the road. I slowed, keeping a sharp lookout but they must have crossed over for I saw nothing until the lights of the road camp, and then the Garnet came into view. I garaged the vehicle and went in, thinking of Mike, remembering the touch and taste of his lips and the feel of his long body pressed against mine.

On Monday evening Mum rang from the Thorntons'. She sounded a little tired and, when asked, confessed to weariness, blaming the way the Alice hospital had kept her hanging around. She was doing well, she said, and was looking forward to getting home in a day or two.

'We'll see, Mum,' I said firmly. 'We're pretty busy at present so there's no chance of me getting away to pick you up. Probably not for a week at the earliest.' Better to let her get used to the idea that she wasn't going straight back to work. 'Anyway, won't you have a follow-up appointment with the hospital?'

'I'll see Dr Clive for that on his clinic run.'

'That's not a good idea,' I said quickly. 'It's three weeks till his next visit. Anyway, what could he do except take you back to town if there's a problem? We're managing here, so there's no reason for you to rush home. Just take things easy and enjoy the rest. Lord knows you're due a spell.'

'Charlie,' she said, with an edge of exasperation. 'I'm perfectly capable of managing my own life. You never used to be bossy.'

'You've never had a heart operation before either,' I said. 'Look, I have to go. Give Rae my best, won't you? Bye for now.'

* * *

Several uneventful days passed. Ute and Eric, I saw, were now taking their meals together, him hanging back in the queue of men until he was last, which gave her the opportunity to collect her own meal and eat with him. The blinis must have made an impression, I thought with an inward smile. Meanwhile, the work on the causeways went steadily forward and the amount of spraying the tanker had done on the route past the roadhouse had even encouraged the growth of green shoots beside it.

'What will you do when the camp moves on?' I asked Ute, as we stacked dirty plates on the sink. 'About Eric, I mean. You seem to be getting along, the two of you.'

She nodded happily. 'Like the burning house, no? He is interesting man, Charlie. Very simpatico.' She swirled dishwashing liquid into the sink. 'When they move they have no cook. Eric says perhaps I cook for them? Your mother is well by then, yes? So, we shall see.'

'Do you really like him that much? I mean, you have to leave this country at some point because of your visa — what happens then?'

She frowned, bringing two vertical lines between her brows, her wide blue eyes thoughtful. 'This we talk about. He is serious man, Eric. He does not make the rush into new things. We wait and we learn each other and then we decide. Is the best way, he says.'

'Umm, I suppose it is. Where's he from?'

She raised her brows. 'Where he puts the hat, he says. He wants no past for there is much sadness in him. His young wife is killed and his little son also. Very tragic. So he lives in the camps. He is the engineer once, but now he drives the machines and lives like the crab in the rock.'

'The crab? Oh, like a hermit, you mean. That is sad.'

'Yes. But is life, Charlie. Comes the big surprise one day when the sky is clear, and is not always nice. Your cousin thinks so too, yes, when they kill her?'

'I imagine she did,' I said feebly. Not for the first time I wondered if it was just Ute's haphazard command of English that was responsible for her unexpected take on living.

18

On Friday morning I was watering the front garden beds when Tom Cleary pulled up short of the fuel apron and beckoned me across.

'I'm not stopping, Charlie,' he said by way of explanation. 'I just wanted to let you know that they've located your cousin's place of residence. I'm being sent to collect her belongings for my boss in the Alice. When they've completed their examination you'll probably be able to have back anything not needed for a trial — if the case ever gets that far.'

'Right.' I absorbed the news, keeping one hand on the door-frame to prevent him taking off. 'How was it found? Where exactly was she living?'

'They had her pic running on TV and somebody recognised her and rang in. It's a flat in Mount Isa. I'm catching a flight over this arvo.'

'I see. I wonder what she was doing there.' I had assumed she would still be residing somewhere on the coast. 'How come you get to be the errand boy, Tom? Couldn't they have sent a constable from the Alice?'

He shook his head. 'Rodeo. They'll need every man they've got for the weekend. They made a hundred or so arrests last year for drunk and disorderly behaviour.' He grinned. 'I'll take the plane trip any day.'

'When you put it like that . . . Well, thanks for letting us know.' I lifted my hand and watched him drive off. The police would be looking for documents, I supposed. Bills, accounts, bank statements — anything that helped to expand their knowledge of Annabelle's life. It was strange to think that faceless officers would wind up knowing more about her than her own family did. It still left the mystery of her handbag's whereabouts though. She must have had one with her, but it hadn't been found at the scene of her death. Unless for some reason the police were keeping shtum about it. Still, there was a lot of bush along the highway and her murderer could have dumped it anywhere. If it hadn't been for the Wilders' penchant for fossicking, Annabelle's supposed suicide would have been accepted and her body never discovered.

⋆　⋆　⋆

The road camp returned to the Garnet for lunch, spruced up in clean clothes ready to hit the road when the meal was over. They were affected, it seemed, with rodeo fever like the rest of the country. Only Eric had volunteered to stay, to keep an eye on the camp, Rob Wyper said, when he paused by the counter to ask if there was anything he could bring out for us.

'Please,' I said. 'If you've room could you pick up twenty loaves from the bakery and a carton of butter from Woolworths? And say, a dozen two-litre bottles of milk? Be nice to have fresh for a change. I'll phone the order through so they'll expect you.'

'No problem,' he said. 'The big esky always travels with me and it'll fit in that. See you Monday, then.'

They left in a burst of noisy good humour, plainly looking forward to the break from camp life. The dust and noise of their going settled until only the throb of the diesel and the piercing call of a peewee broke the sun-filled silence. I yawned and stretched, eyeing Eric and Ute murmuring together at the corner table that had come to be accepted as theirs.

'I doubt we'll see many more callers today, Bob. I might leave you to it and get some housework done. I've been meaning to give Mum's room a good going over before she gets back. The rest of the house could do with vacuuming too. By the way, Mike'll be here tomorrow and he wants a task for the weekend — maybe he could finish the painting?' The timber out front still lacked its final coat. Once that was completed the old place would, I hoped, pleasantly surprise its owner upon her return.

'Long as he knows what he's doing,' Bob said grudgingly. 'I don't want no bodgy job.'

'I'm sure he does,' I protested.

'We'll see.' He sounded unconvinced. I stuck out my tongue at him and left.

There was something soothing about house-work, the repetition of effort that left one's mind free to wander. I vacuumed and mopped, and smoothed chair covers, changed the linen on the beds, and sprayed and cleaned windows and

182

tidied drawers. When the whole house sparkled I dug out a couple of vases from the display cabinet in the lounge and spent an enjoyable half hour selecting and arranging flowers and greenery to fill them. Petunias were ideal, and the bright heads of marigolds made their own bold statement when teamed with sprays of the hardy asparagus fern.

Pleased with the final result, I placed one vase on the kitchen bench and carried the second through to the lounge. To complete the afternoon's work, I turned out the linen chest, separating the towels into neat stacks and aligning the edges of the sheet pile. Some of the doilies had become crumpled in the general disorder and I ironed and changed them for the ones on display, then re-housed the rest in the bedside drawers of Annabelle's old room.

I was turning away when a faint voice called 'Charlie?' For an instant I froze, the hair at my nape standing erect, then common sense re-asserted itself. Annabelle was dead, and anyway the intonation was definitely Ute's.

'Coming.' She was waiting in the kitchen and with mild shock I realised that the sun was setting. 'I didn't realise it was so late.'

'Yes,' she said in her precise accented English. 'Almost the meal is ready. I have come to ask that Eric might eat with us tonight? There is him only and it would be the friendliness to include him, yes? But it is your table, so I ask.'

'Of course, Ute. He can be your guest.'

'Thank you, Charlie. I will tell him then is in the house tonight?'

'*On* the house,' I corrected. 'Otherwise he'll think you mean we're eating over here.'

'On,' she murmured, nodding. 'I will remember.'

★   ★   ★

We actually wound up eating inside the Garnet, for the evenings now were just too chilly to make the back verandah inviting. I pushed two tables together and spread a cloth over them, then switched off the lights above the counter leaving only the eating area illuminated. Ute had made some sort of goulash filled with tiny, flavoursome dumplings — a staple, she said, of her homeland, though lacking an apparently essential herb I'd never heard of.

'Very tasty, anyway,' Eric pronounced, chasing the last of the gravy with one of her dainty little dinner rolls. 'You're a wonderful cook, Ute.'

She beamed happily at him and I thought that his lean face softened as their gazes met, making him look younger. I had put his age at or near forty but now mentally revised it downward by five years. He was a quiet man, not shy for he'd conversed quite well on a number of topics over the meal, but self-contained. Having watched them interact, I thought they just might work with each other long-term. I could see Ute with her strength and common sense transplanting successfully from her European roots, but Eric also managing equally well in another country, for together they made their own island of understanding. There was a growing empathy

184

between them that must lead ultimately to union and I felt a moment's envy. Would Mike and I be as lucky, or was ours only a temporary attraction that would pall and run its course?

At that moment an engine sounded briefly over the diesel's thudding, then stopped and we all heard a door slam.

'Who's this?' I said in exasperation that vanished when the screen door opened to admit Mike as if my recent thoughts had conjured him. I rose eagerly, feeling the smile stretch my face. 'I didn't expect you till the morning!'

'It was a tough decision. Staring at the wall in the men's quarters or company at the Garnet. You won by a short head.'

'I'm so glad,' I said ironically. 'Have you eaten? We're just about ready for sweets.'

Grinning, he greeted the others. 'I won't turn that down, then. Rice pudding once a week, that's our quota at the station.'

His arrival made the evening shine for me. Once the clearing up was over I brought out the battered old Monopoly set I'd discovered in the bottom of the linen chest and even Bob consented to a game. His reason for doing so emerged after much hilarity when we were packing away the banknotes and markers.

'Got your swag with you, Mike?' he asked, swilling down the last of his coffee.

'Yeah, I have,' Mike said. 'I didn't want to put Charlie to any bother.'

'No bother.' Bob's gaze was steely and I was unsure whether to be amused or annoyed as he growled, 'You can bunk down at my place.'

Obviously there was to be no possibility of hanky-panky on his watch.

'Thanks,' Mike said diplomatically.

'Right, then.' Bob got to his feet. 'I'll show you where now. Night all. We'll see yer at breakfast.'

Eric and Ute took their own leave then. I wondered, before finding a torch and switching out the light, if both were headed for the same bed. Without Bob's intervention, I thought, I might at least have got a kiss, even if it was a bit soon to be taking things further between us.

The night air bit coldly and I pulled the neck of my coat closed as I hurried along the path and through the gate to the old homestead. I stepped gratefully into the shelter of the verandah and shone the torch's beam at the light switch, then stopped in my tracks as I heard footsteps inside.

'For God's sake!' How much more telling did Bryan need? Sudden fury welled in me as I snatched the door open, shouting, 'Right, that's it, Bryan. You can get out now! And come morning I'm reporting you to the pol — ' and was knocked flat as a body barrelled into me, smacking my head back against the doorframe. The torch, which had showed only the briefest, jangled image of a dark male shape, flew from my hand, and something pointed and hard hit my cheek as I fell and the intruder rushed past. I yelled in pain and fright as I went down and, through the fading echo of the sound, heard the slap of running feet on the path.

Winded, gasping for breath and terrified, I stayed on the floor, holding my head, which felt as if it had been coshed. But my trembling

186

fingers felt no wetness there and after a moment I crawled to the nearest cupboard and pulled myself shakily up. The torch had broken, as I discovered when I took a step and felt the remains crunch under my shoe. A distracted patting of the wall located the switch and I gasped again as the light came on.

My shining tidy room — in fact, the entire house as I was soon to discover — had been ransacked. The torch *was* broken, but it was bits of vase I'd trodden on. Marigolds strewed the floor along with the contents of upended drawers and cupboards. There was cutlery and tea towels, spilled rice and flour, and loose tea leaves amid a clutter of saucepans, jugs and broken sauce bottles spread over the slates. Only the crockery, ranged in the open-fronted wall cabinet, had been spared — perhaps as a result of my arrival.

The rest of the rooms were in a similar state. Touring them open-mouthed, I saw broken chair legs, cracked drawers, skewed frames where pictures had been yanked from walls . . . Whoever it was (for however irritating his fixation on me, I realised that I couldn't blame Bryan for this) must have been in the house for hours, and the destruction was proof that he hadn't found what he'd sought. Did that mean he was coming back?

The thought galvanised me from the bemusement that had held me as I padded from room to room. Should he return, I definitely didn't want to be there. Grabbing the closest, heaviest implement — a meat tenderiser that had somehow wound up in the hall — I shot out the back door and ran for Bob's place, arriving panting and dishevelled on the verandah of the quarters where he lived.

Jasper dashed at me, growling low in his throat, the warning changing to a tail wag the instant he recognised me. Bob glanced up sharply from the bench outside his room where he was unlacing his boots, then surged to his feet. 'Here, what's up, girl? You look proper spooked.'

'There was somebody — a man — in the house. He knocked me down.' For the life of me I couldn't keep my voice from wavering.

'Whoa there, Charlie. It's okay.' Mike, hatless and with a thick swag already spread across the verandah, stepped forward and put an arm around my shoulders. 'You okay? Did he hurt you? What happened to your face?' Gentle fingers touched my cheek.

'I think I banged it when I fell. I hit my head. But the house! He's trashed the whole place, there's stuff everywhere.' My voice trembled as I fought the tears back. 'I know it's a stupid thing to care about but I'd only just cleaned it and now there's nothing but mess.'

'Right,' Bob said fiercely. 'You stay here with Jasper, girl. We'll take a look — the bugger must've had a vehicle parked somewhere. You sure you're not hurt?'

'Just a bit shaken, Bob.' I pulled myself together. 'But I'm fine, and no way am I staying here alone.'

'She'll be better with us,' Mike said. He nodded at the meat tenderiser forgotten in my

188

hand. 'What were you planning on doing with that?'

I glanced at it and felt my lips twitch. 'Hit him, I suppose. If he stood still or wasn't looking. It was just the first thing to hand.' I let it fall. 'But what could he have been after? I mean *everywhere's* been trashed, even the bathroom cabinet — there's soap, and mirror shards, and shampoo and broken bottles all over the floor! The TV screen looks like he put his boot through it.'

'Talk after,' Bob growled. 'Let's go see if he's stuck around.'

'I don't think he will have.' I found I was clutching Mike's hand and continued to grip it like a lifesaver while the three of us and Jasper retraced my steps to examine the crime scene.

The intruder hadn't returned nor left any clues to his identity. The house, lit up as I'd left it, yawned before us, the screen door through which I'd fled hanging awry, the screws of the top hinge half pulled from the wood. Stepping carefully over the debris, I led them on a tour of the damage, the overturned furniture, emptied linen chest, splayed books, shattered drawers and upended mattresses, cushions and armchairs. The kitchen was the worst, with the contents of broken jars and bottles spread amid spilled implements and dry goods.

Bob, standing in a mess of flour, tea and rice, shook his head, face grim. 'What was the bastard after? Who looks in kitchen cupboards for a safe, for Christ's sake? And if it weren't the safe, what did he want?'

'It's a good thing you weren't here for him to ask, Charlie.' Mike was equally grim. 'Some nutter off his head with drugs or grog — is that likely, do you think?'

'He didn't move like anyone drugged or drunk.' I shut my eyes replaying the brief glimpse I'd had of the stranger and found I could now isolate the separate bits. 'He bashed the torch out of my hand, then knocked me down. I think' — I fingered my face which had begun to ache in earnest — 'that he caught my cheek with his elbow when we collided. I know he went through that door like an express, every bit of him highly co-ordinated.'

'He was thorough, I'll give him that,' Mike said, eyeing the wreckage. 'This lot took more than five minutes. He must've been in here all evening — every wardrobe, every drawer . . . We shouldn't touch anything,' he added as I heaved an armchair right side up. 'You never know, there might be fingerprints. You'd better ring the cop, Charlie.'

'What time is it?' Mum's precious mantel clock lay on the floor, case and glass shattered and hands awry.

'Past midnight,' Bob growled. 'You'd be wastin' yer time. He'll not turn out this late.'

'No,' I agreed. 'Besides, what could he do? The man's long gone.' Tomorrow would be soon enough, as would passing the news on to my mother. I sighed wearily. 'We'd best go to bed. But I'm not staying here. Not by myself.'

'You ain't,' Bob asserted. 'You'll take Jasper and sleep in the spare donga. The old dog'll see you ain't bothered and there's Ute right next to you.'

'I can roll out my swag outside the door, if you want?' Mike offered.

'You'll roll it out here,' Bob told him. 'You an' me are gonna guard the place, in case he comes back. Well,' he added pugnaciously, 'it seems plain enough the bastard wanted somethin' really bad, don't it? The two of us oughta be enough if he's thinking of havin' another go.'

Mike rubbed his head, making his dark hair stand up. 'Right, then. Grab what you need, Charlie — if you can find it — and I'll walk you over.'

'Get the dog's chain first,' Bob recommended. 'We'll tie him outside the door. Ain't nobody gettin' past old Jasper.'

19

The donga was a box-like room containing a bed, wardrobe and a small washbasin and mirror. There were linen and blankets in the wardrobe but when I'd made up the bed I lay wakeful for a long time, stroking my swollen face as I puzzled over the night's events. Bob would, I knew, be out at daylight searching for the man's tracks and those of the vehicle he had used, but even if he found them they still represented anonymous boots and wheels, and would do nothing to resolve the deeper mystery of what the intruder had been seeking.

I must have dropped off to sleep then, for the next thing I knew was a low snarl coming from beyond the door. A pale greyness seeped through the single curtained window. Almost dawn, then. Imagining heaven knows what, I crept from my bed to the door and opened it a crack, telling myself that Ute was next door and I could rouse her with a scream, and anyway Jasper would have his leg off the moment whoever was there got within reach. The suspense of not knowing was worse than my fear. I pushed on the door, then let it swing fully open as I saw who it was.

'Eric! You frightened the life out of me.'

He jumped guiltily, and Jasper lunged, only to be brought up by the chain.

'Hush, Jasper. Sit! That's a good dog. Sorry,' I said belatedly, taking in the import of Eric's presence. 'None of my business anyway.'

He coughed and reddened. 'Morning, Charlie.' He shook his head and said baldly, 'Not that it's any of my business either, but what are you doing here?'

'There was a bit of an incident last night. Oh, do stop it, Jasper! Look, come and pat him and he'll give it up.'

Eric backed up a step. 'Not likely! Let him growl. What sort of incident?'

The door he'd crept through opened then and Ute stuck out a dishevelled head. 'Eric, what is happening? You sound like the bear.'

'That's the dog. Sorry, love. I meant to sneak away but Charlie caught me.' He looked back at me. 'What's happened?'

I recited the night's events and both looked astonished.

'I didn't hear a thing,' Eric said. But he was hardly likely to, I thought with a little spurt of amusement, not with his blonde Valkyrie (and she really did resemble one with her tumbled locks and statuesque form wrapped only in a sheet) to occupy him. Ute, with a frown for the mystery, typically went straight to the heart of it.

'So, he does not rob but makes the destruction. Why?'

'I have no idea. The house is just one big mess, like he was angry — no, scrap that, furious. He even cleaned out the bathroom cabinet! There's toothpaste and shampoo and Lord knows what all over the shower.'

'You will call the policeman, yes?'

'Yes,' I agreed. 'As soon as we've had breakfast

— and that had better be in the roadhouse this morning.'

In fact, I didn't wait beyond getting dressed to do so. Mike had mentioned fingerprints, which probably meant sending for someone. I could be wrong, but I doubted that Constable Cleary would have much beyond handcuffs and a copy of *The Criminal Code*, or whatever it was called, at his tiny station. In which case my plans for an immediate clean-up would be on hold.

Tom asked few questions on the phone, advised me to leave everything as it was and then arrived a little over forty minutes later. He inspected the damage before returning to the roadhouse where we'd already sat down to breakfast. Bob told him what he'd discovered, which was little enough. He had tracked the intruder to his vehicle, which had been left pulled off the road in the mulga a kilometre up the track. It had then been reversed out and driven off, heading for the highway.

'The bastard could be in the Alice or halfway to bloody Queensland by now,' Bob said. 'I hope he is. We don't want him back.'

I felt my heart jump and the blood leave my face. 'You don't think he will return?'

'Depends what he was after, don't it?' he asked. 'Seems to me if he'd found it there wasn't no need to tear the place up like he did.'

Mike frowned. 'Bob's right, Charlie. That smacks of fury and spite. If he'd just taken whatever it was and left, chances are you wouldn't even have noticed for a bit. And then you'd assume you'd misplaced the item.'

'Yes, but what do we have that's worth so much rage? It's not like we've a shelf full of Faberge, or a hatbox of top-secret documents some foreign spy would be after. What do you think, Tom?'

'Where do you keep your safe?'

Bob looked up with a snort. 'Well, it ain't in the homestead kitchen! Not the bathroom neither! It's here, in the storeroom, cemented into the floor. Only way you're gonna steal that's with blasting powder.'

'It seems likely that a thief would try the business first if it was cash he wanted,' the constable said. 'If that's the case, he might target the roadhouse next time, but I doubt he'll be back. So you can't say for sure that anything was stolen from your home, Charlie?'

I shrugged. 'You've seen it — it's more damage than theft. What are you going to do about it?'

'Well' — looking apologetic, Tom set aside the tea mug Ute had hospitably filled for him — 'given that nobody was harmed and nothing seems to have actually been taken, very little I'm afraid. He'd certainly have worn gloves so — '

'He means the rodeo's on and the cops won't spare a man to chase out here when it's not a major crime,' Mike interjected. 'That's about the strength of it, Charlie.'

The constable looked affronted. 'We do our best, but resources have to be allocated according to — '

'And nobody's actually been killed,' Mike agreed cynically.

'But they have! Annabelle was,' I said.

'A separate crime, which I assure you, we are working on. Look, I know it's frustrating and unfair, but that's the nature of wrongdoing. Innocent people are targeted all the time and there's usually very little the police can do about this type of vandalism. If, while you're cleaning up, you do find that items are missing, make a list and I'll send it round the pawnshops. You never know.' Tom stood and replaced his chair, then fitted his hat. 'I'm sorry, Charlie. I'll report it, but realistically there's not much else I can do.'

'Well, that was a fat lot of good,' I said resignedly, watching him drive off. 'It does mean though that I can make a start on the house.'

'I'll give you a hand,' Mike offered.

'And Eric will help also, yes?' Ute asked turning her gaze on her lover.

'Happy to,' he agreed. He coughed diffidently. 'You think the bloke was hanging around waiting for this weekend? He might've thought there'd be only one person here. Or even that the place'd be shut up and deserted.'

'Could be,' Mike agreed. 'You any good with tools? There're a couple of things missing legs and quite a few of the drawers have been damaged as well.'

'I've knocked the odd chest of those together in my time,' Eric said. 'Who hasn't?'

Mike grinned. 'Me, for one. I could plait you a whip but carpentry . . . '

★ ★ ★

We toiled all day and I was dismayed to discover as we penetrated beyond the kitchen just how much the furniture had suffered. Save for a boot-marked crack in the sink cupboard, the damage in the kitchen was confined to foodstuffs and it was easy to imagine a brawny arm sweeping the contents of shelves onto the floor in spite. Elsewhere, however, there was plenty of use for carpentry skills. Eric carried the wounded bits out to the verandah where, with glue and screws and tools from the shed, he set about his repairs. In the lounge I knelt to pick up the carriage clock that would obviously never work again, and tried to straighten the twisted hands.

'Goddamn him!' I muttered angrily. Mum had loved that clock. The little shepherdess that had stood beside it was also smashed. I laid the clock back down to pick up the pieces of the figurine. She had been mended once already, for I had broken her foot off when I was six, but no amount of glue was going to make her whole again now. An aching sadness filled me, and I wept with the shock and outrage that the night's intrusion had brought.

Mike appeared and squatted beside me, putting a comforting arm around my shoulders. 'I know, love, I know. I'd like to break his bloody neck too. Look, I think it might be best if Bob and I move in here tonight. We can't have this bastard chasing you out of your own home. And I can't see,' he added wryly, 'the old boy letting me camp here without him.'

'Not likely,' I agreed. 'He acts like I'm still

sixteen. And what happens tomorrow night when you're back at the station?'

'I'd say that dog of Bob's would be a good stand-in. And Eric's mob'll be here Monday, remember.'

'Yes,' I sniffed, wiping my eyes on my wrist. 'Sorry, it all got on top of me there for a minute. I just wish I knew what this was all about. I mean, I went through this place, top to bottom, only yesterday and I didn't find anything new or strange. And it wasn't just a casual tidy, Mike. I had everything out of all the cupboards and the linen chest, I put in new drawer liners. If she'd stashed *anything*, anywhere, I would have found it.'

He raised his brows in interrogation. 'She?'

'Annabelle. Tom can go on about her murder being a separate crime, but that's rubbish! Of course the two are connected — they have to be. It doesn't make sense otherwise. So this Paul — if it was him, and I think it must have been — was looking for something Annabelle hid while she was here. She and Mum talked, then she was alone while she showered before they left. So she had, what, half an hour in which to do it?' I tapped the floor. 'The slate's cemented in place, the ceiling is all one piece.' Involuntarily we both glanced upwards. 'There're no manholes. It's bush-built so it's not like a regular house. And the other thing is, my cousin' — I termed her so from long habit — 'was a fashion plate. She wore acrylic nails for starters. Not the sort of person to be prising up rocks or digging holes. Wherever she put whatever it was she wanted to hide was a place with easy access.'

Mike frowned, the side of his thumb rubbing at the bristles on his jaw; he hadn't shaved that morning. His arm was still around me and I let myself settle against his shoulder, enjoying the smell of him. 'Okay, supposing she did hide something — but not here?'

I turned my head to stare at him. 'Where, then?'

'Think about it. They didn't drive here all the way from the Alice without stopping at least once. There're no roadhouses, but there are rest stops for travellers, shelters with picnic tables and toilets.'

'Too open and too public,' I objected. They're just frames, those buildings — even the tables are slatted. I suppose you might tape something small under one of them, but how long before some kid spotted it?'

'In the bush, then?'

'It would depend on what the object was, and how sure you'd be of finding it again. If weather affected it, or white ants . . . '

'Yeah, maybe a guess too far . . . But the next question is, why would she do it? I mean, if it was worth killing her over, she must've had a fair idea of the danger entailed in taking it. Would she risk that?'

I sighed. 'I guess we'll never know. Annabelle *was* awfully self-centred. Perhaps she just didn't realise . . . ' I eyed the ravaged room. 'Anyway, we can wonder till the cows come home, but that won't get this mess cleared up, will it?'

'No.' He rose, pulling me with him. 'Time to soldier on.'

20

By evening we could see the end of the task. There were gaps in the rooms where things like the clock and some smashed photo frames had been beyond Eric's resources or skillset, and I had a pile of washing waiting in the laundry. Although a store order was needed to restock the kitchen cupboards, the house was livable again.

'Tonight,' Ute announced as the five of us sat down to dinner — Eric gingerly for he was occupying one of the repaired chairs brought in to accommodate him — 'I move into your house. Eric also. So you have not the fear, Charlie. Until your mother returns, yes?'

It was the ideal solution. Mike would have been better, but that meant uprooting Bob too, and the old man was very set in his ways. He would do it from a sense of duty to my mother, I knew — and hate every confining moment. And Mike would be gone before tomorrow night anyway.

'Thanks, Ute. Mind you, I don't think he'll be back — he must know now there's nothing to find.'

'He might still want to check out the Garnet, though,' Mike said. 'I could roll my swag out over there. What do you reckon, Bob?'

'Wouldn't hurt.' He scowled, pondering the likelihood. 'Man can't tell what the bastard might be planning. I s'pose he might've circled back thinkin' if it ain't in one place it's gotta be the other. If we knew whatever the hell it was,' he ended crossly.

'I've had an idea about that,' I said. 'Could she have been blackmailing him? What if, for instance, he'd done other burglaries — ones she wasn't involved in — and Annabelle had something that could incriminate him, and wanted a safer place than on her person to keep it?'

'So she planned on coming all the way out here when she needed it? Bit inconvenient I'd have thought,' Eric said dubiously.

'But that's the thing. Blackmailers don't actually need their material. It's the threat alone that matters. If you have to expose the victim's guilt, then you've lost out. They won't pay after that.'

We chewed on my words for a while in silence, broken when Bob said abruptly, 'Did yer tell Molly about this lot?' A jerk of his head encompassed the house.

I shook mine. 'Not today. She'll have to know, but I thought I'd leave it a bit — just to prepare her a bit for what's missing. If she gets wind of it now she'll either be in the next vehicle leaving town or fretting herself to bits. She'd had a good day, she said. Been for a drive and a short walk. She sounded quite relaxed, actually. I didn't want to ruin it for her.'

'Yer done right. How long yer reckon she'll stay put?'

I shrugged. 'A week tops? Long enough to get that painting finished out front anyway.'

'What time do you have to leave?' I asked Mike as we were finishing breakfast the following morning.

'After lunch'll do. I'm your man till then. Why, what did you have in mind?'

'A drive if that's okay?'

'Suits me. A picnic job or . . . ?'

'No, just out and back.' I looked at Bob. 'Should be back around smoko time. You can hold the fort till then?'

'Yeah. What are you up to, Charlie?'

'Probably nothing.' With a clatter of cups and plates I cleared the table. 'I'll clean my teeth and grab a hat, Mike, and be right with you.'

Ten minutes later he heaved the drink cooler into the passenger well of his vehicle, leaving the door open for me to get in. 'So, where are we going?'

'Mica Valley. I want to see the spot where Annabelle died. I've never checked to see if the place is marked on the map. If it isn't, how did Paul come to find it? Unless Annabelle led him there . . . and why would she do that?'

Mike grimaced. 'I dunno. You sure you want to do this, Charlie? Maybe we should just drop in on the cop shop and ask Tom instead?'

'And he'll tell us everything the police are thinking? Yeah, fat chance. Look, it might be nothing — probably is — but to me it seems odd that a stranger, someone Bob described as a townie, would go so far off the highway to dump her body. Why wouldn't he just pull off the road somewhere and chuck her under a bush? If it hadn't been for old Len poking around in the valley, chances are she would never have been found. After all, nobody was looking for her out here, not when she was supposed to have drowned off the coast two states away.'

He puzzled over this for a moment as we left the silent road camp behind us. 'So, what are you thinking?'

'I don't *know*.' I heard the exasperation in my tone. 'That's the problem and it's driving me crazy so I thought if I at least had a look for myself . . . ' I sighed. 'It probably won't make any difference but I feel as though nothing's happening. Perhaps I'm just trying to prod things along.'

'It can't do any harm. But I was wondering — you've implied Annabelle wasn't the outdoors type, so would she have known how to get into Mica Valley?'

'Ah.' I considered that. 'Maybe not. Which means what? It *is* on the map, or the track's signposted?'

There were more questions than we could think of answers for and a part of me was irritated that I was wasting time this way when I could just have been enjoying the last few hours of Mike's company. All the stations would, I knew, be straight back into the mustering once the stock camps returned from town, and he would have few free days once that happened.

I said belatedly, 'I'm sorry. We could be painting the front of the Garnet or having flirtatious conversations instead of doing this.'

'Ah, but you wouldn't enjoy them — the conversations — if your mind wasn't on them,' he answered, one side of his mouth twitching up in a smile. 'Of course, I don't know how you feel about painting?'

'I loathe it,' I admitted. 'A friend and I painted a flat once. Put me off it forever. Paint down my arms, in my hair, all over the floor . . . It almost looked worse when we were done than before we began. And that's saying something.'

'Isn't that sort of upkeep the landlord's job? You should've just moved.'

'We couldn't afford to. Anyway, the paint didn't help. Debbie said it just showed up the roaches better. Life in the big city, eh?' I took in the view beyond the window. 'This is a thousand times better.'

He smiled. 'We've still got roaches. Turn over a rotten log even out here, and you'll find 'em. Oh, look!' He was pointing off into the bush beside the shallow creek. 'Emu, with his family.'

'I see them,' I said in delight, counting the stripy chicks as they ran at their parent's heel. There were eight of them, necks erect, absurd little legs following the monstrously larger pair. 'They're so cute!' Something occurred to me. 'The *Advocate* said it was thirty kay from the roadhouse to the valley. Were they just guessing? I mean, we blundered onto it last time from other tracks — we didn't get to it from the highway.'

Mike shrugged. 'It'll be what the cops told the reporter but who knows if it was as the crow flies? I put the trip meter on and we've come about eighteen kay, so keep an eye out from here on. The track might be overgrown, but it was well used once.'

We had gone twenty-eight kilometres before the old track into the valley appeared on our right. It was unmistakable and answered the question as to how a stranger had found it, for the narrow, grass-grown turn-off was marked with a thirty-litre drum, rusted a deep brown. It had its top removed, was half filled with rocks for stability, and had the words *Mica Valley* roughly painted around its circumference.

Mike grunted. 'So, he's driving along with murder on his mind, spots this and decides it's an isolated enough place to dump a body. Works for me.'

'Yes,' I said. 'Only, wouldn't she be suspicious? Surely she didn't just sit there and let him drive her to her death. And they must have been arguing, so she'd have been alert.'

'She mightn't have had a choice.'

'How do you mean?'

'Bob said he was a big bloke, didn't he? And by your account she was tiny. So if they did row and he lost it and hit her she might've been unconscious.' He slowed the vehicle to straddle a bush growing in the centre of the track and I heard it rasping against the crash plate below us. 'Hell, she could even have been dead. Be easy then.'

I shivered, picturing it. The red sand beneath our wheels was giving way to gravel as the range came closer. Soon the track was winding across gutters and over ridges where slabs of broken rock replaced the ever present buffel grass. Euros bounded away and a family of happy-jacks flew, scolding noisily, through the branches of a mulga. I recognised the point where we'd met up with Len and Cora, the wheel marks still plain in the crushed grass.

'There must've been tracks. I wonder if the police photographed them?' I asked.

'It wouldn't prove anything. Could be any four-wheel drive that made them. Besides, we know fossickers come out here too.' Mike's hat tilted as he scratched his ear. 'Have you thought that we mightn't find the exact spot? It's pretty rough-looking country.'

I'd visualised a crime-scene tape outlining the spot, as one saw on TV dramas, but faced with the reality of the range, the rock and stunted scrub and spinifex, I saw how ridiculous that was. Then Mike said, 'I think this is the valley. There's been camps enough here in the past.' We had reached a broad hollow in the hills with a steep wall of the range facing a narrow creek across an open swale that rose more gradually on the far side. Old metal gear, buckets and stretchers, and sheets of iron, rusted to the same colour as the rocks, lay about the workings, now so weed-grown they looked almost natural. The broken remains of a tiny windmill, its vanes missing, stood amid the straggly creek gums, along with the front end of a badly rusted vehicle. And, everywhere, sunlight glinted on scattered shards of mica as if a million bottle tops had been spread across the scene.

Mike, having killed the engine, was looking at

the tracks. 'Come on, then, the next bit's a job for feet.'

Now I was here I felt strangely reluctant. I pointed at the ground. 'Len's, do you think?'

'More likely the police. We'll follow them till they stop. Sing out if you see a boot mark. Len would've described where the body was in relation to the mill, I'd reckon — it's what I'd do with a bunch of town cops.'

We walked through the remnants of old camps and some newer; here and there ash piles still showed where more recent visitors, from earlier in the year, had been. Rain fell infrequently out here and the country wore its history plainly for those with eyes to read it. The air was still and hot within the sheltered valley, but my skin felt cold and my heart thumped with dread. I wished suddenly that I hadn't come, that the violence visited upon this quiet place of bird calls and insects could be left to reverberate away undisturbed until the passing years had buried the last echo, as it had with the noisy, busy miners of forty years before.

Mike seemed to sense my mood. He moved closer and we proceeded in silence until he suddenly squatted to point. 'Here. Two vehicles at least. One pulled off that way, and two lots of boot tracks' — he pointed along the line of them — 'heading that way. There's even an old foot pad, see here? It must lead to another camp.'

'What's that?' Some distance ahead, an anomoly, a straight line buried amid the natural curves of nature, had caught my eye. I stared, trying to make sense of it, and gradually realised that I was looking at a stone hut built against a ridge of tumbled rock. Its roof seemed to fuse into its surroundings and a sturdy wattle bush growing up beside it partly concealed the black hollow of the entrance.

'Will you look at that!' Mike exclaimed, as we moved closer along the pad worn into the soil. 'Dry-stone work. That took a bit of skill.' The tracks he was following made straight for the building, the ground immediately before the hut being scuffed and overlaid by many prints. He reached a hand to stop me.

'This must be it, Charlie. Makes sense when you think about it — a body under cover can't attract birds.'

'Yes.' My throat was dry. 'Give me a moment. I'm going in — I have to see.'

He looked troubled. 'If you're sure. There'll be nothing there, you know. The cops'll have made sure to remove every bit of evidence they could find.'

'I know. But she meant nothing to them — just another case . . . Maybe we didn't get on, but she was my blood, my family. Someone has to care. If we can just die and not matter to anyone . . . ' I swallowed, then finished shakily, 'Even Annabelle deserves better.'

With that I stepped from the bright warmth of the valley into the dimness of the tiny hut and glanced swiftly about me. It was just a small room, three walls and a roof backed onto the rock and earth of the hill. Uneven pavestones lined the floor. Bush rails, riddled with borers' holes, had been laid across the walls to support the rusty iron the builder had overlaid with rock and soil for the roof: insulation for summer heat and the bitter winter nights. There was a hearth below a corresponding hole in the roof where, presumably, a stove pipe had once fitted, and a square aperture let into the opposite wall like a doorless cupboard.

I let out the breath I'd been unaware I was holding and stared at the floor. There was a stain on the pavers and a smell like rotten meat, faint but all pervading, and nothing else. I squeezed my hands together, staring at the stain, remembering what Tom had said about her face having been bashed in. I hoped that Mike was right and she had been killed with a single blow, that the oppressive darkness the little hut radiated was only in my imagination and really held no echo of terror or pain.

'I'm sorry,' I whispered. 'Sorry I didn't know you were my sister. Sorry I didn't forgive you. I'm sorry you're dead, Annabelle.' The darkness and stink of corruption was suddenly overwhelming and I stumbled out, a hand over my mouth.

Mike, squatting on his heels as he waited, shot to his feet. 'You all right, Charlie?'

I drew in a great lungful of air and swallowed a mouthful of saliva. Rather than lie I said instead, 'I'm done here. We can go now.'

21

Not surprisingly my sleep that night brought Annabelle's awful ghost into my dreams. I was back in the foul-smelling hut in the dark when her white faceless form rose before me, but the doorway had turned solid and there was no escape. My own scream woke me, its dying sound no more than a moan in my throat. I bolted up in bed, gasping for air while the drumming of the nightmare's hooves gradually diminished and my galloping heart slowed. At this rate, I thought faintly, Mum's cardiologist would soon have himself a new patient.

Ute and Eric, I remembered then, were in the next bedroom but they hadn't stirred. Relieved and a little envious I slid back down onto my pillow, trying to slow my breathing and regretting that I had no one to hold me against night fears. Mike had returned to Abbey Downs after lunch. I missed him: his warmth, his presence, the way his eyes crinkled when he smiled. Lying there cocooned in the warmth of my bedding, I filled my head with the memories I had of him in the short time since we'd met. His sure strength as he'd wrested the vehicle from the road train's path, the masterful way he'd dismissed Bryan at the barbecue, the laughter we'd shared on the fossick hunt when we'd found my garnet . . .

Realisation flooded through me and next

moment I was out of bed, bare toes curling away from the freezing slates, as I directed the torch's beam at the lacquered box on the dressing table. All too vividly I remembered collecting its scattered bits from the floor after the intruder had been. I had recovered the hair combs (one of them broken), the lipstick, the nail file, the string of coral beads . . . All the little things I had tidied away within it. But I had completely forgotten it was where I had also put the garnet for safekeeping.

It was gone. I wondered how brittle the gem was. It could have been trodden on, crushed underfoot in the clean-up, the dust of it swept away. Perhaps it had rolled into a corner and lain undiscovered? Instantly I was down on my knees, running frantic fingers over the slates, desperately hoping, but all that I found was the smooth edge of the skirting board. Perhaps I had vacuumed it up? I tried to remember when I had emptied the bag from the machine — had it been before or after I'd done the bedrooms? I thought — hoped — it was before. When I'd finished I'd put it away unemptied. First thing in the morning I would check; there was just a chance it would still be there. It had to be! Suddenly the little gem had assumed an importance far beyond its size. Shivering, I returned to bed filled with a wrenching sense of loss as if already aware that the tiny garnet was gone for good.

The remainder of the night passed in wakeful starts that had me lying rigid with pent breath until I was satisfied that no stealthy tread disturbed the sleeping house. I rose tired and headachy, a condition not improved by a thorough search of the dusty hoover bag. Turning the contents onto a sheet of newspaper, I sifted carefully through it with no better results than to set up an itch in my nose that brought on a bout of sneezing. There was no sign of the garnet.

★　★　★

On Monday morning the road camp was back, and as if it were a signal, the tourists began moving again. The next local event would be the race meeting at Harts Range, which would also bring a temporary halt to station work and increased custom to the roadhouse. To me, however, it provided another opportunity to see Mike. Mum would be home by then, I thought. Then I found myself wondering whether or not she liked the tall young stockman. Mike said they had met but to a busy woman knee-deep in kitchen orders, one tanned face beneath an Akubra must look very like another.

Because of the road crew, we ate earlier than usual that evening and I was able to catch the local television news on the roadhouse set. There were items about the rodeo with shots of the champion bronc and bull riders clutching their trophies, a few lines on the Mica Valley murder to the effect that the police had no fresh leads, and immediately after that, a computer-generated likeness of Paul as detailed by Bob: a tall, muscular figure with dark hair, and a threatening appearance. He should not be approached, the newsreader said. He was wanted in connection with a major crime and anyone sighting him should immediately phone Crime Stoppers or contact their local police station.

It didn't take long for talk of the weekend's events at the Garnet to spread among the work crew and I was touched by Rob Wyper's earnest offer to have a couple of 'the boys' spend their nights on the homestead and roadhouse verandahs. 'If you're worried he'll be back, like?'

I thanked him but declined. 'Ute's sharing the house with me and we've got Bob's dog. I pity the man who tries to get past old Jasper!'

'Dunno what the country's coming to,' he said. 'Did you lose much?'

I shook my head. 'Nothing seems to have been taken. But he smashed the place up pretty well. Lucky Eric is so handy. The worst thing was losing the TV. We have to watch over here now. He killed the radio too.' My initial fury had subsided to a tired anger but I could still have cheerfully brained the perpetrator.

'Jesus!' He scratched his greying head, face screwed up in perplexity. 'What did the copper say?'

'Tom? Not much they can do about vandalism apparently, unless they catch someone in the act.'

'That'd be right.' Rob nodded as if in confirmation of the world's wickedness, and the ineffectiveness of the law. Shaking his head in disgust he picked up his packed lunch and left for his work.

Mike rang that evening from Abbey Downs. 'Charlie, how's it going? No more trouble with intruders?'

'No. I think he must have cleared out,' I said. 'The road crew are back now so the place is busy again. But what are you doing at the homestead? I thought the camp was going out?'

'It has. One of the boys had a nasty fall today so I've just run him back. I'll be heading out again tonight, but I wanted to check you were okay first.'

'Thanks.' I felt a rush of warmth for his concern. 'We're fine, truly. Is he badly hurt, your man?'

'Nothing broken, but he's pretty banged up. The horse came down on top of him.'

'Ouch.'

'Yeah, it was a big bugger too, all sixteen hands of him. Harry'll be fine, but it'll take a few days.'

'Shouldn't he see a doctor?'

'He reckons he's okay. He can walk, he's not peeing blood — it's just bad bruising.'

'I can imagine!' I thought of a horse's weight and winced again. 'Well, you be careful, Mike. I don't want that happening to you.'

'My middle name,' he said solemnly. 'Gotta go. See you soon, my love.' He hung up.

I stood holding the silent phone for a long moment asking myself: had he really said that? Just 'love' was a term that everybody used, but 'my love'? Happiness welled within me as I settled the handpiece back on its rest. I'd scarcely lifted my hand away when it rang again and I snatched it up, my feelings bubbling over. 'Mike — '

'Charlie?' It was Mum's voice. 'Well, you sound happy. How're things there — could you get away for a day?'

'Oh!' I tried to gather my thoughts. She didn't know about the intruder, or the damage her home had suffered. I said cautiously, 'How are you, Mum? Sorry I didn't ring yesterday, the weekend was a bit busy.' Rats! Why did I say that? Now she'd ask about it. 'The road crew's back,' I hurried on, 'but it's all under control. So have you seen the cardiologist yet?'

'Yes. That's why I'm ringing. He's cleared me to come home. So if either you or Bob could nip in tomorrow and pick me up, I'll be packed and waiting.'

'Well, that is good news.' *Damn*, I thought. I had wished she'd stay another week, but I knew I wouldn't talk her into it. Of course she'd have to be told about the break-in — she'd see it anyway the moment she entered the house — but better to smooth the way, I thought, with a gradual explanation that minimised the event rather than deliver the news in one blunt tirade, which was more Bob's style. 'I'll come. I'll make an early start and be there by lunchtime. Will you need prescriptions filled? What exactly did the doctor say?'

'What they all say. Diet, exercise, take it easy. I'll worry about that. Who's this Mike — the one you seemed to be expecting a call from?'

'Just a friend. I'll tell you about him tomorrow. How are Rae and Don?' I kept the chatter up for another few minutes before ending the call, then went slowly through the house checking the bare spots on walls and shelves and cupboard tops, as if the overall effect of the missing articles could somehow be diminished by familiarity with their absence.

★ ★ ★

In the grey light of dawn the following morning I was on my way, Bob's instructions the last thing I heard. 'Watch out for them damn road trains,' he said, 'and get that tyre round to the joint where they do the retreadin'.' I had the spare from his old Land Rover to tide me over in the event of a blow-out. 'And you be careful, girl, hear?'

'Yes, Bob,' I said meekly. 'I'll ring before I leave town, okay?'

He nodded, his form no more than an outline in the deep shadow of the shed. I started the engine, flipped the headlights on high and drove off, passing the lighted caravan windows of the road camp. It was bitterly cold. I turned the heater up and wriggled my gloved fingers on the wheel. The day would warm up as the sun rose, but for now the bulky shape of the scrub fringing the road looked vaguely menacing, and the eyes of a wild cat streaking across it glowed malevolently in the headlights.

Bob's warning had influenced my perceptions. That and Annabelle's murder, I rationalised. I had never before felt a moment's apprehension in the bush where the only real danger was the sun, and the odd snake. And there was a far greater chance of dying from traffic-related causes in the city than of suffering a fatal snake bite out here. The few remaining stars were winking out and a dawn wind raised ochre-coloured drifts of dust from the road's verge. The sky gradually lightened and as I flashed past the Abbey Downs turn-off, I switched off the headlights. A little later the shadow of the station wagon appeared on the road as the sun rose behind me and the day of Mum's homecoming had officially broken.

I made good time on the journey, shedding gloves and jacket along the way and pulling briefly into one of the rest stops for tea from the thermos. I did need a break but I also wanted to check that I had been right in asserting to Mike that Annabelle couldn't have secreted anything in such a place. Main Roads, I assumed, had built them and they were all to a pattern, so checking out one would work for all.

It was as I had thought. There was no possible hiding place. Constructed of concrete and steel, they had been built with vandalism in mind, with nothing detachable and everything bolted down. You would need an angle grinder to shift the bench seats and anything short of a bulldozer would fail to move any part of the amenities. Satisfied, I capped the thermos and went on my way.

My first stop in the Alice was to drop off the tyre for retreading. It would come out on the mail truck on Saturday. I pulled in briefly at the bakery to buy fresh rolls, then drove to the Thorntons' where I found Mum occupied in the kitchen at the homely task of shelling peas for Rae, whom I had met out at the letterbox.

'Mum!' She was thinner, I thought as I hugged her, but that was to be expected, and there was a tentativeness about her movements as if she were favouring her body. The surgical wound would still be tender, I supposed. 'You look pretty good considering,' I said, 'and rested, which is great. Are you sure you're up to the drive?'

'Don't be ridiculous, Charlie, of course I am,' she said. 'You look a bit worn yourself. Thanks for coming in. I was thinking of catching the mail but Rae talked me out of it.'

'I should think so!' Rae exclaimed. 'That rackety old truck. Sit down, Charlie. I was just about to make sandwiches, but we'll have your lovely fresh rolls instead, and a cuppa, because you can't possibly leave without lunch.'

I thanked her as she bustled about, turning down my offer of help.

'Sit down,' she repeated, 'and rest. You've had one long drive and there's another in front of you. It'll be ready by the time Don comes in. He's out the back watering the plants.'

'So what's been happening, Mum?' Pulling a chair out, I filched a couple of peas from the bowl as she returned automatically to her task. 'Have the police been round, or is that all finished now?'

'Nobody's bothered me. What's Tom doing?'

'Nothing,' I said more tartly than I intended.

'No, hang on, I forgot to tell you when we spoke last. They did find out where Annabelle was living. Mount Isa of all places! Tom's gone across to bring her stuff back. The cops here will have it now but I daresay with the rodeo on they wouldn't have had time to even look at it yet. And, of course, they haven't found the man she was with.'

'That was always unlikely. How's Bob been, and the new cook? She hasn't pulled out?'

'No,' I said. 'Bob's Bob, same as always. But Ute might wind up leaving because she's fallen for one of the men in the road crew.' I told her about Eric. 'Of course, she'll have to leave the country anyway when her visa runs out, but she'll stay at the Garnet as long as the camp does. She did say something once about maybe getting a job with them when they move on, but I guess that's up to the boss.' I helped myself to a glass of water, adding, 'I'll be sorry to see her go. She's funny, and very practical, and a great cook.'

'She sounds like a real find,' Rae said. 'I just heard the back door. That'll be Don. Right on time, because we're ready to eat.'

★   ★   ★

The drive back was tiring but smooth. I stopped twice at the shelters, once to give Mum a break and the second time for a quick cuppa from the thermos. Seated across from her on the hard metal bench, I drew a breath and said, 'Mum, there's something I need to tell you.'

'Oh, yes?' She withdrew her gaze from the arid landscape to give me a shrewd glance. I wondered if it was my imagination or just the weight loss she'd suffered, but she suddenly looked older than I remembered. 'It wouldn't happen to concern this Mike you sounded so happy about, would it?'

I felt myself flush. 'No, although as it happened he was there at the time. It was Friday night . . . '

The telling upset her. Her colour rose and her work-worn knuckles showed white where she gripped the table's edge. 'In the name of God, why? And if he wrecked so much, how did someone not hear him?'

'The diesel was running,' I said, 'and we were in the Garnet all evening, even Bob. The doors were shut and I suppose the wind was wrong for Jasper to pick up his scent. And,' I added defensively, 'if I hadn't gone home when I did he'd probably have got the crockery too. It's because I scared him off that we've still got plates, if not much else. Everything that could be smashed was. We cleaned the place up and Eric — that's Ute's man, he's very handy with tools — fixed what he could, so it's livable, just a bit short of all your things. I'm sorry, Mum.'

She waved the apology aside to furrow her brow and repeat, 'Why?'

'We think that he was looking for something. I got Tom over but he did nothing. Told me to give him a list of what was taken and he'd circulate it, but unless there was cash in the house I couldn't see anything missing. Though with so much

221

broken I suppose he could have taken something small.'

'But looking for what?'

'It's a guess, but we think it's something that Annabelle hid there. Or that he *thinks* she did. But if so, it plainly wasn't in the house.'

'*We* think, you keep saying. Who's we?'

I felt myself flush. 'Mike and I, Mike Webb from Abbey Downs. Was there any cash in the house?'

'No. Everything goes in the safe. So you're assuming it was the man she brought with her who did this? Paul whoever?'

'Has to be. Why would a perfect stranger stop by to wreck the place? There must be a connection, or it makes no sense.'

'I don't know.' She sighed. 'I'm tired, Charlie. Can we get on? The sooner I'm home . . . I should never have left — that's plain enough.'

'You didn't have any choice,' I reminded her, swallowing the hurt of the implied criticism. 'Let's go, then.'

22

We reached the Garnet in late afternoon with Mum largely silent. She hadn't asked about Mike again and it was hard for me to raise a personal subject in the face of her obvious dismay, displeasure or disappointment — I couldn't decide which — in the way things had fallen out during my brief time in charge. And she was visibly flagging. Reaching home at last, I bypassed the roadhouse, parking near the newly pruned oleander hedge to get her straight into the house.

'You need to rest.' Carrying her bag, I led the way to her bedroom. 'You can see the others at dinner. Shall I make you a cuppa now? It won't take a moment.'

She shook her head. 'I'll just put my feet up for a bit. I'm not an invalid, you know, Charlie. If I want tea I'm perfectly capable of making my own.' There was a snap in her voice.

'I know, Mum,' I said patiently. God! It was going to be a battle every day. 'But remember, you've still got a patched-up heart. Right, I'll leave you to it. We'll be eating in the Garnet, and we've been locking the house each time we leave it, just in case. The key'll be on its hook behind the door.'

Bob was waiting, his face furrowed in concern. 'I heard you drive in. Where's Molly?'

'Resting at the moment. She'll come over later.'

'How is she?'

'Cranky.' I glanced around the room; there were two couples and a lone traveller, whom I found myself eyeing off. 'Who's that, the fellow by himself?'

'Well, it ain't Paul, if that's what you're thinking,' he growled. 'What's going on? Why's she cranky?'

'Why do you think?' I said shortly. 'It's everything that's happened — and me for not somehow preventing it. Though I'd like to know . . . Forget it, Bob. I'm tired, and she's cross about the house, and probably not feeling the best. She'll be over for dinner. I shouldn't bother her until then.'

★ ★ ★

Mum came across to the Garnet having showered and changed; the grey hair along her neck, just as tightly curled as my own, was still damp. Bob looked up at the sound of her step and I swear if he'd been a dog his tail would've wagged.

'Molly! Great to have you home, girl. You're looking good.'

'Thank you, Bob. I'm feeling well. I see you've straightened the garden fence.' Her gaze went around the room over the stocked shelves and tidy racks. 'The whole place looks very neat and sparkly, and I notice that the garden's been weeded as well.'

'Ah, we fixed a few things needed doin', that's all. A screw or two, a lick of paint. Charlie's idea.

224

Gotta say it makes a difference. And she's had the road mob using the water truck round the joint as well.' He glanced at the clock. 'You'll meet 'em soon enough, they'll be in for their dinner any moment.'

I could hear the approach of their vehicles as he spoke and slipped into the kitchen to see if Ute needed a hand. It was a curry night and she was draining rice at the sink, her face wreathed in steam.

'Ha, you are there, Charlie. Today I have moved from the house back to my own room. Is okay, yes? Now the Miss-us is home you have the company, so you will not miss me and Eric.' She shook her head, smiling a little. 'Is wrong name, you know? She should be Miss-me and we are miss-us. Is right grammar, yes?'

'No, you're mispronouncing . . . Never mind, I know it's how Bob says it. But it's Mrs, not Miss-us.'

'Ah.' Enlightenment removed her puzzled frown. 'Always is Bob. He teaches the new words only to make confusion, I think.'

'Everything is confused around here,' I muttered. 'But yes, we'll be fine. I was glad you were there though. It was — comforting. How are things going with you and Eric? Is it serious — or too early to say yet?'

'He is good man. We make the excellent team, you know? Bed is good, also.' She nodded vigorously. 'And you and your Mike? He is the one for you, yes?'

'Maybe. Too soon to know.' Carrying the stack of plates to the hatch, I felt myself colour at the lie. Who was I fooling? Not Ute by the sceptical glance she gave me. I was mad about the man and she seemed to know it. To distract her I asked, 'Has Eric said when the job they're on will be finished?'

'Only that someone called Murphy makes the law that soon they have the major breakdown. This I do not understand, but he says is fact.'

'It's superstition, not fact. He means that things are going so well that it can't last. That they're due an accident because of it.'

She thought this over and shook her head. 'But this is nonsense!'

I laughed. 'Yep, but men believe it. Or pretend they do. And speaking of men . . . ' for the door had opened on the first of the team. 'Here they are.'

★   ★   ★

We made an early night of it. Mum was plainly weary from the trip and, I think, in a state of shock from the ravages committed on her home. She'd spoken to Rob, and thanked Eric for his efforts repairing the furniture, adding, 'It's a shame something couldn't have been done for the mantel clock too — if it hadn't been dumped, of course.'

'Mum,' I said patiently. 'I told you before. It was wrecked. The case had burst open and there were cogs and wheels all over the floor.'

'I'm afraid he made a thorough job of things, Mrs Carver,' Eric said gently. 'I helped clear it up. The place looked like a cyclone had hit it.'

'Well, I still don't see how somebody didn't hear anything. The homestead's only a step away.'

'With the diesel running? Even the damn dog didn't notice,' Bob said. 'C'mon, Molly. It weren't nobody's fault, except the bastard responsible. Thank Christ we were all over here, or else Charlie might've been there in the house when he came.'

His words gave her pause. She gave a quick little jerk of the head as her eyes widened and one hand rose to press against her chest at the thought — or she could just have been holding the site of her scar, I wasn't sure. The action gave her a vulnerable look, making her appear suddenly older. She wasn't. She was still in her sixties, but thin, and pale and tired, she seemed to have aged by a decade.

'Is there any reason to think he'll be back?' she asked.

'Not to the house,' Bob said. 'Where's the point? An' he's in for a bloody great surprise if he tries here. Me and Jasper've moved in.' He glared at me as if it had been my idea to disturb his sleeping arrangements. 'Last night I got to thinkin' we were taking a chance trustin' the locks. I moved me bed in this mornin'. If he comes, he can try conclusions with the dog. That'll settle his breakfast for 'im,' he said vindictively.

'It certainly will,' I agreed. Ute had finished cleaning up. She emerged from the kitchen, switching off the light as she did so, her eyes going straight to Eric, who was still courteously standing before my mother. 'What about it, Mum? Shall we call it a night? I was up before dawn and I'm feeling it now.'

★   ★   ★

But for all that, once I was in bed it took ages for sleep to claim me. I lay thinking of Mike and when my eyes finally closed, I found myself tossing in an uneasy half-waking state, starting at imagined sounds and my rest full of alarming dreams that faded as they woke me. I relived the shock of seeing again that elderly look of vulnerability on my mother's face and from there it was a short step to worrying about Bob, because Jasper notwithstanding, what if the sinister-looking Paul *did* return to continue his search and found him in the way? A cattle dog would stop most people but what if, for instance, he was to come equipped with a tyre iron? Or any other weapon?

I felt as great a sense of responsibility for old Bob as for my mother. In every way that mattered, he was the only real father I'd known, and I loved every hair on his curmudgeonly old head. He had to be seventy-five if he was a day, and for all his macho pretence, he would be no match at all for a killer. And whatever the man sought it was logical, wasn't it, that having failed to find it in the homestead, he would carry the search into the roadhouse? Unless he'd given up? But, worrying it over and over in the darkness, I couldn't convince myself that he had.

I went through it again, the time line of

Annabelle's visit as described by both my mother and Bob. The initial meeting in the roadhouse, the withdrawal to the homestead, then Mum's return, leaving Annabelle alone to shower and change and hide whatever she was carrying. Then her dramatic exit without farewell through the Garnet — back verandah, front door and gone. One place I could definitely rule out was the roadhouse's kitchen. If she had detoured into the storeroom-cum-office where Bob now slept, it would have had to have been a lightning visit. As for the sheds, there simply wouldn't have been time enough for her to trek across to them, search out a hiding place, and return unnoticed.

Therefore, she must have thought it out beforehand, I realised. Picked out a spot that she was certain would be overlooked, and when Mum had refused her she'd gone straight to it. It was the only possible conclusion, though it still didn't answer the more baffling questions of what she'd hidden, nor why.

An old station complex held myriad nooks and crannies in its sheds and outbuildings, but I'd already discarded them. Ditto the house. It had been scoured to the bones. There were the public amenities and the staff dongas, but neither could be considered secure with strangers regularly traipsing through or inhabiting them. Anyway, both were no more than plain sealable boxes possessed of a door and windows.

I sighed with frustration. The whole thing was impossible! It wasn't as if anyone had secrets or treasure to hide out here. The cash from the business was in the safe, and that had only been acquired since the abortive hold-up, so Anna-belle wouldn't have its combination. Briefly, I wondered where Mum had kept the money before. Probably in a locked box that anyone could've nicked. And locked only to keep my father from depleting the contents, not because she feared being robbed.

I would ask in the morning, although first I'd have to convince Mum there was no need for her to bounce straight back into the managing dynamo she'd been before her collapse. The Garnet was running smoothly enough without her labour, so perhaps I could get her to do something sedentary — sewing maybe? She'd bought material to make new curtains back before I'd left home, and I'd seen it still there untouched in the linen chest. Making curtains would be ideal: an easy, undemanding task lacking physical effort. I was still working out the best way to present the idea to her when I dropped off to sleep.

23

At breakfast, which Mum had prepared as Ute had to go straight from her bed to the roadhouse kitchen to cook the road crew's meal, I remembered my question.

'I was wondering, Mum — back before you bought the safe, where did you stash the dosh until you could get it into town? It must've built up into quite a sum each time.' Trips to the Alice would have been rarer when the roads were worse. Every three to four months when I was a child, I'd have guessed.

'The old deed box. It had a padlock and used to live under my bed,' she said. She smiled at Bob. 'I still recall the time we lost the key. It fell out of my pocket. We couldn't make change for a week till you found it near the woodheap. We were at the point of hacking it open with an axe when it turned up.'

'Yeah.' Bob's eyes glinted and he straightened in his chair. 'Then Jim took 'imself off on that trip, remember? Some damn fool scheme to drill for copper, and I made us that strongbox in the summerhouse. Of course, we still kept a bit of cash in the deed box so he wouldn't go looking. Doubt he'd ever have found it,' he added with satisfaction. 'It was a damned neat bit of work, if I say it meself.'

'In the summerhouse?' I was flabbergasted. 'Where, exactly? There's nothing there but the old bench.' And the chair, I mentally added, which used to stand on the verandah.

'It's under the bench, let into the floor. I set some of the flagstones into the lid. Your dad . . .' He coughed apologetically, shooting a glance at my mother. 'Let's just say it weren't wise to leave money lyin' around the joint. He had a nose for it.'

'He helped himself to anything he could get his hands on,' Mum said bluntly. 'That's why we needed the strongbox.'

'Who else knew about it? Did Annabelle? I've been flogging my brains trying to think of somewhere she could've hidden stuff . . . Why didn't you say, Bob?'

He bristled. 'I forgot about it. Besides, only Molly and me ever knew it was there.'

'Huh, I'll bet Annabelle knew too! Come on, show me. It's the obvious answer — the perfect hiding place and she'd have needed only seconds to reach it.' I was on my feet. 'When was it last used?'

'Not since you were a child.' Mum had risen too. 'Lord, I haven't even thought of it for a decade or more. She couldn't have known it was there.'

'You think?' I led the way out the back door and down to the summerhouse, which looked quite attractive now that the flowerbed had been cleared of weeds so the blossoms could be seen. 'Right, Bob. Under the bench, you said?' I seized one end of it and, grunting, he grabbed the other to help move it aside. 'I don't see anything.'

'Yer ain't meant to.' He got creakily down onto

his knees, grabbed a bit of flagstone standing slightly proud of the rest and heaved. It was heavy, I could see, but he slid the lid easily to one side, then glared transfixed into the cavity beneath.

'Well, I'll be buggered!' he said.

'What?' I crouched beside him to stare at the fluffy blue folds of fabric tucked into the space.

'That's my cardy!' Mum, glimpsing it, sounded outraged.

'There's something wrapped in it,' I said. 'Let me see.' I lifted the bundle clear and placed it on the bench. The garment was a pale-blue cardigan knitted in a lacy pattern with little imitation pearl buttons down the front. I unfolded the top layer to disclose a bulging calico bag.

'Tip it out,' Mum said. I obeyed, opening the drawstring to upend the calico over the cardigan and was rewarded with a rain of chains and rings and bracelets, cascading down in a glitter of silver and gold and the effulgent gleam of gems.

'Jesus Christ!' Bob picked up a handful, the delicate links of the gold necklaces incongruous against his leathery palm. 'It's the stuff they stole! Gotta be. How much did they reckon this lot's worth?'

'Over eighty thousand, retail anyway,' I replied, and he whistled as I goggled at the flash of diamonds, the duller glow of square-cut emeralds, the deep, almost purple gleam of sapphires. 'Rubies, amethysts . . . could those be topaz? And platinum, do you think?'

Bob ignored the question. 'No bloody wonder he turned the joint over lookin' for them.'

233

'But how did she get it inside? I mean, you'd have noticed if she was carrying all this, Mum, wouldn't you? And it's too big for a pocket. Surely Paul would have noticed it too.'

'She had one of those roll-on bags they carry onto planes,' Mum said. 'I thought she meant to stay overnight, and then when she said she'd shower before she left I just thought it was typical of her to make use of . . . well, I was too angry really to think much at all. But it must've been in there with her clothes. I suppose she must've told him that she meant to freshen up, so it would seem natural to have the bag with her.'

'Whatever,' Bob said impatiently. 'Don't matter how she done it. We need to get shot of it. You'd best ring the copper, Molly.'

'Wait, let me check if there's anything more.' I still couldn't understand Annabelle's motive for this. The presence of the jewels certainly provided a reason for her murder, but not for her to hide them in the first place. Paul would eventually have noticed the loot was missing, maybe that same day, even.

'There's something here — a card.' With two fingers Mum delicately moved aside a filigreed silver bracelet to reveal a printed oblong in a familiar shade of pale green. 'It's a Medicare card,' she said blankly, 'in the name of Paul A Belligrin. Why in the world should that be hidden with stolen property?'

'To identify him,' I exclaimed. 'Of course! Once the police get that they'll know who they're looking for. They can get his address from the system and track him down. Why, it could be weeks before he even realises it's missing — if you're not visiting a doctor you'd never even notice your card was gone. Not like a driver's licence. The question is, why did she do it? Was it out of revenge, or to protect herself?'

'Could she have meant to threaten him with it?' Mum asked. 'Like informing the police where the jewellery was if she didn't get what she wanted?'

'Don't make no difference now.' Bob grabbed up a handful of jewellery and began stuffing it back into the bag. 'Let's get this somewhere safe till the copper gets 'ere.'

I put a hand on his arm. 'I have a better idea. We'll put it back where it came from. Then Tom can see for himself where it was found. We don't want the cops thinking we knew about this, which they might if we suddenly produce it out of the safe.' I knelt by the cavity again, but before I could receive the bundle from him I glimpsed other items in the bottom of the strongbox.

Hand to my mouth, I stared, then bent to lift them carefully out: a tobacco tin, a musty-smelling copy of *Venture to the Main*, a skipping rope with painted wooden handles and a child's handkerchief with something knotted in one corner. I knew immediately what it was.

'Didn't you have a rope just like . . . ?' Mum began, but her words tailed off as I pulled the knot from the hanky to reveal the plump gold locket that had been my birthday gift. 'Why, that's . . . '

I twisted the tin and the lid came easily away to reveal, nested in their cotton wool as I had always kept them, my little shell family. I touched them gently with one finger: Mum, Dad, Bob, me, and the two little babies with their pencilled eyes (somewhat crooked, I saw) and their tufts of glued-on curls.

'That wicked child!' Mum exclaimed. 'So she did take them, just like you always claimed.'

'Yes.' I riffled through the book, checking the illustrations of the sailing ships, and of the handsome captain with his rapier and cummerbund, which I had coloured in. I'd forgotten that. The book smelled old and musty, and the colours on the illustrated cover had faded. I had loved that book. Gently I laid it back down and looked up at Mum. 'Proof, if you still need it,' I observed dryly, 'that Annabelle knew about your strongbox.'

I replaced the items together with the stolen goods, dusting off the knees of my jeans as Bob lifted the heavy concrete lid into place. We left the bench where it was but even uncovered the lines of the hole were hard to distinguish, for the flagstones cemented into the lid overlapped the straight edges of the cavity. It was a masterly piece of disguise, typical of Bob's fussy workmanship.

Back inside once more, I rang Harts Range to tell Tom of our discovery, which, I pointed out, was certain proof that Annabelle's death was linked to the break-in at the homestead.

'His name's Paul Belligrin, by the way,' I added smugly.

There was a moment's silence before Constable Cleary asked suspiciously, 'How do you know that?'

'His Medicare card's with the swag.' That'd be an expression to trick Ute, I thought frivolously, presuming of course that she'd ever encountered a real swag in her outback travels, for she carried a sleeping bag herself. 'When do you think you can get here, Tom?'

But he needed no urging and was at the door some thirty minutes later with a camera to take pictures of the loot in situ, of the summerhouse itself, of the emptied cavity and, finally, of the jewellery laid out on the kitchen table. He slipped the card into one evidence bag and divided the recovered items between three others, having carefully numbered the various pieces first. All three of us were required to make statements about the steps that led to finding it, which he told us he'd have typed up ready for our signatures when it was done.

'Well, you'd best bring 'em down to us for that,' Bob said. 'We can't all be traipsing up to the cop shop just to sign things. Some of us have work to do.' He sniffed, saying virtuously, ''Specially as we've done all the hard yakka of locatin' it for yer.'

'I hope the police will make public the fact that it's been found,' I added. 'Because Mr Belligrin could come calling again. Especially if he's noticed his Medicare card's missing. He just might work out when and where he lost it.'

'Could you swear to the last time you saw yours?' Tom asked. 'Anyway, that's a decision for

237

my bosses to make, but I shouldn't think you need worry.'

'Well, I hope you're right, Tom. I'll have something to say if the Garnet gets done over too,' my mother promised.

'It won't happen, Molly. He's already searched the place — why would he come back? Well, I'll be off, then, to report this.'

He gathered up his evidence bags and departed, rattling past the road crew's vehicles. Though he was plainly well pleased, Tom's reassurances rang hollow in my ears. The card was the only means the police had of identifying the man wanted for double murder. Why would Belligrin *not* risk returning to find it when, if discovered with the stolen goods, it guaranteed him a life sentence should the police ever manage to catch him?

★ ★ ★

We waited, watching the midday, afternoon and evening news with religious zeal, each day expecting an announcement that the police had recovered the jewellery, but nothing was reported.

'The buggers are keepin' it quiet,' Bob said. 'They don't want him to know he's been rumbled. Means they can't find him, even with his name and bloody address, which they oughta have by now.'

'Yes.' It was worrying. Of course, Belligrin could have left his old address should he have discovered the card was missing and guessed that

Annabelle was responsible. Or the continued media silence could mean he was lurking about the ranges still and had yet to return to his residence. Or he might have skipped off overseas, or headed up to Darwin — the possibilities were endless. If he owned a vehicle the police could circulate the numberplate nationwide ... I shook away the train of thought. It was pointless, I knew, but I couldn't help worrying. I had never felt so exposed and helpless, so open to attack. The Garnet, lapped within the sheltering folds of the range, had always been a place of peace and serenity, of blue skies and bird calls and now, everywhere I looked, I imagined danger sneaking ever closer to harm those I loved.

I wished Mike was with me. I could talk to him at least, air my fears. I wasn't about to upset Mum with them, or worry Bob, who was still manfully guarding the roadhouse each night, and I didn't plan to alarm Ute. Hadn't I told her the bush was safe? And so it was, I silently reiterated, only once you added a double murderer to the equation everything changed.

If Mum had any misgivings over Paul returning, she didn't show it. To my relief she was being sensible about resting and leaving the lifting and carrying of stuff to Bob and me. Something to be thankful for, I thought, finishing up the task of scrubbing the dried mud off the verandah. The daily spraying of the dirt track by the water truck meant that the road crew trekked mud everywhere, but mud, I figured, was better than dust. Mum was presently behind the counter seated in a cane chair Bob had fetched over from the quarters, working on her crocheting. The curtains were finished and she'd moved on without urging to a hobby previously confined to winter evenings, but that now filled the peaceful stretches between customers. She laid down the delicate work as I entered.

'There you are, Charlie. Could you watch the shop for a bit? I want to get the washing off the line.'

'I'll do it, Mum. I'm due over to the house anyway to do the watering. You want a cuppa before I go?'

'Maybe when you come back. The benefit barbecue's this Saturday, remember. I need to make some lists and ring who-ever's turn it is to bring the meat.'

'Surely not,' I protested, 'it's only a couple of weeks since the last — '

'The races,' Mum said. 'This one's early so the two dates don't clash. I find it's best to remind the stations because everyone's so busy with the mustering they're likely to forget it's on.'

'Okay. How much more money do they need to raise to fund this clinic building?'

She pulled a face. 'Years' worth, the rate we're going. The CWA's doing their bit, and the Race Club are pitching in too, but we could do with a really big sponsor to move things along. Meanwhile, you just have to tell yourself that every little bit helps, and it'll all be worth it in the end.'

24

As I had been hoping, the Abbey Downs lot attended the barbecue. I saw Mike's tall form among the hatted group of young men and my heart gave a little joyful skip as he came towards me.

'Charlie! I've been counting the hours. It seems an age since I saw you last. How are things going? How's Molly?'

'Remarkably well.' I could feel the smile on my face. '*And* being sensible, which is more than I expected. She's actually resting, as in lying down for a nap in the afternoon. I thought we'd be screaming at each other by this point but we're rubbing along quite well, considering.'

'Considering what?' He had taken my hand and was passing his thumb over my fingertips, head bent attentively so that his face was shadowed by his hat brim.

'Our history, I suppose. Because as far back as I remember, ours has been a difficult relationship. Sometimes I've wondered if she really wanted a boy because I've always felt I was second best for her.' I gave an unconvincing laugh to cover the familiar hurt. 'I guess we're just incompatible in some way. It happens in families.' I broke off to wave to Rose Pennon, whose pregnant belly preceded her and her family through the gate; Ben and Sue Damson followed them. Both women stopped to greet me and talk. Mike squeezed and released my hand, murmuring, 'See you later,' and went off with Ben and Abe while the crowd grew steadily in size, augmented by the road crew whose evening meal would tonight be taken with the station people.

Ute and Eric were hard at work, the barbecue flavouring the air with the smell of smoke and cooking meat. The inadequate lighting threw heavy patches of shadow across the garden as the figures clumped and reformed, all sooner or later finding their way to my mother, who was buttering rolls in the chair at the table's head.

I checked that the urn on its separate table was working and noticed I'd neglected to bring the coffee tin out. I headed for the kitchen to fetch it, and was cut off by Kathleen Mallory who stepped, unsmiling, in front of me.

'I want a word with you, miss.'

Taken aback by her hostility, I said, 'Good evening, Kathleen. Whatever's the matter?'

'You.' She glowered. 'You've broken my boy's heart, you know that? He's so damned unhappy I can't stand to see it, and if that's not bad enough, you've put his life at risk! All for a silly mistake made years ago. Well, I think he's been punished enough and I'm here to tell you — '

'Whoa up! Is this about Bryan? What rubbish, Kathleen, and quite frankly what business is it of yours? He's not a child, you know — he's responsible for his own actions and if they have consequences he hadn't bargained for, that's his problem, not mine! And what do you mean

— putting his life at risk?'

She glared at me, the fading red in her hair seeming to crackle with the energy of her anger. 'He came off a horse yesterday. He could've been crippled! It would never have happened if he'd had his mind on the job — '

'Oh, for heaven's sake. That's pathetic! And if it's true, then so is he. It's too bad if neither of you can accept it, but it's over. He's no concern of mine. If he was the last man left I still wouldn't want him. I'm sorry, Kathleen, but that's just how it is, and the sooner he accepts the fact the quicker he'll recover.' *If he actually needs to*, I thought. I suspected half of her story was prompted by her own desire to see the last of her sons married. Kathleen was the archetypal matriarch to whom grandchildren were the real wealth of the world.

She said sorrowfully, 'You never used to be cruel, Charlie. It's plain wickedness not to forgive, you know. A real sin. I blame the city influence — '

'Oh, for God's sake. I've got work to do, Kathleen. Excuse me.' Shaking my head, I walked away from her, wondering what Bryan knew about the encounter. Had he really asked her to intervene? I found that hard to believe. Then I wondered if she would try the tale on Mum next, and an unexpected laugh made me snort.

'Something I said?' Mike was suddenly beside me. 'Why are you clearing out?'

'Just getting the coffee. And no, I was thinking about Kathleen Mallory and what a terrible mother-in-law she'd be. Not that I'd ever give her the chance.'

'I'm glad to hear it. Has her sprog been bothering you again?'

'Far as I know he's not here. Poor fellow fell off his horse and his mother was blaming me. For breaking his heart and blighting his future and putting his life at risk. All big, big sins apparently, for which my time in the city is to blame. I expect it's made me hard and shallow and unforgiving, only I left before she got to that bit.'

'I'm glad, because being so hard and — shallow, was it? — it won't matter if I kiss you, will it? I expect you play fast and loose with all the simple bushies you meet?'

'If you say so.' I melted into his arms, my hands on the strong nape of his neck. 'Oh, I have missed you, Mike.' Then with a jolt of surprise that I'd temporarily forgotten, I blurted out, 'We found it! What Annabelle hid. It was the booty from the robbery.'

His lips, which had moved from my mouth to my throat, lost contact with my skin as he raised his head. 'Really? Where was it? Come, sit.' He dropped onto the top step leading to the verandah and pulled me down beside him. 'Hit me with it.'

Coffee forgotten, I told him everything, including the fact that the police hadn't yet announced the discovery of the stolen goods. 'So you'd better keep the fact quiet too. Belligrin might be prepared to write the loot off, but he has to recover his Medicare card. I mean, it links him directly to both murders.'

'Only if he knows Annabelle took it.' Mike frowned. 'I hear what you're saying, Charlie, but he could well be aware it's missing without having a clue when he lost it. I really don't think you need worry about him returning. Look at it from his viewpoint. He's searched the homestead, he knows there's nothing there, and what are the chances of anything staying undiscovered in the roadhouse where people are working and coming and going every day? He'd have to know the business has a safe, but you'd be using that yourselves on a daily basis, wouldn't you? And why would Annabelle have the combination anyway? She wasn't a part of the business. No' — his hand played idly with my fingers as he thought — 'if it were me and I was determined to get my hands on the stuff, I'd be hunting for a hidey hole somewhere close — down the creek, round the soak maybe. Someplace she could reach in a few minutes from the house. But I really think by now he must've written the proceeds off as not worth the risk.'

'Well, I hope you're right. You know, Mike, there were other things in the strongbox too. My little shell people, and my birthday locket. Everything of mine that Annabelle took was hidden in there.'

He shook his head. 'She must've been a spiteful little piece. I suppose your father would've let it slip about the hiding place? I can't see Molly trusting a kid with something so important.'

I snorted. 'He didn't know it existed. I'd think

he was the chief reason Bob built it. Mum wouldn't still have the Garnet if she hadn't kept the cash away from him.'

'Ah. Not much of a bargain, then, your dad?'

'Not in the husband and father stakes anyway. Mind you he could be fun, much more so than Mum, but it never lasted. I suppose you could say he lost interest in things very quickly, whether it was a game with Annabelle and me, or some new money-making scheme he'd dreamt up. When I was a kid I was always thought it was my fault when he got tired of us and walked away. That I must have done something wrong. Annabelle was his favourite, so it couldn't be her.' I shrugged ruefully. 'It's why I turned to Bob. He might've been grouchy, but he was *consistent*, you know? And kids need that certainty in their lives. Besides, I found out early on that his bark's worse than his bite. A bit like a crochety but harmless hound.'

'Huh. Maybe he doesn't like me, but I wouldn't call his brand of harmless friendly,' Mike said.

'Ah, but you're after Molly's daughter, aren't you? And he guards her as well as Molly, good dog that he is.' I giggled in his ear. 'Just like Jasper does.'

'Well, you seem to have him taped,' Mike responded, then raised a questioning brow. 'As a matter of interest, *am* I going to get Molly's daughter?'

'Time will tell,' I said primly, standing up. 'Come on, I started out to do something — oh, God yes, the coffee! Then I'll show you Bob's strongbox. Will you grab a torch from the shelf by the door while I find the tin?'

Spider Webb was standing by the urn when we reached the table. 'Ha!' he said. 'There you are. Thought you was growing the bloody stuff.'

'Picking *and* roasting it too,' I replied. 'Sorry, Spider. But since when have you drunk coffee?'

'Since the damn quack told me to quit the hard stuff.' He spooned enough grounds into his cup to stun a horse. 'What do the buggers know, anyway? Damn killjoys, every one of 'em.'

The party was in full swing, with a radio tuned to a country and western station blaring out guitar music. People were eating and drinking, sitting or standing in small groups, some near the table, others clustered about the barbecue where Ute was forking over steaks to eager diners. Sue Damson was minding the bring-and-buy stall, where several women had gathered. I glimpsed Kathleen among them, mug in hand, glaring at me, and I reached deliberately for Mike, lacing my fingers within his. He grinned, leaning over to plant a kiss on my cheek.

'Are you telling me something?' he murmured.

'Perhaps. And sending that redheaded witch a message. If you can feel something burning your back, it's her. She could glare her way through sheet metal.'

We moved down the yard into the shadows beyond the light's reach where the summerhouse stood. Mike fumbled a tiny torch from his back pocket and shone it on the entrance. The babble of sound from the barbecue became muted by shrubbery and distance as we stepped inside.

'Shine the light over the floor,' I said. 'See anything?'

He took his time before admitting defeat. I squatted down, patting at the floor. 'It's here, somewhere. Ah, got it.' There wasn't much to grip but once I'd shown him the tiny ridge of stone, Mike hauled the lid off and inspected the cavity beneath.

'You'd never know it was there!' He shook his head. 'The old boy's a real craftsman, isn't he? That's heavy too. Makes you wonder how a kid ever lifted it.'

The same thought had occurred to me. Borrowing the torch, I moved it slowly around the edge of the hole, then stopped to point. 'She used a lever. See the mark here? She only had to get it open far enough to drop stuff in.'

'Uh huh.' He replaced it and, standing back up, passed his boot over the join. 'She never intended for you to find it, did she, when she hid your stuff?' He sketched a cross over his heart. 'There, I swear never to let on to another soul the secret of the summerhouse. In case you ever want to use it again for valuables.'

'Idiot,' I said fondly. Well, I suppose we'd better rejoin the party. I just thought you'd be interested.' Really though, in a small way for the secret hardly mattered now, I was demonstrating my trust in him.

'Before we go, there's something I wanted to ask you, after I've kissed you properly, that is.' He proceeded to do so, very thoroughly.

'Oh, yes? I think maybe we'd better stop right there,' I said reluctantly disengaging myself.

'This isn't the most comfortable place for seduction. You were saying?'

'The races,' Mike replied. 'I'd like to take you to the ball, Miss Carver. May I have that honour?'

'Well, let's see, that's difficult. There's you, or old Bob — if he can get away. Hmm. Okay, you're on. Who says women can't make up their minds just as fast as men? Gracious! That's next Saturday, isn't it?'

'Yep. Kevin's got his jockey lined up and the nags went into the paddock ages back. Old Jock's over at the Range supervising their training now.'

'How many are Abbey running?'

'Three. Kevin reckons the chestnut has a chance at the Cup. Anyway, it's the dance I'm interested in.'

'Yes.' It had been years since I'd attended a race ball and a mild surge of panic filled me. I wondered what I could find to wear. I said cautiously, 'When was your last ball?'

'What? Oh, let's see . . . Last year. I looked in, that's all — I didn't have a partner.'

'Do they still hold the Deb and Matron of the Ball?'

'Good God, no! Very seventies, Charlie. Why, last ball some of the girls were wearing jeans. Spangly ones, maybe, but still jeans. I think the gown and gloves outfit has had its day.'

'That's a relief, because I don't have much of a formal wardrobe! Well, I suppose we'd best get back before they come looking for us.'

★ ★ ★

I told Ute about the ball while we were clearing up. 'I'm going with Mike. Why don't you ask Eric to take you? We're usually closed for the races anyway. Mum always attends and Bob runs the bar at the course. You can bet all the road crew will be going too.'

She considered me, head on one side. 'But is very grand, the ball, yes? I have only this.' She held out her hands inviting my inspection of the knee-length shorts and t-shirt she was wearing.

'No, that won't do,' I agreed. 'But perhaps I could lend you something? We're the same height — we could have a look, there's a wardrobe of stuff I didn't take with me. You haven't had a day off since you got here, Ute. And the dance will be fun.' I glanced at the trainers she wore. 'Have you any proper shoes?'

'Yes. The sensible ones, not with the heels for the dancing.'

'That's okay. Nobody's going to look at your feet.' With her striking blonde attractiveness and statuesque figure, that was a given. 'Tomorrow we'll see what we can find. We might need to stitch a bit but we've got a week.'

My own figure hadn't changed in five years, I knew, so my hair, now straggling onto my neck, would be my biggest problem. I would have to pin it up somehow. Finding something with a bodice to fit Ute's more curvaceous form would be harder. Perhaps something of Mum's?

The following morning, I found her at the clothesline folding sheets and asked my question. 'Hmm, I don't know . . . wait a bit, there's that blue chiffon top. She'd probably get into that. I don't know what she'd wear it with though. Not jeans. Why don't you check your clothes, see what would go with the blue? If there's a dress that seems a good match I could whip the bodice off and she could wear it as a skirt.'

'That'd be great, Mum. Are you sure you've time for it?'

'Between you and Bob,' she said dryly, 'I've nothing else. Ute's sleeping with that road-worker, isn't she?'

'Yes, but it's her life, Mum. She's not a teenager. And they seem to be genuinely fond of each other.'

Mum's expression creased into a frown. In the bright sunlight of the garden, the grey of her hair and every last line in her face showed, like a map of the disappointments and hardship she'd weathered through life. 'Hmmph. And you, Charlie, are you sleeping with your young stockman yet?'

I felt myself flush. 'No,' I said steadily, 'but I expect I will be soon. I love him, Mum. I'm not a teenager either, so when we're both ready, yes, it will happen. Did Dad get you into bed before you married?'

Her eyes flashed indignantly. 'No, he did not! How can you even ask! That sort of thing didn't happen when I was young. Decently brought up girls didn't allow it.' Then she surprised me. 'Though perhaps there'd have been fewer unhappy marriages if we had.'

'Oh, Mum. I'm sorry you caught such a rotter. But Mike Webb isn't like him.'

She sighed. 'I hope for your sake that you're

251

right. That top should be on the right-hand side of my wardrobe, folded on the shelf. My shoulders are broader than Ute's so it should be roomy enough across the bust to fit her.'

She was right, for later when the two of us were in my room Ute pulled the soft folds of the blouse over her head and found it fitted perfectly. She turned slowly before the mirror, admiring the results. Her blonde hair was up in a ponytail, which put the firm tanned skin of her neck and shoulders on show.

'Is very pretty.' She smoothed it approvingly over her ribs. 'Soft, like the cloud, yes?'

'We need to find something to go with it.' I opened my wardrobe, pulling out several dresses. 'What do you think? The top's just a tad darker than sky-blue so the green or this ivory-looking one might work as a skirt, do you think? It's broderie anglais. Not too sweet?'

'Is perfect, Charlie! You do not mind I lend it?'

'Borrow,' I corrected automatically. 'No, you're welcome. I don't much like it.' It was the one I had worn to that last dance with Bryan. 'Not really my style — if it ever was. I need something with more colour.' Though I remembered insisting to Mum at the time that it was the dress I wanted above all others. Had it been so Bryan would see me in white as a bride? I had been foolish enough for anything back then.

'So what is it you will wear?' Ute asked.

'This.' I pulled out the soft drape of jersey, tawny gold with a crossover bodice, pleated lightly at the hips, and held it against me. Cora Wilder had been right when she'd advised me to wear topaz or amber. The dress showed off the colour of my eyes, and I knew that under lights it picked out the occasional gold glint in my brown curls.

She nodded, smiling. 'Ah. Sexy, yes? You are the autumn woman in that, strong, a little bold . . . This,' she held up the ivory, 'is for the young girl, but with that colour — he will want you, no?'

I blushed and laughed. 'Well, I hope so.' But Mike's possible response wasn't the only reason for my reaction. I was unused to being thought strong. Perhaps, as Bob had said, my time away had changed me from the doormat my agent had once deplored. 'Let's take that one to Mum — she can measure you and see what can be done about making it into a skirt. Maybe a wrap-around? And I'd like you to have it, Ute — though I expect Mum'll want her blouse back.'

'Thank you, Charlie. We shall be the, how you say, bellies of the ball?'

I went into a gale of giggles that her uncomprehending stare only intensified. I started to explain, then gave up. 'Never mind. I'll get the measuring tape, you bring the dress.'

25

On Saturday evening Bob brought the station wagon round to the front of the roadhouse. He looked very sharp in his race-wear, a pale-blue sateen shirt with an embroidered yoke and a string tie above narrow grey dress pants and polished Cubanheeled riding boots.

'Yer locked up?' He ushered Mum into the front seat while I climbed into the back.

'No, I've left the place wide open, you old fool,' Mum retorted but without her customary sharpness. 'Are you leaving the dog loose?'

'Yep. He can keep an eye on the joint. You right, Charlie?'

'Yes.' I pulled my seatbelt on. Ute, stately and very attractive in her borrowed clothes, had left earlier with Eric in a Main Roads vehicle that he'd cleaned inside and out for the occasion. Mike was already there, having spent the day at the races along with Bob and my mother, while Ute and I held the fort.

'Who won the Cup?' I remembered to ask then.

'Ben Damson. With a big liver-chestnut horse,' Bob said. 'Weren't no competition at all. He just ran away from the field like none of 'em was trying.'

'Well,' I said, 'Kharko. They can afford to breed the best.' The station was owned by the biggest cattle company in the Centre and if the board seemed to pick their managers for their interest in racing, at least it ensured that the local meetings continued, as they hadn't in some other districts. 'Mike will bring me home,' I said, 'so you needn't wait for me. You come back as soon as you like, Mum.'

'I'll stay till supper,' she said. Our contribution to that was sitting behind me, and I twisted about to check that the boxes were secure.

'Well, you're looking very nice tonight,' I told her. 'Don't let her get danced off her feet, Bob.'

He bristled at the thought as I'd known he would, saying darkly, 'You just watch where that young feller puts his hands, girl, an' leave me worry about Molly.'

★   ★   ★

The hall at Harts Range was back behind the police station, a simple shed with a raised timber floor that someone from the Race Club committee had been over that morning with French polish. A music deck had replaced the volunteer musicians of the old days and the paid bands that followed. Somebody had stuck a few decorations up on the walls and strung streamers from the rafters, but the place was basically a big unlined shed. Bemused and a little saddened, I turned to Mike as we walked in, raising my voice over the insistent beat of the music.

'What's changed? I used to think this was so glamorous. It's not even warm.'

'Let's get moving, then — that'll help.' He scooped the wrap from my shoulders and dumped it on the end of the closest bench, then led me onto the floor to join the only other couple dancing. 'As to what's changed,' he murmured into my ear, 'you have, Charlie. Your horizons have widened, that's all. It's no bad thing.'

'I suppose, but the magic's gone.'

'No,' he said firmly. 'That's within us. You'll find it again.'

The floor was gradually filling up around us. I saw Bob and my mother seated against the wall and caught a glimpse of ivory skirt in the midst of the dancers. Eric, animated and dapper in a white shirt and decent pants, looked surprisingly handsome and Ute simply glowed with happiness. Mike pulled me firmly back towards him, turning me under his arm, his own face alight with pleasure. The pressure of his hand was like a firm caress on my hip as we stepped forward together in the Pride of Erin.

'You know you look lovely tonight, Charlie. Good enough to eat. Is it my imagination or is old Bob glaring at me?'

'Probably. He told me to watch you — your hands in particular.' He grinned at that and gripped me tighter. 'So, was the racing good today? I'm sorry you didn't get the Cup.'

'Ah, well, there's always next year.' He winked. 'And I only had five dollars on him, a bit more than the price of a stubby. I'm no gambler. Are you feeling warmer?'

'Yes, I am, thanks. They've shut the doors, which helps.' The music paused and we stood and clapped waiting for it to resume. 'Where did you learn to dance, Mike?'

'Same place you did, I imagine. Bush hops.'

'On the contrary, sir, I had lessons. At boarding school, and then with a drama coach. All actors have to dance, and sing if they can. Oh, good, it's a waltz.' The music had started again. Over Mike's shoulder as we took the first steps I saw Bob rise and bow to my mother with old-fashioned courtesy as he offered his hand. They should marry, I thought, not for the first time, and wondered if he would ever ask her, or if he was content to just love her from afar? He had done it for so long he'd probably never imagined changing things. I wondered if she wanted him to, but surely she'd have found a way to let him know, if that were the case.

I lost myself to the music then. I loved to dance and Mike, for all his claim to having just picked up the knack, was not short of skill. There were fewer modern dances than one would have found in the city, so we foxtrotted and gypsytapped and barn-danced ourselves into breathlessness, Mike refusing to release me to another partner by the simple expedient of staying on the floor until the music started up again.

I saw old Spider waltzing with Kathleen Mallory, and her various sons with their own and each other's wives. And Bryan cutting in on Eric for the barn dance, and Bill Maddison's youngest — a plain, gawky girl, whose hands strangled each other as she waited — finally taken onto the floor at his wife's prompting by George Himan. People were kind. I remembered

257

the agony of my own first time, wondering whether anyone would ask me to dance or if I'd sit partnerless all evening under the pitying gazes of my neighbours.

Supper was held in the side room, the men good-humouredly manhandling the bench seats out to flank the long trestle tables where the food was set out. Mike and I found ourselves seated opposite Mum and Bob, whose gnarled hands were adjusting her lacy black shawl against the icy breeze from the louvred windows behind.

'Will I shut them?' Mike half rose but Spider's sudden presence behind him prevented him from getting out of the cramped seating.

'Bob, there yer are. Where's the Cup at? Young Tom said he handed it over to you to give to me.'

Bob's mouth fell open in almost comic dismay. 'Ah, Christ! I forgot all about it. I slung the box in the Rover and the bloody thing's still there. Jesus! How could I . . . I s'pose you want it now?' He was trying without much success to extricate himself from the bench.

Spider, I remembered then, was president of the Race Club. He nodded. 'Yeah, well soon as this mob's finished with the tucker we'll have the presentation. No worries, mate. If it's in your vehicle, just give us the keys an' I'll grab it.'

Bob was shaking his head. 'We came in the station wagon. The Rover's back at the road-house. Sorry, Molly, I'll have to go back for it.'

'It's okay,' Mike said, finally managing to draw his second leg clear of the bench. 'I'll go. You look after the girls, Bob, and I'll be back in no time.'

'No.' The space that Mike's removal gave made it easier for me to step out from the bench. 'Jasper wouldn't let you out of the vehicle, Mike. I'll come too.'

Bob looked uncertain, half inclined to insist but Mum stayed him with a hand on his arm. 'Thank you, Mike, that's very kind of you. No, let him, Bob. His eyes are younger than yours for night driving. I'll keep some supper for you.'

'For me too, then, please,' I said, turning to follow him, 'I've only had a sandwich.'

★　★　★

It was pitch dark outside with no moon, though the stars, which always seemed closer in winter, glittered like a band of diamonds arched above the range. I pulled my wrap tightly around me and felt Mike's guiding hand on my elbow. 'Watch it here, there's a damn great hole — ' He fell into it as he spoke and swore and I couldn't stifle a giggle.

'So much for your advice. It's nice of you to do this, Mike. Poor old Bob looked so gobsmacked at forgetting.'

'Might improve his opinion of me,' Mike said. 'And while I could've managed, you know, I'm glad you decided to come.'

'You certainly will be when we get there. I wasn't kidding, Mike. Jasper'd have your leg off before he let you set foot out of the car.'

'Nah,' he said. 'He'll be right, he knows me now.'

'As long as one of us is with you,' I retorted.

'You don't believe me, you get out first.'

'Ha!' I caught the glimmer of his teeth in the cab light as he slammed the door. 'Throwing me to the dogs already, eh? And we've only just started courting.'

'Is that what we're doing?'

'Uh huh.' He reached across to kiss me. 'Did I mention that you're looking particularly lovely tonight?'

'You did, but there's nothing wrong with repetition.' I hesitated to ask but then went ahead anyway. 'Has there been anyone for you before, Mike? Anyone serious, I mean.'

'Not really. Oh, there've been girls I've taken out — in town mostly. Your lot are a bit scarce in the bush, as you know, and the drawback in meeting a girl in town is not getting a chance to see her regularly. Next time you go calling she's dating someone else. Out here there's really only the guvvies on the stations and they're a bit young for me. Only kids themselves.'

'Mmm.' I nodded. 'Rose Pennon's governess is just seventeen. Her charges run rings around her. It does makes you wonder — ' I broke off to grab the handhold on the dashboard. 'Watch it. Cattle!'

'I see them.' He doused the lights and slowed to a crawl to let the string of lumbering shapes move across in front of us, the dust of their going tainting the air. Mike turned the lights back on and fiddled with the heater switch. 'Are you warm enough, Charlie?'

'Yes, fine thanks.' We were past the cattle but a faint scent of dust still lingered and I could see the odd motes caught in the headlight's beam. 'Somebody must have gone through before us.'

'Well, it is a highway, my love.' He spoke almost absently and I shivered with pleasure at hearing the endearment again. *I love you.* The words were a silent song in my heart, ones that I would not yet say but hugged to myself like a treasure to be enjoyed in times to come.

Outside the night whipped past, a blur of dark scrub on the edge of the light through which we rushed, chasing but never catching it. We negotiated the detour around the causeway where the road crew were now working, and sailed smoothly over the concrete comprising the finished one. The turn-off was next, and then in short order the road camp, its lights left burning, followed by the darkened roadhouse that loomed in lit sections as the headlights swung across the facade. Mike switched both them and the engine off and the silence rushed in, broken only by the faint *doom-doom* of the road camp's distant diesel. Nothing stirred in the starlight and he turned his head towards me.

'So where's this famous dog that's going to eat me alive?'

Puzzled, I pushed my door open and felt the instant bite of the chilly air. 'I don't know. That's very strange, Mike. He would've heard us coming from miles back. He ought to be here with his bristles up and his growl ready.' I stepped out and whistled. 'Here Jasper! Here boy, to me!'

Nothing happened: no growl, no patter of running feet to greet or challenge us. Even if he'd gone back to Bob's quarters, my whistle, if not the vehicle's arrival, should have brought him to investigate.

'He's not here,' I said blankly, stating the obvious.

'Might be off chasing a euro, or a beast that came in to the trough,' Mike hazarded. 'We can't hang around looking, Charlie. They're waiting on the Cup.' He strode off to retrieve it. The torch flash traced his journey to the vehicle shed while I continued to whistle and call the dog, who still hadn't appeared when Mike returned a few moments later with the cardboard box tucked under his am.

'Got it.' He opened my door, then slid behind the wheel, handing the box to me. 'It's okay, not dusty. I love that dress on you — you look like some young autumn goddess, all russet and gold.'

'*That* certainly earns you a kiss.' I pulled his head down and long moments passed pleasurably until he sighed and put me firmly away.

'We've got to go, love. Old Spider'll be sending a search party after us. I'll camp at the Garnet tonight, so maybe we can carry on from here tomorrow, hmm?'

'Maybe,' I agreed, running my fingers through his dark hair. He turned his head to kiss my inner wrist where the small veins pulsed, then reached to start the engine. The Garnet fell away in our dust, and with my thoughts concentrated on the feel of Mike's lips on my skin, the niggling worry of Jasper's whereabouts was forgotten.

26

Bob was hovering at the door when we returned, the music once again swelling behind him; he fairly snatched the box from Mike's hands.

'You took your bloody time, boy. I coulda ridden there faster.'

'What, on Phar Lap?' Mike quipped. 'And a bit of gratitude wouldn't go amiss, old feller.'

Bob's tanned visage reddened. 'Yeah, well, thanks,' he said gruffly and hurried off. A few minutes later Spider appeared on the dais and the presentations began. Mike and I ate the selection of sandwiches and cakes Mum handed us while the proceedings continued. Ben Damson made a speech, a miniature cup was presented to the jockey, Spider rambled on at length about past race meetings and eventually the cup was christened with champagne. Then the music started up again and those with young children began gathering their kids and belongings, ready to call it a night.

Bob and Mum were leaving too, and Eric called goodnight as he passed with Ute on his arm. I was surprised until I noticed the time; she'd have to be up preparing the men's breakfast within a few hours. The thought brought a yawn with it and Mike looked at me. 'You ready to leave?'

'I think so. Only the diehards will be left soon and they'll mainly be drinking.' Two big fire-drums had been lit near the bar behind the hall, to which some of the non-family men had already gravitated. 'It's been lovely, Mike. I've really enjoyed myself.'

'So have I,' he said. 'Come on, then, I'll get you home. What do you bet old Bob'll be sitting up waiting on you?'

I laughed. 'Maybe Mum'll send him to bed.'

★ ★ ★

Bob wasn't waiting for me to come home, but he was certainly still awake. I saw his shadow cross the light in the shed as we pulled up and said, 'Uh oh, looks like you won your bet.'

However, it was Jasper, not my virtue that was exercising Bob's mind. He came across to the vehicle as I got out, the headlights bouncing off the shiny surface of his shirt.

'Was the old dog 'ere when you come back, Charlie?'

'No, he wasn't. I forgot to tell you, Bob. We didn't see hide nor hair of him. I called him and whistled . . . We thought he might've gone chasing after a euro. They do come in to the trough to drink sometimes.'

'Nah, he wouldn't do that. Not when I left him on guard.' He frowned and scratched distractedly at the nape of his neck. 'Bloody queer, that is. First time he's ever done that.'

'There might have been a dingo bitch hanging around and he got her scent?' Mike offered, reaching into the vehicle to switch the lights off.

I didn't like to suggest it but another

possibility was poison. 'The stations haven't been doing any aerial baiting, have they?'

'No,' Mike said. 'We just got our dates for the 1080 campaign. They start in the district next month. In any case, Kevin wouldn't be baiting this side of Windy Bore so your dog'd be quite safe. He'll be back come daylight, you'll see,' Mike said. 'Got your things, Charlie? I'll walk you to your door. Okay if I roll my swag out again on your verandah, Bob?'

'Yeah.' The old man whistled once, then turned away, saying over his shoulder, 'It's cold as buggery out. You might as well use the end room. There's a bunk in there.'

Mike leant close to murmur, 'I think he's starting to like me,' into my ear and I stifled a giggle as my hand reached for his in the darkness. Privately, I thought the invitation arose more out of distraction over the missing dog than from fondness for my head stockman, but any change of attitude was good. Bob was an important fixture in my life and I needed him to think well of Mike: for him not to do so called my own judgement into question.

* * *

By breakfast time Jasper still hadn't returned. Bob, though plainly upset by his disappearance, affected a gruff unconcern. Handing him his cup, I touched his arm, saying, 'He'll come back.'

'He shouldn't've bloody gone in the first place,' he grumped. 'I've been down to the bore

265

but there's that much comin' and goin' with blokes 'n trucks a man couldn't see tracks unless they were gold-plated.' He glared at Mike. 'How long you stickin' round for?'

'I thought I'd poke off after lunch. That okay with you, Charlie?'

'Good,' Bob said, cutting ruthlessly across my affirmative. 'I got a job that needs a bit of muscle. You can give us a hand, shouldn't take no longer than an hour.'

After breakfast, leaving the men to their unnamed task, I crossed to the roadhouse to help clear up and found Ute at the sink singing lustily to herself in what sounded like German. 'Somebody's happy,' I said, picking up the tea towel. 'Did you have a good time last night?'

'It was very much fun — funny?' I shook my head and she nodded. 'Much fun. Good food also. From where does it come?'

'Well, Mum made ours but everybody takes something along for the supper. It's called bringing a plate.' She frowned on the verge of a question and I said hastily, 'What sort of dancer is Eric?'

'Sort?' She frowned. 'But he is engineer, not dancer, Charlie.'

'I meant, does he dance well? Is he a good partner?'

'Oh, yes, very. We make the good partners. I am very happy, Charlie, because now I will be wife, yes? And maybe make family of my own.'

'What? Oh, wow, he proposed?' At her nod, I continued. 'Congratulations!' I caught her wet hands in mine and we did a little jig. 'So you're going to stay — in Australia, I mean?'

'Yes, but first I go home before I return. But is not for many weeks yet. We work it out, Eric and me. He will stay to drive the machine when I go, then we get married in this Alice. You will come, Charlie? You and Molly and Bob? Perhaps you carry my flowers, yes?'

'Be your bridesmaid? I'd love to, Ute. And it's *the* Alice, not 'this'.'

She flung her arms wide, shook her blonde hair back and beamed at me. 'The, this — I do not care. I am to be wife with gorgeous man. And maybe soon too, you are wife also?'

'Well, I don't know about that.' But the distant possibility was somewhere at the back of my mind and shortly afterwards I took myself off to think about it, ambling down the garden to the summerhouse for some time alone. The shade there, however, was chilly and I moved on, pausing to pull the odd weed and sometimes just standing idly to feel the sun's warmth on my body, my thoughts divided between Mike and Ute's nuptials. Maybe Bob could give her away? Would she want a church wedding or something simpler? We could even hold it at the Garnet with Padre Don officiating it if that suited them.

And where, I wondered, would I choose to get married — supposing Mike asked me? I pushed the back gate open and wandered along the well-worn path to the bore where I could see, through the white trunks of the gums lining Garnet Creek, a cloud of silver and grey swooping and shrieking about the tank and trough.

Galahs were such show-offs! They put me in mind of Annabelle and the thought momentarily dimmed my mood of happy expectancy. How could I daydream about marriage when her battered body still lay in the morgue waiting for the police to release it for burial? Sighing, I sank onto a fallen gum trunk on the creek bank wondering if I would ever be free of her influence. Annabelle was dead and yet she still affected my thoughts and actions. I had been happy a moment before, my world rosy-hued, and now here I was staring glumly at the grey sand of the creek bed thinking that the darkish blob marring the grains immediately below me looked like tar, which was impossible, or blood. As if something had died there, only there were no feathers or tiny bones to point to either owl or hawk having made their kill.

There was too much of it anyway for the victim to have been much smaller than a dog ... My thoughts froze at that point and an instant later I was on my knees in the sand, poking at the grains that had fused together in a brownish mass. It was definitely blood. When I leant above it to sniff, there was a faint but discernable trace of bitter iron in the air and though the sand by its nature could hold no clear tracks, the formless indents around the dark deposit could well have belonged to Jasper.

So, if he'd bled out here — why? — what had happened to his body? My eyes flitting nervously about, I paced across the narrow bed to the far side. An old cattlepad wound down the bank and crossed the sand, and here and there I picked out the distinctive drag marks of euro or goanna tails, but whether the larger tracks belonged to man or beast I wasn't qualified to tell. Bob could, and I almost went to find him before remembering the job he had on that required Mike's muscle. Better not disturb them, then. I could look for Jasper's body myself.

And it wasn't that difficult. Whoever had shot or bludgeoned him — the only ways I could conceive of stopping an attacking cattle dog — must have picked up his body from the creek bed, then dropped it on the bank and dragged it from there. He'd taken it quite a way. The galahs sped off shrieking into the blue as I passed the bore, following the pad beside which the drag marks still showed. I crossed the first stony ridge before the smell tainted the air, just a whiff, but easily recognisable to the bush bred to whom death was a fact of life.

I found Jasper dumped at the end of the drag mark, swarming with flies, his already swelling, eyeless body torn by the birds, and what was left of his mouth still set in the snarl with which he had met his killer. The smell of death was stronger close up, for his body lay in the sun. With a hand over my mouth and hatred for whoever had done it in my heart, I moved upwind from his remains, staring blankly at a gully, choked with scrub and kangaroo grass that led deeper into the range. Who was responsible, and why? There had been no break-in at the roadhouse, so why the need to stop its sole defender? If it had been Annabelle's killer who had found himself challenged by the dog, why hadn't he gone ahead and broken into the place once Jasper was dead? And if it not him, then who? Surely not Bryan who, I belatedly remembered, had been at the dance last night anyway.

I couldn't be absolutely certain that all the road-camp men had attended the race ball — the lights in the camp had been left on, after all — but what reason could any of them have had for doing this? If they'd wanted access to the Garnet they had only to wait for breakfast. Besides, Jasper had been killed out the back in the creek bed, not at the front, the logical point of approach for anyone coming from the camp.

Light glinted on something from across the scrubby gully, there and gone in an instant. It could be anything, sunlight on a turning leaf, or the same thing refracted from a polished pebble. I waited, and when the breeze stirred the dull olive foliage it came again, a blinding wink, like a heliograph, or the reflected light from a tin or bottle. In a place where nobody ever camped? Curious, I set out to investigate.

I stepped carefully down through the tumbled rocks and spinifex of the gully, looking for a way up the other side, crowded as it was with thick wattle growth. Force seemed the only way through, so I grabbed at the stems of saplings, shouldering spiky branches aside and getting scratched for my pains as I climbed up the other side. The glint of light had vanished. Nothing but rock and shiny scree and the tumbled untidiness of curled eucalypt bark and kangaroo grass met my gaze. Then I glimpsed it again, somewhat higher than the ground.

I wondered if somebody could have wedged an empty tin into a mulga fork, or possibly stuck a bottle mouth over a broken branch. I had seen that before, usually near a pub; the decorated growth, festooned from stem to crown with glass, then wittily dubbed a bottle tree. Forging ahead I pushed through the last line of shrubby mulga growth and found myself staring at a vehicle, a Toyota troop carrier, more or less hidden under a camouflage of dead and dying boughs. One of these had slipped off the cab to reveal part of the windscreen, and it was the sun glinting off this that I had spied from across the gully.

I froze where I stood, knowing then that I shouldn't have succumbed to curiosity. The very condition of the vehicle shouted the fact. It had nothing to do with Abbey Downs, whose stationhands had no reason to hide their presence. Taking shallow breaths, I used my eyes and ears, straining to detect any sign of life but nothing save the twitter of birds broke the silence. The camp was deserted. It wasn't exactly a glade — did such things even exist in desert country? I wondered wildly — more a small clearing in the patchy mulga that closed behind it to fence it in. I could see where the wheels had straddled the smaller growth, leaving it half bent still from the vehicle's progress through it. There was more than one set of tracks so the troop carrier had clearly come and gone a few times. There was a sixty-litre fuel drum under the trees and another of equal size beside it, with a siphon hose doubled through the bunghole — the water supply? A rough swag wrapped in a bright blue poly-tarp lay beside it.

Bob had long since taught me to automatically orient myself with my surroundings so that I knew, without having to think about it, that where I stood was perhaps half a kilometre or so south and a little west of the roadhouse. Which meant that the vehicle, a four-wheel drive, had bush-bashed its way from the main highway to reach this point, crossing the shallow Garnet Creek in the process. So Paul Belligrin was back — and not for the first time judging by the size of the ash pile where his campfire had burned. He had probably been coming and going for weeks, unobserved and unsuspected. Given the dust-laden state of the sky, nobody would notice the smoke from a small fire during the day, while after dark scrub and distance would screen the glow. Nor was anyone likely to blunder onto his camp so far from the road. Only fools like me. I stared at the blackened billy as the wind stirred again, teasing the white ash into movement, and my heart thumped in sudden fear. Wherever the man was, he could return at any moment.

Mouth suddenly dry, I whirled about, stifling the urge to run for my life. I must leave no trace of my presence to alarm him. He must remain unsuspecting until I could get word to Tom Cleary. I glanced at the ground, thankful for its rough nature. There had been the sand drifts below in the creek but the grass and bark might have absorbed my tracks there. I would have to check. Then my heart almost stopped and a shocked cry was torn from me as a man's voice said roughly from somewhere behind my right shoulder, 'Where do you think you're going?'

27

I should have run then and risked it, for he wasn't within grabbing distance, but I doubted a rabbit could have kept its feet along that gully side. Even as the thought flashed into my mind he moved, and my limbs froze at the glimpse of the stubby black pistol in his right hand.

Absurdly my first reaction was to think how small it was. I had never seen a pistol before, but I had imagined something larger with a longer barrel. I stared dumbly, rooted to the ground by shock and fear. Belligrin — for it had to be him — was big, easily Mike's height, with a bush of dark hair under a cloth hat, and a scrubby bristle of stubble that, along with the stony dark eyes, lent his hard face a dangerous aspect. His hands were large, engulfing the weapon, and his forearms brawny, covered with dark hairs.

'So who are you — the cousin or the slavey?' he asked.

'What?' I said stupidly.

'Answer me!' he barked. 'Do you live at the roadhouse, or do you work there? Who the hell are you?'

'Annabelle's cousin. And the men know where I am. I told them before I left,' I lied.

'Yeah? That was clever of you, Charlie. You are Charlie, aren't you? Quit lying, you bitch! I watched you come and you were just following your nose. Well, that's bad luck for you, 'cause we'll be long gone by the time they figure out you're even missing.'

Pistol notwithstanding I turned then to run, but had scarcely launched myself down the slope before a steely arm encircled my neck halting me in mid-flight. The jolt almost took my head off. I stamped backwards with my heel and must have connected with some part of him for I heard him swear. I followed through with an elbow to his body, knowing as I did so that my efforts were laughably weak, then my breath was choked off and there was just time enough for my mind to scream *Mike!* before the asphyxiating blackness swamped me.

★　★　★

The world was moving under me, the sun had vanished and everything hurt. Those were my first hazy impressions when my senses returned. Even as I registered them, there was a crash, and my helpless body rose and fell against metal, jerking my arms and banging my hip solidly against some obstruction. I blinked, heart racing again, and tried to orient myself. I was in the troop carrier and it was moving, which accounted for my being flung around. He must still be off the road, then.

Okay, I thought, desperate to impose some sense on my current circumstances in order to retain a semblance of control and not start gibbering with terror, now I knew where I was: I was in the vehicle, the light dim because some sort of shade cloth hung over the side windows, while the rear ones, I found by forcing my head up off the floor for a moment, were smothered in the good red dust of the Centre. So, I was being driven God knew where by a man who had already killed two people. Could matters get any worse?

The act of lifting my head proved that the most injured part of me was my neck. I tried to bring my hand to it and discovered that my arms had been wrenched above my head and secured to one of the seat legs bolted to the floor. At the back end of the vehicle, a similar accommodation secured my ankles. Belligrin obviously wasn't risking me regaining consciousness and launching an attack on him as he drove, supposing I could've got my hand on a weapon. However, such scrutiny as I could manage by skimming my eyes sideways without actually moving my head revealed nothing as useful as a tyre lever or jack handle. The polytarped bedroll was wedged beneath the far row of seats, together with a backpack and a heavy wooden chest (his tuckerbox?) and the ones I lay against had a series of metal lock boxes built beneath them. Down by my feet, the billy I had glimpsed by his campfire rolled insouciantly back and forth across the floor.

I fixated on these details only because I didn't dare dwell on my situation or think about my probable immediate future or I would have dissolved into a terror-ridden lump incapable of helping myself. Not that there seemed much chance of that, bound as I was and with my neck in the state it was in. Every jolt felt as if my head was being taken off. I was almost grateful for the pain; it kept me from worrying about what would happen when we stopped, because I knew he was going to kill me and there was no one to prevent him doing so, for nobody had the slightest inkling of my whereabouts. If, when they grew concerned, Bob or Mike did manage to follow my tracks to Belligrin's camp beside the gully and work out what had happened, I would be miles and hours away by then and probably dead. My breath caught in a little hiccup of terror as I fought down the rising panic.

Where was he taking me? Why hadn't he simply shot me back there and tumbled my corpse under a concealing bush? I should have clamped my eyes shut the moment he spoke and refused to look at him. Or better yet, never have followed the drag marks made by Jasper's body in the first place. Instead, I had seen Belligrin's face, and his own words had linked him to Annabelle. Put simply, it was too dangerous now for him to think of releasing me.

We seemed to travel for hours. At some stage the slow jolting changed to a speedier, smoother ride, as if we were back on the road, then abruptly the pace slowed again and the pitching progress returned. From my supine position I couldn't even guess at our direction, but it seemed logical to assume that the original bush-bashing had taken us around the Garnet to the highway and, having left it, we were now heading back into the ranges. Despair filled me.

We would become the stuff of legend, Annabelle and I, two young women from the one family murdered by the same man.

Abruptly, the vehicle stopped and a moment later the cab door creaked open, and I heard footsteps, though the motor continued to run. My breath came so quickly I was hyperventilating. Was this it? When the back doors opened, would he have the pistol in his hand? My mouth was too parched even to squeak let alone scream, though I knew there would be none but the birds and lizards to hear me. Bug-eyed with terror, I watched the dust slide down the glass as he rattled the door open, then his hands were loosening the strap that tied my bound ankles to the seat.

'Wh-what are you going to do?' I despised the tremor in my voice and swallowed to moisten my mouth.

'Anything you can think of, Charlie, then double it,' he said with a smirk. Both his hands were busy with the buckle, so he wasn't holding the gun. Of course he wouldn't kill me in the vehicle, I realised belatedly as he jumped lithely into it. One of his hands landed on my hip and he slid it slowly up my body, making me cry out as my instinctive attempt to jerk away jolted my neck. 'Maybe later,' he said, leering. 'Bit of a plain Jane, aren't you? Your cousin got the looks in the family. Let's be having you now.'

He wrenched the tie from my arms and my shoulders shrieked in protest as I brought them back down from above my head. My hands were still secured with a broad electrician's tape — the same that he'd used on my ankles, which he now cut free.

'Just till we get you out, so don't be silly now. There's nowhere to run.' He jumped down, caught my right ankle and hauled and with an agonised yell, I was out in a heap on the ground. The pain in my neck brought tears to my eyes and it was a moment before I could take in my surroundings. When I did, my breath stopped for he'd returned us to the little stone hut built into the hill, the site of Annabelle's murder.

'Why here?'

'You'd rather be tied to a tree?' He pulled me to my feet and pushed me towards the entrance, switching off the motor as we passed the cab. 'It'll do while we wait.'

'Wait for what?'

'For the jewels your bitch of a cousin took to be returned to me,' he snapped. 'I can't find them myself so they'd better. She's hidden them somewhere, but they'll find them if pushed to it. You'll write a note, Charlie, to whoever values you most, telling them so. They'll find them and bring them to me or they'll not see you again. Not alive anyway. I'll give them today, so they'd better not waste any of it. One person fetches the package and you die at the first sign of a double cross. Make sure you tell 'em that just in case they're thinking of getting clever and involving the coppers. Get inside now.'

'But . . . ' I turned in the dark little doorway, fervently hoping that my acting was up to the task of projecting bewilderment. 'What jewels? What are you talking about? Oh — ' I managed a gasp as the penny dropped. 'That was *you* who tore up the place? It was, wasn't it?' I cried accusingly. 'Besides, Annabelle — she was only in the house for twenty minutes — just long enough to shower, Mum said. She didn't have time to hide anything!'

I gave silent thanks then that the police hadn't advertised the recovery of the stolen goods. Allowing a hint of curiosity into my tone I added, 'How big a package? You'll have to help if you want them to find it.' Forgetting my injury, I made to shake my head and uttered a little cry of pain and brought my hands up, but bound as they were they could do no more than support my chin. 'You don't know what you're asking!' I let the desperation I felt creep into my tone. 'There're four sheds, and the roadhouse, and the dongas and the dump . . . They'll never search all that in a day.'

If I could buy Mike and Bob more time, I reasoned, they might come up with something. To admit that what he wanted was already in the hands of the police would be to sign my own death warrant. He would immediately cut his losses, kill me and leave, perhaps adding rape to his crimes before doing so. I shuddered and he noticed, his face hard in the gloom of the tiny hut.

'That's their problem — and yours if they come up empty.' He shoved me forward, barking, 'Sit.' I lowered myself carefully to the stained and dusty stone and he taped my ankles again, taking care to finish behind my legs where only a contortionist would ever get the fingers of their bound hands to reach.

'Now I'm gonna bring you writing gear, then cut your hands free, so work out your message,' he said. 'The jewels are in a cloth bag. Not very big, so easy enough to hide. You'll tell them that. And I want it by — let's see, it's ten now — let's say by four this arvo. If they don't turn up, then you're for the chop. Be sure to tell them that. Only one man to bring it. I'll draw a map to show him where. Now, when I free your hands, do just what I've told you and I'll leave you water while I'm gone. But try anything and I can promise that you won't like what I do to you. Understand, Charlie?'

Unable to nod, I said yes submissively, but my heart beat a little faster at his words. If he was leaving to deliver his demand, perhaps my chance would come then. A tiny spark of hope lit the dark pit into which the morning's events had plunged me. If I could somehow free my feet . . . I let my eyes roam over as much of the cell-like enclosure as lay within my line of sight. There had to be something sharp or edged. And if there wasn't? Then I would just have to rely on the men to devise a plan. But first, I was resolved to do my damnedest to escape.

28

After some thought I addressed the letter to Bob. If Mike wasn't at the roadhouse but off somewhere searching for me, Bob or my mother might hesitate to open something addressed to him.

'How will you know that he gets it?' I fretted. With the paper pressed against my thigh, I wrote shakily, *He says he killed Annabelle and will kill me too, unless you find a packet of jewels she hid somewhere at the Garnet and bring it to him* . . . There was more, the time frame and the map showing Mica Valley.

Belligrin didn't bother to answer. I added *I love you* and signed my name. It didn't matter who read it — it applied equally to my mother and Bob, and might well be my last communication with them — but eventually, even if the others had it first, Mike would see it too.

Belligrin read through the note, stuffed it into an envelope and watched me address it. 'Who's this Bob, then?'

'An old man. He manages the roadhouse.' Too late it occurred to me that Annabelle might have told him differently but he just nodded, doubtless pleased by the thought of having somebody elderly and therefore more amenable to deal with. He didn't know Bob.

'Good.' He vanished from sight to return a few moments later with a plastic bottle of water and a packet of wheat-meal biscuits, which he tossed onto the floor beside me. 'See? Obedience pays off, Charlie. If this Bob's as sensible as you, by this time tomorrow it'll all be all over.'

And I'd be dead. I kept the thought to myself and said petulantly, as if I believed him, 'How am I supposed to get the top off the bottle with my hands tied?'

'Use your teeth.' He smirked and left me but didn't go far, for the next thing I heard was a series of grunts until a boulder, the size of a calf, was heaved against the doorframe, blocking out half the light. It wouldn't have stopped me had my hands and feet been free, but bound as I was it made an effective prison of the little hut. Then the throaty roar of the troop carrier sounded and, after a short pause while the diesel motor warmed up, moved slowly away. Without waiting longer, I grappled with the water bottle until I had it between my palms and raised it to my mouth.

Use your teeth, he'd said and I did. The bottle was one of those soft plastic ones. I doubted it would cut butter but I had nothing else to try. The little room was bare — any overlooked artefact from its previous occupation had, I assumed, been taken away by the police along with Annabelle's body. I calculated that I had an hour, perhaps an hour and a half, depending on the method Belligrin used to deliver the note. He was hardly going to walk into the Garnet with it and risk being seen; on the other hand, simply dumping it on the verandah or near the fuel pumps didn't guarantee it would be found. I intended to make the best use of my time even if my feeble plan failed to work.

I had to bend my neck to get at the bottle without spilling its contents, which I knew I'd need for I was already quite thirsty. It was agony, but I persevered, gripping the plastic top in my molars and trying to maintain the pressure of my palms against the body of the bottle. After several attempts I felt the cap begin to loosen and, by moving my hands back and forth to twist the bottle, was finally left with it in my mouth. I spat it out and straightened my neck with a moan, taking a breather before trying to drink the contents, which involved more neck move-ment. My thirst helped, and when the bottle was empty I considered my next step, which was to detach the base from the sides. This time my teeth failed me: I couldn't get enough grip on the slick surface, even when I pressed the bottle flat between my palms. I tried holding it between my hands and flogging the end against the stone wall but the first blow sent the bottle flying from my grip. Swearing, I scooched after it on my bottom and tried something else. I was wearing closed shoes with low, solid heels. Perhaps they would do it?

Positioning myself and gritting my teeth against the jarring my neck was about to absorb, I raised my heels as high as I could and smashed them down onto the bottle. It took several attempts before the first split appeared and, encouraged, I kept at it in a sort of fury, my nerves crawlingly aware of time ticking by, feeling tears of pain and frustration on my face.

Finally, I could stop, the battering having separated a section of the base from the sides. I would like to have lain flat then to ease the sheer weight my head had assumed, but I didn't dare.

I had no way of measuring time but it must have taken me five minutes of manipulation between my teeth and my clumsy hand grip to peel the base from the bottle and retain the latter in my mouth. I could taste and feel the grit of the floor upon it as I tongued the edge clear of my lips and bent my head to rasp it against my taped wrists. I didn't know if it would succeed and had despaired long before the edge of the tape began to part, but it was my one and only shot so I kept at it, ignoring the pain and the saliva that drooled from my mouth.

What felt like eons later, my ears tuned with painful intensity for the first distant throb of a motor, I threw caution to the winds and wrenched at my bonds. The plastic stretched but didn't break and I sawed at them in a renewed frenzy. The next attempt allowed me to reach the tape with my fingers and I spat out my makeshift cutting edge and tore at them, then started on my bound ankles. Twisting them within reach, I used the edge of the plastic to tease the end of the tape free and was then able to get a thorough grip and unwind it. By then I was light-headed from my efforts, but only a broken leg could have kept me in that hut.

Sobbing freely with pain and fear and the relief of my release, I grabbed the biscuits, slid headfirst over the boulder and bolted into the nearest scrub. My very haste was my downfall, that and the fact that I was holding my neck with both hands in an attempt to minimise its jolting, so that when my foot caught on something — a rock or a dead branch — I fell without a hope of saving myself.

It was a long, painful slide to the bottom of the gully. I felt the biscuits, which I had thrust down the neck of my t-shirt, crunch against me as my hat came off. There was a blinding pain in my foot, echoed by the sharp agony of my right knee smacking into a rock and the smart of grazed palms before I rolled to a stop against a clump of grass, gritting my teeth against the renewed assault of agony. Everything hurt, but the urge to flee drove me to struggle up, only to promptly collapse again as my wrenched ankle announced its presence.

'Oh God! Just what I need.' My knee hurt but it was ignorable, as were the pinpricks of blood on both palms. I sat for a moment sick with despair, giddy and light-headed as I grasped my leg, telling myself it was nothing, just a sprain. If it meant crawling I still had to put distance between myself and the hut. I had no idea how long my escape had taken and Belligrin could return at any moment. My hat, I saw, had followed me down. I grabbed it and, with the help of a sapling, rose waveringly to my feet. The pain of that first step made me gasp and the second was no better, but there was no help for it.

Grabbing onto the shrubby wattle bushes and the stems of sprawling mallees for support, I dragged myself on, thankful for the rocky ground that hid my tracks. Bob might've followed the faint traces I left but I doubted Belligrin could — except, of course, that he would expect me to take the easiest route along the gully, which meant I had to leave it and climb the exposed flank of the ridge. My heart quailed at the prospect but it would be better to do it before he returned. If I could get over the ridge and find a place to hide — a nest of boulders or a dense thicket of conkaberry say, where my jeans and green shirt would meld into the shadows . . .

The weakest part of the plan, or at least the hardest, would be climbing the ridge without the help of scrub to hang onto, and added to that was the slight matter of water. I had none and the nearest supply I knew of was at the police station — as good as a million miles away. Looking on the bright side, I thought grimly, if Belligrin caught me I'd have no further worries about thirst. Time to get started, then, but first I needed a stick.

The gully was choked with scrub but it seemed to take forever to find a support that didn't snap under my weight or wasn't too unwieldy for the task. I settled on a mallee branch and with its help started on a diagonal course across the ridge. It was hard going and I was panting and sweating freely before I'd achieved more than a few metres of ascent. Forced to rest, I stood leaning on my helpful stick until a faint rumble in the air vibrated against my eardrum. It galvanised me into action as nothing else could have done. Sound carried a fair distance in the quiet of the range and there was no mistaking the growl of a diesel engine. Blinded with the sweat of fear, I pegged away with my stick amid the rocks and spiny rings of spinifex until I reached the crest of the ridge, and then for the sake of speed and because I really couldn't take another step, sat and shuffled myself down it, going into a free slide at one stage when the rocks changed suddenly to scree.

There was a creek at the bottom, narrower than the Garnet, its banks sparsely lined with the ubiquitous white-trunked gums. Of red clay and about a metre high, the top of the bank was thickly furred over with buffel grass. Beyond it the country opened out in to a small vale dotted with a few corkwoods and a clump of wild orange before humping up again into another bare, grass-grown ridge. No handy rocks or thickets. My heart sank as I contemplated the labour of crossing such an open stretch of country. Then the suddenly shockingly loud bellow of the distant troop carrier had me scurrying to the shelter of the creek bank. I half fell over it and, for lack of any other cover, pressed myself into the narrow band of shadow at its foot where the roots of an old, scaly-barked gum jutted from the bank, forming a hollow in the sand.

My mind, catching up with my body's movement, reasoned that he wasn't close enough to see me, not through a solid ridge. In fact, he didn't know yet that I had gone. Then the engine noise sank to an idle and eventually died, and I held my breath, wondering if he'd just assume that I was still where he'd left me. But I knew he would check: it might take him five minutes or half an hour, but sooner or later the need to torment me or to savour my fear would take him to the hut. Trembling, my eyes squeezed shut, I waited, not moving a muscle, my throat so dry from apprehension that I could no longer swallow.

Lying there, my heartbeat gradually slowed and I began to think again. I was supine against the bank, only half in the shade, and the sunny bits of my body were growing uncomfortably warm. By the shadows I could tell it was near enough to midday, which left four hours before Belligrin's deadline. Would Mike and Bob involve the police? It wasn't as if they could comply with my kidnapper's demands and if either turned up at the rendezvous point without the package, I shuddered to think what Belligrin would do to him. They couldn't even borrow the goods back from Tom Cleary, for he would no longer have them.

A faint yell broke my concentration. I lay rigid, holding my breath, my hearing drowned by the sudden thunder of blood from my racing heart. The sound came again, incrementally louder. My escape had been discovered, then. Gasping in fright, horrified at how little distance I had managed to drag myself if a shout could encompass it, I pressed my body into its pathetic cover and, closing my eyes, waited to be discovered.

29

Belligrin yelled twice more, though I dared not lift my head to check. He sounded so close that he must have been on top of the ridge I had descended, possibly even directly above me.

'I'm going to find you, Charlie, and when I do, I'm going to make you sorrier than you ever imagined you could be. You won't get away from me — your cousin didn't. And when I've finished with you, who knows? Maybe one night your home'll catch fire, and the roadhouse with it. Think about that, Charlie.'

The sun's heat vanished as a cold dread seized me. I heard a stone rattle down the slope and the distant *ki-ki*-ing of a hawk, but he must have kept walking because when his voice rang out again it was fainter. It was hard to breathe through the terror choking me. Would he really do it? I thought of the homestead on fire with Mum asleep inside — though of course she wouldn't be sleeping with me missing, and anyway, the road camp would be there, and the police by nightfall at the latest, so he'd never get near the place. Unless he was vindictive enough to return long after I'd perished and the search was over . . .

I was being ridiculous. Determinedly, I shook away my fears. I was going to get out of this. And right now was the time to move again, while I knew where he was. If I waited I'd never know if he was circling back, which he'd do, I reasoned, once he'd reached his estimate of the distance I'd be able to achieve. So maybe my injury would actually work in my favour. Grabbing my stick, I sat up, cast a cautious glance at the empty ridgetop and hauled myself across the shallow creek, deliberately dragging my feet sideways in the sand in a bid to camouflage my footprints. Hopefully, he'd never think to look or, if he did, he'd be unable to tell the difference between a human's track and a camel's.

I toiled across the vale and up the subsequent slope, accompanying my progress with nervous, backwards glances. The longer it took the more I fretted. It had seemed simple at first — Belligrin's fading shouts had given direction to his whereabouts — but once I could no longer hear him, my mind became prey to doubt. Was he really out of hearing, or had he fallen silent on purpose and was circling back? He couldn't afford to miss the rendezvous with Bob, so how far would he pursue me? It was irrational, but I felt so exposed to his sudden appearance from behind a thicket of scrub or the top of a ridge that, plagued by fear and indecision, I began casting frantically around for another hiding place.

I was hot and very thirsty by then — hungry, too. It was well past noon, the shadows had moved to the far side of the trees, and I'd had nothing to eat since an early breakfast. The packet of biscuits still rode inside my shirt but my anxiety was too great, and my throat too dry, to even consider them. I found a small pebble, rubbed it clean on my shirt and sucked it to keep the saliva going in my mouth and struggled on.

Once, I thought I heard a vehicle far in the distance but that was plainly impossible. I was too far from the highway and, anyway, the blood pulsing in my ears and the stir of the occasional breeze made every sound suspect. Nobody was coming to my aid. I wished now that I had dug in the sand of the creek where I'd sheltered. I remembered the easy way Mike had found the soakage water on our fossick in just such another creek. Perhaps there had been water there too where I had lain, just waiting below the sand for me to dig down to it? The thought was maddening, but it was too risky now to return to test the theory, even if I had been able to.

As it was, I was forced to stop and rest. My ankle, I discovered on inspection, was grossly swollen and had turned a nasty shade of purple. It needed strapping and rest, but the most I could give it in my twitchy state was another five minutes; even as I decided on that, my ears picked up the sound of a human voice, carried on a gust of breeze. It was fleeting, but the burst of adrenaline it provided had me on my feet, hobbling with all speed towards the only cover in sight, a rocky outcrop half screened by a thicket of wattle and deadwood.

Panting and whimpering with pain, I eeled my way into concealment amid the old leaves and fallen pollen, finishing up with one hip wedged against sun-warmed rock and the dried blades of buffel grass tickling my nose. My hat had been pulled off against a branch but I didn't dare move to retrieve it as I pressed myself against the earth. It was warm and very still in the thicket; I could hear only the buzz of insects and see a broken patch of sky visible between the wattle foliage. With slow precision I moved my head to avoid the grass, noting as I did so the occasional blades of maroon through its mostly ivory colouring. Then the voice came again, no longer ranting, but a quiet, conversational tone that was somehow more threatening, along with the unmistakable crunch of boots on gravel. I stopped breathing and had to resist the urge to curl into a protective ball.

I knew I mustn't move. I shut my eyes instead, praying for him not to see as the steps came closer and closer, almost as if he was following my tracks. But he couldn't have been — he wasn't a bushman. Then the swish of grass ceased and a strange male voice sang out, 'Right! Got her.'

Jerking my eyes open, I glared wildly into the brilliance beyond my pathetic sanctuary and saw a stooping stranger peering at me through the wattle. Expecting Belligrin I could only gape. Did the man's presence mean . . . Had he a partner all along . . . ? My mind grappled to make sense of it as I drew my legs up in a vain attempt to work myself deeper into my illusory cover.

Then a voice cried, 'Charlie! Thank God!' and Mike was suddenly there, pushing past the other man to shoulder his way into the thicket. He looked frantic, a pinch-bar of all things hanging from his belt. It caught on a wattle stem and, swearing, he wrestled it violently free before reaching for me. 'Are you okay?' he demanded. 'I've been so worried! We crossed your tracks half a kay back and I didn't dare to hope — but Len swore he recognised the print of your shoe . . . ' And then of course I knew him, the other man. Not some sinister sidekick of Belligrin's but Len Wilder, the gem hunter.

'I'm fine.' I gulped shakily. 'Thank God it's you!' Then, as his arms closed about me, I burst into tears. 'Really, I'm fine,' I sobbed idiotically. 'But I'm so thirsty, and I sprained my ankle. And I thought you were him coming to k-kill me . . . '

'Shh, it's okay, love. I've got you. Come on, let's get you out of here. How did that bastard get hold of . . . Never mind that now. Len, where's the water?'

'Right here.' The old fossicker pressed an army canteen into my hands and everything was suspended while I drank. The fluid restored me and, knuckling my cheeks dry, I sighed and continued to sip.

'Thank you. That's better. But what on earth are you both doing here? I'm still not sure I'm not dreaming — are you real?'

Mike gently pinched my arm. 'Does that feel real? We were heading for Mica Valley when Len saw your tracks. The vehicle's a kay or two back there.' He jerked a thumb behind him. 'The thing is,' he began, picking sticks from my hair. 'Haven't you got a hat? Okay I see it, I'll get it . . . The thing is,' he repeated after handing me the recovered head gear, 'old Len here is quite a tracker and you're wearing the same shoes you had on when we last met. He actually remembered the print on the sole. Pretty good going, eh?'

'Yes,' I agreed. 'But how — I thought you'd left the area, Len?'

'Ah well.' He looked briefly abashed. 'We were camped at the Gem Tree, see — I've found some nice beryls there in the past — and me and Cora had a bit of a row. She's got a tongue on her when she's a mind to sound off, and I sort of cleared out for a day or two to let her calm down. Thought I might as well take a run out to the Harts again, then this bloke flags me down on the road.'

'He delivered the ransom note,' Mike said, cutting the explanation short. 'Belligrin was on the Alice side of your turn-off with a wheel off, pretending he had a flat. Told Len the tyre was buggered and asked him to run the letter into the roadhouse. It was supposed to have a cheque in it for a new tyre. So Len was there when Bob got your note and he offered to help. He knows the area backwards, said he could get me within a few kay or so of the Valley without using the regular track.'

I remembered then. 'I heard you. Only for a moment and I thought I'd imagined it because we're miles from the highway.' My heart had sunk at his words. I said apologetically, 'I don't think I can walk any further, Mike. I'm sorry. Can you get the vehicle closer to me?'

He shook his head. 'There's no time, love. We have to be where he said before four and it's past three o'clock now. You needn't walk a step

— just wait here till we come back for you.'

Panic seized me again and I grabbed his arm. 'No! I can't! What if he finds me again? He's out here right now somewhere, searching . . . Please, Mike, don't leave me. Can't we just go home?'

He shook his head. 'I'm afraid not. We set a trap for Belligrin. Bob's gone to meet him, with a parcel we faked up to draw his attention while we sneak up on him — that's why the timing's important.' He bit his lip. 'We have to be there, because when he learns the truth he might — '

'He will. Oh, God, what have you done, Mike? He'll kill Bob too.' I started to shake, my mind fetching disasters from some dark corner faster than I could view them. 'He's got nothing to lose and you're going up against him with a *pinch-bar*? You're as crazy as he is! Couldn't you at least have got the rifle from the gun safe?'

'No! We thought he had you, remember. And bringing a rifle into the mix seemed a sure way to get you killed. Though, as it's turned out, it might've been a good idea, but it's a bit late to think on that now.'

'And Bob,' I moaned. 'He's old and slow and so damned cranky he's likely to talk himself into a bullet. Why didn't you just call the police?'

Len snorted. 'And have them fart around for hours getting permission and sending for helicopters and what-all? He'll be fine, Charlie. He's got that young feller with him and if we get a move on, there'll be the two of us in the mix as well. So, what about it, Mike? We going or what?'

'But it's kilometres back there,' I protested. 'You'll never make it in time. And what young feller are you talking about?'

'Eric,' Mike said. 'And Len reckons the Valley's just over the next ridge. I know it must seem further but you've travelled a half circle, Charlie. If you really won't wait here, then I reckon we can get you that far between us — what do you think, Len?'

The old fossicker sprang upright from his squatting position and winked at me. 'Of course we can, featherweight like her. Let's get started, boy.'

'Thank you,' I said fervently. 'Help me up, please.'

With a man on either side of me taking most of my weight, we progressed surprisingly quickly compared to my previous efforts with the stick. And quite soon I was mortified to see that Mike was right: if I'd continued on my previous line from where they'd surprised me, I'd have found myself almost back where I'd started. So much for the sense of direction on which I'd prided myself. To take my mind off my ankle, which, even with the weight off it, still hurt abominably, I took a breath to gasp, 'How's Mum coping? I hope she doesn't worry herself into another collapse.'

Len snorted cheerfully, 'Not her. Why, we had our work cut out to stop her coming with us.'

'Or going with Bob,' Mike agreed. He lifted his left hand, the one not holding my wrist that was slung around his shoulders, to glance at his watch. 'She and Ute should be setting off about now to get hold of Tom Cleary. He's our back-up plan. Worst case, he can stop Belligrin on the track and best case, which is what we're aiming for, he'll be on hand to arrest him. Thank God you got away, Charlie. It's made everything so much easier. How did you manage it?'

While they half carried me along, I panted out the details of my escape from the hut.

'Bet that got right up his nose,' Len remarked cheerfully. 'What's wrong with your neck? You look like you're favouring it a bit.'

'A touch of whiplash,' I said. 'He grabbed me round it when I tried to run. One of those holds the footballers get into trouble for. Actually it doesn't hurt as much now as it did. Or maybe my ankle hurts worse. Can we stop a moment?'

Mike glanced again at his watch while I rested my arms. 'Is it far now?'

'Other side of the gully. Time for a piggy-back, Charlie. Think you can climb up and hang on if Len gives you a lift?'

'I'm too heavy for you,' I protested.

'Rubbish. Come on, ally-oop my girl. Time's a-wasting.'

'Well, just across, then.' He half crouched and, with Len's help, I scrambled onto his back, looping my arms about his shoulders while he grabbed my legs. 'For Pete's sake, don't fall, Mike! Maybe you should leave me here?' It cost me something to suggest it but the rocky declivity filled me with misgivings. 'You could break a bone, or sprain something . . . '

'It'll be fine. I've wrestled calves that weigh more than you.' He proceeded cautiously down the slope. I tried to sit lightly and to remember not to choke him with my grip whenever a stone rolled under his boot. Len hovered nearby, a hand out to steady him until, with my heart in my mouth and a final gasp of exertion from Mike, he climbed out the far side where, behind a screen of wattle bushes, I slid to the ground again.

Len eeled away through the scrub to return five minutes later, just as a faint hum broke through the drone of insects. Mike cocked an ear and checked his watch again.

'There's Bob, right on time.'

'The joint looks deserted,' Len reported quietly. 'There's nothing disturbing the birds. I reckon if we head round the slope a bit, we can get down on the blind side of the hut and wait for him there. He might be inside, of course, so we want to keep the noise down until Bob gets here. That old Rover makes enough racket for six. We can make our move when Belligrin shows himself.'

'Okay.' Mike turned to me. 'You'll be okay to wait here, Charlie?'

'Yes.' I chewed my lip. My stomach was churning and not at the prospect of finding myself alone again. 'He's got a gun, remember. You will be careful — both of you? Oh God, I'm sure we should have called the cops in. They train for this sort of thing.'

'The guys with the helmets and high-powered rifles do,' Mike said, 'not the likes of Tom Cleary. We'll be careful, love. You keep your head down here.' And with a brief squeeze of my fingers and a faint rattle of stones beneath his boots, he was gone, Len by his side, the old fossicker turning to wink reassuringly at me just before they vanished into the wattle.

I clenched my hands uselessly in my lap and sat waiting, sick with dread, for their return.

30

The sound of the old Rover grew progressively louder. I wasn't sure if Bob had ever actually been in the valley before. We'd spoken of the little hut to him though, so he'd know roughly what to expect. He should see the mill first, I thought, and that would tell him they were close. The hut itself was hard to spot but Eric, hopefully, would pick it out in time to pull him up. It was important that they kept as much distance as possible between themselves and Belligrin. Surely I had heard that a handgun was inaccurate at anything less than point-blank range? I prayed it was true and that Bob would know it too — and that worry for my welfare wouldn't push him into doing something stupid.

Inactivity was driving me mad. I tried to stand but the pain in my ankle flared into agony the moment I put the least weight on it and I subsided again, panting, biting my knuckles to still my whimpering. A willy-wagtail fluttered down to scold me and between its angry chattering and the blood thundering in my head I missed the moment when the Rover stopped. I listened hard then for the bang of a door or the sound of voices, but if either came, the slope hiding the hut from my sight must have absorbed it.

The little black and white bird flitted from branch to branch in the wattle, continuing to scold. It must have had a nest nearby or else was defending its territory; ordinarily I'd have paid no attention, but its noise made it impossible to listen and I said irritably, 'You're stuck with me, birdie, so either shut up or clear out,' and to my complete astonishment, it flew off. My eyes followed it down the gully and, by the purest chance, fell upon the one piece that had been missing from the whole puzzle, Annabelle's handbag. It lay between the stems of a wattle thicket, a discreet affair of tan and white now soiled and dusted lightly over with debris, the rings on its straps already tarnished.

Belligrin must have stood at the top of the gully and tossed it after he'd killed her. I craned my sore neck, wondering how I could get down there to retrieve it, then I heard the slide of a boot sole behind me and froze, staring rigidly ahead as if not reacting could prevent it from happening.

'Well, well, Charlie,' Belligrin said. 'So here you are. Bitch! I've been chasing all over the country for you. How come you didn't run?'

'I broke my ankle,' I said sullenly. Let him think I had made it no further than this. He mustn't learn about the others, for they were my only hope now. I wished uselessly that I hadn't insisted on accompanying Mike and Len. If I'd stayed where they'd found me . . . But I was here and Belligrin had his hostage back, and dear God! Bob was going to give him some fake parcel and Belligrin had his gun — he'd kill us all.

'Did you now?' Something hard nudged the

back of my neck, then a hand seized my hair, hat and all. 'Wish I'd thought of doing it for you. Up with you, then.'

I screamed as he yanked me to my feet, but the only thing I could do was submit, for he kept up the pressure until I was wobbling on one leg, sobbing with pain, my scalp feeling as if it had been torn off.

Belligrin eyed my swollen foot and put the gun away. 'Convenient,' he said. 'Can't walk on it, eh? Well you're gonna have to manage because I'm not carrying you. Come on.' He grabbed my upper arm and, scrabbling, hopping and crying, I was dragged up the slope. I tried a scream, only half-feigned, thinking to warn Mike of my plight but my captor stopped it with a slap.

'Enough of that, Charlie. I'll gag you if I have to. Got it?'

I nodded dumbly, my face on fire, and he yanked me forward again. 'Come on. A bit of a wait'll keep him worried but we don't want him leaving, do we? You wouldn't like that at all.'

★ ★ ★

The first thing I saw when we came clear of the gully scrub was the old Land Rover parked a short distance away from the hut. The next was Bob turning back from the doorway. He was in jeans and dusty boots, and the usual flannel overshirt he wore in cold weather, open now for the afternoon was warm in the sheltered valley. Hands on his hips, he stared around, a look of puzzled alarm on his face.

'Nothin' and nobody,' he said loudly. He appeared to be alone; I couldn't see Eric and I wondered if he'd dropped him off down the track to serve as back-up.

'Bastard!' he yelled suddenly. 'Where are yer? I'm here. We had a deal, so come on out an' make it.'

'In good time, old man,' Belligrin called, yanking me forward and reaching for the gun as Bob spun around. He showed him the weapon. 'Easy now. You brought what I want?'

Bob ignored the question and started towards me. 'Charlie! You okay? What's the mongrel done to you?'

'I'm okay, Bob.' I gritted my teeth, wobbling where I stood. 'Don't annoy him. Just give him the stuff.' I dared not look at the hut but I tried cutting my eyes sideways at it to indicate Mike's presence; however, my frantic signalling was lost in Bob's sudden surge of fury as he took in my ravaged state and charged towards me.

'He's hurt yer!' he roared. 'I'll kill the bastard!'

'No!' I cried frantically. 'I'm okay, Bob. Really! Don't — '

The roar of the gun froze the words in my mouth. I actually saw a spark leap from the stones a metre to the side of Bob. He stopped as if he'd run into the bullet and Belligrin said tautly, 'The next one won't miss, grandpa.' And then, in quite a different tone that combined surprise with menace, he said, 'What's this? I told you to come alone.'

I suppose it had been too much to expect that Eric, crammed into the footwell of the Rover, would ignore the shot, and the vehicle door had sprung open as he leapt instinctively to his partner's defence — though what he thought he could do with a jack handle at that distance was beyond me. My heart sank as the gun rose again, this time aimed not at Eric, but me.

'Drop it or I'll put one in the girl.' Belligrin's ugly tone left no room for doubt and Eric obeyed instantly, casting the steel from him as if it were red-hot.

'Good, now if there's no more of you wanting to be heroes, bring me my package. And don't move a whisker, grandpa,' he added for Bob's benefit. 'When I'm satisfied you haven't pulled anything you can tie each other up — unless I decide to shoot you instead. That'd be easier. Either way, Charlie's coming with me. I'm thinking somebody as stupid as you obviously are just might have been dumb enough to call the cops.'

'No cops,' Bob said. 'All right, give it to 'im, Eric, but leave the girl. Take me instead.'

'I think not. A broken ankle makes her nice and biddable, which I'm betting you aren't, grandpa. Am I right, Charlie?'

Through stiff lips I said, 'He's old. Please don't hurt him.' All hell was going to break loose the moment Belligrin opened the package Eric was bringing towards him. It looked realistic enough: whatever the contents were, they'd been placed in a plastic bag that was well sealed with tape — the broad, extrasticky type that called for scissors or a sharp knife. I guessed it was a deliberate ploy to delay its opening, but it would only buy us a moment or two at best.

Then Eric stumbled. It looked so natural that it had me fooled, but not Belligrin. The parcel shot from his hands as he fell and landed half a metre to the side of its intended recipient, who made no move to retrieve it. Eric had both palms flat on the soil ready to spring but Belligrin had failed to follow the script that called for his temporary distraction. Instead, feet firmly planted, he waggled the gun, saying coldly, 'Get up. You just earned yourself a bullet. Now pick the parcel up — carefully, mind — and hand it to me. Then get over beside the old guy.' He glanced down at the tightly sealed package he now held and nodded to himself.

'Trust that little bitch. Right, now listen carefully, Charlie. You're gonna reach into my pocket and get my knife out, then open the blade for me. Nice and slow. No sudden moves because up this close I'm not gonna miss grandpa or his mate. Got it?'

I nodded dumbly, wet my lips and put a shake in my voice as I asked, 'Which pocket?'

'That's my girl,' he said with a smirk, 'sense at last. Left hand, vest.'

I looked at Bob and raised a trembling hand to the pocket in question. Belligrin was wearing a sleeveless vest of lightly padded cotton, one that zipped up the front. It hung open at present, which put the pocket at an angle to my hand. I'd been standing so long on my good leg that it was shaking with weariness and I didn't have to feign my sudden loss of balance. I clutched at Belligrin to prevent myself falling.

'Sorry,' I mumbled desperately, praying he would realise it was unintentional. Apparently he did, for no sudden blast occurred. Eyes on Bob, trying to signal my intention, I fumbled for the pocket's opening, bending my wrist awkwardly to make what I was about to do believable once I'd closed my fingers over the hard shape of the knife and withdrawn it. I swayed against my captor again as my hand came out, then cried out as the knife dropped, and I let myself fall on top of it, shrieking with the very real pain of my wrenched ankle as I landed.

Which was when I heard Mike and Len make their move. From where I now was on the ground — both my and Belligrin's backs had been to the hut — I couldn't see, but I was fully occupied anyway, sobbing, 'I'm sorry! I'm sorry!' as I rolled frantically to grab at the knife. My hands were sweaty and shaking and my first grab at it missed, but on my second try I got a grip on it and my thumbnail into the little hollow made for the purpose, and succeeded in opening the longest blade. It was a stock knife, of a type I knew well for Bob carried an identical one, and I knew that particular blade was almost the length of my forefinger. It mightn't kill but perhaps it could cripple.

I saw Belligrin jerk his gaze from me back to his other captives, then whip about to look behind him as I clutched the knife and lifted it towards him. Seated, I couldn't reach higher than his thigh but that would do. Drawing a breath, I screamed, 'Run!' and drove the blade as deeply as I could into his leg.

I expected to get shot and I can only suppose that stress and terror for Bob had made me hysterical, or surely I couldn't have done it. My tears had been faked but it wouldn't have taken much right then for me to cry in earnest for I had never been more frightened or felt as much pain in my entire life. My scream got both men moving, which probably saved a retaliatory shot from coming my way.

Belligrin yelled in surprise as the knife went home. He roared, 'Hold it!' and then the gun went off as he made a sound like 'Oof!' and staggered sideways, hit by a fist-sized rock, hurled by Len. I heard the clatter of boots on stone and twisted about to see the pair of them running flat out towards him, Len aiming another rock and Mike with a two-handed grip on the pinch-bar.

Belligrin brought his gun hand up and I screamed a warning for, by then, less than a metre separated him and Mike. I heard the hollow crack of steel meeting bone somewhere around Belligrin's knee and an instantaneous retaliatory explosion as the gun went off again. The world seemed to freeze for long seconds before Belligrin tumbled slowly sideways, the gun spiralling away through the air. Then the bar fell from Mike's hands as he ploughed face first into the ground, to lie as motionless as a pole-axed steer, his head a bloody mess.

31

Full-blown hysteria took me over then. I remember crawling, scuttling sideways like some limb-deprived crab to reach him, heedless of guns and killers. I remember a wailing cry that must have erupted from my throat and a harsh voice bellowing, 'No you don't, you bastard!' as the gun flew past me, driven by a kick from one of the men. I watched Mike's life-blood pool on the thirsty soil, my hands fluttering uselessly over the dark mass of his gory head while my heart broke in two.

An agony of sorrow filled me. 'Mike! Oh God, what shall I do? Mike!' But he lay still, his strong body lax against the red earth and already a fly had come to buzz about him, drawn by the blood.

'Get away!' I screamed, swatting at it, and then Bob was there, trying to lift me.

'Come away, girl.'

I glared at him. 'No! Give me your shirt.' Another fly had followed the first. I couldn't bear the thought of them touching him. 'Now!' I yelled, the tears streaming down my face. Wordlessly, Bob shrugged out of his overshirt. I dabbed impatiently at my wet eyes to clear them, but still the tears brimmed like rain as I wiped the blood away from his head, pressing the absorbent flannel against the wound as it continued to flow. 'He died trying to save us.

Because that monster was going to kill us all,' I cried. 'You know that, don't you? He was never going to let any of us live — and now Mike's dead ... ' Another sob broke from me. It seemed my fate to cry for men I couldn't have.

'You've got that wrong, love.' Len was suddenly beside me. 'No way is he dead, not if he's still bleedin'. Here, let's have a gander.' He peeled my hand away and lifted the sodden shirt to inspect the wound, parting the torn scalp with grubby fingers, something I'd failed to do. 'Thought not.' He nodded with satisfaction. 'See here? The bullet's just gouged a bit o' bone outa the side of his head. Scalp wounds always bleed like crazy,' he said authoritatively. 'The extra blood must be there to grow your hair — or keep your brains working, I guess.' The feeble joke passed me by unnoticed as I stared at him, a sudden wild hope replacing despair.

'He's alive? You're sure?'

'Of course. Here, you don't believe me, feel this.' He pressed my blood-stained hand against Mike's sun-warmed back and, holding my breath, I felt the faint movement of his.

'Oh, thank God!' Forgetting my ankle, I made to scramble up, only to desist with a yelp of pain. 'We have to get him to Harts Range and call the doctor. They've got an airstrip and a phone. Oh, hurry, hurry!'

Eric, who was sitting on a groaning Belligrin and using his own belt to tie the man's hands behind him, said, 'What are we gonna do with Sonny Jim here? I think he might need a doctor too. Mike caught him a good 'un with that bar of

310

his. Wouldn't be surprised if he bust his knee. And he seems to be bleeding from the other leg too.'

'Good,' I said vengefully, wondering where I'd dropped the knife. 'I don't care if he dies! In fact, I hope he does. I stabbed him. Let him wait for the cops — they can see to it. Mike needs immediate attention.'

'An' you, Charlie,' Bob said. 'We'll take him in the Rover. Let's get you in first.'

'Hang on.' Eric's head had lifted. 'Vehicle coming. This'll be the cavalry now.'

It was. Tom Cleary came charging up the track, heedless of its inequalities, his vehicle lurching and shuddering like a live thing. And behind him where his dust ended, and driven at the same reckless pace, was the Garnet station wagon with Ute at the wheel and Mum in the passenger seat, clinging onto the doorframe. They all debouched at once, Tom's furious questions completely drowned out by Ute's thankful shout of, 'Eric, my heart, you live still!'

'Of course I do,' he said rather testily. 'I'm fine, Ute, but Mike isn't. He's been shot.' To Tom he said calmly, 'Why don't you stop shouting the odds and take charge of your prisoner? I'm sick of sitting on the bastard. He's broken Charlie's ankle and put a bullet in Mike. We need to get 'em both back to your airstrip asap.'

'I ought to arrest the lot of you,' Tom said angrily, 'taking the law into your own hands this way. You should've called me immediately . . . Is this him — Belligrin?'

311

'Yes,' I said. 'You can add kidnapping and attempted murder to everything else he's done.' I wanted to scream at him rather than explain but instead I said urgently, 'Mum, can you please organise Mike into the station wagon? He's been shot in the head and he's unconscious.'

'Charlie! You're okay?' Her eyes ran over me, wincing as they encountered my discoloured, badly swollen ankle. She knelt beside me, gathering me into a fierce hug. 'I've been so worried! What did he do to you? Is your ankle really broken?'

'I think it's just sprained. And he didn't do anything except tie me up and threaten me.' I could see she didn't believe me. 'He didn't touch me, Mum, if that's what you're thinking, though he threatened to, but I got away first. And fell down the stupid bloody hill, that's how I hurt myself.' I sniffed, feeling my treacherous eyes welling up again. 'It just hurts so much and I thought he'd killed Mike, and he was going to shoot us all ... We've got to get Mike to a doctor!' I cried fiercely. 'Why won't anyone listen? The bullet didn't go into his head but he could still die!'

'It's all right, Charlie,' she soothed. 'We will. And you too. Thank God I didn't stick to Mike's plan. We were supposed to wait but I couldn't, so we came early and it's just as well. Right, you sit still and I'll get your young man loaded up. He can lie along the back seat if we bend his legs up.'

'No, I've got a better plan. Get Bob to help me to the vehicle first. I can sit with him, cushion his head — God knows he doesn't need it banging against the seat.'

So that was what we did. Ute drove, muttering strange words in German or Polish whenever the vehicle hit a bump, while Mum sat tensely beside her, eyes glued on the driving mirror to watch how we were faring. 'You're very stiff,' she observed at one point. 'Did he hurt your back, Charlie?'

'My neck. He grabbed me by it. It's better than it was, still sore though if I jerk it.' A wheel thudded into a pothole as I spoke, making me catch my breath. 'Like that.'

'I am sorry, Charlie,' Ute called back. 'Is damn hard, you know, to drive in this bugger-all where the road is not good.'

'What?' Mum frowned blankly.

'Never mind,' I said hurriedly. And to take my mind off my worries about Mike, I asked, 'What was in the packet they made up for Belligrin? Which he never got to open, by the way.'

'Jasper's chain, inside a cardboard packet. Custard powder I think,' Mum said vaguely. 'It was all done very quickly. The chain was there on the bench and about the right weight. The packet was just the first one Mike grabbed from the cupboard. He chucked the contents in the sink and jammed the chain inside it. We still don't know where the dog is,' she remembered.

'Jasper's dead.' I looked anxiously down at the unconscious man whose head I cradled. The bleeding had stopped, though I still held the soaked flannelette bunched against the wound. The cloth had stuck to the drying blood and I

313

feared to pull it away. 'Belligrin shot Jasper and dragged his body into the scrub over the creek. That's how he got me. I was following the drag marks when I stumbled onto his vehicle.'

'We couldn't work out where you'd got to,' Mum said. 'I thought maybe you'd had a fight with Mike and gone off to cool down. It's what you always did when you and Annabelle . . . Then that fossicker, Len, turned up with the letter. I was all for calling the police but Mike wouldn't have it — Bob, either. He said they'd bugger about till they got you killed.' She was obviously quoting, and she paled, remembering, her hand creeping up to her chest. 'I've never been so terrified. If I'd lost you . . . '

'Well, you haven't, Mum. Don't get upset please, remember your heart.'

'Charlie, you are my heart,' she said baldly. 'You're all I have left.'

The words jolted me, both from their meaning and the intensity with which she had said them. 'I'm not,' I protested feebly though the sweetness of hearing them rendered my automatic denial meaningless. 'You have the Garnet, and Bob.'

'And neither would be worth spit without you,' she said fiercely. 'I couldn't have borne it if I'd lost you so soon after your coming back to me. First the op and then this . . . '

'Oh, Mum, I'm sorry.' I stretched a hand forward as far as I could and she moved awkwardly about in her seat to reach back and take mine. Her clasp was warm and strong, her upside-down hand thin and sinewy within mine. 'I didn't stay away because of you. I just never felt you needed me in your life.'

'Well, I do. We're too alike, Charlie. We don't show our feelings. But it doesn't mean — it's never meant — that I don't love you. Your father found that hard to accept too. He said I was emotionally crippled, and my being so had damaged you. I think it was why he preferred Annabelle. Emoting was her forte. I always wondered why it was you rather than her who wanted to act.'

Because, I saw in a sudden flash of insight, playing a part made it easier to pretend all the things I felt but had trouble saying or showing. Then Mike's head moved against my thigh, driving everything else from my mind. He moaned once but remained comatose. I slid shaking fingers along his neck, feeling for a pulse, my voice catching in sudden terror.

'I can't find it.'

'Try just under his jaw,' Mum said. 'Use your whole finger, not just the tip. Got it?'

I obeyed and breathed again. 'Oh, thank God, and here's the road.'

'Now we go very fast, Charlie,' Ute promised. 'Hang onto the hair, and we will be there before you find out.'

There was something wrong with that sentence but I couldn't puzzle it out now. Bracing my feet against the floor, I looped my arms around Mike's body and we tore down the highway towards the police station, leaving the vehicles behind us buried in our dust.

32

What was left of the day passed in a daze of nerve-stretching anxiety as we waited for the flying doctor and irritability on my part at what seemed like endless paperwork. Tom had his own priorities and was desperate to get some sort of statement from me before I escaped into town. Then Doctor Spears, as thorough and imperturbable as when he'd come for Mum, insisted on examining me too before loading both mine and Mike's stretchers into the plane.

'I've sprained my ankle,' I said crossly, 'and hurt my neck, that's all. I'm fine. Mike's been shot, for heaven's sake. Can't we just go?'

'As soon as I've checked you over,' he replied, flashing a torch in my eyes. 'Hmm, well you seem okay, if a little stressed. I'll just strap you in: we don't want you falling off, do we? Molly, I'd wait a few hours before ringing the hospital. Charlie will be fine but they won't be able to tell you much about Mike until he's had a scan done.'

'Thank you, Clive.' Her face was anxious as she reached to clasp my hand. 'Try not to worry, Charlie — he's in good hands now. I'll be in tomorrow. I'll see you then.'

At long last the door thudded shut, and Doctor Spears and his nurse belted themselves in as the engines turned over, then ran up to screaming point; finally, we were moving. Mike hadn't stirred again since that moment in the vehicle and I was desperately worried about him as I felt the wings lift, heard the thud of the wheels clunking into their wells and let go of the breath I'd been holding.

*   *   *

There was, of course, more paperwork at the hospital. Mike's stretcher vanished down a corridor while I was answering questions about us both, then my pulse, temperature and blood pressure were retaken and I was wheeled off to the X-ray department to wait my turn in the queue.

Visiting hours that evening brought Rae Thornton to my room. 'How are you, Charlie? Molly rang — she told me what happened. I was never so appalled!' Her thin gold wedding band caught the light as she greeted me and took my hand in a warm clasp. She was wearing a soft pink blouse that went well with her silvery hair. She glanced at the support collar I wore. 'You injured your neck as well? My dear, what a frightful experience for you all, but you're safe now.'

'I don't know that Mike is,' I said. 'They haven't told me anything.'

'I'm sure the staff are doing their best for him.' She sat on the visitor's chair. 'They must be confident he'll recover or he wouldn't still be here.'

'What do you mean?'

'Well,' she said, 'I understand he has a head

317

wound, and as we don't have a neurological specialist in the Alice, they'd have flown him out, to Adelaide I imagine, if there was need of one. So that's a good sign, isn't it?'

'Yes, of course! I hadn't thought of that.'

'No,' she agreed. 'Sometimes, when we worry, we can't see the wood for the trees, so to speak. Is there anything you need that I can get you?'

'No, that's okay, thanks. Mum's coming in tomorrow. I expect she'll pack a bag — I came without so much as a toothbrush. Nothing seemed to matter,' I confessed, 'except getting Mike to hospital. He saved us all, you know . . . '

I found the words spilling out as if Rae's common sense and kindness had released some sort of emotional valve in me. I had answered Tom's questions earlier, sticking strictly to the facts and grudging every second it took, but now I told Rae everything I had experienced that day; the terror of being held captive, my adrenaline-fuelled flight from the hut, the relief of Mike and Len's arrival, along with my bitter regret that I had refused to stay where they'd found me.

'Because he wouldn't have been hurt, then,' I explained. 'When he fell and I saw the blood, I was sure he was dead. I thought the bullet had gone into his head.' My voice trembled and she clasped my hand.

'But it didn't. And in any case, you can't know how it would have ended if you hadn't been there. It's even possible your action of stabbing the wretch threw his aim off enough to save Mike.'

'Do you really think so?'

318

'Yes, I do. You can't blame yourself for the crimes others commit, Charlie.' She patted my hand. 'I'm sure Mike would tell you the same. So you've grown fond of him, have you? I hoped you would. And Molly tells me there's another couple pairing up at the Garnet too?'

'Ute and Eric, yes.' I smiled shakily. 'They got engaged at race time. She's great — you'd like her, Rae. Her English is hilarious but she's fluent in several other languages, so mixing up her expressions the way she does isn't surprising. She and Eric go together like hand and glove.'

Rae nodded. 'It's nice when you find your life partner, even if she had to come all the way from — where was it?'

'Poland.'

'Such a long way! And from what Molly tells me you may have found yours, too. I'm glad for you, Charlie.' She beamed at me and I blushed and demurred, though not very convincingly.

'I'll think about that when he gets better.'

'We'll pray for him and I'm sure he'll be just fine. I'll leave you now. You won't be in here long, so remember we have a spare bed when they discharge you. And give me a ring if there's anything I can do.'

'I will. Thanks for coming.' I smiled at Rae as she got up and brushed my cheek with a kiss, then listened as her footsteps joined the general exodus down the corridor. Shortly afterwards a nurse came in to do her observations and ask if I wanted the light off. I agreed and she lowered the bed to a level position and left, leaving me to find a way to accommodate the stiff neck collar and the uncomfortably flat hospital pillow in a manner not incompatible with sleep.

★ ★ ★

The days started early in hospital. By the time I'd eaten breakfast and been helped onto a shower chair in the bathroom, with a towel and a fresh hospital gown awaiting me, and had my bed made, it was still only eight o'clock. Time stretched endlessly ahead. The nurses who had replaced the night shift knew nothing about Mike and none of them had leisure just then to inquire, but she'd ask Sister later, the one called Jenny promised. She vanished through the door, pushing the sphygmomanometer before her, and I heaved a frustrated sigh. Mum would be on the road by now, but it would be hours before she arrived. I had nothing to read and no way to get off the bed. My strapped foot still throbbed when I moved it, but the doctor would be doing his rounds at ten, Jenny had assured me, and he'd tell me how long I had to keep off it.

An hour later she was back, wearing a conspirational air and pushing a wheelchair. 'Time to get you mobile, Charlie. I'm popping you down to Physio so they can fit you with some crutches.'

'I haven't seen the doctor yet.'

'Oh, that's okay. Plenty of time before he gets to this ward. And there's a policeman who rang up to find out if he could visit.' She dimpled at me. 'Sister told him not before ten unless he wanted to be run over by a cleaner's trolley.'

We were rolling down the corridor towards the lift when its doors began to open. Seeing it, Jenny whisked the chair about and pushed me through a swinging door into a room set up with a bed, a large overhead light and an open-fronted cupboard whose shelves were filled with a variety of boxes. 'Where are we going?' I asked as she continued through and out the door on the far side.

'Just a shortcut. It's down here a little way, and just round the corner. Here we are.' A nursing station came into view but the only occupant had his head bent over something and didn't look up as Jenny pushed me into a room where Mike lay asleep with a bandaged crown. 'Ta-da! Now we haven't long, Charlie, because you really are expected in Physio, but hey, what's a few minutes? He came to last night. Mr Webb,' she said firmly, leaning above him. 'Wake up, Mr Webb, someone to see you.'

Mike's made a noise like 'Huh?' and then his eyes opened, widening as they caught sight of me. 'Charlie?' he said uncertainly and blinked as if to confirm what he'd seen was real. 'It *is* you!' He lifted his head, reaching out a hand, which I clasped in both of mine. 'I've had the weirdest dreams.' He winced as he spoke, laying his head carefully back on the pillow.

'I'm not surprised. I'm so glad you're okay. How do you feel? It looks like they've shaved your skull, on one side anyway.' I squeezed his hand. 'Oh, God, when Belligrin shot you I thought it was all over. I was sure you were dead.'

He forced a grin. 'Bullets bounce off me — didn't I say? Did they get him?'

'Oh, yes. He's in police custody. Probably the first criminal Tom's ever busted. Eric sat on him, I think.' I gave a shaky laugh. 'Bob might've kicked him once or twice, and I'd already stuck a knife in his leg — and all before Tom even got there. Really, he didn't stand a chance.'

'He doesn't deserve one. Murder, kidnapping, robbery . . . ' His voice faded, then he said carefully, 'I dreamt I was kissing you, Charlie. Is that part of the weird stuff or is it true? I can't seem to sort things out just now.'

'It's true.' I leant towards him, 'No, don't move. We did this once or twice,' I said as our lips met. 'Can't you remember?' With a lurch of my heart, I wondered if his confusion was normal or a symptom of underlying brain damage.

'Bits and pieces, but I'm glad that bit was real.' He caught my hand and pressed it to his lips. 'I'll probably remember it all later — thinking hurts right now.'

'Then don't. Go back to sleep. Rest and get well.' Jenny had released the brake and was about to drag me off. 'I'll come back after. Love you.'

His eyes crinkled. 'I think I recall that bit too. Something about the girl of my dreams and — and rubies?'

'Physio,' Jenny said, firmly wheeling me away, but outside the room she heaved a sigh. 'That was *so* romantic. What did he mean, rubies? Your favourite stone, are they? He's a bit of a hunk, isn't he?'

Ignoring the question, I asked some of my own. 'But what about his memory? Will it come back? And why does his head still hurt?'

'He's been shot,' Jenny said. 'For the brain, that's like someone pounding on his skull with sledgehammers. I expect he'll have headaches for a few days yet. But he's awake, he's talking and making sense, so he's not really damaged. He's very lucky. An injury like that could've addled his wits for good. The doctor will tell him so.'

'Yes, I know it,' I said soberly. If things had fallen out differently we could both be dead — like Annabelle. I shivered at the thought, and was reminded of the policeman who was coming to talk to me later that morning.

When he arrived he introduced himself as DC David Morgan. I was sitting in the visitor's chair, my new crutches by my side and a cotton blanket pulled over my lap. He glanced around, said, 'Back in a tick,' and left, returning with another chair that he plunked down opposite me. 'Right, how are you today, Miss Carver?'

'Not too bad, thanks. DC — is that detective constable? I didn't know you had rankings — I thought you were all just detectives.'

'Uh huh, we do. So I just wanted to run through things with you. Have to make sure we've got the charges against Paul Belligrin right, you know.' He smiled, a movement involving his lips but not his eyes, which held a hard, unnerving light. I was glad I had nothing to hide for I wouldn't have cared to lie to him.

'I did tell Tom everything I could remember, you know.'

'That'd be the constable at Harts Range? Uh huh, well you must have been pretty shaken up then, being hurt and all, so it'd be understandable if you forgot a few details. So, starting from the beginning, where and how did Belligrin get hold of you? Not at the roadhouse?'

'No.' I wondered briefly if he'd read Tom's report at all, then realised it was a ploy to get me talking. 'It was because of Bob's dog, Jasper. I was down by the creek behind the roadhouse and I saw the blood in the sand . . . '

'Who's this Bob, then? Just tell it like it's the first time I've heard any of it, okay?'

I sighed. 'Right. Well, Bob works for my mother . . . '

It seemed to take hours. I wondered that he took no notes and some time later, as he kept stopping me to clarify points, saw that he was unobtrusively recording my words. When I asked whether he should have asked my consent first, he shook his head. 'Makes it easier is all. When we're done, it'll be typed up for you to sign — if you're not happy, you don't sign it. Though that does mean we'll have to do it again. Now, getting back to the hut, can you remember exactly what he said about your cousin?'

'She wasn't,' I interjected irrelevantly, 'my cousin. She was my half-sister.'

He frowned. 'I don't think that's in the file.'

'Oh well,' I was vaguely annoyed at myself for having mentioned it and sighed. 'Family secret, you know. My father seduced his brother's wife, the result was Annabelle, and Mum raised her when she was orphaned. I didn't actually know the real truth of it until a couple of months ago.'

'I see. Like that, was it? Well, we haven't been able to establish it but we're assuming she and Belligrin were in a sexual relationship. The post mortem showed a pregnancy, which suggests they were. About twelve weeks if I remember right.'

'Oh.' I don't know why I was so shocked. It was the nineties, after all. Perhaps it was pity for the unborn child, or horror at the thought of its own father killing it. 'Dear God! Could Belligrin have known about it?'

Morgan shrugged, dismissing a question he obviously didn't consider important. 'Okay, Miss Carver, if we could just get back to the hut for a moment. Now, you said the plan was for this Mike and Len to wait out of sight . . . '

He left at last and, awkward on my crutches, I got myself back to bed, where I must have dozed for a while. The neck collar had ensured I'd got little sleep the previous night, but it was more comfortable now with the head of the bed elevated. I woke when Jenny returned on her rounds and saw that it was nearly twelve.

'I don't suppose you could take me back to Mike's room?' I looked at my crutches. 'I'm not sure I could find it on these.'

'I don't see why not.' A dimple appeared in her left cheek as she smiled. 'I could send your lunch tray over too, if you like?'

'You're a jewel,' I said gratefully. A thought occurred to me. 'The police haven't been to see him, have they?'

'No. The doctor told them they'd have to wait.

No point making his poor head worse, is there, if he's only got a patchy recall?' She was sympathetic and I wondered if it was Mike's condition, or the fact of his being a hunk that made her so. She was younger than me and quite pretty. No. I stifled the thought; I was finally beyond all that. Poor, dead Annabelle no longer had that power over me. I pitied her now, which I hadn't done before, and even wondered if she had lived and borne the baby, whether we might someday have buried our differences, something I had never considered possible. Not to the point of becoming friends, perhaps, but enough to allow me to have known the child. I would have liked that.

33

Mike was sleeping again when Jenny wheeled me into his room. I propped my crutches against his bed and shook my head when she made to wake him. 'It's okay, I'll give him a shake when lunch comes.'

Before that happened, he blinked awake, the skin about his eyes creasing into a smile of welcome as he saw me. 'Charlie, you're back. What time is it?'

'Midday, near enough. Lunch'll be along soon. I thought we might eat together. How's the head?'

'Oh, a bit achy.' He grimaced. 'I keep dozing off. Poke me if I do it again. What've you been up to?'

'Physio' — I indicated the crutches — 'and talking to a detective. The hospital's keeping him away from you for the present but he'll be back later on to get a statement.' I paused to grab a sliding crutch. 'Mike, he told me that Annabelle was three months pregnant when she died, so Belligrin killed his baby too.'

'Jesus!' He frowned. 'It doesn't make it any better of course, but it mightn't have been his.'

'No, I suppose not. I just assumed . . . It's so wicked! That baby was my niece or nephew. And now I'll never have the chance to know it,' I said sadly, then the rattle of wheels sounded in the corridor. 'Here's lunch coming.'

327

We ate, speaking only of inconsequential things. I told him about Jenny sneaking me in earlier for my unsanctioned visit. 'She's a bit of a rebel, Jenny, *and* she thinks you're a real hunk. So sheila alert, mate.'

He grinned. 'Where in God's name did you get that phrase from?'

I screwed up my nose, thinking. 'Danny Bader, probably. He rather fancied his chances with anything female — saw himself as God's gift to womenkind.'

Mike frowned. 'Oh, yes? And who was he exactly?'

'Just an actor back in Melbourne. We knew each other slightly. Not my type, so you needn't worry. He'd go, *Sheila alert! Save me, God!* any time a girl walked past.'

'Sounds a right pillock.'

'He was.'

'So what is your type? You've never told me much about the life you had in the city, Charlie.'

'Because,' I said slowly, 'it was unimportant. I mean, at first I was all fired up to become the new Nicole Kidman, but that didn't last. Acting's a pretty hard field to break into when your talent is mediocre at best. It took me a while to realise that and to become sick of the novelty of my so-called freedom, sharing sub-standard flats with other hopeful girls like me. The leaky taps, the freezing rooms — Melbourne's cold like you wouldn't believe — and always scrambling to find my share of the rent . . . Looking back now, I think I hated most of it — except the acting, but that wasn't going anywhere.' I sighed. 'Maybe if I wasn't so stubborn I'd have given up sooner. It all seems so unreal to me now, particularly blokes like Danny. He was riddled with doubt and insecurity — the rest was all facade, and very wearing, you know?'

'He still sounds like a pillock.'

'That's because you're a hulking bushy, all muscle and get-go.' I grinned at him. 'By the way, Rae Thornton came to see me last night. Wasn't that sweet of her? And Mum'll be in this afternoon sometime. I'll probably be discharged tomorrow. Have they said how long you'll be here?'

'Another day or two, I'm guessing.' He yawned and fell silent and when I glanced his way next his eyelids had closed again. I sat, watching him sleep while the catering staff removed the empty dishes and the rooms and corridors around me settled into quietness. When he woke again it was with a grimaced apology. 'This is ridiculous! I can't seem to stay awake. I'm sorry, Charlie. When I get out of here, I'm going to take you out for a romantic dinner to make up for it. Think you'll be in town that long?'

'Count on it,' I said. 'I'll stay for you.' He sat up in the bed then, pushing his pillow behind him, so I manoeuvered myself to his side and pulled his face down for a kiss, then rested my head against his shoulder. 'We're so lucky to be here and more or less intact.' I shuddered. 'We came so close to losing each other.'

'I know, love. Don't think I don't.' His arms tightened around me just as Mum came into the room, followed by Bob.

'They told me we'd find you here — ' She broke off, adding dryly, 'I see you're both feeling better.'

'Heaps, thanks.' I smiled. 'Hello Bob — I didn't expect you to come in too. Who's looking after the place?'

'Well, I weren't letting Molly make the drive on her own,' he said fiercely, 'and her just outta hospital.' I grinned as Mum, standing behind him, rolled her eyes at me. 'Ute and young Eric've got it under control. How you doing, son?' He came across to shake hands with Mike. 'How's the head?'

'Getting there, Bob. Here, sit down Molly, and Bob, maybe you can get a chair from another room?'

'She's right, I'll stand.' I caught his callused old hand as he moved away and pulled him down for a hug. He flushed, saying gruffly, 'What's that for, then?'

'Because I love you?' I had never actually told him so before. Mum was right, I reflected, I was no better than her at displaying my feelings. But that was going to change. Loving Mike had shown me how simple it really was. 'And because you came for me when I was in danger. You and Eric and Mike, Len too — you were all so brave and wonderful that day. When Mike and I get married, Bob, will you give me away?'

His eyebrows shot up to his hairline. 'Hang on, Charlie! He seems a decent enough young bloke, but how long have yer known him to be talkin' about gettin' married? Bit soon, ain't it?'

330

'Well he hasn't actually asked me yet,' I confessed. 'But I think we're heading that way. So will you?'

'Yeah, well maybe,' he growled and I heard Mike chuckle behind me.

'Thanks, old feller. She'll probably refuse me if you don't.'

★　★　★

At the visit's end, Mum pushed my chair back to my room. She'd packed a small bag for me and now moved about tidying its contents into the cupboard while I used my crutches to visit the bathroom and get myself back onto the bed. Bob had lingered with Mike saying he wanted a word. I could make a fair guess at the subject and was torn between amusement and dismay. To banish it, I told Mum about DC Morgan's visit and what he'd let slip. 'It turns out Annabelle was pregnant, Mum. Remember, we wondered why she wanted money? Maybe that was the reason.'

'She was?' Mum looked dismayed. She sat in the visitor's chair, my toilet bag forgotten in her lap. 'Foolish girl! Why didn't she say? I'd have helped her if I'd known . . . '

'Not the way she wanted,' I reminded her. 'She wasn't after a baby shower, for heaven's sake. For all we know she might have wanted the money for an abortion. In fact,' I added, 'that's probably the answer. She was never very maternal — at least I never thought so.'

'But a lot can change in five years . . . ' Mum began, then shook her head. 'No, you're right.

Somewhere along the way I made a big mistake with her. I don't know — maybe she needed more love than I could give her.'

'Don't go blaming yourself for Annabelle's shortcomings, Mum,' I said sharply. 'We're all responsible for the decisions we make — it's those choices that frame your life, not whoever parents you.'

She shook her head. 'It might look that way from the outside, Charlie, but it isn't always so.' She glanced down at her hands, which were smoothing the plastic of my toilet bag, petting it as if it were some small animal, and visibly steeled herself. 'Take me. I've never spoken of this to a soul before, but as a young girl my father sexually abused me.'

I gaped at her, not believing my ears, but she was nodding.

'You think that didn't change me? I thought I could put it behind me, move on, you know, but it wasn't possible. He ruined sex for me, and marriage. Your father told me I was frigid, that I'd never loved him, but the truth was the whole bed thing repulsed me. And even now the very thought of — of that, of being touched that way . . . Of course we had sex, you're the proof of that, but I never enjoyed it and I couldn't pretend I did. I thought, when I met and married Jim, that I'd finally escaped. My father was dead, nobody knew about what he'd done and here I had a new life just waiting to be lived. But it was spoilt before it ever started. So you see, there are some choices that you don't get to make.'

'Oh, Mum! Didn't you tell Dad what had been done to you?' I knew nothing of my maternal grandparents save that my grandmother had died young in childbirth and Grandfather Graham in a mining accident when Mum was a girl. She had answered my questions the one time I had asked what had become of them, and had never mentioned them again.

'Of course not. I couldn't. Times were different then, Charlie. Respectable girls were expected to enter the married state as virgins.'

'But it wasn't your fault!'

'That I was spoiled goods, you mean? That wouldn't have mattered. The time to tell him, if I was going to, was before the wedding.' She sighed. 'And then there wouldn't have been one. And I needed him. I was alone in the world — unskilled, working in a boarding house for little more than my keep when we met. I thought he was the answer to a prayer. If I'm honest, I didn't actually love him, but I liked him well enough, and I thought that love would come.'

I shook my head. 'Thank God times have changed. How old were you when your father — ?'

'The first time he did it? Eleven.'

Horrified, I said, 'Couldn't you have told someone — the police?'

She sighed. 'The two of us lived in an old hut on a mining field in the desert, Charlie. How would I have got into town to see a policeman? My home had cracks in the walls, a dirt floor, and a long-drop dunny out the back. If you wanted a bath you bucketed water to fill a tub. I

333

scrubbed my father's clothes and cooked his meals and whenever he wanted sex, he came to my bed, which was a swag on the floor. There were two other families on the field but I didn't know the women, so who was there to tell, supposing I hadn't been too shy, or far too ashamed, to breathe a word about it? And he was always sorry afterwards. He said he couldn't help it.'

'Huh!' I said angrily, 'The man was a paedo. He should've been locked up.'

'Well, he also said if I told they'd put me in a home, and with my mother dead he was the only security I knew. Every time it happened he'd swear he'd never touch me again, but a week or two later he'd be back. It wasn't as if there was a door I could lock against him.' She sniffed and I realised that tears were running silently down her cheeks.

'Oh, Mum, I'm so sorry. Why didn't you tell Dad this — after you were married, I mean? Make him see how it was?'

She took the tissue I gave her and wiped her eyes. 'Because of the guilt and the shame. I can't explain it. My father did it, not me, but I still felt as if it was somehow *my* fault. It crippled me emotionally. Which is why, in case you're wondering, there'll never be anything between Bob and me. I know he loves me, and for his sake I'm sorry that it's so, because he deserves better, but I'll never marry him. He accepted that a long time ago and has settled for companionship. It might be selfish of me, but a friend is better than loneliness.' She gave a final sniff and crumpled the tissue. 'Well, now you know. We're all as our pasts have made us. And I know mine must have contributed to Annabelle's problems, because Lord knows she had them.'

She seemed to give herself a mental shake then, as if disposing of the uncharacteristic stew of emotions she'd displayed, said practically, 'Bob's at the backpackers' tonight and I'm staying with the Thorntons.' She eyed my crutches. 'Now that you're more or less mobile, I'm guessing they'll let you out tomorrow.'

The time for confidences was plainly over, so I nodded, though there was more I wanted to ask. 'But I'm staying in town until Mike leaves too, so if you want to get back sooner, I'll find my own way home. Is that okay?'

'We'll work something out,' she agreed. Then, seeming to realise that she still held my toilet bag, she tutted and rose to put it in the bathroom. When she returned, she'd washed her face and patted her greying curls into place as if the past half hour had never happened. Composed and in control again, she kissed my cheek. 'I'll see you tomorrow, then, Charlie.'

'Yes, see you, Mum.' Saddened and amazed, I returned the embrace and watched her leave, reflecting on how little one ever knew about another, even those whose familial ties were closest, and whose lives one had judged to be open, if difficult, books.

34

I had an unexpected visitor that evening in the shape of Len Wilder, who tapped on my open door and entered, hat in hand. 'Came up to see Mike,' he explained, 'so I thought I'd look in, see how you're doing.'

'I'm fine, thanks, Len. Take a seat. I'll probably be out tomorrow.' I'd removed the neck collar without incurring a reprimand and now pointed to my crutches. 'I'm sort of mobile. How's Cora?'

He grinned. 'She's settled down. Bit like a wattle fire that woman, flares up quick, but it doesn't last.'

'Well, that's good. So you came all this way just to see Mike? That was kind.'

He shrugged. 'I drove his vehicle in. I couldn't leave it out in the scrub, and he's gonna want transport when he gets out of here. Just dropped in to tell him where it's at. The copper came in too, so I'll get a lift back to the Gem Tree with him tomorrow afternoon.'

'Why's Tom needed in town?'

Len shrugged. 'Who knows? Procedure, I reckon. It'll be the biggest case the cops have had in this neck of the woods. The bloke committed double murder — damn near a triple one. Young Mike's real lucky to be alive.'

'I know.' I shivered. 'When I saw him lying there with all that blood . . . Thank God you

336

knew what to do. It never even occurred to me to check his pulse.'

'Yeah, well, back in the day I was an ambo. I guess the training never leaves you — it's sort of automatic, you know.'

'Really?' I was impressed. 'So how did you get from that to camp cooking? Mike mentioned you'd worked in stock camps.'

He hesitated and I said quickly, 'It's none of my business. I expect I was surprised or I wouldn't have asked.'

'That's okay.' He turned his hat about and shrugged. 'No secret really. The job burned me out. It's stressful enough dealing with strangers, you see some awful stuff, especially with road fatalities. It's the kids that get to you. Of course it's got its good side too — saving folk, getting them to help in time . . . But one night I was called out to a head-on and found my best mate and his family in the wreck. He had a road sign speared clean through his body and his little girl was dead.' Len grimaced. 'One of her arms was in the ditch. That did it for me. I quit the following week, just after their funerals.' He stood up. 'Anyway, you and Mike survived so at least your story's had a happy ending. Something to tell your grandkids when you've got 'em. I'll be getting off now. Might see you out at the Garnet sometime, eh?'

'I hope so, Len. And thank you for all your help. You were splendid.'

The colour rose under his tan and he shook his head, shrugging off the praise. He was an interesting character, I thought — artist, bushman, trained paramedic, and shrewd with it. I wondered what Mike had told him, for I was almost certain that he'd used 'your grandkids' in the collective sense.

★   ★   ★

After the doctor's visit next morning I was free to go. I pegged my way along the corridor to Mike's room to tell him and found him sitting in the chair, restless and bored. He rose at my entrance, gesturing at the chair, but I chose to sit on the bed instead.

'Easier to get back up. How's your head feeling today?' I noticed that his bandage had been replaced with a dressing and nodded at it. 'That's an improvement, but it does highlight your very odd-looking haircut.'

'You're not kidding.' He kissed me and grimaced. 'I feel fine but they're still keeping me in for another twenty-four hours. A precaution, the doc reckons. And he's insisting on a further week off work.'

'Well, that makes sense,' I said mildly. 'You can't wear a hat till the wound closes and you don't want to be getting dirt and sweat in it. Why don't you come home with me once you're out? You can lie around getting fat or serve behind the counter, whatever you feel like.'

'Sounds good. Thanks, I'll take you up on that, Charlie. How about dinner tomorrow night, then we can head back the next morning?'

'If you're sure, Mike. Why don't we just wait and see? You might be a bit shaky still.' I looked

338

down at my wrapped, shoeless foot. 'And I certainly don't feel up to a glamorous night out. More like a pizza on the couch. Maybe that'd be better, and save the dinner for another time? I wouldn't mind truly, as long as you're on the couch with me.'

He grinned and kissed me again. 'Right, so the first order of business will be to find accommodation with a couch.'

'Or you could just bring the pizza round to the Thorntons'? Rae has a very nice lounge suite.' I glanced at the clock. 'And now I have to go. I told Bob I'd wait for him in the cafe and the wardsman is probably chasing around looking for me right now.' Mike's look changed to one of puzzlement. 'The wheelchair,' I explained. 'They never let you walk out of these places. I shouldn't keep him waiting.'

'All right, love. I'll see you whenever, then. Pizza it is.'

★   ★   ★

Ten minutes later, I wriggled thankfully into a comfortable position in the station wagon's seat as the hospital vanished behind me.

'Yer got enough room there?' Bob asked. My crutches were in the back and he'd stuck a toolbox, padded with a couple of cornbags, in the footwell to rest my bad leg on.

'Yes, it's fine thanks, Bob. You're heading home today?'

'Yep.' He squared his hat on his head, adding gloomily, 'God knows what sorta mess those two'll have the place in. I just hope Eric hasn't buggered up the diesel.'

The diesel that ran the generator was, according to Bob, only kept alive by his arcane knowledge of it. I guessed he'd be more disappointed than not if Eric had succeeded in keeping it running.

'It'll be fine. Ute could manage an army, let alone a roadhouse.'

'You think?' He didn't, obviously. 'So you're still plannin' on comin' back, Charlie?'

'Of course I am, you old grump. What else would I do? And before you ask, I'll be back Friday if Mike's up to it. He's off work for a week, the doctor said, so I've invited him to stay.'

Bob grunted. 'Yeah, well, I s'pose you could do worse than 'im.'

'So you actually like him?'

He gave me a dour look. 'I never said that. But at least he ain't a know-all like most young fellers. That's something.'

I hid a smile at this rousing encomium and said encouragingly, 'Well, it'll give you a chance to get to know him better. Because he's going to be around for a while — a long, long while, I hope. And I've been wondering, Bob, now that they have her killer, what do you reckon are the chances of the police releasing Annabelle's body? I think it'd help Mum if we could have a funeral, so we could get on with our lives and put it all behind us — am I right?'

'Yeah, yer are.' He indicated as he turned into the Thorntons' street, squinting at the houses. 'This the one? Right.' He directed the car into the driveway. 'I already asked the cops, an' we can bury her whenever we want.' He opened his door. 'Stay there till I get hold of your crutches. Molly's at the funeral joint now, gettin' a date an' sortin' things before we leave.'

Rae and Don came hurrying out then to usher me inside and there was no time for more talk about it. Bob drove off to collect Mum from the funeral parlour. They returned briefly, stopping only long enough to say goodbye and collect Mum's bag.

'So when's it to be?' I asked hurriedly between exhortations to stay off my feet and not to let Mike drive until I was perfectly certain he was fit to do so.

'Sometime next week. Don will decide as he's taking it. We've already had one service, so perhaps people won't bother for this, but I'll have to let them know so they have the option. Take care, Charlie, and we'll see you in a day or two.'

She kissed me and left, accompanied by the Thorntons, while I stayed in my seat, listening through the window to their last-minute exchanges, the slamming doors and then the engine starting up and fading away down the street.

35

Three days later Mike and I were back at the Garnet. Home had never looked so good.

'It's like I've woken from some nightmare,' I confided as Mike pulled in clear of the fuel pump apron. 'How's your head?' It was a question I had asked perhaps too often during the trip out, for he answered with somewhat laboured patience.

'It's fine, thank you. It doesn't ache, I'm not dizzy, nor am I experiencing any trouble with my vision. Can we please just forget about it, Charlie?'

'Sorry. It's just that my ankle still hurts and I simply fell over — you were shot!' It worked as I'd known it would; the moment of irritation was subsumed in concern for me.

'Just wait there. I'll get your crutches, or I could carry you in if you like?'

'I don't want to give you a hernia,' I said. 'The crutches will be fine.' My foot had, in fact, improved, but was not yet up to bearing my weight.

Ute grinned and gave a piercing whistle as I clomped my way through the screen door Mike held open for me. 'Charlie, you are here! And Mike! Your head is well again? I have made the big prayers for you both. So, God hears, I think.'

'That was nice of you,' I said as she flung her arms exuberantly about me. 'Careful, don't knock me down.' Mum and Bob had arrived by then. Mike pulled out a chair and I sat, returning their greetings and inquiries.

'Just another day or two,' I told Mum, 'then I can toss these.' I tapped the aluminium crutches. 'Well, actually they have to go back to the hospital. I suppose Sid can deliver them for us.' To Bob I said, 'Yes, the trip was fine. Not much traffic. Diesel's still working, I see.'

He scowled at me and went off to organise a cuppa.

'How's Eric?' I asked Ute. 'And the road crew? They must almost have finished the job by now.'

'Is one week more,' she said. 'And Eric is wrong, the Murphy man did not come so all is well. They go where is more work to make. And me also, soon.' She nodded. 'This I have told to Molly. Is ten days but your foots will be better then, yes? And you will cook instead, Charlie.'

I worked through this as I picked up the mug of tea Bob had provided and took a sip. 'So you're going with the camp as their cook?'

'But no, no. Me, I go home, to Europe, to make the organising. I sack myself from my job but I must tell them, yes? Is only polite, Charlie. And also that my family, my friends, know that I leave them for always, to marry and live in the great bugger-all with my man. Then I come back. First is the notice to Molly, then is the plane trip and the goodbyes. And while I am not here, Eric will make the asking of your government, yes? For the papers and the marrying so I am not, how you say — illegal person here.'

'Right.' It was a typically energetic plan. Very Ute-like. 'We shall miss you,' I said. '*I* will miss you. You've become part of the old Garnet.'

'And me also, Charlie. You are my first friend in this country so we will keep the touch when I am back and married. And Eric and me, we come often to visit you here. We drink the beer and talk about our men, and how I teach you to make the rolls, and the day you get stolen away, yes?'

I pulled a face. 'Well, maybe not the last bit, but the rest, you bet.'

Her brow began to furrow and I said hastily, 'Never mind, it just means okay. We'll certainly do that.'

She beamed, satisfied, and returned to the kitchen.

★　★　★

By Saturday my discarded crutches were handed to Sid, who promised to personally deliver them to the hospital. By then the covering on Mike's head wound had been reduced to a half-dozen steri-strips, and a fuzz of dark hair had started to grow back over the area. He fitted his hat on rather gingerly still, but his headaches had stopped. He wasn't yet up to heading a ball in a soccer game, he said, but was otherwise as fit as a mallee bull.

'Oh yes?' I pulled his head down to inspect the wound. 'It *is* healing, but it looks a bit raw still. I think you should wait until at least after the funeral before you start work again.'

This ceremony was to be held at two o'clock on Thursday. We travelled into Alice in two vehicles with Mum and Bob in the station wagon, and Mike and I in his Toyota. I hadn't expected many of the locals to turn up — as Mum had said, they'd already attended Annabelle's memorial service — but old Spider Webb came, and George and Bess Himan. I was surprised to see Rob Wyper in the church, barely recognising him out of his shorts and blucher boots, but he had come to town to pick up a machinery part, he explained, and thought he'd pay his respects. And to my immense surprise, both Len and Cora Wilder had turned up, arriving just behind us.

'I thought you'd be out in the hills hunting gems,' I said, greeting Cora. 'Nice to see you both again, and very good of you to come today. Especially as you didn't know Annabelle.'

'But we've met you,' Cora said, 'and then you had such an awful time with that terrible man. Len told me all about it. How are you both?' I could see her sneaking peeks at Mike's head where he stood talking to her husband, but his hat covered the wound.

'We're both fully recovered, thanks,' I said, 'though it might've been a different story without Len's help. Come and meet my mother, Cora. And do you know Rae Thornton?' I gave Mike, who looked up as I turned away, a little wave, marvelling that we were so attuned to each other's presence that we could actually feel when one of us drew apart from the other. Like quicksilver, our bodies yearned to join, but we hadn't managed it yet.

A few people had sent wreaths. I collected the cards after the service, finding one from the Maddisons of Arcadia, another bearing the names of Ben and Sue Damson, and the largest of all, a ring of green ferns and white chrysanthemums from the road camp. Our own offering of yellow roses looked paltry beside it.

Mum had asked Rae to arrange for refreshments following the burial and these were available in the church hall. 'Though really,' she had said ruefully, 'there're so few of us you could all have come to the manse.'

'This is fine,' Mum replied. 'The sandwiches are very tasty, and the little tarts. Where did you get them?'

Mike and I left them talking. We were travelling back in the same order as we'd come the moment the wake ended, to the Abbey Downs turn-off anyway, where he would take his leave. His recuperative week at the roadhouse had flown by, though we had done nothing in particular save to rest as our hurts healed and the terror that Belligrin had caused gradually receded. I still occasionally woke with a racing heart from murky dreams of capture and heartbreak, reliving again the awful sound of the shot and Mike's fall, but picturing him alive and still dossing down in the quarters with old Bob always calmed my fears.

Finally, the mourners all left and Bob, who had slipped away earlier in the station wagon to do the banking and to collect the small store order that fitted snugly into the back section of the vehicle, returned.

'All set,' he told us. 'Yer right to go, Molly?'

Mum assenting, we made our farewells to Rae and Don, who had waited with us to lock up the hall, then took our leave, Mike and I leading the way in the Toyota as we wound our way through the streets and out onto the Stuart Highway.

'So when do I get to see you again?' I asked as we powered along the bitumen.

'As soon as I have a day free. Though that probably won't be before the next benefit night,' he added ruefully. 'If I'm away much longer, whoever's running the camp in my absence will have it for good.'

'It's not your fault you were shot!'

'It's not Kevin's either, love, and he's got a muster to finish. I'll phone and let you know as soon as I do. You'll still be at the Garnet?'

I inhaled loudly in exasperation. 'Why does everybody think I'm leaving? First Bob and now you. Of course I'll be there, you great booby. Where else would I be?'

'Okay, don't eat me,' he said mildly. 'I just thought you may not feel too comfortable going back. You've been through a pretty terrible time after all, and with Ute leaving any day . . . '

'Men!' I exploded. 'I can tell you right now, Mr Webb, and you'd better pin it in your hat, that Carver women are made of sterner stuff. If you want a delicate damsel in your life, I'm afraid you've come calling at the wrong house.'

He grinned. 'Good to know. In that case we've something to discuss but we might leave it until we reach the turn-off, hmm?'

I eyed the strong line of his jaw and the taut tanned skin of his cheek where the little mole sat. 'What exactly? Why not just tell me now? Maybe it's going to take a lot of discussion.'

'Perhaps it will, but all in good time,' he said and thereafter refused to be drawn on the subject.

My spirits sank as the kilometres sped by. When we reached the turn-off, he would have to leave, and who knew how long before we could meet again? I wished that we had spent a night together, or even a stolen hour of two, but our injuries aside, it had been impossible in town and, anyway, Mike had exhibited a totally unexpected old-fashioned streak on the subject of sex unsanctioned by marriage. 'It's not the dark ages, *and* we're practically engaged,' I had protested. 'Don't you want to?'

'Of course I do. I can hardly keep my hands off you, Charlie, but there's Bob. Let's not wreck things between him and me, love. You're as good as his daughter and I don't want him hating my guts for the next ten years, okay?'

'Wimp,' I had muttered, but that was how matters stood between us still. I hoped, meanly, that he was as frustrated as I felt. At least it made a change from Bryan, though that reflection had done little to still the yearning within me to belong, in all senses, to Mike.

The sun was almost gone when we reached the spot where the Abbey Downs track speared away from the highway. Mike pulled off the road, let the diesel motor idle down, then switched it off.

'Well, here we are.' He opened the door and got out to rummage in the load, returning after a moment to slip back behind the wheel.

I put my hand on his knee. 'I'll miss you, Mike. What did you want to discuss? Mum and Bob'll be here soon, not to mention we've had the past week to talk ourselves blue in. So why now?'

'Ah, but I hadn't seen Len then, and that, my love, was what I was waiting for.'

He drew a wad of tissue from his pocket and, peeling it apart, revealed a ring: a silver shank set with an oval, amber-coloured stone, surrounded by a ring of smaller brilliants.

'Not diamonds,' he said apologetically as I gasped. 'They're topaz and citrine, sourced and set by Len. He only finished it last week. He came to the funeral to give it to me. You told me we were practically engaged . . . well, I'd like to make that official, Charlie. So, would you consider wearing my ring?'

'Oh, Mike! It's beautiful.' Unaccountably, tears sprang to my eyes. 'Of course I will.' I offered my left hand and watched him push the ring the length of my finger. 'It even fits! How — ?'

'Lucky guess, I reckon.' He kissed me lingeringly, his voice suddenly husky. 'I do love you, Charlie. I think I fell for you the day we went ruby hunting, remember? And you made that slap-up lunch.' His voice suddenly regained its teasing note. 'I said to myself then, 'A sheila who can feed a man like this is worth hanging onto.' Ow!' He rubbed the rib I'd pinched.

349

'Serves you right. When did you commission Len to make it?' I moved my hand, watching the stones flash as the light hit them. 'It's a lovely ring. He's really, really talented. Cora showed me hers but I had no idea he could do such delicate work. It must be harder to shape an oval than a circle, wouldn't you think? And there are all those amazing tiny little settings as well.'

'The old boy knows his stuff,' Mike agreed. 'And I asked him to make it after Belligrin snatched you. While we were roaring through the scrub to rescue you, actually.' His tone sobered at the memory. He rubbed a hand over his face, saying, 'It was an act of faith. You *had* to be safe, and in a crazy way it seemed to make a sort of bargain with Fate to go ahead and order it then. I said, 'I'm going to marry Charlie. Will you make me a ring to give her?' And he agreed, just like that, while we were tearing through the mulga hitting every bloody rock and gully in the Territory, 'Course I will,' he said. 'Cora'll know what'll suit.' And obviously she did, as you seem pleased enough with it.'

'I love it, Mike. And you too.' I kissed him. 'She told me I should wear topaz or amber, you know,' I added, 'so she must have remembered.' I shook my head. 'You're amazing! To think of such a thing at such a time. Why weren't you, I don't know, making a plan instead?'

'Because, my heart, I'd already made it. I knew I had to have you in my life, so I was going to get you back from that bastard no matter what, and when I did I was going to get my brand on you.' He picked up my hand and kissed my ring finger. 'And now I have.' His eyes went to the driver's mirror. 'Dust coming now, so they won't be long. Talk it over with Molly, love. See what she thinks about an earlyish wedding — end of the season, maybe? Will that suit you? You might think me a bit slow off the mark but I don't want to wait a day longer than we must. There're a couple of married men's cottages at Abbey Downs — the mechanic's currently got one — so maybe we could get the other? But we'll sort all that out. Come here.'

The kiss lasted until the station wagon drew up beside us. 'You'd better get moving,' I said regretfully as I got out of the vehicle. 'You'll be in the dark as it is. I love you, Mike.'

'And I you.' His fingers slid gently over my cheek. He leant to shut the door I'd left open and straightened again, his right hand reaching for the key. 'Take care, love. Remember, you're precious to me.'

'And you be careful with your head. Keep it clean.' My voice wobbled. 'I'll miss you, Mike. Bye.' I stood, blinking furiously, stepping back from the dust as he raised a hand to us all and drove off. When the sound of his engine faded I looked again at my ring, then pulled open the passenger door and climbed into the back seat to acquaint Mum and Bob with my news.

36

Ute left us the way she had come, via Sid's mail truck. Eric and the rest of the road camp had moved east up the highway by then to the far side of Kharko, gravelling and rolling a badly cut-up section of road fronting the Arcadia turn-off. Eric didn't return to the Garnet to see her off.

'For why?' Ute had said, blue eyes opening wide, as she tossed her backpack onto the load. 'When I am back he comes to the airport. The greet is more important than the goodbye, yes?'

'If you say so.' I hugged her. 'Safe travel, Ute. When do you fly out?'

'Is a Saturday. The bus makes its arrive then in Cairns.'

'Well, I hope everything goes well for you. I can't wait for the wedding. You'll be the first bride ever to be married at the old Garnet.'

'Is your turn then, yes?' She held her hand out and I matched it with my own, both of us momentarily contemplating our rings before she turned to pull open the truck door.

I nodded, little cheered, for I was missing Mike. After some consideration we'd settled on a weekend in October for our wedding when, according to him, the stations would have finished their stock work. Don Thornton would marry us, Mike's family had been sent invitations along with the rest of the district, and we'd decided on Darwin for our honeymoon.

Bob of course, had to find something to grizzle about and picked on the general upheaval and amount of extra work the wedding would entail. 'Be hot as blazes in October, Molly,' he grumbled. 'An' you'll already have worn yerself out with that other pair. If they wanna get hitched, let 'em do the job in the Alice. Ain't one weddin' enough for you to be handling?'

'After Eric helped to save Charlie's life?' Mum asked reproachfully. 'Besides, Ute has no one in this country but us. Of course she must have her wedding here! I'm surprised at you, Bob. She was a tower of strength when we needed her, and the best worker we've ever had. So I mean to see that she has a wonderful day — it's the very least we can do.'

'Bloody woman mangles the language every time she opens her mouth,' he grouched, determined to find fault.

'While your German and Polish is so good, isn't it?' I said sweetly. 'I've had an idea, Mum. Why doesn't Bob give Ute away too? She's got no one else to walk her down the aisle.'

'Hey, hang about there, miss!' he blurted, his face assuming a hunted look. 'Have a bit o' sense, Charlie. For starters we ain't got a bloody aisle!'

'We could make one though — I've pictured it. What if we set up Don's little altar table in the summerhouse and Eric waited for her there? We could make a pathway between the chairs for you to walk her down from the verandah.'

'An excellent idea,' Mum said warmly. 'They'd

be in the shade for the ceremony there, and we could tie crepe bows on the chairs, and string the coloured lights across the garden.' She was nodding while Bob scowled ferociously at me. 'It'll have to be a late afternoon do, anyway. So will yours, Charlie — we'd have trouble keeping the food and drinks cool otherwise. Not to mention the guests.'

'So it'll be like a practice run for you, Bob. You can make a speech too — get your hand in for my turn,' I coaxed.

'I s'ppose yer want me to do tricks as well,' he snarled. 'What am I, a performin' clown?'

'No. But you're the closest thing I've got to a father, and I can't get married without you,' I said. 'Besides, you wouldn't add to Mum's stress and workload by leaving it for her to do, would you?' I was shameless in my demands. 'It'll be the happiest day of my life, and Ute will feel that way too. She really, really wants to get married, you know. It's a small thing to ask and we'll both always remember that you did it.'

Mum had a little smile on her face, which, fortunately, Bob didn't see as he growled and fussed until finally caving in. I kissed his cheek. 'I just remembered something Mike told me when he rang last night. He's got a pup for you if you want it. The mechanic at Abbey Downs has a blue heeler bitch. He begged one of the litter for you when he got home from hospital. She pupped the very next day and it seems yours is a male. He'll be old enough to wean pretty soon. The mother's a good guard dog, Mike says.'

'Now there's a bloke with more sense than a chicken. If you'd listen to 'im . . . *He* wouldn't be worryin' a man to make speeches.' No two ways about it, my lover's careful strategy had paid off with Bob.

'He likes you too,' I said, and was rewarded with another scowl.

★ ★ ★

Bob named the pup Jake. When I asked why, he simply shrugged. 'Good enough name, ain't it?' He was a comical-looking little fellow, sporting a thick blue coat with one flyaway ear permanently cocked and an inquisitive nature. He dogged his master's bootsteps about the place and bade fair to take after his mother's guard-dog reputation, for the first time he encountered a stranger he backed up, bristling, until his rump encountered Bob's boot, then snarled, displaying all his baby teeth. I laughed to see it.

'Got yourself a tiger there,' Rob Wyper observed, slamming his cab door. 'How's it going, Bob? Hello, Charlie.'

'Hi Rob. Where's your crew? Or have you finished the job?'

'Nope, bit of a breakdown, plus we're short a man with Eric away, sorting out his bride's residency permit. He's a changed fellow these days — looks like I'll be losing him anyway when it's all settled,' he said gloomily.

'How's that, then?'

'He told me he'll be giving up the road work. Talking about getting back into engineering. The bugger'll wind up being my boss, see if he doesn't.'

'I expect he wants something better than camp life for his wife,' I said. 'You coming in?'

'Might top up first.' He had pulled in beside the bowser, so I left the men to it, smiling to hear Jake's baby growls resume the moment Rob moved his position. Bob would have denied it with his dying breath, but he already loved the pup and was building the same bond with him as he'd had with his predecessor. He was a dog man, Bob, and the creatures knew it and gave him their hearts and loyalty without reserve — seemingly for little reward as he never, publicly anyway, paid them much attention.

★   ★   ★

The next event was Ute's arrival, scarcely twenty-four hours after her return to Australia. Eric accompanied her, along with a suitcase containing their wedding clothes and gifts for Mum, Bob and me. Mum's was a silk scarf, mine an amber pendant on a silver chain, and Bob's a box of Swiss chocolate.

'So you have the little bit of Europe here. From Paris, from Hungary and the cows of the Swiss, yes?' Days of constant travel seemed to have had no effect upon her. Her blue eyes sparkled and her energy seemed undimmed. 'Eric is gone to his work but I stay and help. I will make the eats so all is ready for Wednesday, when is wedding. This is correct, yes?' She fluttered her hand. 'The many days, so quick you know. I lose them.'

'I'm not surprised,' I commiserated. 'After all the travelling you've done, I wouldn't know if I was Arthur or Martha.'

'But I am Ute — oh, is another of your sayings, yes? This I am learning now.'

'It's nice of you to offer, Ute, but there's no need for you to cook, we can do it. It's *your* wedding, after all,' Mum began, only to be firmly overruled.

'But no. Already it is settled in the stone. We have brought the foods for the nibblers, which I prepare. The blinis and the little — how you say?' She couldn't find the word and pursed her lips, gesturing with her fingers. 'Light, like the air kisses, you know, with the curl of salmon, or the special cheese on top.'

'Snacks?' Mum suggested.

'But yes. Only not the sandwich. And no dead horse — no, not even for Bob.'

'We've made the cake,' Mum said. 'I hope you'll like it. It's only two tiers with plain icing and some decorations that Rae found for us. You'd best come and see.'

'I know already is perfect,' Ute declared, and repeated the assertion once she saw the cake with its plain white icing banded with silver ribbon and topped with the miniature bride and groom. 'It is *magnifique*, Molly! You are great friend to me. I make the picture to send home of Eric and me and this so beautiful cake. You have my very much thanks.'

'That's all right,' Mum said. 'Now instead of

standing here, why don't we have a cuppa? Eric, wherever he's got to, must be parched. And then you should rest for a bit. If you're not worn out, you ought to be.'

★ ★ ★

Settled into her old room, Ute did in fact sleep the rest of Monday afternoon away, while, between chores, I folded white crepe paper into rosettes, which Mum then stitched together. They would be fixed to the chairs intended to line the aisle Bob would create once he'd had finished mowing and watering the lawn. The lattice of the summerhouse where the ceremony was to be held — Mike's and mine too — shone white with fresh paint. The little table that would serve as Padre Don's altar just needed flowers, but we could use the wattle, I said. It was blooming everywhere at present.

'That won't last,' Mum objected. 'It never does. There'll be blossom all over the cloth.'

'I'll grab some at the last minute. It won't droop before Don gets them hitched, and then it doesn't matter. I wonder how many will come?' Rather than issue invitations, we had simply announced at the last benefit night that the wedding was taking place, but we expected the full road camp and at least a handful of the locals.

'They'll come — they ain't turning down a free feed. You can lay a quid on that,' Bob observed cynically. Bess Himan had promised to provide the meat so we could definitely count on

358

her and George, I thought, and Mike, of course, as well as the Thorntons and whoever else Eric may have asked.

★   ★   ★

The Thorntons flew in around noon on Wednesday and from there everything went to plan. It was a warm, clear-skied day with new growth on the creek gums and a brilliant blaze from the wattle. It perfumed the air and laid a speckled carpet of gold below its canopy. Ute looked radiant in a short white dress with her blonde hair piled high and held by a glittering comb; she carried a gilt horseshoe and a tiny white-jacketed bible in lieu of a bouquet. Eric plainly thought her a splendid sight with her bare tanned arms and shoulders and brilliant gaze. I supported her at the makeshift altar in the amber dress I'd worn to the dance, while Bob, dapper in his sateen shirt and grey trousers, made a passable fist of his speech. The wattle I'd picked failed to droop and enough people had turned up to make a good showing in the decorated seats. Ute's 'nibblers', though eyed warily at first, were quickly demolished and rounded off with a quantity of quiches and other easily prepared eats.

Some people had brought wedding gifts, which, when the newly made couple finally departed for the Alice, I promised to pack and hold for them.

'You'll never get to the Alice tonight. It's past ten already.' I spoke into the dim circle of torchlight, for I had accompanied them out to Eric's vehicle, and was helping him remove the assorted cans that some of his workmates had tied to the tailboard.

'No matter, we've got a swag. Thanks a lot, Charlie. It's been a great day and it's meant a lot to Ute, and to me, what you and Molly have done for us.'

'Is the best day ever,' Ute agreed. She'd changed into jeans and now turned on her heels, spreading her arms wide to take in the glitter of stars above us, the soft breeze on our faces and the distant music flowing from Don's fingers on the piano accordion. He was taking requests and the crowd were singing along. 'Me, I am married wife. And now I get to sleep maybe, under the stars. This I have never done.'

'First time for everything, wife.' Eric ushered her into the vehicle, the cab light shining on their animated faces before the door closed. I waved as they drove off, then returned to find Mike and rejoin the party.

37

Later, as the two of us stood in a little island of privacy beneath the coloured lights, Mike said quietly, 'It was a great day, Charlie. A credit to both your and Molly's efforts. I hope our wedding goes as smoothly.'

'It will,' I promised. 'Maybe Ute will help with the catering — she's some cook. For all his talk of wog tucker, I noticed Bob putting away the hors d'oeuvres at a decent rate. Have you heard from your parents?'

'Of course. Mum said she'd sent an RSVP — hasn't it come yet?'

'Maybe next mail. Tell me about them — I can't even imagine what they're like and they'll be my in-laws!'

'You'll like them,' he said confidently. 'Dad's easygoing, and Mum's . . . well, she's Mum, you know — nice, average, I suppose, kind. Everyone likes her.'

'The point is — will they like me?'

'What's not to like?' He kissed me. 'You'll be Dad's favourite daughter-in-law, and Mum'll love anyone who loves me. She's over the moon about the wedding. I think she thought the three of us were going to stay bachelors. She had hopes for Dan — he had a girl for two years, but they broke up after they'd been living together for six months. Of course she didn't approve of that, but she'd have forgotten about

361

it if he'd married her.'

'Well, if I only have to marry you to win her approval . . . That's okay. When can I see the house?'

'First free day I'll be over to get you. Don't expect too much,' he warned, sounding suddenly worried. 'There's no garden, not even a lawn. The house is just two small bedrooms and a kitchen.'

'That's okay. We can easily live and eat in one room, and there's a bedroom each for when we row. It does have a bathroom though? I rather like being clean.'

'Yep, with hot water when you light the donkey, a flushing loo and a laundry out the back . . . power when the diesel's running. And what's with the rowing? We won't.'

'Of course we will. There'll be times you'll be cranky, and occasionally something will upset me. It's only natural. Every couple rows — ask your mum if you don't believe me. How long have your parents been married?'

He blew out his breath. 'Jeff's thirty-two so . . . thirty-three, thirty-four years maybe? I've never inquired. Why' — he ruffled my curls — 'do you think we can top their record?'

'Definitely. I'll be trying for sixty — that'll only make you ninety, after all.' I leant into him, murmuring into the swell of the music that covered our conversation. If we'd had a floor instead of lawn we could have danced.

Then, like the abrupt arrival of a cloud before the sun, my happiness was momentarily pierced by the thought of how easily all of this could have never happened. If Annabelle hadn't died, then I wouldn't have come back when I did, and I might never have met the man whose life I would now share. Fate or chance had brought us together, the odds against our ever meeting astronomical. It was scary to even think about the many ways we might never have met. If Mike hadn't taken the job at Abbey Downs, if I hadn't needed a lift home from the Alice . . . But having triumphed over these probabilities and come together, I was suddenly, fiercely resolved that nothing would ever sever us.

I turned within Mike's arm lying loosely about my waist to loop my hands about his head and pull it down to meet mine, glimpsing beyond the dark outline of his hair the heavens lit by the million pinpricks of distant stars. Despite the odds, the universe had been on our side and that had to mean something. We had met, and he was mine until death parted us.

I kissed him then and told him my deepest truth.

Acknowledgements

I shall lift up mine eyes unto the Hills and give thanks for their often useful (and sometimes zany) suggestions. I should also like to thank my hard-working editor, Amanda Martin, for being particular and highly professional, my publisher, Ali Watts, for being there, Sarah Fletcher, dedicated proofreader, and the rest of the crew who design and print my books.